In The Vale

This book is dedicated as ever to Muriel with my love,
and to the memory of Meic Stephens

In The Vale

Sam Adams

First impression: 2019
© Sam Adams & Y Lolfa Cyf., 2019

Cover design: Y Lolfa
Cover illustration: Chris Iliff

ISBN: 978 1 78461 728 8

Published and printed in Wales
on paper from well-maintained forests by
Y Lolfa Cyf., Talybont, Ceredigion SY24 5HE
e-mail ylolfa@ylolfa.com
website www.ylolfa.com
tel 01970 832 304
fax 832 782

PART ONE

I

In June 1775, Thomas Jones, yeoman farmer of Llangan in the Vale of Glamorgan, whose scattered strips of land, in the age-old manner, together amounted to thirty-nine acres, wrote to his older brother in London –

My Dear John,

It is several years since I first besought you of your kindness to take into your household for a time our only daughter Sarah, when she reached years of maturity sufficient to be useful to you and to benefit from the experience. She is now sixteen, in good health, sturdy enough and, I think (as a father would you will say), wise beyond her years. She is generally of a cheerful demeanour and has proved herself competent in all those tasks her mother and I have set her. She is yet a country girl, but one I feel sure will not sink into despondency at being transplanted to the town. I should not confess it, even to you, Dear Brother, but she is my favourite. I beg you will take her in and care for her, and help her achieve that ease in society and knowledge of fine things that life in London with the kindest and ablest of teachers must surely bring.

Your grateful and affectionate brother,

Thos:

Seven years had passed. The carriage slowly climbing the steep hill winding up from the cluster of cottages at the crossroads in Ystradowen had only one occupant, a young woman, who, having been thrown vigorously from side to side as the wheels of the vehicle struck now projecting stones and now holes worn deep in the mud-slick surface, had pressed herself into a corner to mitigate the shocks. She was fortunate she told herself, that the winter had been mild, for this lane under snow would be well-nigh impassable. As the vehicle lurched she glimpsed through its windows shaggy banks topped with dripping leafless hedges. Of what she wondered? Mostly hawthorn probably; it was usually hawthorn, she recalled – here hacked low to promote denser growth when spring came again.

Spring would come, here – and to the teeming thoroughfares of London. The thought was accompanied by a sudden sense of emptiness, of loss. In London, she had become her own woman – hardly a woman of the world, but one confident in her own abilities, and cultivated, her mind opened to culture in a way she could never have dreamed of had she remained on the farm in Llangan.

She and Uncle John had parted tearfully, for they had become very fond of one another. They were (for modesty she hesitated to think it) like-minded in their regard for things of beauty. As she was about to board the mail diligence at the Swan with Two Necks, an enormous coaching inn at Paddington, he had, rather formally, presented her with a parcel that was stowed carefully in the box upon which the blunderbuss-armed guard sat. Then he had embraced her and wished her God speed and embraced her again, before she climbed into the coach. On the journey she had travelled in pleasant enough company and, once the initial shock of the impetuous onward dash of the vehicle had subsided, on the whole quite comfortably, from London via Bath and Bristol, and by ferry across a mercifully calm Severn Sea.

Her uncle had been very kind to her and generous with his time, more than keeping his end of the bargain made with her parents. She had left Llangan mild-mannered, dutiful and possessed of that stock of knowledge common to country girls used to the domestic round, the garden and the farmyard. Beyond that she knew her letters, could count and calculate and, in the family tradition, was a seamstress of some skill. The Joneses had long established connections with the drapery business and the land; some, like Sarah's father, farming freeholders, others shopkeepers, a few both. And, she remembered, there was a link her father spoke of from time to time, usually on winter evenings, rubbing his chin and gazing rather ruefully into the fire, a link too distant to afford any but the faintest hope of position and wealth, with a branch of their family that owned Merthyr Mawr, a grand estate a few miles west of Llangan. As she grew older, she began to understand that the remote prospect of a fine mansion amid rolling meadows, with woodland and sand dunes over the hill, and the blue sea beyond, was the reason her parents were ambitious for her to make a good marriage. She was not a beauty, as she told herself when she looked in the mirror, not even pretty, but well formed and neat in appearance, and quick in apprehension. She was to follow the path taken by many, many others, into domestic service, but not in the Vale. She would go to London and the home of a relative, from whom she could hope for an education as well as a living, and, perhaps, the prospect of meeting an eligible young man.

The draper's shop at the corner of Sackville Street and Piccadilly had been grander than she had dared imagine and the apartments above, her uncle's home, were spacious and so handsome that, even after several months' sojourn, they seemed almost otherworldly. There was nothing in the longhouse at Llangan, solid and comfortable as it was, to compare with John Jones's large, high-ceilinged rooms with their tall windows looking down upon the bustling streets, elegant furnishings, silk damask covered walls and, most wonderful in her eyes, the pictures that hung against the gleaming silk. Tables, chests and cabinets with ormolu handles and ornamentation glowed dark red and chestnut brown in every room, save one, where five tall bookcases filled with leather bound volumes stood against the walls. It seemed to her a place of extraordinary luxury, as indeed it was, most of all on winter evenings, when the window shutters were closed and the rooms were bathed in firelight and candlelight.

'So you are Sarah,' he had said by way of greeting on the day of her arrival, holding her at arm's length and looking at her closely, up and down, as though he were examining a bolt of cloth or a painting. 'I shall call you Sally. And you must call me Uncle. That will do for a start. Now we shall take tea: you like tea?'

Two servants, William and Alice, who were husband and wife, shared all domestic duties and waited at table. They and two apprentices, who assisted in the shop, had their sleeping quarters in garrets under the roof. There was no mistress of the house, for John Jones had never married. On her seventeenth birthday, by which time she had become familiar with the place and its routines, and been quietly judged competent and quick to learn, her uncle announced that she was to be thenceforth housekeeper. William and Alice, who had been in his service for several years and were well content with a master who was undemanding and often travelling abroad, to Ireland, where there was a branch of his business, or France, where he did much of his collecting of art and furniture, might have complained about this change in arrangements and wondered what it would mean for them. Sarah took her new responsibilities seriously and worked diligently to please her uncle; nothing less would have satisfied him. Whatever their apprehensions on this account, whatever they muttered together when alone, the servants chose to say nothing to their master or the young woman thus peremptorily set up over them. The new housekeeper had already learned enough about managing their working day and they put up with her keener scrutiny of the performance of their duties. Her supervision of the household accounts went harder with them, but they bowed to her demands rather than risk losing a comfortable place.

Although he did not often talk about his own life and career, gradually Sarah learned that, having served an apprenticeship in Bristol, John Jones found a position in London and quickly made himself indispensable in the shop where he was employed, which specialised in army officers' uniforms and accoutrements, like the polished mahogany and brass-bound travelling boxes for which his shop was famous. In a few years he was able to set up in this military business on his own account, and in another decade, such was his success in obtaining contracts to supply uniforms, to purchase the premises he occupied when Sarah came to join him and furnish them to his taste and greatly to his satisfaction. He had a circle of close friends, whom he entertained from time to time, but otherwise lived simply. He was comfortable in his own company surrounded by the rare books, paintings and elegant French furniture, which were his passion.

The day's work done, 'Sally,' he would say, pointing to a small detail of a scene or the brushwork in a painting, 'come and look at this.' With quiet insistence, he opened her eyes to a fuller understanding of the arts of painting and sculpture and the crafts of cabinet-making and fine furniture. He taught her to see – and, in time, to find almost as much delight in objects of refinement and beauty as he found. The pleasure in books was harder earned, for most of the volumes that loaded the bookcases were old and not easy to read, many in Latin. Twice each year they had all to be taken from the shelves for careful dusting and replaced in precisely the same order. Then she felt the weight of the great folio volumes in her arms and, under her fingers, the tooled and gilded leathers that bound them. Some were hundreds of years old, her uncle patiently explained, as he showed her elaborate title pages and the dates when they were printed. Books, too, were beautiful, for their solid, lustrous presence and the lingering odour of ages in tobacco-smoke-filled rooms that accompanied them.

The streets of London were not like this, she thought, as the carriage lurched and jolted. But, in all her years there, she had not explored those streets widely. This had, at first, been a source of disappointment and some annoyance to her. At home in Llangan, when her time was her own, she had wandered freely. As a young girl, with fair, beribboned hair, she knew and was known by everyone. On fine days in late spring and summer, daily tasks done, she would often walk to the church, where so many came to hear the sermons of the rector, the Reverend David Jones, that from time to time, he was obliged to preach in the churchyard, the church being too small to accommodate so great a host of worshippers. In those girlish years, Sarah would not enter the church alone, for on the limewashed walls, at some season for which she could never prepare herself, faintly, as through an engulfing mist, with an unquenchable instinct of their own, would grow images of men and women being cast into a fire and thrust down, down, by horned demons and a dancing, grinning skeleton.

It was the churchyard that attracted her. She would walk the great circle of its wall, pausing here and there to consider a tombstone and sound out slowly its message of sorrow and hope. But always the circuit ended at the stump of what had once been a tall decorated slab of stone topped by a wheel bearing a sculpted image of Christ crucified, arms spread wide, almost wing-like, to embrace on one side a curious bird-headed figure (a devil, her father said) and on the other a man stabbing at His side with a spear. It was cruel, and she did not want to look at it, but always her footsteps led her there and always she did look with fascinated revulsion. As she grew older, childhood fears dissipated, she walked the village still when she was free of domestic duties, her hair heavy and plaited now, and darkening to light brown. There would be an exchange of greetings and gossip with many of those she met, for she was confident and of a friendly disposition.

She had grown out of girlhood in London, had come of age indeed, but her uncle would not countenance her leaving the house alone and, in time, she accepted this restriction. She had, from the first, been accompanied to merchants of foods and wines, or candles and other necessities in nearby streets, by William or Alice, and her uncle, treating her on other occasions more like a companion than a servant, escorted her on walks along streets of fine houses and to places of interest or recreation – Old Bond-street, Great Jermyn-street and south to St James's Square, as far east as Leicester Fields and then north to Soho Square. Or they would set out west to Green Park and along a path in the heathland of Hyde Park as far as the Serpentine river, strolling arm in arm, like father and daughter, Uncle John occasionally pausing to speak to someone he knew and introducing her. But she never encountered the young man of means and ambition her parents hoped would enter her life, because her uncle took such pains to ensure she was sheltered from those who might deceive her and exploit her innocence.

At the back of the shop was a yard with a stable and a coach house, and occasionally, with William holding the reins, they went by carriage rattling up a cobbled alley where the horse's hooves struck sparks from the stones and out eastwards along busy thoroughfares by way of High Holbourn to Little Britain, then down Aldersgate Street and Paternoster Row to the great domed mass of St Paul's. In these parts of the city it had long been her uncle's habit to visit booksellers. Some, like Edward Ballard, a bald, rotund man, in Little Britain, knew him well and greeted him like the old and valued customer he had become. Nearby was another friend, James Wiltshire, his short-sighted bookbinder, wrapped up in top coat and scarves in his icy workshop, bent over a bench among rolls of leather, sheets of marbled papers, presses, and the dies and hand tools of his trade, but the journey would always end at old John Newbury's establishment in St Paul's Churchyard, a broad street arcing the cathedral, where there was an immense collection of ancient books exhaling a musty odour of old paper and ink and dust.

Newbury, with his flowing white locks and immensely bushy

white eyebrows, was often to be found in the midst of his shop, reclining in one leather armchair, his right leg supported by another, the foot swathed in protective bandages. He was a martyr to gout, he told the quiet, scholarly men who shuffled around the loaded shelves. Sarah recalled the occasion when he beckoned her uncle to bend closer and dramatically lowered his hoarse voice to say, 'I have volumes here from the son of an eminent family fallen on bad times, whose father acquired them at the Richard Mead sale some thirty years ago, very rare and interesting – medical treatises, beautifully bound for Mead himself – would make a handsome addition to your library. Look beneath my chair. Won't let them out for hoi polloi, you know, to finger them. What think you?'

'Sorry to see you laid up again like this,' John Jones had whispered in return. 'Mead certainly a fine man, wonderful physician – but medical books not really my interest. Rare you say? Very old, I'll wager. Thank you for the nod in my direction. I'll think about them, truly, and if I can see how they might add to my collection, I'll come and look them over.'

'Can't promise to hold them back for you – have other favoured customers. But you do that. Very fine I assure you, richly illustrated.'

'I may have missed an opportunity,' her uncle had said, ruminating aloud as they left Newbury's. 'Old medical books are not easily come by. Ah well. Now let's give ourselves a treat.'

So saying, he had led Sarah, as usual, over the broad, busy road to St Paul's coffee-house to partake of refreshment, hot chocolate for her at that wintry time of year, punch for him, and conversation with some of his cronies, always older men, who spoiled Sarah with the flatteries of older men and made her glow harmlessly. And now, when she had expected to be overjoyed at coming home to the Vale, she thought of those excursions with that sudden rush of loss that visits us when we leave the old and pleasant and familiar for we know not what. Would she return to London with its thronged thoroughfares, its gaudiness and noise, day and night – and the noxious odours of the Thames and pervading presence of soot in the air? Would the time before her ever be as full?

The carriage jerked and slid around a bend and then, on a firmer, paved track passed between pillars at an open gate and rolled up to a broad doorstep surmounted by a pair of columns and a door of indeterminate colour in the fading light. It stood ajar by the time Sarah had descended and her bags and the wrapped gift from her uncle placed beside her. Her first deep breath of air on stepping down from the coach was of such purity and sweetness it made her senses swim, and then she almost swooned. The man who greeted her in waistcoat and breeches was tall and straight, his own thick hair (he wore no wig) combed back and tied with a ribbon at the nape. Candles already lit in the entrance hall revealed dark brows and eyes, aquiline features and full, almost womanly lips.

'You are surely Sally,' he said. 'We have been expecting you. I mean the children, of course, have been waiting to see you. But Thomas Digby has fallen asleep – which, perhaps, is just as well. You will be there when he awakes. Frances would not sleep. I shall have her brought down anon. Joseph – ' he called to a figure hovering behind him, ' – look to the baggage. Meanwhile,' with a small inclination of the head, not quite a bow, 'I am Richard Aubrey. Welcome to Ash Hall.'

Sarah had been brought home by a concatenation of circumstances. During the years of her absence her father, in his late forties, had become suddenly less vigorous, so that her brother, Stephen, named – hopefully – for the distant cousin who owned Merthyr Mawr, had taken on an increasing share of the work. In expectation of profit, and ever mindful of the supposed wealth of a kinsman, no matter how remote, Thomas Jones had invested money and, at those times of the year when farming made few demands on him, not a little time, in nearby lead mining and smelting works, until his wife said he was doing altogether too much for his own good. His lassitude and unease with himself suggested she was right. The occasional letter from Llangan made no mention of it, but family contacts in the drapery trade had passed the information from one to another, together with reports of her mother's anxiety at this unlooked for change in her husband's vitality, until it had reached John Jones's ears. Such was his fondness for Sally, he had almost suppressed it: he did not want her to be hurt by the news, still less to lose her. To think of her, capable, cultivated and charming as she had become, returning to a humble farmyard existence pained him.

Then intelligence arrived concerning a family in the Vale with which he was acquainted through his business as tailor and army clothier. Sir Thomas Aubrey of Llantrithyd and (by the advantageous marriage of his grandfather) possessor of ample estates in England and Wales, he considered a friend, a rather grand friend to be sure, and they did not meet often, but when they did it was always cordially on both sides. Not long before, the connection had brought into the shop the baronet's son, also Thomas, a sturdy army lieutenant about to embark for America, to purchase one of the fine campaign boxes for which John Jones was famous, and the soldier's father had come to settle his son's account. Sir Thomas was of middling height with a long muzzle, rather sheep-like. Beneath the enveloping heavy woollen coat in which he had been travelling, he was richly attired. His manner was easy and in his relations he was exceedingly pleasant. He was accompanied by John, his eldest son and heir, a man of different cast, hawk-featured and negligently elegant, who had become an MP in 1768. He did not disguise his boredom, peering about and poking with his cane among the wares displayed, but Sir Thomas was perplexed and glad of the opportunity to gossip. Thus it was John Jones heard of the misfortune that had befallen Richard, Sir Thomas's youngest son, whose wife Frances had died of a fever shortly after giving birth. The couple had already a daughter of two years or so and that this second child was the son they both longed for had been greeted with rejoicing, but their happiness quickly turned to anxiety and then to grief as Frances sickened and, a week later, died. The babe was put to a wet nurse and, oblivious of the sorrow that had followed hard upon his entry into the world, thrived.

'A wet nurse is sufficient for the present,' said Sir Thomas, 'but Richard has to consider what will happen when the child begins to grow. And there is also his sister, already two years old and walking, or rather tumbling, about and beginning to prattle. Servants can look to their clothing and feeding, but they need a mother, or, in these most unhappy circumstances, someone who will care for them as nearly like her as possible and has, though this one could hardly hope for, the sensibility, delicacy and refined taste that poor Frances possessed. I fear Richard has lost an irreplaceable paragon, but if you know of such a one ...'

I think I do, John Jones said to himself, then, although he regretted it almost as soon as he uttered the words, 'I think I do,' he said.

If Sally were to leave him, as some day she must, he reasoned, this would be a place of the quality he would be content to see her occupy. He was quite sure she would meet the highest expectations of Sir Thomas – and of Richard Aubrey, and that she would be happy in a fine house in the Vale of Glamorgan, serving a family with ancestry and noble connections. He did not want to lose her, but this employment would take her closer to her family home and answer any concerns that might arise about her father. He could not allow himself selfishly to deny her these opportunities.

'I believe you will find my niece Sally – Sarah, I should say, Sarah Jones – who comes from Llangan in the Vale, where my brother farms, and has been my housekeeper here for the past six years – is the very person you seek.'

Urgently called to the shop below, Sarah, in an apron with her sleeves rolled to the elbow, her brown hair undressed, tousled, descended the stairs to be met by two unfashionably bewigged gentlemen. She curtsied and, despite herself, brushed her hair quickly from her forehead with her hand, and blushed. Yes, she was well, she thanked the gentlemen. Yes, she was happy as housekeeper in her uncle's home, which she agreed was very fine, nay, beautiful. Yes, she was fond of children, though she saw none in her present employ. She was conscious of the gentlemen's eyes over her and blushed again. They examined her rather as they would a horse: she was a young woman, slender and straight, of middling height, clear-eyed and with good teeth, who spoke modestly and was not shy of work. Sarah, glad to be dismissed, curtsied again. As she turned to the staircase, she heard the languid, careless voice of the younger man, 'Not a pretty one – which is no bad thing in the circumstances.' And his father's admonitory 'Hush!'.

Her decision to leave London had not been taken easily. One evening, soon after the visit of Sir Thomas and his son, Sarah found her uncle comfortably seated in his library. There were books at his side, but he was smoking a long-stemmed clay pipe and gazing thoughtfully into the fire.

'Ah, Sarah,' he said, 'I was thinking of you. I do not doubt for one moment your ability to become, as it were, another mother to the children of Richard Aubrey. And I saw at once that Sir Thomas, who is an astute judge, was greatly taken with you – as indeed I had every expectation he would be. I am certain it will be arranged and you will return to the Vale – if you wish it. Selfishly, I would prefer you to remain here, but I shall not with hoops of love, loyalty or duty bind you to stay.'

Sarah, who had come to bid her uncle good night, stood silent, with head bowed. 'Sit here a while with me,' her uncle said. 'You have met Sir Thomas and his older son, but so brief a meeting will have told you little about the Aubreys. They are of ancient stock, claiming descent from French nobility who accompanied William of Normandy in his conquest of England in 1066. The true star in their family firmament was Dr William Aubrey, one of the finest legal minds of the reign of Elizabeth. He was from a branch of the family that settled in Brecon. His fame was such, I was told, a monument was raised to his memory in St Paul's, but it was, alas, destroyed in the great fire of 1666. A son of the lawyer, named Thomas, married Mary Mansell, heiress of Llantrithyd, in the Vale, and *their* son, John, who had supported the Royal cause through the time of Cromwell's Puritans, was created baronet by Charles II. Do you follow me? It is not easy to keep track of all. Well, there has been a succession of heirs to the baronetcy all named John – as stout and honest a name as you could wish' – he smiled – 'and one of them married an heiress of considerable estates at Boarstall in Buckinghamshire and near Oxford … I fear I have lost you.'

The pipe was refilled and, as smoke once more spiralled into the candlelight, he began again. 'It matters not. This last wealthy couple were the parents of Sir Thomas, whom you have met, with his heir, yet another Sir John. It may be you have heard – or will hear – some tittle-tattle about Sir John. He appears a stout and worthy gentleman but, if the gossip is to be believed, there is another side to his character. He is reputed a member of the Hellfire Club – a band of rakes led by a man called Dashwood, who meet somewhere near Aylesbury, in Buckinghamshire, where they behave in a scandalous manner unworthy of their names and station in life. Boarstall is also near Aylesbury, which perhaps explains how Sir John became ensnared in this disreputable business. But Richard, the youngest son, is of a very different cast of character. Like his great ancestor, he is a man of learning, a scholar, who was brought up largely at a mansion near Oxford. And so it was at Oxford he was educated and, until his marriage, not three years ago, he was a Fellow of All Souls there, residing at the college. It seems he became friendly with two brothers of an old and honoured family from Meriden, in Warwickshire, named Digby, and through them met their sister, Frances. In short, a marriage was arranged that was to everyone's satisfaction. Richard was, I think, thirty-five; Frances in her late twenties – a good age to settle down, I am sure people said. Sir Thomas gave the couple Ash Hall, as fine a house as you could wish, in the Vale of Glamorgan. When it seemed Richard had little to look forward to beyond old bachelorhood in an academic cloister, he was suddenly married, with an estate to run and, quite soon, the beginnings of a family. And then … the tragedy. It was, by all accounts, a happy union, though most distressingly cut short – cynics might say before disillusion could replace the first felicities of the bond of marriage. But who am I to speak of such things?'

He smiled self-deprecatingly and the question hung in the air. Coals shuffled in the grate and resettled, emitting a feeble flare of flame. Sarah observed he did not expect an answer. 'Thank you, uncle, for helping me to understand. Shall I call William to tend the fire?' she said.

'No, my dear, I shall finish my pipe and repair to bed. And you will tell me in the morning whether you will stay by the side of, I fear, a maudlin old man in London, or … or, I suppose, go home.'

As she opened the door, Sarah heard her uncle's long drawn sigh and then he blew his nose. Barely a month later, she began her journey from London and on the third day arrived at Ash Hall.

In what remained of that first evening at Ash Hall, Sarah gathered an impression of spacious accommodation, and furnishings that, while not nearly so refined as her uncle's, were yet handsome, if somewhat uncared for. Richard had welcomed her with restrained warmth. Although his demeanour suggested he bore still a heavy burden, he felt, he said, a weight lifting from his shoulders, for his father had assured him that Sarah Jones, of a Vale family, who carried with her from London the highest recommendation of a man of taste and discrimination, would be the nursemaid and governess of his children he so desperately needed. Sarah had bowed her head to hide her blushes. She would strive her utmost to live up to her uncle's good opinion, she said, and would be glad to meet her charges at the first opportunity. Since, by the time she had changed from her travelling clothes and taken a little light refreshment, Julia Frances, too, had fallen asleep, that was delayed. Richard had looked at her closely; he hoped profoundly that this would be for the best, but had nothing more to say. A few days, a week at the most, would reveal whether his father's praise of this young woman had been extravagant, his confidence in her misplaced. And if that proved to be so, she could return to her family; Llangan was only a few miles away. Fatigued from her long journey, Sarah was glad to follow a maid bearing candles and a footman carrying her baggage up a broad curving staircase to her room.

The keen early light of a clear frosty morning disclosed a small room, yet with a high ceiling, for this was not in the servants' attic quarters but on the floor below, where family and guests slept. A communicating door gave entrance to the children's room alongside. Sarah dressed hurriedly, for although this chamber was well, if plainly, furnished, it had no fireplace and was bitterly cold. Strangely forested silver landscapes were etched on the inside of windowpanes, echoing the dimly perceived frost-decked trees in the garden beyond. A melancholy complaint from the other side of the connecting door quickly followed by an infant wail told her the day's work had begun. She wrapped a shawl about her shoulders, eyed again the unopened oblong parcel that was her uncle's parting gift and hurried to the door. She knocked softly and entered a somewhat larger room where coals sputtered with low flames in a small fireplace.

The infant's cry had stopped almost as suddenly as it had begun and Sarah quickly understood why. Thomas Digby was sucking hungrily at the breast of a plump young woman swathed in a patterned blanket, his arms and fingers, legs and toes all moving together, as though, if he could, he would somehow clamber into her. This was Jennet, his nurse, who was gazing down on him almost in wonder. She was, Sarah duly discovered, from Ystradowen, the village below the manor house, where the men in her family, like those in her husband's family, were all farm labourers. Three days after Thomas Digby Aubrey entered the world, her first baby had died at birth. Her parents and in-laws were known to the Aubreys and this news had quickly reached Ash Hall, so that, when, soon after, Frances died, an elderly servant of the manor house was despatched to speak to the grieving mother, who was known to be clean in her person and restrained in her manners. She was reluctant to leave the ruinous cottage where she lived with her husband's family in their winter penury, but the promise of payment greater than the menfolk earned on a good day overcame all doubts. For herself, she pleased Richard Aubrey by being quiet and neat, and he provided her with fresh clothing. She was bewildered and rendered almost speechless by the sudden change, but quite soon the far greater comfort of her surroundings and a creeping sense of fulfilment brought by the sucking of a babe, though not her own, invaded her. The household servants understood they should attend to her needs, because she was the new heir's lifeline and, as days passed, by degrees her anxiety at the utter strangeness of her situation diminished. She slept in the same room as the children and at the merest whimper from the baby swiftly put him to her breast. Sarah had heard not a single cry through the night.

Julia Frances was standing, swaying sleepily, one hand on the blanketed knee of the wet nurse, inscrutably watching her brother feed. She was dark and brown-eyed, like her father. Sarah gathered her in her arms and bore her off through the open door into the adjoining room, where she placed the child on her own bed, and pulled the blanket around them both, talking quietly about the morning and the frost in the trees. What did one do with a child who has lost her mother? The answer seemed to be to keep her warm, and speak gently to her. In a little while Sarah's eyes fell on her uncle's gift, which lay on a side table near the bed.

'Shall we open the parcel?' she said. The child looked up at her and said nothing. 'Will you help me?'

The object was the size of a large book, but not nearly as heavy. Sarah reached out and lifted it on to the bed before them. 'Shall we open it, Julia?' The child nodded and placed a small, plump hand on the outer layer of brown paper. 'Let's see – can you help me?'

In a few moments the string binding had been untied and they both pulled at the loosened wrapping. Two more rustling layers of stout paper lay about them on the bed before the child, whose interest had increased throughout the operation, pulled away a final gauze-like sheet and disclosed a small painting within an exquisitely carved and gilded frame. 'Cows,' she said. And indeed, there were cattle, drinking at a pond, and trees heavy with foliage bowing over, and blue above the trees and in one corner a sunstruck edge of cloud. 'Trees,' said the child, pointing.

'Isn't that lovely,' said Sarah, gazing rapt at the peaceful pastoral scene. In the bottom left hand corner of the painting was a signature: G. Morland. 'Ah, uncle, dear uncle, how can I repay you?' The tremble in her voice made the child look up and study her face, with a small frown, seeing tears in her eyes.

Sarah breathed deeply. 'You must call me Sally,' she said. Then, laying a gentle finger on the child's breast, 'You are Julia, and,' pointing in turn to herself, 'I am Sally.'

They looked together at the painting – the cattle, trees bending over limpid water, blue above and the glowing edge to the patch of cloud. The child, at ease, leant against her and Sarah, her arm about the small warm body, held her close.

Sarah soon felt at home in the comfortable surroundings of Ash Hall, a large square house standing on an eminence, looking south over Ystradowen and the town of Cowbridge towards the sea. She was surprised to find that on clear days it was possible to see the coast of Somerset across the broad estuary of the Severn from her bedroom window. This long view was obscured from the lawn at the front of the house by a stout stone wall and a clump of low trees. Mr Aubrey told her he planned to remove both wall and trees. He had seen at Meriden Hall in Warwickshire ('Where my wife came from,' he added, his voice almost a whisper) how the construction of a ha-ha gave the same utility as a wall in preventing stock from entering the garden, and an uninterrupted view across the wider landscape.

'It was my intention to accomplish this in readiness for the coming of spring, when my wife and the new babe could have the pleasure of the garden and the beauty of the view beyond. Even though she has gone, I will do it for her sake – and for my son,' he said, 'whose inheritance this place will be.'

As the months passed, he kept his word, and more. Much of the stone was reused to enclose a kitchen garden at the rear of the house and, a little later, espaliered fruit trees were set against the new walls and a narrow plantation begun, including some sweet chestnuts, as protection from northerly winds. Another new wall bordered the property on the eastward side, beyond which lay the road Sarah had travelled on that first evening, which seemed already distant, so unexpectedly full was her life, and within it a flower garden arranged in four rectangles separated by low box hedges.

It had taken almost half a year before Sarah had felt settled in London with her uncle. Perhaps that was due partly to her youth and the wrench of leaving home, and the great distance she felt from Llangan; and perhaps it owed something to the quiet and rarefied splendour of the rooms above the shop at the corner of Sackville Street and Piccadilly. Her return to the Vale was different. Though not at Llangan, she was at home once more, among voices and customs, weathers and places which were familiar. Though narrower in its reach than attending to the varied needs of her uncle's home, her new occupation, caring for Richard Aubrey's children, was, she knew, the greater responsibility. He put his trust in her and did not interfere. What she and Jennet would do with the children daily was for her to decide and, although it was never asked of her, still less required, she sought an opportunity to recount to him at the end of each week what had been done and how the children fared. On those occasions when he was engaged elsewhere and she could not see him, she wrote reports for him. Days might bring moments of confusion and anxiety, but as she saw the children grow in stature and understanding of the world, and in affection for her, she felt nothing but delight.

Ash Hall was a bright house, especially on the south side, where five tall windows on the first floor matched five more below, two of which opened outwards from the largest room in the house, like two pairs of doors, on to a veranda and a level field of close-trimmed grass beyond. There was space enough and to spare for the master, his two infant children, Sarah and Jennet, and six servants, two of whom were usually employed outdoors. The furniture was mostly aged black oak glowing with the sheen of many years' beeswax polishing, and well-worn, stuffed leather from the great Aubrey house at Llantrithyd, which was little used since Sir Thomas resided at his Boarstall estate and visited the Vale only a few times each year. The same, older and far grander Llantrithyd mansion also supplied family portraits on the walls, some from the time of the Tudor monarchs. Through the winter well-tended coal fires warmed the spacious rooms on the ground floor. Coal was worked only a few miles away in the hillier country to the north so that there was a plentiful supply for the purpose and, Mr Aubrey explained, for burning limestone later in the year to make lime for dressing the fields in readiness for sowing.

In those first months, Aubrey was constantly busy with the improvements that he and his wife had planned and he was determined to carry forward. Labourers and masons were hired and he spent his days working alongside them, to hasten progress, he said. Each day at dusk he returned to the house exhausted, supped alone and retired early to bed. He was a man in his prime and as capable of the work as any, but there was no need for him to do more than direct the labour of others. Why then? He gave himself little time for his children, except on Sundays, when he would kneel to embrace Julia Frances, smile upon Thomas Digby and say a kindly word to Sarah and Jennet. On these occasions they observed how low his spirits were. Did he set out so to fatigue himself with daily labour that he would, at least for that time, forget his loss? Or, Sarah wondered, did he feel responsible for the death of his wife, and was punishing his body in daily penance to purge his guilt. She determined that she would strive to renew in him a father's love for his children.

She and Jennet talked together, though at first the nurse had very little to say. She was not sure how old she was, nor did she know the date of her birthday. She thought she was nineteen. She was dark haired and pink cheeked and her brown eyes were diffident, but Sarah saw how dexterously and tenderly her hands caught and held and lifted the baby, and with what ease she cradled him in her arms and held him to her breast, motherless child and childless mother rapt in silent communion, and wondered whether she would, or could, possess the same maternal skills, whether indeed, even if she did possess them, they would ever be called upon in tending a child of her own. Jennet's wages and, occasionally, certain small surpluses from hen house and garden, went directly to her husband's parents, for it soon transpired that he had left the family home to seek work elsewhere. Weeks passed bringing no news of him; but then, he had not learned to write, nor could she read. Preoccupied with the baby who had so quickly replaced the one death snatched from her, she did not appear distressed by this turn of events; at least she said nothing. In the almost mute weeks before Sarah's arrival, while scrupulously attending to the infant, she had needed to be bullied into eating for his sake. Sarah's calm assumption of authority, extending even to the other servants, and withal, her gentleness and ease with the children, worked a change in Jennet's demeanour. She responded with cheerfulness to Sarah's good cheer and, though still shy, smiled readily. Thomas Digby, too, well fed, waxed bonny and content.

Governess and wet nurse spent their time together, mutually dependent and close. There were times when the children were unwell or unhappy from falling over or having had some desired act or object denied, but they were brief. Sarah loved them almost at once: Julia clung to her and Thomas came as happily to her arms as to Jennet's, except when he was hungry. By August, when they often walked the lawn at the front of the house together to survey the latest stages in the construction of the ha-ha and new walls, the baby, wrapped securely in a light shawl wound around Jennet's body, as Sarah had so often seen in Llangan as a young girl, was attentive to sights and sounds about him. On his round face the first faint impressions of individual character were beginning to be etched, while Julia, steady and light on her feet, chattered about the trees and flowers and the birds, and the men working, her Papa among them.

On such occasions Jennet delighted in hearing Sarah talk about London – the size and magnificence of the buildings, the busyness of streets crowded with people and carriages, the opulence of shops and the goods they offered, the street hawkers and performers – all the sights and sounds of the great city, which left her open-mouthed with wonder.

'Is everybody rich there?'

'Oh, no,' said Sarah. 'There are many ragged beggars, and vagabonds and thieves. And some parts of the city, where my uncle would never take me, nor allow me to be taken, are full of filth and vermin. William and Alice, his servants, knew about these places, for they were brought up in London, and told me of them, but they, too, would never venture into them. The houses, they said, are full of people, from cellar to roof, and stinking, and they throw night soil into the street, which is only a little narrow lane, and always dark because the houses on both sides are so tall – and we heard of houses falling down and killing everybody in them.'

'Ach-y-fi,' said Jennet, wrinkling her nose and, 'Oh, the poor people.'

'Yes,' Sarah continued, pleased with the effect of her narrative, 'London can be a very smelly place, especially down by the river, where I did go from time to time, but it is a very grand river, with all the boats and ferries, and so wide, from here right over there.' She pointed vaguely in the direction of Ystradowen, while Jennet gasped in awe.

'And you lived down there Jennet?'

'Yes, our cottage, I mean my Dada and Mama's, is a bit behind the church. It's not very big, and the roof's leaky, but it's all right.' She glanced behind at the broad, many-windowed façade of Ash Hall.

'Does your husband come from Ystradowen?'

'Evan? Yes, just along by the crossroads, though I don't know where he is now.'

She paused and Sarah wondered whether this thought

grieved her companion, and would perhaps make her weep, but there were no tears. Instead she looked down at the baby, nestled in the shawl, asleep now, and went on, 'His Da is a bit lame. He doesn't get a lot of work, especially in the winter. They don't even have chickens. We've got a few chickens at home – and a share in a pig.'

Sarah considered this, and could think of nothing more to say. Nor would Jennet volunteer more information about her home and daily life before the loss of her own child and sudden translation to Ash Hall. The contrast was great and Sarah divined her reluctance to say more arose from a sense of loyalty to her parents, and to Evan and his family.

Thomas Digby had been baptized at his mother's bedside the day following his birth. The Reverend George Williams, curate of Ystradowen, had left the small grey church with its stunted tower and curiously twisted, sagging roof and struggled against a biting wind up the steep lane to Ash Hall. Sarah heard from servants, and later from Richard Aubrey himself that the curate, frail and aged beyond his years, had yet greeted the new life placed in his arms with warmth and benign tenderness. Father and mother together named the child, joining the names of their families in him, and he, being baptised with water, waved his arms and kicked his legs and wailed, at which all smiled happily, the parents, the curate and two old servants proud to witness the rite. Barely a week passed before, with profound sadness, the curate dragged himself up the hill once more to comfort the bereaved husband.

Ten months later, on the first Sunday in September, it was decided the child should be taken to the church to certify his baptism, as the prayer book directs. On the day appointed, the sun came up haloed like a lamp in soft grey mist. The hill on which Ash Hall stood soon cleared, but from her room Sarah surveyed a broad grey river filling the valley below, from which the church tower and the leafy tops of the tallest trees rose like half-submerged rocks and shoals. By noon the last wisps of mist had disappeared and the day was bright and warm again. It had been a fine summer; haymaking had been completed early and the harvesting of oats and wheat was proceeding apace. 'God be praised,' people said, 'we shall not lack this winter.' Mr Aubrey, his building projects almost complete, much to his satisfaction, greeted governess and nurse and his children with smiles. Julia ran to him and he lifted her and kissed her on the cheek and said what a good girl she was, and put her down, stroking her dark hair as she stood by his side. He was neatly but soberly dressed, the dark frockcoat and breeches signifying he was in mourning still, but he held himself straight and tall, like a man hale and in good heart, and again the sensuous lips parted in generous smiles. Although his sense of loss was undiminished, this would be a happy occasion.

The carriage had been called and he helped Sarah and Jennet and the children settle within. Sarah kept Julia safe with an arm around her shoulders, while Jennet held the baby close and upright in her arms by the carefully wrapped shawl. The conveyance lurched and clattered down the hill between hedgerows and dust rising from the horse's hooves and carriage wheels fell soft upon dry hawthorn, tall grass heavy with seed and the leaves and flowers of campion and thistles and knapweed. Another, far grander carriage was drawn up near the church and a groom held the halters of two matched bays. At the lych-gate, Sir Thomas, in full-skirted green coat with white ruffles at throat and wrists, was waiting. He embraced his son, acknowledged Sarah with a smile and hoped she was well, and bent to kiss his granddaughter. Come from Boarstall on a visit to view his Vale properties, he was glad to combine this necessary business with the church baptism of his grandson, and so it had been arranged.

The rumble of carriage wheels, thudding hooves, whip cracks and loud bellows, 'Clear the road! Aside for Lady Margaret!' scattered a dozen or so interested onlookers to crouch close beneath the hedges on either side as two lathered greys rounded the bend at speed and were brought slithering to a halt by the coachman, standing, legs braced, in his box, hauling on the reins.

'Stand aside, stand aside!' he shouted again, to the empty road as he leapt down and strode to the carriage door and handed down the lady within, her face mostly hidden by an extravagantly large bonnet oddly tilted as though by the impetuosity of her arrival. It was Sir Thomas's spinster sister, Margaret, daughter of their father's second marriage who, Sarah learned later, had leased much of the Llantrithyd estate from her half-brother and was deferred to by all. Small and plump, she was simply attired in cream silk that glimmered in the sun. Richard Aubrey bowed and addressed her with deep respect. Although sorely tempted, such was the elaborate courtesy of this greeting, Sarah dared not study her beyond first impressions of the dress and the bonnet, which, when adjusted, still revealed little of hair and features, save a wide, thin-lipped mouth, the tip of a nose and becoming paleness. But Margaret was much taken with the baby and determined to have him in her arms. Careless of her dress, and heedless of his protests, she appropriated Thomas Digby from the reluctant Jennet, who was at the same time essaying a curtsey to the grand lady.

'An Aubrey, every inch an Aubrey,' said Margaret, from the depths of her bonnet, 'I would know those lips – and that frown, anywhere. I do believe he is going to cry. Here, take him.'

Restored to Jennet's arms, the baby protested loudly, until the nurse's quite violent rocking and cooing, restored his placid humour. The birds resumed their singing and a mild breeze ruffled the leaves of the tall churchyard elms, casting shadows across sun-silvered walls and bent and sagging stone-tiled roof sprinkled with yellow coins of lichen.

'Come,' said Sir Thomas, leading the party along the path through the ancient graveyard.

They were received with ceremony at the church door by the Reverend George Williams, but this was not the ageing and feeble man Sarah had expected to see. At first she wondered whether some miracle had not occurred to restore the curate to health. But clearly this was a young man, no older than herself. As though in answer to her unspoken question, he addressed himself to Sir Thomas and Margaret Aubrey: 'I know my father would have wished to be here to receive Thomas Digby before the congregation as one of the flock of true Christian people but, alas, he was received into the bosom of his Christ not two months ago. I mourn him still. I have been instituted curate here in his place by Richard, Bishop of Llandaff, and God's Grace, and, with your permission, will this day conduct the office of baptism according to the rites of the Church.'

'Amen, and amen,' said Sir Thomas, leading the way into the church.

III

A SHARP RAP at the window made the kneeling man look up through his fingers. He trembled. Had God answered? He lowered his hands and, wincing, raised his head. The shape at the window was not of God-like stature. Through his tears and the distorting glass, a blur of white and black filled one small pane: it was the magpie.

Before he had time to struggle to his feet, the vague shape fell backwards and away into dusk. In this room on the dark side of the house, close under the hill, gloom had already gathered in the corners and was making towards him; an early rushlight glowed on his desk, where the Bible lay open.

Prayer, long, on his knees, had done nothing to ease his anxiety, for he was sure all was not well with him and that time, his time, was short. For some weeks he had slept badly, a sense of impending calamity haunting him accompanied by the strangest, alien odour, as though there were a crack in the wall of Hell through which a puff of noxious fume would from time to time waft into the blackness of their bedroom. Oh yes, Hell was very close; he had never been surer of it.

Again, that very day, with the faintest first light, as he had raised his head, a thunderclap of pain split his skull like an axe, pursued by anguish as of a knotted cord drawn into the socket of his left eye and on through the endless maze of his brain until he retched and moaned. As Esther struggled with trembling fingers to light the bedside candle, he had sunk back to the pillow, not daring to move while the pain echoed and flashed. Sometime later – had sleep or unconsciousness intervened? – he had opened his eyes on the whitewashed beams, each with its blue shadow, crossing the ceiling above him, and so had risen, very slowly, with great care, fearful lest an unguarded movement would reawaken the cause of his agony. With the same slow deliberation, he had dressed and descended the narrow stair step by stone step to the brushed and sanded flags of the kitchen. The fire had been lit, their sons, George and Richard, precious survivors, had taken the bay mare and left for the glebe, and Esther, hand to cheek, brow furrowed, had watched while he lowered himself to the straw-seated chair at the table's head. What would he eat? Nothing. Tea? The merest twitch of assent.

With the tea had come unbidden a small bowl of bread and milk. It awakened a memory: he was a child again at his father's table, and his mother, tenderly solicitous, bending over him. Was it the flavouring of memory that this time transformed the everyday taste, the softness, to manna in his mouth? With each morsel he felt stronger and clearer in his intention.

'Esther,' he whispered, reaching for her hand and putting it to his lips, 'my dear Esther, I believe I know what must be done. If you will place the tea on my desk, I will sit there a while and, with God's help, write to the Bishop.'

But he didn't write. Not then.

That May morning, leading the sturdy draught horse already harnessed for the plough, George and Richard tramped the muddy lane from the whitewashed farmhouse at Maendy across Newton Moor where an army of fresh green shoots was rising amidst the splintered brown waste of last year's bracken. Above, the sky was pale blue, but to the south and east a thick line of cream edged with red marked the horizon. The magpie, which had been watching from the garden hedge in expectation of titbits, followed from perch to perch, a harsh rattle reminding them of its presence. Patience exhausted, it flew down, settled momentarily on Richard's shoulder and tugged at his hair. He brushed the bird away.

'Go! Away with you! Would you make me bald?'

'I warned you no good would come of your kindness,' said George. 'If it was clumsy enough to fall from its nest, it would have been better left to find its own way back. Or in any event left. You have made it too familiar with humans.'

Richard shrugged. As the younger by five years he was used to his brother's admonitions, and the tone of voice accompanying them that had in it more of sorrow than anger. George sounded like their father, and indeed looked like him, lean, round-shouldered, fair, the nose rather bent and prominent, while he was shorter, squarer, dark-haired and, at seventeen, already swarthy. Their father had said very little of late and that in whispers. Even in church, he performed the familiar rituals of prayer and preached in a voice so low that some older members of the congregation could not forbear calling 'Speak up, Vicar'. He seemed to fear raising his voice lest it should wake something terrible lurking within him. Although nothing had been said, Richard felt his father had been seized by an affliction that was slowly drawing the life out of him. It was difficult to know what to do, except follow George in the daily routines of husbandry on the farm and the glebe.

The change that had overtaken the household, his father's

silent suffering, his mother's anxiety, had not been lost on George and, with his concern, a greater sense of responsibility had come upon him. But since his father had given no sign, no instruction, he too could think only of the day's tasks demanded by the passage of the seasons.

The magpie's insistent call faded as they crossed the moor, passing the fingerpost pointing to Llansannor, their father's home village, where, they well knew, in the almost circular ancient graveyard, with the great house just beyond the wall, lay the remains of four small children, their brothers and sisters. Nearing Penlline, the lane climbed steeply and passed between tall trees and hedges so high and weighted with foliage they bowed inwards, hiding the sky. In the damp warmth of May, blossoms on the hedge banks, primrose and dandelion, bluebell and celandine, strained up towards chinks of light in the canopy. The brothers barely noticed, for in the green shadowed stillness of the place, where no breeze penetrated, iridescent flies swarmed, circling maddeningly about them as they walked. It was easy to understand why many of the villagers believed old tales about the woods being haunted by bejewelled flying serpents (ungodly foolishness their father said). The horse, as irritated as they were, rolled her eyes, flung up her head and would have turned and bolted, but George, who, from years of work in the fields was stronger than he appeared, took a fresh grip on the halter and held her. Richard broke off a slim leafy branch and wafted it constantly about her head to give her a little relief.

'This is a deathly place,' George murmured and, despite the humid warmth, he felt suddenly a chill of premonition: that bird, and this infested hole. 'Oh, Father,' he whispered. And still the flies sought corruption and the hedges rustled like wings above him. At length, the lane widened, and junction with the village street brought respite.

From above, the seven-acre glebe sloping gently away from the stone wall surrounding their father's church and its graveyard near the crown of the ridge, would have appeared broadly wedge-shaped. In full, clear day the view extended to the west over neighbouring villages, Llangan and Colwinston, and as far as Merthyr Mawr, no more than flashes of reflected light five miles away. It was time to plough summer fallows ready for sowing with rye grass and clover. The ploughmen staked out the ground for a straight furrow and hitched the bay to the wooden plough. She knew the pattern of the day as well as they, and once she felt the plough handles raised so that the blade bit into the warm, moist soil, set off at a steady walk towards the distant hedge, while the earth, opening and curling over like a dark brown wave, unwound in a long line behind. The brothers laboured and rested in turns, while the bay plodded on, the nodding of her old head becoming more pronounced hour by hour. Sweat polished her and oozed white from under the black harness. At the end of a furrow they paused to wipe her down with handfuls of long grass while she snorted and dribbled. Through the long day, wave by wave, a brown tide slowly spread across the field.

At Maendy, Esther found her husband deeply asleep, his head resting on his folded arms upon the desk, the cup of tea cold where she had left it. He had chosen a sheet of paper and the ink and pen were ready, but he had written not a word. Although she had made no sound, a sense of her watchful presence stirred him. She hastened to place an arm about his shoulders, saying 'Hush, hush', as she would to a sick child. Nevertheless he started and, with a gasp of pain, grasped his head as though he would crush whatever malice lay within. And then, despite himself, he wept.

'My dearest, we must do something. Surely, you will let me ask doctors to help. Could you not send a plea to your Williams kin in Cardiff? I know their patients speak well of them.'

With the slightest shake of the head he whispered, 'No, they are too distant, too busy with the many calls of their practice in town ... too expensive. I cannot expect remote relatives to come gratis to my aid. And I am not certain there is anything they can do to help me. It would be paying for nothing.'

'Call Bevan then? He is but two miles off and would come quickly. Let me send for him, beg him to ease your pain.'

He looked into her eyes and again the axe struck, so that for a time he could not speak: 'Yes ... call Bevan. Ask him to come ... quickly, please. I begin to fear I shall run and dash my head against the wall.'

Bevan, a broad, squat man, in old age, white-haired, ruddy-cheeked, with a great bush of white beard hanging down his chest, came to Maendy farm in a pony-trap carrying a weighty leather bag of tinctures and instruments. He knocked the half-open door and, without waiting for voice or sign from within, walked into the kitchen. Esther was standing behind her husband, who sat at the scrubbed deal table with his head again resting on his arms. It was warm within. Light full of motes from an untended fire entered the long, low room through two windows, brushed the tall back of an old settle and the tops of the backrests of three oak chairs, and touched with gilded fingers a pair of brass candlesticks on a narrow shelf above the inglenook. In shadow on the seat of the settle, a full moon of fresh milk lay still in a broad, shallow bowl.

The patient, who had barely moved at the sound of footsteps, raised his head as the door creaked and opened wide. Bevan looked at him. What were the symptoms he asked; how long had they persisted? He bent and cupped his ear to listen to the whispered account of strange odours detectable by the sufferer alone, of agonising headaches set off by the slightest jar, turning his head or raising his voice, or simply nothing at all, plaguing him by day and night.

Bevan stroked his beard, deep in thought. 'What you describe must be the consequence of pressure within the skull,' he said, ' – pressure such that the brain is assaulted and reacts as you describe.'

'Can you stop the pressure?' Esther said, close to tears.

'Stop it? I don't know, but I believe drawing away blood will relieve the symptoms. There are still the questions of how much blood, and from what site it could be most efficaciously withdrawn. My instinct tells me a small quantity, at least to start. It is rather unusual but, for obvious reasons, I suggest it should come from the temple.' He turned to Esther. 'I shall need your help. Do you think you will be able to hold the dish?'

He rummaged in his bag and produced a pewter bowl. On one side the arc of a circle had been cut from the rim and opposite this bite a flat hand-grip extended. 'You hold it by the handle, so,' said Bevan, passing it to Esther. 'As you can see from the shape, it is better suited to withdrawing blood from the arm, but we must improvise. That is why I shall need your help. First bring me some clean rags.'

Esther nodded. How could she refuse? Returned to Bevan's

side she could faintly discern the incised marks of a scale in the dull silver sheen within the bowl. 'Yes,' said Bevan, 'you see there how I shall determine the letting of four fluid ounces – enough I think for now. And we shall see how the patient responds. You must sit up now, Vicar. You have heard what I said. I shall need you to sit as straight and still as you can. Yes, your head back a little, so. And Esther will help. Come, hold the cup under the left temple – not so close that I cannot address the site. There, yes, there … and tilted a little towards the head. Yes. Now do not move it. You have seen blood letting before; there is nothing to fear.' He extracted a knife from a pouch and wiped the blade thoughtfully on his sleeve. 'Let us find the vein.'

He rubbed the temple gently, raising the vein, and then taking the knife with one extended finger guiding the blade as though he were at table, punctured the blue thread. As blood spurted bright red from the incision in small pulsing jets, Esther gasped.

'Esther,' Bevan hissed, 'now I need you. Hold the cup, I must see how much. Four ounces. Enough.' And he pressed on the vein with a broad thumb. 'Quickly, the rags. Now hold them there, firmly, let us say for five minutes.' He produced a pocket watch.

'It is done, Vicar. We must pray that this alleviates your pain. If so, at the very least, we can repeat the operation to give you some ease.'

As Esther led him to the door he added, 'Let him rest where he chooses, though bed will be best. I will leave this flask with you. It contains tincture of the opium poppy, exceedingly bitter to the taste. If the pain returns, give him a little – no more than twenty-five drops every four hours, and only if it is needed, in a glass of warm water, honey and cloves. Let us hope it will not be needed.'

The next morning George again crossed Newton Moor and climbed the hill to Penlline village. He was alone, for Richard was weeding the young barley crop in a field close to the farmhouse. His companion in labour was one of a pair of oxen from the hovel, which needed the flick of a long, thin whip on its flank as a reminder to lift one broad hoof after another as it moved as though half asleep slowly through the dank green tunnel, impervious to circling flies. With the same measured pace the share would spill out fresh furrows through the day. It was as well less than two acres remained to be ploughed.

As he leant to the plough, George pondered the future with disquiet. He had observed the rapid decline of his father, whom he had seen that same morning, deathly pale, sipping medicine left by Bevan. He was sick and often in great pain; earnest prayers for his recovery had so far been unanswered. What if he were to die? The lease of the farm extended another four years. While he lived, the benefice of Penlline and his curacy at Ystradowen would pay the rent and rather more, while the glebe and the farm together could, if the harvests were fair, more than supply their needs. But his father's death would end the incumbency and remove the glebe. Old Sir John, who owned their farm and land, would not quickly force them out, for the Aubreys were fair and it was in their interests to keep good tenants. But when the time came, the rent would have to be paid, and he, George, would be responsible for paying it. To the rhythm of the ox's plodding progress he began to calculate an income deprived of the Penlline living. No matter how hard he and Richard worked the farm, it would be difficult to hold on to Maendy. Sooner or later the stock would have to go, the horses and oxen, their half-dozen milk cows, a score of sheep. He and Richard would be reduced to hiring themselves out as labourers to work for others. Of what use then would be their schooling, the reading and writing, the arduous hours of Latin and arithmetic?

Richard walked the barley field behind the farm. Armed with weeding stick and hoe, head bent, he scoured the soil between whiskered green barley shoots. Before he set out, George had been more schoolmasterly than usual, reminding him earnestly that, encouraged by the damp warmth of early May, weeds were springing up apace and already threatening to choke the crop. 'Yes, I know,' he had protested, 'I have seen them, and you have told me all this before, many times.' But he recognised a more urgent tone in his brother's nagging and easily guessed the reason. He, too, was concerned about their father's sickness, and not from filial love alone, for he understood that the Church was his father's life and the better part of the family's livelihood. He saw their mother was beset by anxieties and he grieved for them both.

Out of sight in the hawthorn hedge already heavy with white blossom, the magpie rattled, and seconds later in a flurry of wing beats it was on his shoulder pecking at the wide brim of his hat. 'You are faithful while I feed you, yes, I know,' said Richard, bending to his task, while the bird flapped its wings and adjusted its claws to hold on. 'But really this is too much. Have you brought ill-fortune down on us? Some would say so. Some would say I ought to get rid of you – shoot you. And that would be an end of it. Here, take this.' He broke some crumbs of bread and cheese from the cloth-wrapped bundle he took from his smock pocket and tossed them on the ground, where at once the bird settled, and leaning on the hoe, viewed with a fresh sense of wonderment the iridescent glossiness of its back.

'There will be no more,' he said. 'Whatever saving and befriending you have brought, it has not been good. You must go, and I warn you, stay away.' When the bird had pecked up the morsels and would have returned to his shoulder, he shook it off and clapped his hands until it flew to a distant hedge.

It was tedious labour, scratching and scraping out meadow grass and poppies, digging around the roots of broad-leaved charlock and pulling the plants free of the soil, hacking and hoeing thistles. There were indeed many weeds already flourishing as George had said. Without help, it would take all day and perhaps even much of the morrow to tackle this, the smallest and highest of their fields. Their father said (and George repeated) that hiring labour now, when time was on their side, for work that was not arduous, was wasteful. At haymaking and the reaping of wheat and mowing of oats and barley, which all had to be done at the right time and speedily, then they would call on friends for help and hire labourers. Richard straightened his back and scanned sky and sea to the south, a merging of hazy blues suddenly slashed across the horizon by a line of light. Did that have meaning? The silent question dropped into the labyrinth of his brain and he bent again to his task.

Hearing the clatter of the horse and trap approaching, Esther met Bevan in the yard outside the house. She was pale and drawn, as before. There had been little change in her husband's condition; he was tortured still by sickening waves of pain, but the opium tincture brought relief and he had watched her beseechingly as she measured it out for him drop by drop.

Bevan was thoughtful. 'I am sure release of pressure from the plethora of blood in the skull is the key. We must try a more drastic measure, and I shall need you, Esther, to be doubly vigilant. Do you have a bowl, one as big again as the bleeding cup we used yesterday? Bring it to me. Do not mention this to your husband, but I shall withdraw as much blood as will induce syncope. Do you understand what I say? I shall bleed him until he faints away.'

Before Esther could protest, he continued, 'I want you to persuade him and help him to lie on the table, and then to hold the bowl as you did yesterday, and be ready to support his head when he faints so that I can stop the flow. Now bring me some rags.'

The Vicar swayed to his feet and held the edge of the table while he sought his balance. Lack of food and sleep had weakened him. As though he were a child, Esther held him in her arms and thus he allowed himself to be laid on his back and she lifted his legs on to the table. He did not ask what was to be done, but lay still as a corpse on the deal planks, gazing upwards into the murk of the smoke-stained ceiling.

'It will be like yesterday,' said Bevan, looking down at him. 'You will feel the merest prick. And Esther will be close at hand. Lie still for us.'

The eyes of the patient did not move; he gave no sign that he had heard. The knife did its work and the bright red blood pulsed out, splashing into the white earthenware bowl that Esther held with mounting horror. What if he did not faint? The eyes were still wide, but a new and dreadful pallor was invading cheeks already pale. With no warning, the head sank away from the bowl and the blood spurted down greying hair and in a scarlet arc across the scrubbed boards.

Esther was unable to suppress a cry and Bevan, poised by her side, leapt to staunch the flow. 'It is well. Dispose of the blood and wipe those stains,' he said. 'I have done as much as can be done.'

When George and Richard returned Bevan had gone. They found their father still lying upon the table, his head swathed in bandages. He was awake but silent and too weak to rise, and their mother, seated close by, little better. Esther stirred herself and tenderly the three raised the still figure and, as best they could, half carrying him, the young men brought their father up the curving narrow steps to the bed he and Esther had shared for twenty-four years. Esther removed the bandages and he lay back on a pillow. It was late afternoon and outside the weather was fair. The bedroom had been warmed by the sun. A small, open window, low in the wall, allowed a stir of air into the room, and a little light. In turn, the sons bent to kiss their father's grey cheek, noticing as they did so a sticky rust in the matted grey hair brushed from his left temple. He made neither sound nor movement, but an hour later, with dusk beginning to thicken and blackbirds hymning the day's end, they heard a low moan from the room above and then an anguished howl.

The next morning the doctor returned to find there had been no improvement in the condition of his patient, whose night had been made tolerable only through doses of the opium tincture rather stronger and more frequent than Esther had been told to allow him. The vicar lay in bed, barely conscious.

George and Richard, delayed by their mother, stood near the door. Bevan looked grave. 'I have been reading about symptoms such as those you describe,' he said, addressing the still figure. 'They can be associated with what is called a fungoid tumour in the brain. I have to confess I am as ignorant of the cause and origin of such dreadful intrusions as I am of their treatment. Let us for a moment assume it is a tumour, a growth on or in the brain, how could we treat it? Bleeding, as we have proved, has little or no effect. If we could find it, see it, could it be removed? Could I cut it out?'

The vicar gave no sign he understood or had even heard. Esther sobbed and covered her face in her apron. George and Richard bowed their heads and remained silent.

'This sort of thing has been done,' Bevan continued, ' – and long ago in the past. The Romans had a brass tube about five inches long and an inch in diameter, with saw teeth at one end, which by pulling cords they could cause to rotate at such speed the teeth bit into the skull to remove a disc of bone and so expose the brain beneath. Now I don't have such an instrument, and if I did would not know how to use it. Nor would I know where in the skull to excavate. All I can do is hope that those steps already taken will in a day or so bring improvement, and in the meantime help alleviate the pain with opium. But there are doctors in Cardiff and elsewhere, more knowledgeable than I, who might be able to help you. Have you understood, Vicar?'

The man beneath the bedclothes turned slowly and faced the wall. There was nothing more to be said. Bevan raised his top hat to Esther, and nodding to the two young men, made his way down the stairs and out of the house. In a few moments, with a creak and a clatter of hooves, the trap moved away.

George broke the silence in the bedroom. 'We must take advantage of this fair weather. I have finished ploughing the glebe and will join Richard in the top field,' he said.

The figure in the bed moved, turned to them a thin, worn face pale and striated as limestone. The colourless lips barely moved as the ghost of a voice left them. 'Yes,' it said, 'you must do all possible to secure a good harvest. And it is time that I, too, ceased this useless, maundering idleness. Esther, help me please with a little of that potion and your arm on the stairs. I shall go to my desk.'

The vicar sat, pen, ink and paper before him. He knew that his living at Penlline, with the tithes and what his sons' industry won from the glebe, would be lost on the day he died, and he was sure that could not now be long delayed. In the time remaining to him there was something he could do that might offset those foreseeable losses. Much would depend on his older boy. He recalled how, from George's seventh year, he had daily schooled him in letters and figures, taught him how to work in the garden and, later, in the fields, how to plough, how to mow, before he went to the school at Cowbridge. He had done as much for Richard. They had not disappointed him, but he could not hope now to raise up each in his turn to a manly understanding of the world and Christian duty, as he wished and had always intended. But he could perhaps place George on a path towards betterment.

He had been persuaded to take a spoonful or two of bread and milk and a few sips of tea. No stronger, but a little more fully awake despite the opiate's dulling of his senses, he began to write.

'To the Right Reverend Father in God, Richard Lord Bishop of Llandaff.'

He surveyed the words sprawled on the page. Was that his hand? It was the writing of someone who hardly knew how to write, someone without control. He grasped the pen more firmly and scratched more slowly –

These are to certify to your Lordship that I George Williams Vicar of Penlline in the County of Glamorgan and your Lordship's Diocese of Llandaff do hereby nominate and appoint Geo: Williams to perform the Office of Curate in my Church of Penlline aforesaid, and do promise to allow him the yearly sum of twenty pounds for his maintenance in the same, and to continue him to officiate in my said Church until he shall be otherwise provided of some Ecclesiastical preferment unless by fault by him committed he shall be lawfully removed from the same. And I hereby solemnly declare that I do not fraudulently give the Certificate to entitle the said Geo: Williams to receive Holy Orders, but with a real intention to employ him in my said Church according to what is before expressed. Witness my Hand this 26th day of May in the year of Our Lord 1786.

Again he scanned the page. It was a shameful scrawl, but he could do no better. The Bishop knew him well enough and would surely understand that it had been written in extremis. He signed at the foot of the sheet, 'Geo: Williams, Vicar of Penlline'.

Although his voice was little more than a whisper, Esther who had been listening for the slightest sound hurried to the room.

'Help me seal this,' he said, 'and see that it goes at once to Llandaff. Our George is but twenty-two, young for what I intend, but I trust Bishop Richard, if he knows I am no longer capable of serving church and parish, will indulge me in this and waive the rules. Please, another glass of the potion.'

I V

THE CORTÈGE CRAWLED over Newton Moor, a thin, black disjointed snake under blazing sun. Neighbouring farmers and members of the church at Ystradowen, where the late Reverend George served as curate, had paid their respects to the coffined dead and fallen into step behind the slow moving cart on which he lay. On either side the common rolled itself into shallow purple hollows and little grass-topped island mounds amid rushes, clumps of gorse patched still with yellow flowers, and dense bracken that surged here and there to the edge of the road. From solitary trees, black shadows flowed across the way and seeped into the dust. The birds were silent, but back from the road a few labourers were gathering bracken for winter cattle bedding and bickering in Welsh, and their voices and the rustle of cutting, like the choppy rush of wave on wave, and the tinny hiss as they sharpened the blades of their hooks, rose above the hum of insects in the ears of the mourners. The shuffling procession wound with the road between greyish low banks and then passed almost hidden where the massed dark green fronds, limp and barely stirring in heat, closed in, head high. What could be glimpsed of distance shimmered or was hung with haze. About the hooves of the horse, the slow-turning wheels of the cart and the feet of walkers' dust rose and fell silently. It was the first week of August.

George and Richard trailed behind the cart that carried

their father's coffin, draped in a dusty black cloth frayed at the edges. Wisps of hay that had escaped a perfunctory brushing hung about the cart. It had been wise, George thought as he walked, to cut the hay early. They had been blessed with a warm, damp spring followed by sunny weeks during which fields and hedgerows became lush with growth and the temperature had risen steadily. It could not go on and the rain, when it came, would be heavy he felt sure. He and Richard had helped neighbours as eager as they were to make the most of the fair weather, and had been helped in their turn. Day after day they had risen early to be out in the field soon after dawn with the grass still dew-damp and webs of low mist along the hedges. Without thought they had fallen into line and into the rhythm of cutting, the scythe close to the ground, arms straight, the body twisting left to right, slicing the grass neatly, adding stroke by stroke to the swathe lengthening across the field. And in the afternoons, the smell of the fresh cut grass filling the air, with a new rhythm they raked and bent to heap it at the end of each swathe into sweet green mounds, which others gathered into mows. For a month or more plentiful hay had been stacked in the tithe barn and in thatch-roofed ricks in two fields. The beasts would not go hungry.

Richard, his eyes on the swaying, creaking cart and the parish pall spread upon the simple pine box beneath, pondered what their father's death would mean for them. He had heard how urgently at the last his mother prayed God to grant her husband release from suffering, and had seen, when his time came, how she was prostrated with grief. They had knelt together at the bedside where his father's corpse lay stiffening, and he had helped George raise her and draw her from the room when it seemed she would weep her life away there.

On another rare visit to his Welsh estates, Sir Thomas Aubrey had come in his carriage to Maendy to view the land his family had owned for centuries. It was a good year; he found it well kept and productive. When George asked could the lease be transferred to his name, as he had discussed with his mother and brother, Sir Thomas leant on his cane and thought a moment. He was inclined to be sympathetic, he said, and thought again. 'Yes,' he had said finally. 'How long has the lease to run? Six years?'

'Four,' George had replied.

'When that time comes we may need to reconsider. What about the Penlline glebe?'

'That will be lost to us, I fear. The new incumbent will surely wish to farm the land himself. Although Richard and I have long laboured in those fields, as curate, I have no say in the matter. Nor do I yet know who is to be appointed. If he is of generous spirit, he may wish to let some of the land to me, but I cannot say I expect it.'

'No, no,' Sir Thomas had murmured, thoughtful again, ' ... but I shall see to the lease.'

Richard knew without the Penlline glebe and the tithes his father collected from the parish it would go hard with them simply to pay the rent. Only a few months ago he had learned of the letter to the bishop, nominating George curate of Ystradowen at twenty pounds a year. But the twenty pounds, not a penny of which had entered his brother's pocket, should have come from his father, and now the living would pass to another, whom they would find, perhaps, less inclined to maintain George as curate.

Richard loved his brother, yet he was envious when, after a day's work in the fields, George sat secluded at their father's desk, reading their father's books and sifting through many tumbled pages of notes and observations he had made in his years of service to church and parish. More than that he envied George the cassock, their father's cassock, frayed and worn as it was, the outward sign of his sudden elevation to a curacy. He envied, too, how his brother's voice echoed in the church, and how the congregation silently obeyed his call to prayer, his spiritual injunctions. Uncertain though this new position, this calling, was, to Richard it seemed raised up and desirable.

But today George was not wearing the cassock. He would have no part to play in the funeral, which would be conducted by the aged vicar of Llansannor and, although he had met the Reverend Griffiths, he felt on this occasion an overwhelming humility and diffidence about his newness to the cloth. But he had determined that he would, if he could, leave a mark of his father's passing at the church. He felt for the carefully folded paper in his coat pocket, and with a shiver, though not of fear, sensed there momentarily the clasp of his father's hand.

At the fingerpost the cart turned sharply right and the bereaved, close behind, heard an unmistakable muffled thump from within the coffin. Richard sought his brother's hand. 'Hush,' George whispered, 'it is just the movement of … It's nothing.' In another hundred yards the Penlline churchwardens and a small band of parishioners fell silent as the loaded cart approached and with a quiet exchange of greetings fell in among the perspiring followers in ones and twos trailing behind as they moved between flowery banks surmounted by overgrown hedges. The church bell began to toll, its bronze notes falling slow, one by one, always the same through the heavy air. It was not far to the old manor house set grandly among its trees and then past it, around another corner in the narrowing lane, to the church, where, at the thatched lych-gate the vicar waited.

The Reverend Griffiths, white-haired, bent, in cassock and surplice, greeted the mourners with a slight inclination of the head and solemnly clasped the hands of George and Richard.

'I am glad your father has come home.'

'It was as he wished,' said George, 'for here,' he glanced around him, 'lie his parents and theirs before them, and our own brothers and sisters.'

'All is ready for him.'

The churchyard lay in dappled shade beneath its ancient yews and a screen of tall limes bordering the great house beyond its walls. Neighbours hurried forward as George and Richard drew the coffin from the cart and together they bore it into the church porch. It was a light burden, as though empty, as though spirit and body had already departed. George recalled his loved father near death, shrunken and skeletal, and thought suddenly of the vastness of this life, the intricate web of experience from infancy to our dying day, and then how infinitesimally minute it was compared to the life beyond. Unseen in the umbrageous depths of the nearer yew, a magpie rattled.

The church of Saint Senwyr was small and low beneath the beams of its arched roof. The bell fell silent. Out of the heat and brightness of the day the cool gloom within was balm. The shuffling of feet on the ancient pavement and the settling of bodies in simple pews were the only sounds. The mourners, many of whom had not before entered the church, gazed blankly at the unadorned altar and blanched walls, faintly patched here and there with the red and blue light cast by small coloured windows. The Reverend Griffiths, murmuring prayers, led the coffin bearers from the porch down the nave past rows of bowed heads into the chancel, where to the right, before the altar, two paving stones had been raised and a narrow grave dug. Looking down, Richard saw mingled in the pile of excavated sandy earth fragments of old bones and his swarthy face grew pale.

Creaking and scraping, the coffin was lowered into the pit and in the silence that followed the high and faltering voice of the cleric uttering the familiar committal prayers rose and echoed among the rafters. Soon, very soon, the mourners were once more in the churchyard, breathing deeply, stretching, talking cheerfully one with another about crops and families, gladly aware of the body that contained their immortal souls. George took the vicar gently by the elbow to lead him aside.

'Thank you,' he said, 'I am very grateful for this last act of friendship to my father. But there is one thing more I would beg of you.'

He reached into his pocket, squeezed reassuringly the ghostly hand there and drew out the folded paper. 'My father has a place close to the altar in the church where he was baptised. It is as much as he could have desired. No, more than that. He, in all humility, would not have dreamed of it. Nor would he have made this request: is it possible a memorial inscription could be placed on the wall nearby, in stone or brass? I would like to say I have the money to pay for such an inscription, but at present I do not. But if I knew the churchwardens and most assuredly you, Reverend Griffiths, would countenance an addition such as this to the interior of your church, I would work day and night to have one made. I have drafted the text in readiness. Would you be so good as to consider it?'

He unfolded the paper and handed it to the cleric, who read aloud softly: 'Revd George Williams, Vicar of Penlline, who lived at Upper Maendy in the parish of Ystradowen in the county of Glamorgan and diocese of Llandaff. Departed this life 5th August 1786 at 4 o'clock p.m. and was interred on the 7th within the chancel of Llansannor (the south side of it) by the Revd David Griffiths, vicar of the church of Saint Senwyr in the same county and diocese.'

A breeze had arisen, enough to stir to rustling the lesser branches of the churchyard trees and fill out the folds in the vicar's surplice so that it rose in a white cloud about him. He patted down the billowing cloth and looked up, 'I do believe the weather is about to change.' And then, 'A fair hand, indeed – very like your father's. Yes, I am sure this, or something similar, would serve admirably, and, speaking for myself, would be happy to see it – if a place can be found for it within the church. But you are right, the churchwardens will need to consider – and the bishop too, I think. You will not mind if I present it at my next meeting with the churchwardens?' He refolded the sheet and, hoisting the surplice, thrust it into the pocket of his cassock.

George regarded the old man doubtfully. The answer had been no more than he expected, but there was no encouragement in the level tone of his voice. And he had never once mentioned, though he certainly knew of it, the curacy at Penlline. 'Thank you,' he said. 'I must join my brother and express our gratitude to those who have been our companions in sorrow today, and as a final act of friendship have accompanied my father's coffin to its resting place. I hope to hear from you – about the memorial.'

'Yes, yes, of course,' said the Reverend Griffiths, already turning and shuffling away.

V

EVAN, JENNET'S HUSBAND, had left home soon after she was summoned to the big house on the hill, not saying where he was going, though it was assumed he would seek work as a coal miner: there were pits not far off at the northern edge of the Vale. Months had passed and still he had not returned. At first, almost daily, she had expected him to appear at the door of Ash Hall to claim her, but as no oral message had come to her, no sign of any kind, she began to wonder whether he would ever return.

'Perhaps he has gone up into the valleys,' she would say. 'I've been told people are looking for coal up there, but it's a wild place. And then it's not so very far, and surely he's not working all the time. He could come back for a day to tell his Ma and Da and me what he's doing. But perhaps he doesn't want to come back. Perhaps he's found another woman up there.'

And from time to time she would ask herself why he had gone so suddenly, when she needed him most. 'I don't think it was my fault,' she told Sarah quietly, downcast, 'because I tried very hard. I did everything Evan's mother and the old woman told me, and the little boy never once cried. And I felt so sad for him, and for Evan.'

Thomas Digby, aged fourteen months, was weaned. Having bred teeth readily with the aid of a silver-mounted coral and rattle, he had enough to chew effectively and from time to time to cause his nurse sharp pain and tenderness, which she bore stoically. Without a wife and many miles distant from his mother-in-law, Richard Aubrey sought local advice on the matter. Jennet, the youngest of her family, seemed bemused by the question and could not, or would not, offer an opinion. Sarah, for all her maternal instincts, was equally at a loss. Spinster Aunt Margaret, wisely asked as a courtesy, opined that once there were teeth, of course the child wanted solid food. Older maidservants, who had raised families, said they had stopped breast-feeding early, because they were constantly busy and had no time for it. They then gave their infant children pap, a mixture of flour or breadcrumbs cooked in milk or water. One suggested adding egg and honey to make it more palatable for feeding. At first Thomas, used to the warmth and comfort only Jennet supplied, protested vehemently and long, so that Mr Aubrey relented and to the nurse's delight permitted her to continue feeding him, but at fourteen months she stopped.

Soon afterwards, Sarah, returning from a walk with Julia along the roughly paved paths of the demesne, for it had been a drenching winter, found Jennet in the children's room. Thomas was sound asleep, and she approached quietly. The nurse was standing at the foot of the cot, looking down at the beautiful child. It was a strangely moving tableau in the partially curtained room where yet stray beams of low afternoon sun penetrated. So it was, Sarah saw a tear form at the edge of a lowered eyelid and, catching the light, fall like a diamond to the plump breast of the young woman.

'Why Jennet, whatever is the matter?'

'I shall be sent away soon. I know I shall be sent away. He doesn't need me now. Anyone can feed him,' she whispered, 'and I don't know where I'll go.'

'Go? Surely not.'

But Sarah understood well enough the young woman's plight. She had one purpose only in the household and, since Thomas could be spoon-fed, was essaying to feed himself indeed, though he had difficulty in finding his mouth, the service that once she alone could supply was no longer needed. Where she would go, if go she must, was a further cause of distress. Poor, honest Jennet felt out of loyalty she should support Evan's aged parents while waiting for him (and that might be for ever), but Sarah was sure she would be happier returning to her own mother and father.

Drawn through the connecting door into the next room, the nurse hid her face in her apron and wept.

'You must try to tell me what you would prefer,' said Sarah, embracing her, 'and I promise I shall do what I can to help.'

Jennet's response was unexpected: 'I want ... I want ... to stay here ... with Thomas and Julia ... and you.'

Sarah and Jennet were perforce much together, as the children's needs dictated, and almost from the outset had been entirely at ease in one another's company. Jennet, like a docile younger sister, yielded all choice and resolution to Sarah, who, for her part, was conscious not only of a sisterly bond with Jennet but also, whence she knew not, responsibility for her. Thus, at the next opportunity, when she gave Mr Aubrey her customary account of what the children had been doing and how they fared, she resolved to mention Jennet's earnest wish. He had been engaged outdoors in foul weather much of the day, attending to estate business, and, having supped, was standing with his back to a blazing coal fire. Nearby, a high-backed leather armchair had been drawn up, and a small table bearing a few books and, deep ruby in the firelight, a glass of wine. A large gilt-framed mirror on the mantelshelf above the fireplace reflected flaring candles around the heavily curtained room, and the shoulders and dark pigtailed hair, in a military manner thought Sarah, of the master of Ash Hall.

Richard Aubrey felt the business of the day had gone well; he was beginning to feel better content with life. Standing straight, his hands clasped behind, he was rather taller than Sarah recollected his brother to have been and, with his aquiline features and delicately curved lips, more handsome – a thought that had not before occurred to her.

'You find me among my books,' he said, pulling a chair forward from beneath a library table. 'Come, sit you down.'

A large glazed bookcase occupied much of one wall of the room. 'Are you a bookish sort of person?' he asked.

'No, but my uncle is. He encouraged a similar interest in me, but I hardly dared enter his library unless he was present, so precious are its contents. He has many, many books – and is constantly buying more. I once told him it was like an illness with him, but he only smiled.'

'These,' said Richard Aubrey, gesturing towards the bookcase, 'are the companions of my days as student and then teacher at the college of All Souls in Oxford, mostly the ancient languages, a little theology, and a little law to please my father. I'm afraid I have no time for them now.'

'If you will permit,' said Sarah, 'I should like to begin reading to Julia. It is not my intention yet to teach her, only to read to her. She listens most attentively to stories I tell her that I remember hearing when I was a child, and I believe if I read the stories from a book, she will begin to understand what pleasure is given by reading. But,' glancing at the tall bookcase, 'I hardly expect to find suitable tales in your library.'

'Books from All Souls of the Faithful Departed? No, I think not.' And he laughed, tilting his head into the leather chair back. 'Nothing nearly so enjoyable, but I can readily obtain what you need.' His dark eyes shone.

Sarah had not seen Mr Aubrey laugh before. She had thought him earnest and dedicated, and old beyond his years. The transformation within had, no doubt, been gradual, but suddenly he seemed to have broken free of the hard frost of long mourning and become himself again. She dared ask the more difficult question:

'Jennet no longer nurses Thomas, but she feeds him with a spoon and helps him feed himself. They make a very pretty picture together, because he knows her so well, and trusts her. Will you allow her to stay and give him the affection and guidance one so young needs?'

'Stay? Yes, of course she shall stay – if that is what she, too, desires: I would not attempt to stand in the way of her returning to her family. Yes, let her stay and assist you, at least until Thomas is breeched, and then we shall see. Are you content with that?'

'Very content,' said Sarah.

Her smile told him that was the answer she had been hoping to hear.

George received the curacies of Ystradowen and then Llansannor at his father's urgent prayer to God's servant, Richard, Bishop of Llandaff. He had attended the grammar school at Cowbridge, was literate, God-fearing, familiar with the Bible and offices of the Church, as the son of a long-serving minister of the Gospel should be, of unsmirched character, serious and thoughtful. He wrote with a fair hand, had by rote the orders of various of the services in the Book of Common Prayer, spoke with a clear and carrying voice. He looked well enough in his inherited robes, old and worn as they were, and was soon at ease in his new role, which was as well: at twenty-three he was a youthful curate to be left to perform his duties unhindered by help or advice. He continued to live with his widowed mother and his brother Richard at the farm known as Maendy Uchaf near Ystradowen. By toiling through the seasons in their few fields, the brothers maintained themselves and their mother, the poor remnants of their family. The months sped by and, lacking the slightest prospect of the betterment of their condition, neither had any thought of marriage.

He had been quickly disabused of the belief, or hope, that the curacy of Penlline, where his father had been vicar, would fall to him. The new incumbent would not hear of it. The absentee possessor of the livings of Ystradowen and Llansannor received the great and lesser tithes of both parishes at his handsome home fifty miles away at Abergavenny. Rector of Llanelen, he was so busy he had never once visited his parishes in the Vale, but was pleased to confirm his satisfaction with the existing arrangement of George's curacy at somewhat less favourable terms than his father had previously set down: fifteen pounds per year for each.

Still better off than he feared he might be, the first task George took upon himself at Ystradowen was a survey of the parish register. It was, he grieved to see, in a bad way. Damp had invaded and carelessness defaced a few pages, while several others were torn at the edges, for what purpose or by what mishap he could not imagine, so that entries were damaged and a few lost. He found the first baptism recorded in his father's hand in 1763, the year he was born. Why yes, of course, he thought, having thus become curate of Ystradowen and, perhaps, Llansannor too, his father was bold enough to marry, and so he was conceived. As he turned the pages he remarked the change in his father's hand in recent months; his bold penstrokes of earlier years had become tentative and, nearing the last, weary and falling away. He noted, too, one by one, as they came into the world, the baptisms of the children of the Reverend George and Esther: William, Thomas and James, Ann and Hannah – all dead while still young, and Richard, his dear surviving brother. Three of these entries were on damaged pages and he determined not to risk their loss to future generations. On a fresh page he recopied neatly, with great care and a little flourish, his own family, together with a note explaining his action, which he signed: 'Rev. George Williams, Curate, 1786.' He closed the register with a sense of satisfaction and, bubbling beneath, a droplet or two of pride.

So busy were his Sundays there was barely time to sup with his mother and brother. His determination to hold services at both churches meant that he tethered an elderly but game cob, bought cheaply of a distraught hill farmer at the end of a fair in Cardiff, to the railings of the church while he led the faithful in their morning prayers at Ystradowen before galloping, in all weathers, cassock hitched up to his waist, to Llansannor to perform the same rituals for the congregation there. His intention had been to preach, as he had witnessed his father do many times. For this he considered himself well prepared, since the only fortune his father had bequeathed was an ample supply of sermon notes on biblical themes and the good life.

But soon the necessity for haste, if he were to give of himself even-handedly at both churches, and the apparent indifference of listeners, led to the curtailment of his pronouncements from the pulpit to a few sentences that might announce or mark a significant day in the Church year. Neither congregation protested. He celebrated Holy Communion at each church three times a year and took pains to greet churchwardens and remind them of his readiness to be informed and advised by them. He was equally assiduous in visiting the sick, often quitting the plough, sowing or harrowing, mowing, hedging or mending fences to wash himself clean, put on clerical dress and go forth with prayer book to call at outlying farms and ruinous cottages where the old, the sick and the needy awaited the word of God. He became accustomed to the sour odour of sickness in rooms over-heated and airless, or beaded with damp and chill, like a foretaste of death. It was on one such visit he met young Richard Lewis.

The boy, who might have been fourteen, was lodging with his grandmother at a farm that had seen better days in the south of the parish within a mile or so of Cowbridge. He had come from his home at Llancarfan at the bidding of his mother to help her mother, a widow in her declining years and much reduced circumstances. When she married Edward Morgan, Elizabeth Lewis had been a catch. She was of a family claiming connection, albeit distant, with Lewis of the Van, a great landowner in the previous century, whose broad estates in the Vale had been divided and divided again with each generation until the legacy of many of his descendants consisted of little more than the roof, often a humble roof, over their heads, and family pride. Elizabeth brought with her a dowry sufficient for her new husband, with a little money of his own, to purchase the farmhouse where she still lived and the fields that surrounded it. But he was not a successful farmer, having as a young man cultivated habits inimical to thrift and good husbandry that he was unable to change. He was a merry, talkative drinker, a sporting man and a gambler, with many friends who, when the weather changed, were not to be found, or confoundedly busy. Elizabeth bore him three pretty daughters. They loved their father, because he was affectionate, indulgent and, at times, jolly and amusing, though those occasions, frequent enough when they were young to tide them over his periods of withdrawn introspection, became fewer with the passage of each year. All three were married young, taking with them little beyond their comeliness and an optimism that had somehow survived the vicissitudes of life with their father. What little purpose he had seen in orderly living, when they left home, departed with them. Gradually, he sold his stock, mortgaged his unproductive land, drank punitively, alone and morose. On a late spring evening, early dark, the sky massed with heavy clouds, thunder in the air, and the earthy odour of heavy raindrops in dust rising about him, he fell, or was thrown, from his horse and split his skull on a tall roadside stone, reputedly Roman. The arrival at a canter in the yard outside her door of the lathered, riderless horse alerted Elizabeth to a mishap. With some difficulty, neighbours were gathered to search for the fallen and he was found the following morning, stiff, drenched with dew, half in a ditch beside the bloodied stone.

Mary, the middle daughter, who had married a distant Lewis cousin, learning that her mother, living alone since her husband's accidental death, was unwell, sent her son to ease her solitude and give what assistance he could. Family pride customarily inclined Lewis parents to make sacrifices to provide an education for their male children, and Richard was no exception. With twin cousins of like age from a somewhat wealthier twig of the family tree, he had received a grounding in the Classics from a private tutor, whose hero was the Athenian orator Demosthenes, and briefly attended the school at Cowbridge. But he lacked the cleverness that might have elevated him to the law or the Church and returned to Llancarfan to work on a neighbouring farm. When George met him at his grandmother's sadly dilapidated home, he was a thin, overgrown youth with a turn in one eye, roughly cropped hair the colour of old straw that started from his skull in all directions like ruined thatch, a long, pale face and prominent Adam's apple. Summoned by George's knock at the door, he spoke little and uncertainly, his voice wavering between manly bass and hoarse falsetto.

The bare room within was filled with acrid smoke from a smouldering fire of green wood, over which Elizabeth, a bundle of all her clothes, crouched in a low chair. She was aged beyond her years. The curate offered her the consolation of prayer, but she would have none of it.

'I prayed to God throughout my marriage,' she said, ' – prayed He might visit my husband with good sense, and preserve us all from penury, but you see what we have come to. And Edward, who was all affection, and might so easily have been a good man, He saw fit to snatch from me. I am beyond caring for myself, and will not call on others to care for me.'

She would not be reconciled to her condition or to her Maker. The gangling boy cast his pale, wandering eye from one to the other and around the echoing room, and said nothing. George rose, a gloomy sense of failure, and of obligation thwarted, thick, thick as the smoke, about him. Wrapping his threadbare cassock around his own meagre body and a strip of brown woollen stuff about his neck to keep out the cold, he bowed to Elizabeth, opened the creaking door and stepped into the windswept empty yard. He did not visit the farm again. Soon after Easter, Elizabeth Morgan was dead and the property in other hands. The boy, Richard, returned to his family in Llancarfan and years were to pass before he once more entered the life of the Reverend George Williams.

In occasional letters to her father Sarah conveyed little beyond her contentment with her position at Ash Hall. Her father's replies were brief. They said her mother and her brother were well but revealed nothing of the declining health and low spirits of the writer, other than in their oddly disordered appearance. The loops of loosely formed letters seemed to be reaching out to her, but what should she do? To leave Ash Hall and return to Llangan would sharply end the life she had made for herself. There would be no going back; nor could she expect to be welcomed once more at the London home of her uncle, which already seemed far off in time and distance. Occasionally, alone in her room, perhaps awakened early by a slant of sunlight through a gap in the curtain striking the wall above the marble topped table where a jug of water stood in a bowl, a sponge and soap alongside, she wondered what would become of her. She enjoyed the confidence of Richard Aubrey and found increasing pleasure in the children as they grew in understanding and interest in the world about them. And she had the trust and affection of Jennet, who, assured of her place, worked happily beside her. Before London, she had not thought of a future beyond the farm, and now as she gazed inwardly into the past, she wondered what would have become of her. She would have married, perhaps. She remembered boys from neighbouring farms, Jenkin Andrew, Joe Cook, Watkin – what was it? Thomas? – with whom she sometimes spoke as their families walked together from church. They might well be married now, with children of their own. The thought brought a pause in her reverie: children of their own. She shook her head and brushed back her hair with her fingers. What did that matter to her? She was more settled than she had ever dared dream. She thought how she would kneel while Jennet ran a comb through Julia's freshly-washed, gleaming dark hair, and how when she opened her arms the little girl in her white nightgown, with glowing eyes and such smiles, ran to her and clasped her about the neck and kissed damply her cheek, and her heart swooped suddenly like a swift in flight. So with each day Julia was dearer to her, her friendship with Jennet more cheerful and warmer; and, as he left farther behind the dismal time of mourning and became more readily approachable, her respect and regard for the master of the house grew.

After she had spoken with Mr Aubrey about reading to Julia, Sarah wrote home to ask if aught remained there of the chapbooks wherein she had first learned to read. By way of reply she received a brief letter and a small package. The letter, from her brother, Stephen, said her father was a little indisposed and unable to write, but otherwise all was well. That was disquieting, but surely, she thought, if her father were really unwell, she would be told. When unwrapped, to her surprise, the package revealed the horn-book her father had used to teach her the shapes and sounds of letters, for it was to him she owed her precious ability to read and write. There it lay in her lap, not much bigger than her hand, with the little handle, holed at the top, a ribbon, blue still within the knot and elsewhere faded now almost grey, threaded through it, by which she was wont to attach it to her apron strings. She smiled at the tiny engraved pictures beneath the silky layer of horn and traced with the tips of her fingers the outlines of Aa, Bb, Cc … as she had done hundreds of times sitting on her father's lap or alone in a sunny window corner, so many years ago. And she shook her head at the sweet, sad memory of it.

At their next meeting, she took it to show her employer. 'Ah,' he said, 'I once had one of those. I remember it well, but I have no idea where it is now. Long ago cast into the flames I suspect. I can tell you were a careful child, for this has hardly a blemish. I'm afraid I used mine as a bat.' He held the horn-book by the handle and made a little striking motion. 'I blame my brothers,' he said. 'They encouraged me to smite small balls with it.' He mimed batting again and laughed.

'I was very fond of mine – this one,' said Sarah. 'I used to hang it at my waist. With your permission, I should like to give it to Julia, so that she may, perhaps, begin to learn her letters.'

'Yes, yes, of course you may. And what of chalk and slate? I remember those, too. I cannot think what age I was, but I believe you have brought Julia to a state of readiness for such things. I shall see they are obtained.'

He was true to his word. A few days later Sarah found a paper-wrapped parcel in her room containing a small slate in a neat wooden frame, some lumps of chalk and two newly-purchased chapbooks, one of rhymes for children, the other the story of Dick Whittington and his cat. She could not wait until their regular meeting to thank Mr Aubrey but went at once in search of him.

He was on the veranda at the front of the house, the grass beyond a well-watered rich green and trees already thickly leaved, speaking with one of the wealthier neighbouring farmers about sharing in the purchase and carriage of coals both needed for burning quarried limestone, the kilns being ready. A great deal of lime would be spread on the fields and many journeys made through the month of May to lay in stocks of coal from pits, the nearest about five miles off, the farthest twice that. Aubrey saw Sarah's breathless approach and wondered what was amiss.

'No – nothing.' She curtsied deeply to both men, embarrassed, her cheeks red. 'I am very sorry … will you permit me to leave?'

'Tell me first what has brought you here in such haste.'

'I wanted to thank you for the slate and chalk – and the books … they will give us such pleasure. But I should have waited. Please forgive me.'

'It is of no consequence. We have almost finished our business – isn't that so Perkins? You had better return to Julia.'

The other man mumbled and turned aside. It was not what John Perkins had expected in the household of an Aubrey. But soon they had indeed finished their arrangements and shaken hands. Richard, alone, thought about what had occurred, and about Sarah, her animation, her flushed cheeks.

When next they spoke, it was Aubrey who sought her, to tell her Sir Thomas, his father, was about to visit his Vale estates. He had been unwell during a long and dismal winter in Buckinghamshire and this sharp reminder of mortality had made him anxious to return to Llantrithyd, for what might be (How could one tell?) the last time.

'He is now in good health, I am given to understand,' said

Aubrey, 'but – and I would not repeat this to another – I do not trust my brother's judgement in such matters. In any event, it is not unfinished business that brings him back here; he simply wants to meet again some tenants he counts as friends, or at least old acquaintances, and of course, to embrace those of his kin who still reside in the Vale.'

Sarah nodded. She had met Sir Thomas, and his elder son, briefly – she felt herself colour at recollection of that first interview in her uncle's shop – but could find nothing to say, and Richard, she thought of him as Richard, continued.

'There are a number of matters I need to discuss with my father and this visit provides the opportunity, but I cannot be at Llantrithyd to greet him as I would wish because of a meeting of the magistracy in Cardiff, which I must attend. I would like Julia to represent me – I know he will enjoy that – and you must accompany her. I shall write and advise him of this and to arrange to see him instead on Thursday. Your duty will be no more than to present to him his grandchild. He will be pleased to see how Julia has grown. He is a kindly man, and it is good, too, that she shall meet him. I am half inclined to send Thomas Digby along into the bargain, but that would be asking too much of you, and possibly of him. My two are his only surviving grandchildren since my brother's boy died, most unfortunately, still very young.'

Again Sarah had nothing to say, except that she was very happy to have his trust in this as in other matters affecting the children, but later, alone, she wondered at the ease of his manner and the candour of his words.

On a warm, fresh morning, the sky clearing after overnight rain, Sarah and Julia set forth in the carriage, the child's father having left for Cardiff earlier on horseback. The windows of the carriage were open and the jingle of harness mingled with birdsong for them. Rocking as on a boat, they plunged the steep lane between foaming banks of flowers, Julia holding close to the fringed silk shawl over her nurse's shoulders. Then they were at Ystradowen and beyond, on a smoother road of crushed limestone where gradients were gentle and the muffled hoofbeats lulling and, passing beyond Cowbridge, they entered another lane broad almost as the road, with well trimmed thick hedges and so past the church and rectory to Llantrithyd Place.

'Y Plas.' The driver's voice came through the window, and Sarah glimpsed his hand pointing. But she had already seen. It was, she thought, truly beautiful. Some of the once familiar streets of London were lined with tall, grand houses, sumptuously elegant, like her uncle's home, but far larger, the homes of lords and wealthy merchants with business interests growing in the tropics. This was different. The house, an ancient dwelling, from the time of the Tudor monarchs, lay in a shallow green bowl, glowing in early summer light. Their way lay on a gentle curve down the grassed and tree lined slope through an open gate between massive, square pillars into an open courtyard. The sun, still rising behind the thick-tiled roof and tall chimneys, slanted across the north wing of the main building, while the south lay suffused with shade. The carriage slithered to a halt on thick gravel before a handsome porch set in a tower and two servants ran to secure the horse and help the passengers descend. The heavy, studded door stood open before them.

Sarah, with Julia holding her hand and pressing close, entered a grand hall panelled with oak to the ceiling. Heavy beams crossed overhead, scrubbed flagstones lay beneath their feet and gilded armorial escutcheons lined the walls on either side of an enormous fireplace cased in marble, its great iron basket empty now. The panelling gleamed darkly in the pale light of windows either side of the room, neither yet catching the sun. A broad oak staircase rose to the floor above. It was cool after the warmth of day. A liveried footman appeared and led them to the parlour where, he said, Sir Thomas was waiting to greet them. This smaller square room was bright with light from three windows, the largest a curved bay with eight lights looking out onto the court. Here, a fire glowed in a fireplace where marble caryatids on either side supported a tiered shelf, above which hung the portrait of an ancestor, though Sarah could not say which. Sir Thomas, in a blue velvet cap and a voluminous gown of the same material that enveloped him from neck to ankles, was seated in an armchair near the fire and did not rise to greet them as Sarah curtsied and Julia looked at him with dark, wide eyes.

'Sally,' he said, lifting his arms wearily in a gesture of welcome, 'forgive me. I seem to lack the vigour to offer the courtesies I would wish to extend to you, and to Julia, my dear granddaughter. Will you come and embrace your grandfather? Come kiss me here?' He laid two fingers on his cheek. 'Come … come,' he said, opening his arms to her and smiling.

To Sarah's surprise the child, who had continued holding her hand, released her grip and trotted to the stranger in the chair, submitted to his gentle embrace and kissed him.

'Why, you little darling,' he said, 'I believe you have the looks and sweet charm of your mother. Oh dear, how sad … And is Sally kind to you? Do you like Sally? Yes, I'm sure you like her and of course she's kind. Will you do something for me? Will you tell your father that I shall be very happy to see him on Thursday?'

Julia still looked at him wonderingly, the tip of a finger between her lips.

'I shall remind her and we will tell him together. Won't we Julia?' The child nodded.

'Come, Julia, come sit by me a little while,' he said, making room on the chair and patting the space beside him on the broad leather seat. With an effort he lifted her to join him and, having placed a protective arm about her, motioned Sarah to take the chair the other side of the fireplace.

'Now you shall tell me what improvements my son has made at Ash Hall and what you and Julia have been doing together.'

Sarah saw before her a figure much changed from the spry, composed gentleman who had witnessed Thomas Digby's admission to the congregation at Ystradowen. He had the pallor of one who had not been outdoors for some time, and even as he sat, his lean frame sagged, the head heavy, tilted forward, and his eyes, sunken in dark pools, were unnaturally bright.

She told him about the works that had been undertaken – the ha-ha, the new walls, the protective screen of trees, the kitchen garden, and then, as he nodded approvingly, saying nothing, how Thomas had grown beyond expectation and was already walking, and how Julia was learning her letters and sat still and silent listening to stories following the words in the book with such rapt attention.

'You are a good little girl,' said Sir Thomas, pressing her to his side, and she leaned against him contentedly. 'It is tiresome, I know,' he continued after a few moments, 'you and Sally having come so far to see me, but I'm afraid I grow weary, why, I cannot understand, since I have done naught but sit here. Perhaps it is time to go to bed – isn't that funny, going to bed in the middle of the day – to see if the repose denied me throughout the night will visit me now.'

The child, finger still to her lips, said nothing, but a servant approached and Sarah rose.

'Why don't you and Sally take a little walk in my garden before you go home,' said Sir Thomas, 'but will you give me one more kiss before you go?'

He bent his head towards her and the child kissed his cheek and wriggled off the chair to take Sarah's hand.

'Good-bye, dear Julia. Good-bye Sally – Jenkin will escort you on the garden walk and attend to your needs. I am deeply sorry that I cannot join you.'

Their way to the garden lay through an unexpected door in a panelled wall to the left of the ornate fireplace. Sir Thomas's eyes had already closed before Sarah, with Julia in her arms, stepped down onto a gravel path that led along the north front of the house to well-kept formal gardens with terraces, walks, orchards and water channels. The sun was high but there was a breeze and cloudlets tumbled in the blue above. The demesne sloped gently away to the south and this was the way they walked. Groves of trees rose from black troughs of shadow, heavy with foliage, dense greens of every shade, shifting in the sun and wind, and raised and swayed their slenderer arms slowly, like dancers. Behind them, the servant explained, lay the walled deer park, and before them a stream ran down a shallow valley into a pond fringed with ash trees, where they paused for Julia to watch fish gliding through the shaded water. Then Jenkin took them up the other side of the valley to a little empty tower where, at a false doorway, a stout wooden seat had been placed, and they sat and looked down on the Plas. This was where the Master liked to come, Jenkin told them.

Sarah understood immediately why they had been led along Sir Thomas's favourite walk to the seat beside the squat tower on the hill. Below them lay the ancient great house amid gardens, groves, ponds and meadows, threaded with glittering streams and canals. It was, she thought, enchanting, touched with radiance and grace. Julia, by her side and tired now, leaning against her, was part of this, and she the most fortunate of women to have had, if for this day alone, a fleeting sense of belonging.

Jenkin carried the little girl along a fresh path back to the house and, feet crunching gravel, between the long arms of its north and south wings to where their carriage was waiting. There was no one to say good-bye, but Jenkin smiled and waved to the sleepy child as they moved off.

Three months later, in September 1786, came news that Sir Thomas had died.

The Reverend George Williams, curate, sought the blessing of God Almighty on the congregation at Ystradowen and there was a loud Amen from the two dozen or so faithful, followed by a collective sigh, as of relief it was over for another week, then rustlings, the clatter of clogs on stone floor, and in another moment cheerful, neighbourly voices breaking out as though unloosed.

George was moderately satisfied with the way the service had gone. It was mid-October, the day of St Luke the Evangelist, who had been summoned from tending the sick to be a physician of souls. The gospel passage, which he had taken as his text, told of the sending out of Christ's apostles, 'Therefore, said he unto them, The harvest truly is great, but the labourers are few; pray ye therefore the Lord of the harvest, that he will send forth labourers into his harvest … Carry neither purse, nor scrip, nor shoes, and salute no man by the way. And into whatever house ye enter, first say, Peace be to this house. And if the son of peace be there, your peace shall rest upon it … And in the same house remain, eating and drinking such things as they give: for the labourer is worthy of his hire.' At Maendy Uchaf, George had considered how apt the verses were for workers in the fields whose harvest labours were but recently accomplished. Pen in hand at the old table, windows open for the unseasonable warmth, he had glanced at his mother nodding in her chair before the empty grate and Richard, across the scrubbed boards, bent studiously over his Bible. They knew what it was to bring in the sheaves; knew, too, that despite the harvest, they were close to the holy penury described by Saint Luke.

'The labourer is worthy of his hire,' he had said aloud, so that Richard looked up and his mother stirred. 'What think you of that? Are not those words meant for my congregation?'

Richard had smiled. 'I trust they will recall them when the time comes to collect the tithes.'

'Well, yes, Amen to that, even if we are unlikely to receive more than crumbs that by chance may fall from the table of the Headmaster in Abergavenny. It would be pleasant to be received everywhere, or even occasionally, with smiles. I will speak to them about the year's good harvest, and about God's harvest of souls in which I pray they and we are numbered.'

His appeal to their common experience had caught the attention of his parishioners, and perhaps would have held them longer had it not been for the prattling of a child, hidden by the pew, at the back of the congregation. The mother, whom he could not see clearly, her face shaded by a broad brimmed hat, had tried to hush the little girl, as he was sure it was, but the spell once broken could not be conjured again. He had heard of great preachers addressing hundreds, thousands, who flocked to them, and had wondered whether he possessed that power. Within a few weeks he had known he did not – and neither had his father while he lived. It was not a question of Christian faith, sincerity, love of one's neighbour, an intensity of desire to garner souls to God's harvest, but of some all too human capacity that might be used for good or ill, which he recognised here and there in others, but, alas, not in himself.

The woman and talkative child were among the last to leave the church and, hastening as usual to the congregation awaiting him at Llansannor, George met them at the gate, where a carriage was drawing up. Then he saw it was the young woman who was caring for the children of Richard Aubrey, whom he had met at the baptism of the younger child, Aubrey's son and heir. His bow hid his blushing confusion, for this was an entirely unexpected encounter, and his words tumbled out:

'I hope I may see you again … when, perhaps, I am less pressed …'

'Julia's father has agreed she should begin attending church services, so I fear this is not the last time we shall interrupt you. But we will try to be good, won't we Julia?'

The little girl looked up at the man in the green-tinged black cassock and nodded seriously.

In another moment, no further word said, they were in the carriage and away. George, his mind full of the chance encounter, rode less furiously than usual and found, when he arrived at Llansannor, a congregation more restive than he would have wished. After the service, without the planned sermon, he apologised to the wardens for his lateness. He had been detained, he said, by the unexpected addition to his congregation at Ystradowen of a member of the Aubrey family.

That was the truth, he told himself later, if not the entirety of it, which would have involved admitting he had been struck by the slender form and neat attire of the woman who held the hand of Richard Aubrey's pretty daughter – and, he added inwardly, the modest confidence of her demeanour, as of one without self-importance, yet sure of herself. He could not recall having heard her name, but determined to discover it at the next opportunity.

At morning service each Sunday in the months that followed, George looked for the quiet young woman and the little dark-haired girl and was rarely disappointed. They were always among the last to arrive at the church and, as before, took places unobtrusively at the back. At first other members of the congregation turned to stare at them, but soon their presence was accepted as normal. Womenfolk of the village made no acknowledgement on passing them, but some men, tenants of Aubrey, George thought, nodding in their direction, touched their forelocks.

Although he found he increasingly wished it, George rarely met them and when he did there was time only for an exchange of greeting and perhaps a word about the weather. He became determined at least to know her name and on a chill morning the following March, having cut short his sermon, he followed them to the lych-gate, where they stood sheltering from the wind as best they could beneath the pitched roof of thatch. He bowed and, seeing the carriage approach, introduced himself hurriedly. He was conscious of being calmly appraised and would have hurried off at once but for the young woman's smile. She was Sarah she told him – or Sally – the name first given her by her uncle in London and adopted by the Aubrey family, because it was by that name she had been introduced to Sir Thomas when he called one day at her uncle's shop. But she was Sarah (she pronounced it the Hebrew way), Sarah Jones, from Llangan, where her family had a farm. And then the servant was lifting the child, helping them into the carriage.

'Goodbye – and thank you,' said George, although he did not know what he was thanking her for, as the door closed and the vehicle jerked and moved away.

Later, alone, he thought about Sarah, or Zara, or, indeed, Sally. Without being fully aware of it, for several months he had been looking over the heads of those parishioners filling the front pews to observe her. He knew her form having seen her lightly clad on warm Sundays; he knew the particularities of brown hair, quite golden in sunlight, darker eyebrows and blue eyes, short, straight nose, small chin, the occasional smile at something said by the child. He recalled those moments before the two were bundled into the carriage and the sensation of being scrutinised, the little girl's frankly curious, dark eyes looking up, first at him, then her. He planned a conversation, which began 'Good morning, Miss Jones, would you mind if I addressed you as Sarah? How are you this fine Sunday? How is little … ?' He realised he did not know the child's name. He would ask his mother.

But it was hopeless: there would never be time for quiet, ordinary conversation. She was not the usual servant in a big house. She had the calm of one accustomed to being among and speaking to people of standing, gentry folk. It was more than he had any right to expect that she would take an interest in a shabby curate, rough-handed and weather-beaten from work in the fields.

VI

RICHARD AUBREY LEANED on the broad wooden gate
entrance to a field where the flowers of spring and
summer had gone below ground and the grass was fading. The
hedges, too, had thinned to long lines of scrawled calligraphy,
the last will of a dying year. First frosts had fallen hard during
the previous week. Richard was low-spirited, had been so since
the funeral at Llantrithyd, for his father had been brought back
to the ancestral home for burial.

Sir Thomas's death had not been unexpected. From the
moment he received Sally's report of a man suddenly aged and
enfeebled he had feared the worst; what she described was not
the trifling indisposition his brother had suggested. His own
meeting with his father soon after revealed how frail he had
become, how fatigued and breathless. There was talk of travel
abroad to famous watering places, but he said it was too much
to contemplate: the journey to Llantrithyd, God knew, had
been almost unbearably arduous. In the end he had gone to
Bath, but it did no good, and he simply faded away.

Although they had spent little time together in the last
twenty years, since his departure from the family home for
Oxford, there had been no diminution in Richard's respect and
love for his father, who had been a patient guide throughout
his youth and considerate of his needs thereafter. His being
there, in the Vale, he owed entirely to his father's concern to

see him properly housed in a manner that fitted his station and with productive land in his care.

'The seclusion of college, your book learning, are behind you,' he had said, 'you will have a wife to support and, God willing, soon a family.' They were standing together on the terrace before Ash Hall, a fine but somewhat neglected property. 'This land,' he gestured with an outstretched arm, 'properly managed, will serve your needs. But you have much to learn. In my view, the most important thing is to judge people soundly and get the best out of them. I hope and believe you already have those skills. Let your tenants and neighbours know you will be firm and fair – and do your share. Choose your friends and servants carefully. Don't demand of either what, at a pinch, you would not be prepared to do yourself. Be loyal and expect loyalty. Do not tolerate slyness or laziness. Remember, you are a gentleman. That means you must behave as a gentleman, and so you will be perceived and treated by others. This land,' pointing again to the acres surrounding them, 'is your livelihood. You must see it is well tended; it will repay the care you give to it. Don't be afraid to question those who know these parts about husbandry, stock and crops, and don't rely on one voice only: it does not pay to have favourites. Whatever the source, weigh carefully the advice you are given.'

It was rather like Polonius admonishing his son, Richard had thought, but he did not resent the lesson and vowed inwardly he would follow his father's precepts to the best of his abilities. At that last meeting in the bedroom at Llantrithyd Place, his father, propped up and supported by pillows, had shown how pleased he was to know what had been done in the development of both house and land. That Richard had overcome the grief of widowhood to achieve so much was a great satisfaction to him, and he said he had been pleased to see how Julia had grown in stature and sensibility. He was glad Sally Jones had proved herself as capable in caring for the child as he believed she would be when he first saw her. 'Judging people, you see – very important,' he'd added before lapsing into silence.

As the youngest of three brothers, Richard's way through life had not been clearly signposted. John, the eldest, had spent two years touring France and Italy in some luxury, preparing for his inheritance – the estates in Buckinghamshire, Oxfordshire and the Vale that were his birthright. A career in the army beckoned Thomas and he had distinguished himself as colonel and commander of men in the war in America. But what would he, Richard, do, having followed them to the university at Oxford? As he contemplated the empty field, dusk beginning to thicken and a dozen or so black birds rising up and flapping about a clump of tall trees beyond the farther hedge and resettling silently, he thought, when all was said and done, it might have been better had he stayed at All Souls. The life suited him. He found pleasure in study, and did not lack energy, but no grand ambition stirred him. Perhaps he would eventually have become vicar or rector in some pleasant Oxfordshire village where his father had the advowson rights, and then … yes, perhaps married, to have a companion in later life. To have a family? H'm. He had started along that sequestered path contentedly, with a Fellowship of All Souls, granted because his father was able to prove the family lineage back to Archbishop Chichele, founder of the college more than three centuries before. Sir Thomas had been delighted to see how he had studiously prospered, in a few short years becoming Dean of Arts at the college. The country parish was postponed, indefinitely.

There, at All Souls, he would surely have remained, but for the merest chance of falling in with a student from Magdalen, a few steps farther along the High Street, who, like him, was strolling towards the Cherwell bridge and the water meadows. It was a fine September evening and they began talking. Richard was surprised to find his companion was several years younger, for, as he was hatless, it was plain to see he had lost most of his hair and, as though to compensate, a great bush of brown beard hung down his broad chest. By the end of their walk, Richard knew him as Wriothesley Digby. As his name suggested, he too was of an old and distinguished family, with extensive property at Meriden in the county of Warwick. His father, the Honourable Wriothesley Digby, a barrister, who had preceded him at Magadalen decades before, was the son of Baron Digby of Geashill. He and Richard had much in common and soon became friends. Wriothesley introduced his younger brother, Noel, also at Magdalen, to their company. Noel was yet to achieve his majority, but they were all three alike in temperament and interests and often walked out together or, in inclement weather, met in one another's rooms for a convivial glass of wine and conversation and to read and compare books. Then, in May 1779, the brothers were visited by their sister, Frances, a year younger than Wriothesley, and very different in appearance, small and shapely, with thick black hair swept back from her forehead and dark blue eyes that danced when she was amused. At that first meeting, Richard recalled, he had been almost struck dumb, and had anxiously pressed the brothers afterwards to tell him whether Frances had not thought him the most complete ox. No, no, they assured him, smiling broadly, she had been impressed by his thoughtful demeanour.

Although he claimed his unwonted silence was due to embarrassment at the unexpected presence of a young woman, when he anticipated only familiar male company, he had, in fact, been spellbound by Frances. She had accompanied her father, who was in Oxford on legal business, and had seized the opportunity to see her brothers briefly before travelling on to spend a day or two with a family friend living nearby at Stanton Harcourt. Richard wrote to Frances apologising for being less than helpful in making her welcome at Oxford. Why, he might have shown her the wonders of All Souls, had he but thought of it …

It was the beginning of a correspondence and, quite soon, meetings, which Richard was quietly eager to initiate, at first through her brothers. He was a capable horseman and, with his mind fixed on the goal, not dismayed by the seventy-mile journey to Meriden. As most young men of family and position, with albeit a modest income, he was not entirely innocent of experience of the fair sex, but his family had not pressed him into an early relationship with one of his own class for the sake of his or their betterment, and opportunities to meet such a one in the normal course of events were, for an Oxford scholar, rare. Indeed, with each passing year he had become more deeply embedded in the affairs and male society of All Souls, until bachelor existence seemed increasingly inevitable and even a matter of indifference.

The entry of Frances into his life changed that. She was a young woman of taste and decorum, played harpsichord and flute pleasantly, led a blameless Christian life, as befitted one whose ancestry included several distinguished men of the Church, and was devoted to her parents and home. Her father having borne with equanimity her courteous rejection of several suitors from the local gentry, in her early twenties she remained unmarried. Richard, some eight years older, appeared to her a man of pleasing disposition and, she reflected, tall and rather handsome. Furthermore, now relaxed in her company, he had revealed himself firm and clear in his views, and one who spoke eloquently and, on occasion, humorously. She decided almost at once that she liked him and their acquaintance developed. Their families supported the match. Sir Thomas and the Hon. Wriothesley found they conveniently had business to attend to in London, met there, and drew up a marriage settlement. Richard would give up his fellowship at All Souls to become a gentleman farmer on Aubrey property in the Vale of Glamorgan, while the dowry Frances brought with her would provide for the refurbishment of their home, Ash Hall, and improvement of its lands.

In July 1780, Richard and Frances were married at the parish church in Meriden. It was a private, family wedding, which Richard's brothers were unable to attend because business detained them elsewhere. Wriothesley and Noel, friends of the groom and brothers of the bride were, of course, present. Another brother, Kenelm sent a message wishing them both long life and happiness with an elaborately chased silver salver of substantial weight. Kenelm was with the East India Company and lived in Madras and sumptuous ease, a host of servants attending his every need. Husband and wife could not fail to remember him each time their eye was caught by the gleam of silver on chest or table, and from time to time Richard wondered whether his own talents, employed overseas, would have brought him a fortune to match that which would one day fall into the lap of his brother John. After the wedding the couple journeyed south to meet relatives in Oxfordshire and Buckinghamshire, then west to Llantrithyd and, at last, loaded with gifts, to their new home, overlooking the village of Ystradowen in county Glamorgan.

All the circumstances of his meeting with Frances, their courtship and marriage, were fresh as yesterday in Richard's memory, for their time had, indeed, been short, tragically short. He pulled his topcoat closer about him against a sudden chill breeze and bowed his head in prayer. When he looked up, brushing the blurring moisture from his eyes, it was to see a pale half-moon hung low in the sky. He turned from the gate, shaking his head. He was not alone and unblest, as self-pity had prompted him to think. He had house and land, unencumbered; he had his health, thanks be to God, and he had two children, in both of whom he could discern, as it were, the signature of his late wife. He could not but reflect that he had also been fortunate in the choice, his father's choice, of Sally Jones to care for the children. It was on Sally, her person and her merits, his mind turned as he strode briskly towards home.

With the death of his father Richard Aubrey was deprived of the being in whom, from childhood, he had placed the most complete trust. He had servants and tenants but, transplanted as he was from Oxford to the Vale, no one he could invite to listen to, still less deliberate upon, things that touched him closely. His Aunt Margaret, to whom the leases of much of the Aubrey property in the Vale had been assigned, might have fulfilled the role, but she lived at Llanmaes, near the coast, some distance off. He had met her only a few times, knew her hardly at all and could not be sure where her sympathies lay when it came to matters affecting him and his brothers. He had been a sociable fellow at All Souls, but the society of the college was of a mannish, bachelor sort, and the conversation of a scholarly kind, when it wasn't shallow or silly – the silliness of idle men, some of whom seemed three-parts stranded still in boyhood. After marriage, suddenly in a new place, with new responsibilities, distant from family and friends, he and Frances had clung to one another. It was a time of sharing secrets and making plans, and then Frances, in whom his future hopes lay, had been snatched away. For a time he could not bring himself to think about the children. He had been too distressed to consider marrying again, for the sake of Julia and the baby. Besides, his previous life had not included a circle of acquaintance among whom a likely candidate might have been found and there was no one he knew in the neighbourhood remotely eligible.

With much of the planned work in and about the house completed, Richard had time in the early evening, by lamplight and firelight, to enjoy the company of his children, especially Julia Frances, whose prettiness and lustrous eyes drew from him unexpected depths of care and affection. Observing her reciting her letters or rhymes she had learned, or following Sally's reading of stories with rapt attention, was strangely moving. How was it, he thought, a grown man could be drawn and held by such a simple scene? But it was not the child alone that charmed him; it was the woman and child together, their heads bent close, oblivious of him, concentrating on the page before them. As he watched, hardly breathing, he found he was entranced, too, by stray wisps of hair at the young woman's nape, escaped from her careful combing and pinning, and curling softly upwards. It evoked a fascination, a melting tenderness within that almost betrayed him; he so longed to reach out and touch her bare neck. The child's sudden laughter at a turn in the story broke the spell. In this fashion, he learned to enjoy his children. He told himself it was for them he had planned and laboured as he cleared his mind of depression, and Sally Jones had much to do with this. In a shorter time than he had thought possible, she was no longer a servant in his household, but the surrogate mother of his children, loved by them, and respected by the other servants, indoors and out. (He had no doubt she would be fiercely supported by Jennet, if ever the need arose.)

The pall of grief that had enveloped Richard was the heavier because of his loneliness, for he had no one, relative or friend, with whom to share his thoughts. As month followed month, and one year slid into the next, he discovered he trusted the nurse-governess and began taking her increasingly into his confidence. She possessed a quality of attentive silence that made unburdening himself to her come easily, so that on those occasions when they met to discuss the children's progress, he would from time to time turn to his own concerns and plans. She rarely offered an opinion, but was ever a sympathetic listener while he laid bare and clarified his thoughts.

One winter evening, the wind buffeting the house and trees creaking in the darkness beyond the windows, so that for warmth they were seated either side of the fireplace, after talking about Frances and Thomas, as Sarah was about to excuse herself from her master's company, Richard said, 'Wait a while, I don't believe I have told you about my brother, Thomas. His is a strange story and, though I cannot be sure how or whether circumstances could change, it may affect me nearly.'

The narrative had long fascinated him, and watching her eyes widen as he unfolded it for her stirred a bubble of excitement in his breast.

'Thomas, you know, is almost four years my senior, and I always admired him, because he was strong and capable at all the rough-and-tumble things boys get up to. He paid me little attention, but I used to watch and try to emulate him – which is something I never thought of with John. Well, after Oxford, in the early 1760s, he bought a commission in the army, which my father had recommended as his career, and quickly found the life suited him. In recent years he has been fighting in the war in America. I met him when he returned and heard from his own lips what it was like. I suppose he felt I had grown up and he could speak to me openly. Do you know aught about America?'

'Only that my uncle's business in London benefited from the need to clothe and equip many young men who, like your brother, were bound for America – and how their numbers increased when the war began! I'm afraid my uncle rather welcomed the war. It increased his business tenfold, and he would smile to think of the books and paintings and precious objects he would be able to buy, without for a moment considering that many of those who visited his shop would be killed or horribly maimed. He wasn't without feelings, as I knew from the way he took me in and taught and nurtured me. But he was in business to make money and, without a family to support, he spent it on things that gave him pleasure.'

'I cannot blame him for that,' said Richard. 'Indeed, I rather envy a man who can dedicate himself to making money, and does so successfully. I am not that way inclined. Nor are my brothers. With us it is land, and rents, and legacies – which amounts to waiting for people to die. Not a comfortable thought. Be that as it may, Thomas went off to America in 1772 and was there when the rebels declared their independence of Britain, and before that, as I heard from his own lips, he was present when the first shots were fired at Lexington. By all accounts, he fought and led his men with distinction during a succession of victories later that year, which promised to make the enemy eat their declaration. But then, at the battle of Saratoga, when the pendulum swung the other way, and when France and Spain joined in on the colonists' side, our forces were hard-pressed. Thomas told me of hot, enervating summers and dreadful frozen winters that went on and on, and the misery of the men, and deaths from disease far exceeding losses in battle. Towards the end he was a colonel at Fort Detroit, a stronghold on a commanding eminence above a great river of the same name that soon flowed into an enormous lake. And that lake was but a puddle compared with others he heard of from scouts who had penetrated farther into the wilderness or come south out of Canada. I listened keenly to what he said but could barely comprehend his report of vast distances, dense forests stretching black from horizon to horizon, and Indian tribes with savage customs and impenetrable languages – who were fortunately more inclined to support the British than our enemies, but resented all strangers to their territories and could never be trusted.'

Sarah gazed at him and shook her head in wonder and near disbelief. 'How did he survive such trials?'

'A good constitution certainly helped, but above all fortune smiled on him and, when he did fall ill at Fort Detroit, a young woman from the village below the fort nursed and tended him so that he recovered while others of the garrison languished in fever, grew ever weaker and died. It was a terrible time.'

'And what of the young woman?'

'Ah, what, indeed: Thomas married her.'

Sarah could not forbear and clapped her hands. 'What a wonderful story!'

'Well, I suppose, yes,' said Richard. 'But it was, you know, very far from home and my father did not greet the news cheerfully, for we knew nothing of the bride, Elizabeth – Elizabeth Irving, of a Scottish family, I believe – or the circumstances of the wedding. It was, Thomas has assured us, conducted by a clergyman, but not in a church, or even a chapel, there being no such thing in a wilderness. The houses of the village about the fort were, doubtless still are, simple cabins built of felled trees, of which there is an endless supply. The place is an outpost at the very edge of civilisation. In consequence, the ceremony was conducted in my brother's room at the fort – where there were witnesses enough but, alas, no parish register in which to record the deed. So my brother, his wife and their little boy returned to England … without proof of the marriage. And the clergyman cannot be traced – may be dead for all we know. It is a rather delicate situation, which the family is striving to keep to itself.'

He looked searchingly at Sarah, suspecting for a moment that, carried away by the excitement of telling the story to a rapt listener, he had overstepped the bounds of discretion.

'I understand,' she said. And his anxiety subsided.

On their father's death, brother John had taken possession of baronetcy and estates, as was his right. He was five years older than Richard and, when they were boys together, had often asserted his greater age and bulk by shrewd and sly blows, while Thomas, who was only a year younger than John and by chance or nature much the same size, stood moodily aside. Richard became used to the subservient place he occupied, while John had first choice of everything. His was the largest pony and when, on occasion, by superior horsemanship, Thomas won a race, John would complain his brother had cheated and insist they exchange mounts.

While Thomas went up to Oxford, John departed on his grand European tour and returned with some knowledge of French and Italian, and exotic tastes in revelry and young women. After he in turn had sampled Oxford, expenditure of several thousands of pounds on the purchase of votes and refreshments for voters bought him a seat in Parliament at Wallingford, and an educated taste for self-indulgence earned him membership of the Hellfire Club, where discussion of politics went hand-in-hand with dissipation. Richard knew little of all this apart from what was contained in a few boastful letters from France or Italy addressed to Thomas, which he had been allowed to share: unedifying tales of drunken mishaps and the pursuit of young women married to complaisant older men.

When, later, rumour rippled up the Thames valley to Oxford from Medmenham concerning men of wealth and position who called themselves Knights or Friars of an order that swore allegiance to Venus and Dionysus, he did not at first realise his brother was of that company. The simple fact was, apart from casual bullying when they were young, John, almost always at a distance, led a very different life and largely ignored him. Richard was not given to frivolity, still less crapulent and libidinous behaviour. They had only kinship in common and, with their father's death, even that tie was weaker. What his brother would decide about Llantrithyd Place and other Aubrey properties in the Vale was of importance to him, but should he act in anticipation of change? It was at this time he turned again to the one person he felt he could trust to air his concerns.

'John, my brother,' he said to Sarah one still evening of constant drizzle, the tall windows almost as fogged with wet inside as they were without, ' – he has no heir, you know. Truthfully, he has been of recent years so unkindly served by fate or fortune that I cannot help but feel profoundly sorry for him, though in our younger days he gave me no reason to love or admire him, and we soon went our different ways. On the rare occasions we write to one another, it is invariably to expedite some business. We meet yet more infrequently, and when we do, as at the funeral of our father, find we have little to say. Yet, as he is my older brother, I care for him and would not wish him ill.'

'We cannot choose our kin,' said Sarah, 'as we do our friends. We stand with them as family, but no law says we must love them.'

'John did not attend my marriage to Frances, nor did Thomas for that matter, and I did not hold it against them. I was present when John married Mary Colebrooke, as were many others. Her family had long been wealthy bankers in London and they had a house in the classical manner at Gatton in Surrey. It was at Easter, an early Easter that year, 1771, but a fine day. I didn't linger in the neighbourhood and remember little of the occasion now, except the magnificent house on a hill overlooking its park and a lake, and the crush, the unholy crush I am tempted to say, in the ancient church where the ceremony was conducted. So John and Mary were married and settled at Boarstall. All seemed well. Before the end of the year they were celebrating the birth of a boy, who was, of course, named John. But no other children were born in the years that followed … and then there was the most appalling calamity … I hardly know how to tell of it now. But – he, young John, was five, and for his breakfast he was to have a dish of gruel. The oatmeal was prepared as usual with milk and set before him. He tried a spoonful and said the taste was strange, he didn't like it. This perhaps appeared an act of disobedience by a spoilt child. In any event, his father insisted that he eat it all – and, tearfully, protesting still, the child did. In a short time he was convulsed with pain and stricken with terrible sickness. Father and mother were alarmed. The doctor was sent for, but before he arrived the boy's condition had worsened. What had the child eaten? Why, simply gruel. But when the bowl of oatmeal from which the breakfast had been prepared was produced, it was at once recognised as that in which arsenic had been liberally sprinkled to serve as bait to poison rats. Nothing could be done. The boy's death was hideous, the parents' grief beyond imagining.'

Sarah had become pale, one hand pressed to her lips the other to her breast, the stir of coals in the grate the only sound in the silent room.

Richard began again, quietly: 'My brother has never spoken to me of this. How could anyone, implicated however innocently, as he was, in such a tragic event speak of it, ever? No, it was my father who told me lest, in ignorance, I should hurt John or his wife by asking after the child. It was my father, too, who divulged that, soon after the death, my brother razed to the ground the house where it occurred.

When I think of that terrible time, as I have done this evening, I wonder what it meant for the marriage. John buried his grief in his politics – he had always spent much of his time in London – but what did Mary do? I think she may have wasted away in mourning. Before three years had passed she followed her son into the grave.'

'Oh, how dreadful. I weep for Mary.'

'News of these events spread, as they usually do, at first through the servants and then John's wide circle of acquaintance. He was obliged, my father said, to tolerate the sympathy and condolences of well-meaning friends. And there were those who said it was a judgement – that my brother paid, is paying still, in this life, for the sins of his youth. They are canting hypocrites. To be sure, his life has not been wholly innocent: even now he has under his roof a child – his child he has acknowledged – born out of wedlock to a young woman of a French noble family, whom he met on the grand tour. Perhaps he should pay, but how could it be right to punish the child and his mother for the youthful indiscretions of the father?'

Sarah pondered the question. Is there justice in this life? What had Richard Aubrey done that his wife was taken from him, leaving an infant boy and his sister, two innocents, motherless? Does God have a plan? The death of Frances had brought her to Ash Hall, placed in her hands the nurture of those children, and on this evening, with the damp air clinging to the windows and gathering in droplets that trickled down like tears, the task of listening while the master of the house unburdened his mind. She looked at the man, the curve of the eyebrows, the strong straight nose, the delicately shaped lips, as he, too, sat pensive.

'I know not what to say,' she said. 'In church we are told there is a higher purpose we cannot hope to understand.'

Richard appeared not to hear. 'I did not attend his second marriage,' he said. 'Very few did. While not secret, it was conducted very quietly. He married his ward, Martha, who is also our cousin, being of our mother's kin. I met her once, by chance rather than design – a fair young woman. Why, yes, young: she is a full twenty-five years younger than my brother. Though husband and wife now five years or rather more, they have no children. John, Sir John, I should say, is a Lord of the Treasury and occupied with parliamentary duties ...'

After the death of Sir Thomas Aubrey, several months passed before Sir John, his heir, sixth baronet of Llantrithyd, decided it was time he visited the ancestral home. He left parliamentary politics and his business affairs in London reluctantly, and determined to spend no more time in Wales than was strictly necessary. Richard viewed his coming with some trepidation. It appeared to him that, if his brother wished the family to maintain their position of influence and authority in the Vale, since Thomas, now Lieutenant-Colonel, had expressed his determination to remain in the army, it was only reasonable *he* should occupy the Plas (as his servants insisted on calling it), to maintain house and demesne. If, on the other hand, John was careless of severing roots in Wales and planned to sell the entire estate to expand his property in the English counties, then his position was precarious. He did not have the wealth to purchase Ash Hall and its land and had no expectation of receiving them as a gift.

The visit provided no clear answers to these questions. When he was sure his brother was sufficiently revived after his long journey, Richard rode to Llantrithyd to greet him. Their meeting, the first since the deaths of their respective wives, was amicable. John, with the understanding of loss his own experience had brought, was at first unexpectedly gentle, but his sympathy had no length to it. He was impatient to be done with the formality of exhibiting himself in Wales.

'What is to be done with this house?' Richard said at last, having despaired of the matter being otherwise raised.

His brother shrugged. 'I have no plans for it. My life is largely spent in London, where my duties at the House and in the Treasury keep me pretty busy, and if I'm not there then you will find me at Boarstall, or perhaps Chilton or another of my Oxfordshire estates.' He paused. 'Time will take care of Llantrithyd,' he said.

Perceiving that John did not intend summarily to dispose of the Place, and had no plans for any part of his Welsh property, Richard contentedly resigned himself to a future at Ash Hall, a comfortable and pleasant enough dwelling, especially as he had improved it. Soon after, conversation exhausted, they parted with cool cordiality.

For a short time the great house at Llantrithyd, though some visitors, peering round doors and looking into corners, thought it a little shabby, was again vibrant with warmth and light. The baronet, who had travelled alone, held court and gentry families and tenants from all parts of the Vale came to offer condolences on the death of his well-loved father, and wish him long life and happiness. Robert Jones of Fonmon Castle, whom Sir John had been hoping to see was, alas, abroad, in France (having fled, he was surreptitiously informed, to evade creditors). The ageing Thomas Edmondes of Llandough Castle, whose father had been a close friend of his uncle, baronet before him, limped forward with a courteous greeting and engaged him in earnest conversation about the politics of the Vale, of which he knew nothing and cared less. A crowd of tenants anxious to learn about future rents were quickly passed over: 'I will attend to all such matters in due course, as leases expire. There is no point in anticipating. Mr Mumford, my agent, will speak with you, each and every one.'

Then came the welcome relief of a short, red-cheeked gentleman farmer, John Perkins, and his wife Elizabeth, a plump, merry woman some years older than her husband, whom he was given the freedom to address as 'Bessy'. Bessy, it transpired, had previously been the fourth wife of the rapscallion rector and Lord of the Manor of Gileston. When they were wed she had been twenty-two, her husband seventy-three. 'He lived on, lively enough, until he was eighty,' she said, with some pride, 'and left me *very* well provided for.' Sir John, highly amused, gave several dozen bottles of beer, intended for distribution to the tenants, all to Perkins.

He left Llantrithyd once, to call on Aunt Margaret. The three-storey stone house at Llanmaes, which he had once thought impressively large for its single occupant and her servants, now appeared rather mean. As for the mistress of the house herself, his late father's half-sister, she was small and fat, and with that wide mouth, he thought, resembled nothing so much as a frog in a wig, albeit with airs above her station. Her briskness irritated him. She was an old woman, and a busybody, in whom, unaccountably, his father had reposed much trust. They spoke briefly of leases and other financial matters touching the Vale estates and having reiterated his intention to leave the Place unoccupied for the time being, and the land unsold, still leased to her, he left. The next day he set out for London.

Richard's circle of acquaintance gradually increased. It included fellow magistrates, whom he met at sessions at the Red House in Cardiff and in Cowbridge at the Bear. At first he found these new duties amusing.

'You know my Welsh is limited to commands to dogs, horses and farm labourers,' he told Sarah, 'well, today we had a woman before us who was said to have called the Doctor's wife a harlot – and offered to prove it – in Welsh. This was a bit beyond me, but all was explained. The doctor was beside himself, but I couldn't help wondering what lay at the bottom of it. Why would an apparently respectable woman say that sort of thing, even in Welsh? Was there a grievance felt so strongly that nothing but public calumniation of the good doctor's wife would answer? Or was she, the wife I mean, incontinently betraying her husband with all and sundry? And then there were the young men who twice on the road between Cardiff and Cowbridge, after the fair, with scores of people trooping homewards, goaded their stallions to fighting, the horses prancing and biting one another, then rearing up and lashing out with their hooves most furiously, and everyone scattering like chaff before the wind, women and children crying out, men shouting and cursing, little short of a riot. Twice! And the foolish, drunken miscreants apparently caring not a jot. They will get the whipping they deserve.'

He frequently sat with another magistrate, Bloom Williams, apothecary-surgeon of Cardiff, whose father, now dead, had been well known as an apothecary before him. Williams, he told Sarah, was short and stout, of unprepossessing appearance, but energetic and determined to make his way among people of influence. He had been helpful in the early days of Richard's experience in the magistracy, and had a remarkable capacity for remaining awake and alert during long hours of intensely boring business.

'Do you know I have spent half the day dealing with complaints about dung?' Richard said on another occasion.

'Dung? Is that, too, the business of magistrates?'

'Why, yes. We have to consider complaints about the stopping of gutters, the blocking of drains – through accident or carelessness – and about buildings left in a ruinous state, an eyesore and a danger to the public at large. Then there are people, who should know better, unhitching horses and abandoning carts in the middle of the road, or leaving trapdoors open in pavements. Heaps of timber or stone appear in the street overnight – and dung: endlessly we hear of piles of dung blocking narrow ways. Very unsavoury. And reprehensible behaviour, but who to blame? – that's the question. I think there must be a whole tribe who secretly go about collecting dung for the very purpose of unloading it in the streets of Cardiff.' His brow furrowed, he looked perplexed, exasperated.

Sarah bent closer over the needlework in her lap to hide her laughter.

'It's hopeless,' he said. Then he, too, gave way to laughter.

VII

O N HER EIGHTH birthday, it being Sunday, Sarah took Julia to church as usual. It was eerily still, a chill January day, the sky dense and leaden, trees and hedges robed in white caught statuesque in frozen gestures, the surface of the rutted lane iron. Blankets and brass foot-warmers filled with hot coals had been placed in the carriage. The blankets were brought with them into the church, where the air was frigid. Well wrapped as both were in fur-trimmed hooded capes, with woollen stockings and mittens, the cold nipped noses, toes and fingertips. Soon, like the dozen parishioners who had braved the day, they too clung together for warmth. Beneath aged cassock and surplice, the curate wore almost all the clothes he possessed, and shivered so that the Word of God issued from his lips quavering uncertainly. He hastened through matins and begged forgiveness for his despatch, saying it was to send the congregation with God's blessing the more speedily to their homes.

The coachman, having dashed back to Ash Hall and the servants' kitchen fire, lingered there, not expecting the service to end early. He was struggling into greatcoat and freshly-warmed boots when with clatter and scuffle and hasty goodbyes the church emptied and the worshippers hurried away followed by clouds of breath. Sarah knelt at the church door, Julia, whimpering with cold, close in her arms, the blankets trailing around them.

'My dear, dear child, I was not wise to bring you today,' she said. 'Yet it seemed a fitting way to begin celebrating your birthday. The carriage will come soon.'

Having added threadbare cloak and scarves to his attire, the curate joined them in the doorway. 'Come within,' he said, 'I'll wait here to tell you when the carriage is approaching – though to be sure it is hardly warmer inside than out. Did I hear it is the little lady's birthday? Please allow me to wish her,' his teeth chattered, 'a very happy day. God grant her warmth – soon – and future health and happiness.'

Sarah looked closely at the hollow-cheeked, pinched face of the curate. He was concerned for them, an honest, caring man, one who would strive for the good, and with a shy charm beneath the shabbiness.

'Julia thanks you for your greetings,' she said. 'You will understand she is not disposed to be conversational just at present, but there will, I'm sure, be other occasions. Thank you, too, for your kind offer. We will perhaps step in from your doorway.'

Placing an ancient, black, felt hat on his head and with another scarf pulling its broad brim over his ears and tying it in place with a knot under the chin, the Reverend George stepped outside and peered in the direction from which the carriage would come. 'I feel sure it will snow,' he called over his shoulder, and, a little later, 'I believe I hear the carriage.'

In a few minutes more, it stood before the lych-gate, the horses huge in a fog of their own heat nodding their heads and stamping. Fresh coals had been added to the foot-warmers and soon woman and child were wrapped in blankets inside, where their feet buzzed with something between pain and pleasure. The curate waved and shouted

'Good-bye, good-bye ...' but there was no answer from within as the carriage rattled away.

Before it had gained the hilltop and the gates of Ash Hall, snow began to fall.

At first, small flakes eddied and spiralled, idly, singly, uncertain of direction in the still air, but past midday, the sky more intensely dark, white lines ran along previously unobserved contours and edges, paths had ermine borders. Inside the house, curtains were closed early, oil lamps and candles lit, and baskets of logs and buckets of coals drawn to hearths ready to replenish fires. The daily servants and labourers were sent home earlier, while it was still just light. Sarah recognised it as a wise and generous decision, typical of the natural kindliness of their master, and it was accepted with gratitude.

Mr Aubrey requested dinner at half past four o'clock in the library, where the table had been placed closer to the fire and screens arranged to hinder draughts from door and windows. Afterwards he called for the children to be brought to the room, so that they should join him to mark Julia's birthday. They came with Sally and Jennet, who was especially welcomed, and all partook of apple tart and custard. Although tearful throughout, Jennet ate as heartily as any. Julia sang 'Sing a song of sixpence, a bag full of rye', at which Thomas Digby laughed and clapped, and afterwards her father gave her a small gold ring set with a garnet gleaming dark red in the lamplight that she would wear on a fine gold chain around her neck until she was bigger.

As well as Julia's birthday, the occasion marked Jennet's last day in the service of Mr Aubrey. Thomas, recently breeched, appeared taller – almost a young man, his doting nurse thought. She was leaving, not because she was no longer needed, but because she had won the love of Howel, one of the farm labourers, a sturdy and reliable man, unmarried and much the same age. For a long time Jennet had kept him at a distance while she waited for news of her husband. But Evan had not returned, nor had there been any sign of his continued existence. His father had died and his mother accepted that her son had gone to what she hoped was a better place, whether in the mining valleys or the grave. When told of the new relationship, she bore no ill-will to her daughter-in-law, though she inwardly hoped Jennet would help to support her as before. In the absence of proof of Evan's death, the couple could not be married, but Mr Aubrey was easily reconciled to the prospect of them living together and found opportunity to provide for them tenancy of a cottage at Ystradowen. Howel would continue to work on farm and garden and, having more than fulfilled her part of the bargain struck five years before, Jennet would leave with his blessing and a silver shilling to say how grateful he was that she had nourished and cared for Thomas. Soon afterwards, clinging close to Howel's arm, their way lit by a burning torch of pitch and cotton tow held in his other hand, Jennet left Ash Hall.

In the early hours snow began to fall in good earnest. In her cold room, blankets closely wrapped about her, Sarah slept fitfully, for the wind roared about the house and rattled the tall sash window. When, after what seemed a tedious time of half waking and odd, oppressive dreams, she was at last fully awake, it was to the realisation of change. The wind had dropped, it was unearthly still and silent, and the room was suffused with white light that seeped through gaps in the curtains. Outside the cocoon of her narrow bed she knew it would be intensely cold and she lay there waiting for the sound of the children's voices.

Her thoughts flowed from snowfalls of childhood to her mother and father, and brothers – yes, two brothers, James and Stephen, James little older than she, whom she played with, who had fallen ill and died when she was – seven was it? – or eight? – the same age as Julia. Thinking of Julia propelled her into the present. Julia, who seemed almost her own, so close were they, was a great part of her happiness at Ash Hall. Such beauty in one so young was a rare gift, and with it a loving nature, devoid of mischief and spite. Her mother, her true mother, must have been the same, Sarah felt sure. No wonder Mr Aubrey, Richard, mourned her so long, and missed her still she had no doubt. He was a good man, she thought, a good man – and a handsome man – oh yes, handsome. A small surge of warmth rose within her and she smiled to herself, and took a deep breath of the chill air outside the blankets. He was a good man, and she admired him, and loved to hear his laughter. She was glad the long mourning was over and that he took pleasure in seeing his children grow – and, it seemed, in talking to her. That she had never expected, no, never expected.

Small, sleepy voices from the adjoining room ended her reverie. She gathered the blankets about her and hurried, her stockinged feet already beginning to chill, through the door to join them. It was not warm, but warmer than her room. There was barely a glimmer in the hearth.

'We won't wait for Mary,' she said, and bent to add slivers of wood to the fire and blow it into life, before adding more wood and when it was well alight placing carefully into the flames some lumps of coal from the bucket.

'Shall I read to you while we wait for the fire to be really warm?'

'Yes, yes!' the children cried, and Thomas scrambled from his small bed to Julia's somewhat larger and, despite his sister's protest, forced his way under the blankets.

'Now, if you are polite and quiet together like that,' said Sarah, 'I can begin. Otherwise … '

They lay quiet and she read the adventures of Tom Thumb and Dick Whittington while the fire gathered itself and the coals caught. Soon Mary came, well wrapped in a shawl, her clogs clattering on the boards, saying 'Good morning, good morning! There's such a lot of snow outside – you're better off where you are,' and knelt, raking out the ashes from the previous night and shovelling them into her bucket and feeding the fire with more coal until it was a blaze.

Then the children got up and all dressed and Sarah took them to the frost-etched window and made a spy hole with her breath and wiped it so that they could look out onto a world transformed. At the front of the house snow had been swept into two great waves, their crests frozen on the point of breaking, trees rose from unplumbed depths of snow to exhibit bare branches and twigs redrawn with thick white lines, the ha-ha had been reduced to a shallow dip in a field of brilliant white that overwhelmed hedges and, sweeping down the hillside, faded into a misty grey distance. The children thought it was a fairy land. And so it was, full of strange delights to the eyes, for an hour – no more! Beyond that, it became a misery of penetrating cold.

Each door, opened in turn and hurriedly closed again, revealed a wall of snow had surrounded the house under cover of darkness. Cattle were lowing and, at Mr Aubrey's command, a narrow path was carved from the back door, which gave onto the vanished kitchen garden, to byre and stable. The pump was frozen and water for the beasts and for the kitchen was made by melting snow in the great laundry tub.

Sarah thought of Jennet waking in her new home with Howel. He would surely see that they were well supplied with fuel to keep the cold at bay. And, in turn, she would tend him and feed him, and embrace him with her love. But there were many others in the village down below, the old and sick, those in dilapidated cottages, those in hovels, who would view the winter morning with horror and despair. And she thought of Llangan under snow, her own father, grown sickly, her anxious mother, her brother and farm servants labouring against the weight of fallen snow. How fortunate she was. She took the children into the kitchen where a great fire glowed and, once breakfast had been cleared, they sat with her at the corner of the long oak table closest to the open hearth. There they read together, Sarah and Julia taking turns and Thomas watching closely as their fingers moved from word to word. Later, while Thomas practised his letters with horn-book and chalk on a new slate, Julia took ink and paper, and the pen Sarah had cut for her, and wrote a letter to her father:

Dear Dear Father

Thank you very very much for my beutiful present I love the ring very much the stone shines a beutiful red. The snow loked beutiful this morning but it is very cold I hope you do not have to go out.

Your loving daugter

Julia Frances Aubrey

At first, everyone seemed energised by the drama, but soon the change it wrought to their lives, the increased difficulty of daily tasks and the sense of being confined by snow became tedious. More paths were made, men moving slowly along, hidden to their thighs and often to their waists, as they struggled, shovelling through the snow. When the way to the stable was clear, Mr Aubrey attempted to ride out to see that all was well at Llantrithyd Place, but he had not reached the lane before the horse floundered in deep snow and took fright. When coaxing and spurs failed, he gave up. Though not long after midday, it was already getting dark. The wind was rising and blowing fallen snow in icy pellets. He was glad to sink his face into his scarves and let the horse have its head as it followed the trail it had pushed and trampled through the endless white back to the stable. His return was greeted with joy, because fears had been whispered about the danger of his undertaking. He was colder, he said, than he had ever been in his life, and sat silent for a long time, thawing his limbs before the kitchen fire, while the cooks and remaining servants busied themselves.

The lamps were lit and the bright glow of the fire cast moving shadows on the walls. The children were quiet, as though subdued by the silence and weight of snow. Thomas played with a few toy redcoat soldiers, thin, like silhouettes, moving them within the frame of his chalk slate and drawing lines for them to jump over or march around, while Julia concentrated on her needlework, carefully cross-stitching the letters of the alphabet onto a square of linen. Sarah, seated between them, poised to attend to their needs, was becoming confused by *The Life and Opinions of Tristram Shandy, Gent.*, which, at his suggestion, she had borrowed from Mr Aubrey's library and had been reading for some time. It was strange, unlike any book she had read before: Tristram barely appeared in it and of his opinions she could find nothing at all, but Richard – Mr Aubrey – had assured her it was a fashionable success in Oxford and London. 'You must let me be your teacher,' he had said, 'for I found it richly amusing.' Now, still and thoughtful beside the fire, he watched from time to time the little group seated at the table, his dark-headed girl with her heart-shaped face and pursed lips, absorbed in her task, his young son, dark too, marching his men in the confines of the slate and chalked lines, humming to himself and leaning against Sally, who looked down on them both and smiled, he thought, a satisfied smile.

It was more than he could have hoped for in those terrible days when he watched helplessly the strength fade in his wife's limbs and the hope and light fade from her eyes. Thomas could know nothing of that; all the affection he experienced had come from Jennet and Sally. And Julia had no true memory of her mother: a faceless figure perhaps, ghost-like before her passing and, he hoped most fervently, the warmth of a motherly embrace. From the start, Sally had been more than nurse and governess to her, had given her tenderness and affection – not a mother's love perhaps, but how far short of that he couldn't tell. She was, after all, a farmer's daughter from the Vale, albeit one that had received some education at the hands of a clever uncle of aesthetic tastes. He could see clearly she was warm and practical and he did not doubt her capacity for love, demonstrated almost daily before his eyes, as she cared for his children: *cared* for them. She had the capacity for a kind of love that was brave, sensible, cheerful. Yes, that was it, cheerful – and enduring. How wonderful it must be, he thought, to be loved like that, firmly, without nonsense. He watched again and saw the satisfied smile, and how the boy, sensing her glance, looked up and smiled at her, and she took one hand from the book and passed her arm around him and pressed him to her side, and Richard hurriedly bowed his head to hide his tears.

The fire in the children's room had been well tended, Mary told him, and safely banked for the night with small coal. Mary, whose wrinkled face easily creased in toothless smiles, had been a servant at Ash Hall many years, long before Richard became master. Small and, layered with petticoats as she was, still of stick-like slenderness, her bare forearms mere skin and bone, she was surprisingly strong from long hauling buckets of coal about the house, and proud of her skill in lighting and tending the fires. 'It's cold going up those stairs,' she said, 'but they will be warm enough in bed. And I've raised the ashes again in the library and put fresh coal on. It should be fine by now.'

'Good. I shall have my dinner there – and Mistress Sally will join me. I need to speak to you,' he said, turning to her, 'once the children are in their beds.'

The meal had been cleared and they were seated still at the library table. Sarah folded her hands in her lap and looked up expectantly.

'Are you going to help me understand what Mr Sterne is about in his book of Tristram Shandy?' she said. 'Or does it concern the children? I hope you are not displeased at the letter. I let Frances pen it entirely by herself.'

'Both,' said Richard, ' – or really, neither. I am more than happy with the way the children are growing in your care, how sensibly they behave, how they are learning to read – and to write. I shall preserve carefully, like a precious ancient text, that first letter from my daughter. As for Mr Sterne, a merry cleric,

I shall not stand between you and him. Let him win you over, or fall by his own eccentric wit. No, I wanted to ask about your personal comfort here. It may seem strange after – how long is it? Five years? Six? – I should express an interest in your well-being … beyond what is usual between master and servant. But I don't think of you as a servant. The children's closeness to you, and their importance to me, defines a different relationship. I am not doing this very well … I merely wanted to say that I am aware your room has no fire – no fireplace, indeed – and that it must be bitterly cold. While the children were yet very young, it was proper that you, and Jennet, for the time she was with us, should sleep near them lest there should be need of you during the night. I think that is no longer the case. I shall have you move to a room, somewhat larger, and more comfortable, where there is a fireplace.'

A quick frown, and signs of unhappiness in Sarah's eyes, told him she was about to protest. 'The chill is nothing,' she said. 'I love my room and its nearness to the children. At the slightest sound, a cough, a cry in the night – from a pain or a bad dream – and in a moment I can be at their side.'

'Yes, I know, I know. But you will hardly be much farther from them than you are now. Your door is the other side of the corridor, opposite theirs. And you will please me by occupying a room more suited to your position. All the servants look to you for guidance. That was not what I intended when you first came here. You were not employed as housekeeper, though I was given to understand that was the position you occupied in your uncle's house, but as nurse and governess to my children. And you have far exceeded that. I see it daily: you have become another mother to Thomas and Julia. Late in the day, perhaps, I say it behoves me to provide greater comfort for you, as a sign to all of the esteem in which you are held. And,' he smiled, 'you will surely be gracious enough to accept that.'

It was the gentle voice as much as the spoken words that brought a sudden warmth to Sarah's cheeks, so that she bowed her head. 'Yes,' she said in little more than a whisper, 'yes, of course. I shall do as you say, and I am conscious of the favour you show me, and very grateful.'

On first opening the door of her new room, she gasped: a fire glowed in the ornamented grate, candles flickered in brass candlesticks either side of the mantelshelf and on an open, mirrored dressing table. The confused thoughts this unexpected vision brought included a momentary flash of irritation, that she had somehow been betrayed into impropriety. It was surely not right that the room had been prepared for her by Mary and other servants working secretly at their master's bidding. She had no special claim to be so favoured, no desire to be placed above them. And how could she repay such generosity? She could do no more, or with more goodwill, more tender care and affection, than she did now. In another moment her perplexity melted in delight of this gift.

She leaned her back against the door and drew deep breaths. When she had cleared her vision, she saw the room was unlike others in the house. It was furnished differently. A linen press against the farther wall, like the elegant dressing table, was of reddish mahogany, as, too, was the writing table between the tall curtained windows, and pretty giltwood chairs were placed before both dressing table and desk. Unlit candles stood pale in brass wall sconces, a gaudily fabric-covered wing chair had its back to her near the fireplace, and a cheval mirror occupied another corner, obscuring a communicating door. Turkey carpets lay on the painted floorboards either side of the bed, which, although not perceptibly larger than the one she had slept in since her arrival at Ash Hall, was curtained. It was a lady's room. Could it have been furnished for Frances Digby, perhaps before her marriage? She shook her head and put the thought from her mind.

Taking up her candle, she crossed the landing to her former place – cold, bare, a room with the feeling of emptiness about it. Her clothes, her few possessions were no longer to be seen. She quietly turned the handle of the connecting door to look in on the children, as she had done hundreds of times before. Both were sleeping soundly. Returned to her new warm room she found her belongings had been neatly stowed in drawers in the dressing table and the far larger drawers of the linen press. Nothing had been forgotten. The precious gift from her uncle, the painting by George Morland, hung between the sconces. Recognising it in the shadow, she remembered how well her uncle had taught her. The giltwood chairs might well be French, or perhaps made in imitation of the French style, she thought: Uncle John would know at a glance. In her bed, its curtains not entirely closed, because she would not be parted from pleasure of the fire's glow and its faint reflection in mirror, ruddy mahogany and gilt, she thought how fortunate she had been. She had not sought the advantages that had come her way, and this latest sign of Mr Aubrey's approbation aroused mixed feelings of gratitude and concern. She would have to think of ways that would justify her acceptance of favours she believed were beyond her just deserts. Puzzling her new situation, she sank beneath the blankets.

An icy dawn had broken, but there was still little sign of daylight when she awoke to find Mary, whose knock had roused her, bent to the fire. In a few minutes the servant had brought it to a cheerful glow. Sarah sat on the side of the bed to thank her and was shocked to silence when the old woman, bucket in hand, gave her a little bob and hurried through the door into the dimly candle-lit corridor beyond. When not long afterwards she drew back the heavy drapes that covered the windows, she looked out on a snowy landscape in which the slate roofs of the stables were barely distinguishable, vertical stones that topped the wall of the kitchen garden stood like a row of black teeth above the endless white, and a little farther off the bare, black arms of the sweet chestnut trees at the top of the lane saluted her.

Her first thought was for the children. They should see she was still near them and, once they were dressed, she brought them to her fireside. There, even before their breakfast gruel with honey, Julia read a little from her book of nursery rhymes. It was thus Mr Aubrey found them, Sarah seated in the wing chair before the fire, Thomas on her lap, watching closely, while Julia stood at the chair arm reading aloud. It was some moments before he could speak.

'I see you are all comfortably at home here,' he said. 'Good, good. Shall we go and break our fast? What clumsiness! – mine I mean. It is still desperately cold outside, we need food. Come,' with arms wide, 'let's to the kitchen and eat.'

The pattern had been set. Henceforth Sarah's room was also, during the day, when they were indoors, the children's room, a comfortable schoolroom and playroom. An ill-matched but convenient oak chest was brought in where their things were stored. Sarah was content, being able now to convince herself she was no longer especially favoured, but that was not the servants' perception of her status.

For an entire month, winter was unrelenting. Deep frosts spread a glistening crust on the white surface of the changed world. The lane, filled up with snow, here and there to the full height of the hedges on either side, remained impassable. Movement was easier on some fields sloping down to Ystradowen, where the snow had been blown to hedge margins and piled there in great drifts, leaving shallower accumulations elsewhere that a careful rider could negotiate. Eventually, treacherous icy paths wound their way to Cowbridge and to Llantrithyd. Mr Aubrey set off again for the Plas, saying it was unlikely he would be back that same day, much as he wished it.

Two days and two nights passed and still he had not returned. Sarah hid her anxiety from the children and kept them busy with work and play as best she could while insisting rooms were kept warm for them and food prepared as usual. On the morning of the third day, encouraged by a lull in the gale, a few of the day men braved icy, narrow paths through deep snow to Ash Hall. They stood in a huddle outside the back door, stamping their feet. Finding the master was not at home, 'What shall we do now?' they asked. Slither their way back home again, without having earned a penny? The kitchen maid, who had answered their knocking, turned to Sarah, at the head of a small table drawn close to the hearth where the children were finishing their breakfast. Together, the other servants turned and looked at her, and the men in the yard peered in. After a moment's thought, she told one to lay in more sawn logs for the fires and bring coals nearer to the door, and the other two to clear the stable yard in readiness for the master's return. 'And please close the door,' she added, 'or we shall freeze inside.'

Just past midday the men working in the yard came to say

they had finished their tasks – was there anything else? The kitchen maid ran to fetch Sarah, who came into the kitchen clutching a shawl about her, her breath already visible in the instantly chilled air. She observed their pinched, pale faces and frosted beards, and their relief when she dismissed them. She didn't wait to see them hurry off.

Unable to leave the confines of the house, or even move more than a few yards from a fire, for all Sarah's efforts to instruct and amuse them the children were fretful and gripped by lassitude. They had an early supper while warming pans were put into their beds and their bedroom fire made up and, after a last story about Jack and his adventure with an immensely tall beanstalk and a giant who lived in a castle in the sky, which Sarah remembered from her childhood, they went contentedly to sleep. At nightfall the wind rose from the north and snow whirled by the windows, whether fresh or blown from drifts it was impossible to tell. All the servants were once more gathered in the kitchen, where a great fire blazed, and yet the air was chill in the farther corners. With the noise of the wind no one heard approaching hoofbeats on the icy path, and the servants looked fearfully around at a muffled thud against the door. Had hoary old winter himself arrived demanding to be let in?

'Open the door,' cried Sarah, 'for God's sake, quickly.'

Unlatched, the door swung open with the wind's blast and a figure wrapped in cloak and scarves crusted with ice fell in over the threshold. Someone screamed. 'It's Mr Aubrey – he's dead.'

The door slammed shut. In the confused hubbub of wailing and shouting that followed, Sarah knelt by the prone figure, pulling at the bundle of frozen clothing until she had turned him on his back, hauling away layered scarves, already dripping with melting ice. The face was deathly pale, the body, corpse-like still, and the eyes open, staring with huge pupils, but there was the faintest sign of breathing – a breath, a breath, a long pause, a breath.

'He's alive,' said Sarah, who had been holding her own breath until she almost fainted away. 'There's a fire in his room?'

'No, Mistress Sally. He didn't come back this morning and we didn't think to see him today.'

'We must get these wet, frozen things off him. You,' she motioned to the two men hanging back at the fringes of the group, 'carry him to my room, undress him at once, quickly, and place him in my bed. Someone light the candles, and Mary, tend the fire there – now.'

The servants had been standing, some wringing their hands helplessly, until stirred to action by her urgent cries. Younger women scurried to light the way and the room above and in a moment their dying master had been lifted and carried upstairs, followed by Sarah and Mary with coals for the fire.

'Lay him on the carpet by the bed. Strip him. Come, come! You must get those wet clothes off to save him.'

She watched as they struggled with boots and stockings, buttons and sleeves until she almost wept for anguish, but at last it was done and the marble form of Richard Aubrey lay still at the bedside.

'Lift him, lift him, man – into the bed. Now, out. All of you – out.'

The two menservants backed away sheepishly and Mary, rising from the hearth where the fire, replenished, was burning well, called to them, 'Dewch o fa'ma,' and pulled them out of the room.

Under the bedclothes, the man lay still as before, staring at nothing, his breath faint. Sarah knelt by the bed, begging God to tell her what to do. And suddenly she knew. She rose, hastily took off her gown, her stays and petticoats and, in her shift and woollen stockings, entered the narrow bed. Clasping the rigid form in her arms, she pressed herself fiercely against its deathly chill and prayed the warmth of her body would bring life. 'Live,' she murmured in the frozen ear, 'live … live for your children … for me … live, live,' on and on, until at last the turmoil of events and fatigue overwhelmed her and she fell asleep.

She was awakened by a stir in the body beside her. Mr Aubrey, sleeping now, had turned so that he faced away from her. Still she pressed close and, with a surge of inexpressible joy, recognised that his back possessed its own natural warmth. She had never before lain with a man and, the awful prospect of the previous night having dissipated, observed dimly in the light of guttering candles Richard's broad shoulders and solid, smooth flesh with something akin to wonder. The bed curtains had not been closed and a glance told her the fire had burned low. Slowly, carefully, she removed herself from the bed, dressed, and with infinite pains repaired the fire as quietly as she could. When flames began to flicker she raised herself from the hearth, and then at once sank to her knees and gave thanks to God. It was still dark, the wind no longer shrieked but harsh gusts buffeted the house. Those were the only sounds. She set fresh candles in candlesticks and sconces and the room was soon cheerful with light and warmth and the promise of life continuing.

Then, thinking of the events the previous evening, how distraught she was, she wondered at her assumption of authority, and how the other servants obeyed her. She had never before spoken to them in that way, but they were terrified, as she was, by the lifeless figure fallen on the threshold, and needed only to be told what best to do. They would soon put it behind them. She sat for a while in the wing chair by the fire, but when there were more signs of stirring from her bed, she awakened the servants with the news that Mr Aubrey had recovered, thanks be to God, told his man to gather fresh clothes for the master and place them at his bedside, and the cook to prepare a warm, nourishing drink. Mary was already in the kitchen, raising ashes, cleaning the cavernous inglenook and piling fuel on a lively fire. Daylight eventually disclosed a landscape still in the iron grip of winter, snow swept by the night's wind into fantastic shapes of crests and hollows, icicles hanging a foot or more from eaves, the line of bare, black trees like frozen sentinels descending the lane.

In two days of home warmth and nourishment, Richard Aubrey was his own man again and ready to tell his story. He recalled setting out before midday, but the lane leading away from the Plas was blocked, as before, and the path by which he had picked his way there had been hidden by fresh and wind-blown snow. He found himself out of sight of the mansion house, alone in an endless white expanse where almost all familiar landmarks had been erased. Having, he thought, ridden miles out of his way, he dismounted and for some time trudged to rest his mount, for there was still a long road before them, could they but find it. At length he struck upon the turnpike for Cowbridge and beyond and made his way slowly towards the crossroads with the sign pointing to Ystradowen that he longed to see. By this time it was afternoon, the sky darkening and the wind strengthening and, on foot again, leading the horse, he would have missed the turning and trudged onwards to God knew where had he not stumbled against the fingerpost, which was three-quarters buried in packed snow. Before he reached the village the horse was struggling against a bitter gale as well as the precarious footing. So they slipped and slithered on. The rider, shivering and then numb with cold, and blinded by icy pellets, gave the beast his head, hoping, and then praying, its knowledge of where the stable lay in this blank wilderness was superior to his own sense of direction.

'Well, so it proved,' he said, 'though I was unaware of it. The poor creature stopped and I slid or fell from its back. I suppose the weight of clothing prevented me from breaking bones as I fell, but I was not fully conscious and lay there for a while, the wind howling about me, thinking, "Those are lights, but I don't really want to move ..." I might easily have died outside my own door, but something, some guardian angel surely, made me struggle to my feet – and that is all I remember.'

He did not voice to the assembled servants, harkening open-mouthed to his tale of near tragedy, his initial bewilderment at coming to consciousness in Sally's bedroom and Sally's bed, but waited until he could speak to her alone. By then some inkling of what had happened when he fell through the door had been conveyed by remarks from one or two of the servants, particularly old Mary, who habitually talked while she was busy at a fireplace sometimes in Welsh, sometimes English or a strange mixture of both, not conversationally, but rather to herself, though anyone with a mind to was welcome to listen.

Sarah had said nothing, but when, in the usual way, she came to speak to him about the children, he asked her directly what had occurred.

'You were frozen, death-like in appearance, and I feared you were dead indeed, but I saw signs of breathing and the servants then hastened to help you.'

'You told them to take me to your room?'

'Yes, because yours had no fire. You were not expected that day. The men carried you upstairs, and put you to bed.'

'And that's all?'

Sarah nodded, and looked down at the table between them where some pages of Julia's writing practice lay. But she could not hide the sudden warmth that flooded her cheeks.

'I was undressed? I found myself unclothed when I awoke. How did that occur?'

'I truly believed you were in mortal danger ... and if your clothing, which was soaked and frozen all through, was not at once removed so that you could be wrapped in blankets, then you would ... die. I told the men to undress you and put you into the bed.'

'You were probably right. I know of men – and women, whole families, perishing ... in their cottages, in weather less severe than we have suffered these recent days. You were wise to order the servants as you did.'

Sarah remained with her head bowed. 'I am happy you are here among us. I thank God for it,' she murmured.

'Yes, indeed. But one further thing bothers me: a dream, or something like a dream. As I was beginning to revive, or perhaps when I woke momentarily, I seemed ... my body seemed ... to be clasped in an embrace, a warmth, close, very close to me. If it was a dream, it was a rare and beautiful dream, and I shall never forget it. I think perhaps it saved my life. By the by, Sally, since I was in your bed, where did you sleep?'

Sarah remained silent, not knowing what to say, sensing Mr Aubrey was watching her closely. Should she tell him the truth? And how might it be received? He could readily accept he had been undressed by his menservants, but what if he knew she had been present, indeed, had hastened the men in their task? That he might well consider improper. And as for embracing the naked body of one's master … what kind of woman would he think her if she were to admit it?

Richard wanted her to tell him it was her body that had restored his to life. He wanted to ask whether, in the close confines of that narrow bed, she, too, had been naked, a thought that had excited him since his return to full health. But he understood her suffering and confusion.

'There are of course other bedrooms,' he said.

Sarah nodded, and he saw her relief. Rising, she said, 'Shall I leave these pages on which Julia has worked so hard? She was very pleased to know you would be looking at her writing.'

'Yes, of course.' He smiled, 'I shall look at it with great care – as you would expect of a former Fellow of All Souls.'

A wind from the south had brought rain and brooks were beginning at last to trickle beneath their layers of ice. The snow was thinning to sparkling lace at edges and gradually receding, exposing here and there the swollen carcasses of sheep, which as evening began to fall appeared like stepping stones in a faintly glimmering grey tide.

Sarah was in her room. It was a black night, no moon, nor stars, rain again pattering against the tall windows of the silent house. The cold was no longer penetrating and instead of hurrying beneath the bedclothes, Sarah was seated, reading, in the wing chair near the fire. Hearing the click of a lock and the creak of a hinge, she turned to find her door still firmly closed and, puzzled, addressed herself once more to the book in her lap. A voice, hardly more than a whisper, directly behind her chair, startled her.

'Sally, please – don't be alarmed. I wanted to talk to you.'

Richard had come, on stockinged feet, wearing a dark red banyan and embroidered velvet cap, through the connecting door she had never seen open and had taken as part of the furniture rather than a means of access to her room. She was alarmed, so much that she trembled and her voice quavered. 'What's happened? Are the children unwell?'

'No, they sleep peacefully. There's naught amiss. I simply needed … to talk – to you.'

He stood, tall and elegant in the patterned gown, across the fireplace from her, rather like an eastern prince, she thought. One arm resting on the narrow mantelshelf, his familiar features haloed by candlelight, he was watching her closely, tenderly, with dark eyes.

'It was you,' he said, 'I am sure it was you … who lay beside me and gave me your warmth. I rose like Lazarus from an icy grave, but it was not a miracle, it was strong, sensible, loving care that brought me back to life. No one else here could have accomplished that.'

'I prayed, oh, how I prayed that you be spared.'

'Prayer alone is never enough. The supplicant must be ready to serve as an instrument of God's good will.'

Not knowing how to reply, Sarah remained silent with eyes downcast and was startled again when suddenly he was close to her, kneeling at the arm of the chair, reaching for and, though she would have withdrawn it, holding her hand.

'Dear Sally,' he said, lifting her fingers to his lips, 'you restored my children to me, for in my grief I had neglected them, and through them gave me reason to live and plan for the future. You brought back to me the joy in simple things I never thought to find again. For all that, too, I am forever in your debt.'

'It was, I'm sure, no more than anyone would do, granted the good fortune to serve you. If what I have done pleases you, I am happy …'

'Enough of service. Come,' he said raising her to her feet, 'let me show you my room. Pretty as this is, you will see we can be more comfortable there.'

As he led her to the door, which had remained ajar, Sarah saw, fleetingly, as though figures in a half-remembered story, their reflections in the cheval mirror: a handsome Prince of the East drawing by the hand a maid in long white shift and floating shawl. She barely noticed the room they entered, although it was larger, the fireplace grander, the bed wider and heavily curtained. They did not speak, but the sounds they uttered were as of those who had long endured hunger and thirst and were at last feasting and being satisfied.

Through what remained of winter, Ash Hall and the management of its land slowly resumed their normal pattern. Farm labourers had much to do to repair the damage wrought by ice and snow to stock and property, and indoors there were still fires to care for, garments to be darned and mended, food to be cooked. The little scullery maid prepared vegetables, plucked poultry, washed dishes and scoured pans endlessly.

Housemaids, shooed out of the kitchen, dusted and swept, made beds, cleaned windows and stairs.

Sarah kept a watchful eye on all and continued to care for and teach Julia Frances and Thomas Digby. She gave no sign in her demeanour and relations with the other servants of what had occurred. For his part, Richard Aubrey, too, remained as before, pleasant to all and otherwise inscrutable. At night, in her room, Sarah waited for the click of the lock and the sound of the door behind the cheval mirror opening, and from time to time she was not disappointed. Whenever it did, they met and embraced like old friends and lovers, and there was great warmth and tenderness between them. In the third week of April, on a day when the sky was dark with rain falling thick and straight to earth like a shower of arrows and then suddenly bright, washed clean, she knew beyond doubt she was with child.

VIII

SARAH WAS NOT surprised by her pregnancy. She had been brought up on a farm and knew from early childhood why the ram was admitted to the field where ewes grazed, why the bull was led by the nose to the heifers, though once he had caught wind of them it would have been difficult to stop him, why the stallion was put to the mare. But she was for a time uncertain what she should do, to whom she should turn for advice. No one among her fellow servants answered this need, and she knew no one outside Ash Hall, save Jennet perhaps, who would be excited, full of concern and eager to help, but not with advice.

The answer came one night as she lay in Richard's arms. Sarah, thinking it was time she returned to her own room, wondered what her father and mother would say if they knew she sometimes shared the bed of the youngest son of Sir Thomas Aubrey.

'Richard,' she whispered, 'it is many weeks since I received a letter from my father. The dreadful winter has come and gone and I begin to wonder … '

Richard sighed and turned from her, breathing deeply. He was asleep; he had not heard. She raised herself on her elbow and looked at the handsome profile, the dark hair on the pillow, and would have kissed him had she not feared to wake him. She took her candle and made her way silently to her own bed. She would speak to him the following day.

With morning her plan had hardened to resolution. While the children, attended by the cook and kitchen maid, were having their breakfast, she went into the stable yard. On their hill, the early mist had risen, though it lingered still in hollows and above copses about the village down below. The sun was warming the red crest tiles and purple slates of the stable roof and leaves on the sweet chestnut trees were beginning to unfurl. Richard had ridden out early, inspecting fences and the state of banks and ditches and, as was his custom, he was brushing the horse, his favourite, the dark bay gelding that had brought him home, more dead than alive, through the winter storm. The last of its rough winter coat had gone and under the vigorous brush its sleek flanks rippled like dark water moved by a breeze.

'Good morning.' Richard's smile was warm. 'What think you of this beast?'

'Very fine,' she said. The tall horse nodded. 'I see you agree,' she added, stroking its velvet nose.

'Mr Aubrey?'

He looked at her. 'Why the formality? We are alone here. The horse will tell no one.'

'Please,' she said, 'will you permit me to visit my parents? It is many weeks since I last heard from my father and, while I blame myself for not writing to him to find how well, or ill, they survived winter and the floods that followed the thaw, I feel it would be better if I could, for a day only, see them again.'

'Why, yes, of course, Sally. Llangan isn't far – and you must have the carriage to take you and return you safely here.'

'I shall walk …'

'No, I forbid any such undertaking.' He smiled, 'It would

demand hours of your time – and a long rest afterwards. I – *we* cannot easily do without you for more than a day. Howel will escort you in the gig, and wait ... while you take tea – or whatever you intend, and bring you back. And we shall be impatient until you are here once more.'

Two days later, the weather still fine, the carriage took Sarah down the steep lane and through the village to the crossroads and speedily west along the turnpike some five miles to another crossroads and north along an increasingly familiar narrow sunken way to Llangan and in a few minutes more to the farm, the whole journey little more than an hour.

Ten years, more, had passed since she had left, but the farm before her was much the same as that which lingered in her memory – except that it was smaller, meaner, shrunken by time and her acquaintance with the thoroughfares of London and the houses of the Aubreys. In the yard she found a young woman, hardly more than twenty she guessed, and with child, as she was, but far more obviously so, tossing scraps from a bowl to a flurry of hens and an imperious cock. A farm servant, thought Sarah, as the woman, startled by the sudden arrival of a stranger, and bereft of words, fled to the open door followed by the flock of clucking chickens. In a moment, another, much older, woman stood in the low doorway raising her hand to shade her eyes and peering out.

'Who is that?' she said. 'What do you want?'

For several heartbeats they looked at each other trying to discern some sign of the familiar beneath outward appearance. Then it was the voice that convinced Sarah, her mother's voice.

'Mam, it's Sarah,' she said. 'I've come to see you and Dada.'

Still the old woman peered, as though not trusting her sight, at a straight, slender lady, in bonnet and travelling cloak open over her shoulders, and beyond, in the lane, a carriage with a man holding the reins of a chestnut pony.

'Sarah? What are you doing here? Who's that man?'

'I've come to see you and Dada. Mr Aubrey said I could come – in the carriage. And that's Howel, who works on the farm, and I think would be glad of a drink after the journey. Is Dada here?'

Without another word, the woman turned and disappeared into the gloomy interior, where, after a hesitant pause, Sarah followed. The sound of an upstairs door closing told her the younger woman had no wish to be seen. The square room with its bare stone walls, no larger than her room at Ash Hall, was, as all else at the farm, strangely diminished, but otherwise much as she remembered. It seemed inhabited by a damp chill despite the low fire smouldering in the hearth. Her mother crouched there stirring the coals and resettling the kettle to bring it to the boil.

'Don't mind Elen,' she said, ' – a shy girl. You see how she is. She'd rather keep out of the way. She's Stephen's wife, good as gold, but shy. You know.'

'I am very glad for Stephen,' said Sarah. 'Is he out working with Dada?'

Her mother continued poking the fire, adding a few chopped sticks and then a larger, misshapen lump of wood that had been drying in the hearth. At length she looked up.

'Your Dada's gone,' she said. 'It was the winter – nearly killed all of us. But he hadn't been well, ever since getting into that lead business. Left the farming to Stephen and spent all his time up in Llanharan. Didn't do him or us any good. Gave all the money to the doctor, and for what? But the winter … he couldn't take it. Died in February – and you should have seen the trouble they had digging the grave. Ground like iron.'

For a moment, Sarah was silent. Then, as memories of her father, clever, gentle, so insistent that his daughter should learn to read and write, rose up, she was overwhelmed by grief, and sat, head bowed, rocking herself as the tears fell. Why had they not written to tell her of her father's illness? But, of course, her mother could not read or write, and Stephen, who had not welcomed her father's teaching as she had, was clumsy and ill at ease with pen in hand. And she, preoccupied with all that had occurred at Ash Hall, was more to blame …

'There, there,' said her mother, without feeling. 'Don't fret. It's all over. We carry on. Stephen has the farm to look after, and a wife, and soon now a babe. We'll manage.' She scanned Sarah briefly from neatly dressed head to well-shod foot. 'And you look well. A lady, Elen said. I'll take a drop of beer out to – who did you say?'

By the time her mother returned Sarah had composed herself and decided she did not want to linger. She had come, she realised, chiefly to see her father, to share with him the story of her long years of absence from home and family, and to thank him, for he had made her journey into the world possible. Her mother had always been impatient of the fatherly care given to a mere girl, and even perhaps jealous of her learning skills she had never acquired. And now she was oppressed and embittered by her sense that her husband had deserted her.

It was to her father that Sarah would have turned for advice. What, she wondered, would her mother say? Her expectations were not great, but, rather resignedly, she decided it could do no harm to find out. When they had drunk their watery tea in silence, Sarah said, 'I feel certain that I, too, am carrying a child.' Her mother's eyes widened. 'It will be several months yet, but, yes, I shall have a baby. I came here today … I wanted to ask you what you think I should do.'

'Do? You've done enough already.' She poked the fire vigorously and sparks flew from the smouldering log. 'Your father told me you were a servant at the Aubrey house – in Ystradowen, was it? They won't have you with a baby in tow. You are wed? It's your husband's business to tell you what to do.'

Sarah stiffened. Was there any point in going on? 'No,' she said, 'I haven't married.'

'Then who's the father? You do know who's the father? He's married already I suppose. One of those backstairs scrapes.'

'No, he is not married.' The truth, Sarah thought. 'And there was nothing backstairs about it.'

'Then marry. Now, before it's too late. Save what's left of your name.'

'I may not want to marry. I may want to go away to have the child. I thought once I might come here.'

'Ah, so that's what's brought you here after all these years. You would carry your little burden, your little mistake, here – and give us the work while you play the lady with the Aubreys.'

Her mother was suddenly breathless and began coughing. Leaning forward, she spat a hissing globule into the fire. She gasped, 'Want, indeed. There was too much want when you were a girl. Your father was too good to you. If it's advice you're after, go to your uncle in London, or your father's sister in Pencoed. Ask them.'

'I am sorry not to have seen Stephen.' Sarah, very pale, rose quietly. 'Please let him know I wish him and Elen well, and the baby.'

In another minute, and without a glance behind, she was in the gig, wrapped in her cloak, and on the road back to Ash Hall.

Sarah mourned her father and blamed herself for not having seen him once at least while he yet lived. She did not know he had been ailing, as her mother described, though she had sensed some indefinable change in him from the letters she received. After church the following Sunday, while the children (for now both Julia and young Thomas accompanied her) waited in the carriage, she confided her unhappiness to the curate. George took her hand in his rough hand and studied her face with such tenderness that her eyes filled with tears. 'God is with you,' he said, 'I know. I too have lost my father, one who cared for me and took pains to teach me – through whom, indeed, I am here today. It is his cassock I wear. When it is God's will to take a loved one from us, we must accept His will. We grieve for ourselves, for the loss we feel, but they are with God. They forgive our lapses in love for them when they were here with us, as God forgives us. The love of your father, and of your Heavenly Father, go with you.'

It had been an unhappy return to Llangan. Her mother's scornful anger had been a shock, but Sarah had not returned empty-handed. She had been reminded of the affection and kindness of her uncle, and of an aunt who lived a few miles west beyond Llangan, whom she could not recall from childhood, but knew to have been close to her father. She wrote to Uncle John, telling him of her father's death and asking the name of his sister, to whom she intended to convey the same sad news. He replied sharing her sorrow at their bereavement and enclosing information about her aunt. She was Jane Griffiths, whose husband farmed Pen-y-lan, on a hill above Pencoed village. 'Should you travel that way, she would I am sure welcome you,' he wrote, 'though not with as much joy as I would welcome you here.'

Sorrow for a time distracted Sarah from her more immediate predicament, but she could not quell the thought that each day she drew nearer to the time when her pregnancy would become obvious to all. Her uncle's words brought some small comfort; there was one to whom she could perhaps turn when her time came. His love and tender regard were extended to her still – but as a maid, she thought, not as a woman soon to bear a child, and she remained deeply troubled. She had no doubt she would have to leave Ash Hall, where she had been happier than she dreamed possible, and be parted from Richard Aubrey and his children, whom she had grown to love as her own. And what of the child she carried, Richard's child? Should she make some excuse and go away, leaving him in ignorance, or should she tell him, as her mother said and, if she could, shame or coerce him into marriage? But there, she knew, the problem lay: even if Richard loved her, as from time to time she felt he did, he would not marry her. A man of his rank in society did not marry the governess of his children. She remembered Richard's brother had conceived a daughter out of wedlock, and had not married the woman – though he had brought up the child. It was that thought in the end that persuaded her she should tell Richard, so that, no matter what happened to her, their child would have, she truly believed, a good father, and at least some of the advantages of wealth and position.

She was prompted to tell him when next they were together

in the big, curtained bed, but put the thought firmly from her mind. It smacked of wheedling. Instead, when a day or so later they were talking in the library about Thomas Digby's progress with letters and numbers, she said, 'I shall be having a child in, I think, seven months.'

At first Richard appeared dumbfounded by the revelation, but he quickly came to his senses. 'Yes, I understand. Together as we have been, it could hardly turn out otherwise. We must think what is best.'

'I shall leave before my condition becomes plain to others of your household. I cannot pretend it will not be hard to part from Julia and Thomas, but they are well started now and will, I am sure, continue to thrive, no matter who comes in my stead.'

Richard leaned back in his chair staring upwards at the ceiling until Sarah thought it best to withdraw. She had risen to her feet when he said, 'Don't go ... sit, sit a while longer. Let me think.'

The room was still, holding its breath in the flickering candlelight. At length he said, 'I do not want to lose you. Nor would I stain you with the name of concubine. Others might, but I will not, and I think it would be no more bearable to you, for you are good and honest. Allow me the space of a day, perhaps two, no more. I must see if something can be done to keep you as close and as long I would wish.'

The next morning, when Sarah came into the busy kitchen with the children, she was told that Mr Aubrey had taken an early breakfast and left to visit his aunt.

Margaret Aubrey was, in old age, a formidable lady. What might have been becoming plumpness when she was younger had declined into a wrinkled corpulence, which, however, had not slowed her trajectory through life. She had copious energy, rarely sat still for long and, when in her carriage, insisted on travelling as swiftly as horses and driver could manage. She was said to bounce when excited and, on rare occasions, with rage when frustrated. Long accustomed to deference, she had an air of superiority. To Aubrey family members in Glamorgan and their dependants, she was the matriarch. To everyone she was known as Lady Margaret. It was natural that Richard, in need of counsel, should address himself to her.

He was not expected, but advised of his approach. Margaret left the library, where she had been dealing with letters from tenants and lawyers on an array of estate matters. Hardly a day passed without some such correspondence, the inevitable consequence of being the leaseholder of seven thousand acres of the Vale. Most of this work she did herself, with the occasional assistance of an amanuensis, for she was perspicacious and over the years had acquired business acumen to match any.

Having decided to meet her nephew in the first-floor sitting room, she called her maid, who ran to fetch and fit for her a fine peruke and place a fringed silk shawl about her shoulders. When Richard was announced she was seated in an old and ornately-carved cushioned armchair. He bowed and stood, ill at ease.

'Well?' she said. 'You surely haven't come to Llanmaes to look at me. I haven't seen you in many months. How is that young son of yours? Well, I trust. The fate of the Aubrey title could yet depend on him – as you are aware. But it's for the future to decide. I don't know what that brother of yours is up to. Come, come, what's brought you here this morning?'

'Aunt, it is a personal matter – of great sensitivity – on which I need … I would be most grateful for … your advice.'

'Does it touch upon the family? Yes? Well, go on, I'll not interrupt.'

'Do you perhaps remember the governess of my children? You met her once.'

'No.'

'Ah – well, she is with child.'

'So? Why should that have brought you here? If she is already so far advanced she can no longer do her work, send her on her way – and the fellow she has been consorting with. There are governesses aplenty to take her place.'

'I am afraid, Aunt, I am the fellow.'

'All the more reason to get rid of her – and quickly. Send her back to her family, or anywhere. Give her a few shillings if you must, but get her out of Ash Hall. I do not understand how your brother can give house room to his French bastard; do not you fall into the same trap. Doubtless the woman – what's her name? – lured you into this situation in expectation of gain. Don't give her that satisfaction. Are you sure the child is yours? If she has been free with her favours with one man, there may well have been others.'

'Please, Aunt, forgive me: I cannot allow this calumny. She is entirely honest and honourable. She came at my father's recommendation – and you will know him a man of sound judgement – from her uncle's home in London, where she learned taste and discrimination. Her name is Sally, or more properly Sarah, daughter of a farmer at Llangan. She has proved an excellent governess and, far more important than that, she has been as a mother to my children, who are very attached to her. And I am attached to her, too. I mean I have the highest regard and affection for her.'

'More fool you!'

'She has saved my life, twice. When I was reeling, hopeless of a future after the death of Frances, her steadiness, her sensibility, her calm and caring address to the children's needs, brought me to my senses, drew me back from the black emptiness of my existence.'

'A paragon.'

'Yes, Aunt, truly: do not mock. And when, having ridden through the winter storm back to Ash Hall from Llantrithyd, I lay dying, I say with utmost seriousness, dying, on my own threshold, it was she preserved me by ordering the servants, who were wringing their hands, not knowing what to do, and then most chastely warming my frozen body and restoring it to life.'

'Very well, you have reason to be grateful to this woman. I will not pursue the matter of you lying with her. But there was a consequence of that action. Do not think of marriage, unless you are prepared to sever all connection with this family and take her away, far away from here. Then you must consider what will become of Julia, a pretty little thing, and Thomas, that precious boy of yours. Are they to join Sir John and his bastard in Oxfordshire – or wherever he holds court these days? And how are you going to feed and clothe a new family? Without land and rents, what livelihood do you have?'

'You are cruel, Aunt. You tell me what I cannot do. Tell me what I can.'

A silence fell, during which the sun, which had been creeping around the house, found the first of the room's three windows and sent a steep, mote-filled shaft of light across a polished oak table to a sideboard beyond.

'Very well, Richard. I cannot but say I am disappointed, because I saw in your marriage to Frances an example to set before your brothers. Not that they would take much notice. This is what I would advise. Find the woman a husband, quickly. Is there a likely man in the village? Whether you, or she, tells him of the baby I care not. Give them to understand that, out of gratitude you will help them, see them settled in some comfort. That will gain you the satisfaction of keeping Sally or Sarah nearby, for a time at least, while your children may have some need of her. Then you can hope that both she and the man she marries will be discreet and not abuse the trust you place in them. And you must look about you for a wife. Surely there is someone in the Vale ready to take on a handsome fellow like you.'

As Richard rode homeward, afternoon spring sunshine warm on his back, he pondered his aunt's counsel. 'She's right, of course she's right,' he said aloud to himself. But he was prepared to swear, throughout the time she had been at Ash Hall, Sally had not walked out with any man. The only man she had mentioned in their conversations, and that was because the children regularly went to church with her, was George Williams, the curate at Ystradowen.

FOLLOWING HIS VISIT to Aunt Margaret, Richard swore an oath, privately, that he would henceforth deny himself the pleasure of the womanly warmth he had so eagerly received. Although Sarah waited long into the night, the connecting door between their rooms remained locked. When she spoke again of leaving Ash Hall, he said he would not hear of it, and at other times, when they met below stairs, while feigning contentment with his own lot, he said he grieved to see her downcast. She was in need of a change of routine, perhaps teaching and caring for two children, delightful as they were, was sometimes more burdensome than she would admit, especially as she was in a delicate condition. At this she became tearful, but he persisted, suggesting that, to allow her a little more freedom, to meet other members of the congregation, perhaps to walk a while in the fine weather, a maidservant should accompany her and the children to church. Having gathered that Sally had a sympathetic interest in the Reverend George Williams, he hoped that with a maid at her disposal she would begin to know him better.

Sarah knew full well a change had occurred in their relationship. She did not tax Richard with this: he was master of the house and of her destiny, and she had been blessed with good fortune in serving him. She did not suspect him of a stratagem in encouraging her to take her time at church and, having assured herself of the children's safety in the carriage with the maidservant, was glad to meet parishioners, although they remained humbly shy in exchanging greetings with her. She did not realise that, although she was simply, if neatly, attired, her calm demeanour, her slim, straight form and ease of manner told them she was different, in their minds a lady.

For his part, the curate was delighted to find her unencumbered by the young Aubreys and, having learned this new arrangement to give her a little leisure was likely to continue, hastily set about freeing himself of the responsibility of officiating at Llansannor. During the long weeks of winter cold he had striven to meet his obligations at Ystradowen only to find the church empty, or a congregation that could be numbered on fewer trembling fingers than grasped the icy rail that ran along the top of his pulpit. Llansannor at that time was no more within his capabilities than the Russias, though the churchwardens there showed little understanding of his predicament. With this new incentive, the sacrifice of his share of the lesser tithes seemed to him worthwhile. So it came about that within two weeks, the May month weather still fair, he had begun to accompany Mistress Sarah some distance up the lane towards Ash Hall. At first they spoke of the winter. He told her of the trials he and his brother, Richard, had endured trying to save their meagre stock, and how, despite their best efforts, they had suffered losses. She murmured her sorrow at this, but did not speak of the night when Richard Aubrey nearly died of cold. Their conversation turned from the seasons and farming to family: they had both lost dearly loved fathers who had taught them the pleasure of reading and given them a start in life. They discovered in themselves enough common experience and shared interest to talk easily and began to know one another.

When Richard Aubrey asked if, as a result of the brief episodes of liberty from her responsibility for the children, she had met anyone of interest, she admitted she had, and that the young curate who had officiated at the baptism of Thomas Digby (of whom he denied any recollection) was agreeable company. Richard said he was pleased to hear this, but the pleasure was feigned. Alone in the library, an unread book before him, he admitted he was jealous – jealous of a shabby, lean, impoverished curate, whom he recalled well enough. That was not the way to behave he told himself. It was an unworthy emotion and could set all at risk: he would suppress it. To speed Aunt Margaret's plan (and speed was of the essence) he must encourage Sally's friendship with the Reverend Williams and do all possible to ensure it prospered. As old Burton said (he thought, recalling a favourite book during his days at All Souls), a man who is melancholy and idle is the more likely to be jealous. His melancholy at the prospect of losing Sally he could do little about, therefore he resolved to act. When next he spoke to her he confessed he did, after all, remember the curate at Thomas Digby's baptism – indeed, had thought at the time he was deserving of preferment and, having been reminded of him, would see what could be done about it. This she could not forbear hinting to the Reverend Williams on their walk the following Sunday, and it spurred the curate to greater effort in church and among the poor and sick of the parish. The effect, though not large, was almost instantaneous: his congregation increased and he met more politely raised hats and friendly greetings as he went about his business. On Sundays, as they walked together, Sarah, too, noticed this and quietly rejoiced at it.

As was his wont from time to time, Richard called at the children's room, *her* room, and watched quietly as she instructed them and then while the three played with the dominoes he had bought for just this purpose at a knicknackatory during a recent brief visit to Bath – an expensive whim, fruitless in the outcome, prompted by his interview with Aunt Margaret. When the maid took the children downstairs for lunch, he detained Sarah and, grasping her hand spoke earnestly: 'We must address the problem of the baby you are to bear.'

'I think not,' she said, withdrawing her hand forcefully, so that Richard was startled. 'I know I have to leave before it becomes obvious to all, and if my mother will not have me, I shall go elsewhere. I do not ask anything of you and will not betray our ...'

'Love' she was going to say, but held her tongue. She would have left at once had he not closed the door firmly and stood there before it, reaching again for her hand, which she withheld. Although he did not understand why, Richard could see she had been hurt and almost wept at it.

'Sally, dear Sally, forgive me. Forgive my clumsy speech. I do not want you to leave. If it were my decision alone, I would have you stay for the children's sake – and mine, most assuredly mine too. I wish I could say family doesn't matter, I shall make my choices where I will, do what I please, but my aunt has shown me that it *does* matter. There is a very great deal at stake. Nothing is certain yet, but I must think of my son. My brothers have been – what can I say? – perhaps wayward, thoughtless sometimes, but I am not like them. All I want is to do what is best for you. Please let me say this: I would have you wed, comfortably, and living nearby, so that Julia and Thomas Digby may still call upon you when they need that affection they have learned comes so readily, so sweetly, from you. And if I cannot have you by my side, give me yet the painful pleasure of seeing you prosper (if I have my way) in the loving care of another.'

'Leave me a while,' said Sarah. 'Would you be so kind as to ask one of the maids to bring me tea here. Say I am a little indisposed ... but I shall be well soon.'

That evening, the children safely abed, she came to Richard in the library to tell him she understood and would, if she could, do as he wished. She had spent a little time in the company of the curate at Ystradowen, an agreeable young man of about her own age. He was unmarried and, as far as she could tell, unpromised, indeed unattached in any way save to his family and his calling. If he asked for her hand, and she had no way of knowing he would, she would dedicate herself to working by his side, as she must, because he laboured for small returns in his parish and the few fields of a farm, the tenancy of which he and his brother had inherited from their father.

She held up her hand, seeing Richard was about to interrupt. 'Please, a moment more and I have done. The baby, our baby: if we, the Reverend George Williams and I, marry, I shall need to tell him of the child I carry, with a binding promise that he will tell no other soul – and we must see what the future brings.'

Richard nodded, drew breath, then, finding there was nothing he could say, bowed his head, and Sarah quietly withdrew.

Alone, later, again she pondered her condition. That she carried another's child could not long be hidden from George; it would be better, therefore, to confess the fact before they married. If he then abandoned her, she could not, nor would she, blame him. But if he stood by her, she would be faithful to him till her dying day. As for naming the child's true father, to George or anyone, that she would not do. Let those who would gossip and surmise, that would remain deep buried within her.

Each Sunday, as before, at the end of Morning Prayer, the children having departed with the maid in the carriage, Sarah and George walked together. The third Sunday following her talk with Richard Aubrey was a day of heavy showers during one of which they sheltered under a hedge, the curate's cassock thrown over their heads and shoulders. As they stood close and still, the rain stabbing through the thin fabric above them and puddling around their shoes, George said, 'In weather like this I usually run for the nearest cottage and beg a moment's respite from the storm, but today I am more than glad to remain here.' After a pause he added, 'I would be happy to stay anywhere in your company.'

Sarah turned to him a flushed and dewy face and smiled. 'Let us hope then for a little more comfort than this hedge affords,' she said.

Catching the softness in her voice, George sought and found her cool, damp hand. 'Could you be content to share a curate's life? I can offer you nothing but hardship now, and little prospect of betterment, but I promise you a loving heart.'

The clatter of a carriage approaching down the hill prised them apart: Howel had been despatched to rescue Mistress Sally.

'I shall need time to think,' she said, hurriedly divesting herself of the drenched cassock, and then, as horse and vehicle came into view, 'No – no thought. If you are sure you wish to marry me, no matter what – well, yes. Yes, I will marry and stand by you, whatever the future may hold.' And she stood for a moment in the still falling rain, looking at him, bedraggled under the hedge.

For some time after the carriage had, with difficulty, turned and moved away, the curate remained under the dripping hawthorns staring wonderingly at the spot where she had spoken those unexpected, improbable words. Then, laughing aloud, he ran splashing down the lane.

In the weeks that followed events occurred unplanned by him, in which he seemed swept up and carried along. A farm servant from Ash Hall brought a peremptory written request that the Reverend George Williams of Maendy Uchaf attend the presence of Mr Richard Aubrey.

The curate arrived at the day and time specified and was conducted to the master of the house in his library, a room larger than the entire ground floor of his own home. He was not invited to sit, for Mr Aubrey, ill at ease and irritable, was striving by the exercise of will and rational thought to suppress his emotions. 'You know Mistress Sally has no father,' he began. 'It falls to me to decide whether you are a suitable match for her. What do you have to say for yourself?'

'I have known Sarah – ah, Sally – for some time, as a member of my congregation, with your children. It has been a joy to see them at my church.'

'Yes, yes, go on.'

'I cannot say I have entertained thoughts of marriage. That seemed beyond the bounds of possibility. But from the start I greatly admired her kindly care for the children, her mildness, her composure.'

Richard was suddenly weary. 'I haven't time for … ,' he said, and then, 'You can maintain this woman? Do not imagine you can live on her wealth: she has no dowry. You have income? Land perhaps? Are you ready to work – to keep her?'

'I will do all in my power.'

'I'm sure. But that's not what I asked.' He paused, but no response came. 'Nevertheless, if she is prepared to go through with this,' he added, wearily, 'so be it.'

He turned his attention to papers on the desk before him. After some moments in which no further word was said, George, sensing that, brief as it had been, the interview was over, left on tiptoe, closing the door quietly behind him.

He continued to see Sarah with the Aubrey children at morning service on Sundays, and to walk with her after the service, a habit that caught the attention of others and began not unkindly gossip and rumours in the village. It would be nice, people said, if the curate and the Aubrey governess were to wed.

There was little talk of marriage between the couple. It was as though both understood such arrangements as were needed were in the hands of others. Rather, they spoke about their families and their younger lives, which had a good deal of mundane experience in common. They were setting in place foundations on which a relationship could be built. And then Sarah knew full well how greatly changed her life would be as the wife of a curate, and she carried within her a secret she was as yet unwilling to share. Eventually, she told George about the years spent with her uncle in London. He had not known of this. Only Jennet among the villagers knew, and she was wisely discreet about her service at Ash Hall.

Sarah's descriptions of the great city and the elegance of Uncle John's home dumbfounded him. He said he feared

Maendy Uchaf would be a grave disappointment to her, although the farm would be theirs to occupy as his mother intended to move to Cowbridge, where she would live with a sister, widowed like herself. And his brother Richard, too, once he knew of the forthcoming marriage, had begun looking elsewhere.

'I would not have them leave for my sake,' said Sarah, 'not ever, but we surely have time to think again of such arrangements when we are married.'

In the second week of August another message arrived, inviting the Reverend George Williams to meet Ambrose Portrey Esquire, of Llanmaes. Again the curate climbed the long, winding lane to Ash Hall, where he was led to a small sitting room. Within he found a stout, expensively attired gentleman of middling age, bewigged and resplendent in richly embroidered waistcoat, standing at a window looking out onto a path at the side of the house edged with raspberry and gooseberry bushes heavy with ripening fruit. Richard Aubrey was elsewhere; they were left to introduce themselves. Ambrose Portrey had come on a mission at the request of Lady Margaret Aubrey. He understood that the Reverend Williams was to marry Mistress Sally Jones, of whom he had heard many good things – the Reverend could consider himself most fortunate in the match – and, to further this excellent cause, he would accompany the Reverend to Llandaff to obtain a marriage licence directly from the Bishop.

George felt his head spin, grasped the arm of a chair and sat heavily. In his conversations with Sarah neither had mentioned a date for the ceremony. He had assumed it was yet several months off, and would be preceded by the reading of banns in the usual way. Obtaining a licence had not occurred to him; it would involve expense he could not afford.

Portrey waved aside the objections he could see about to be uttered. 'These arrangements,' he said, 'are being made by Lady Margaret, as a mark of her gratitude to Mistress Jones for all she has done for her nephew's children. There is no need for you to be concerned about expense – or any other matter. I have already informed the Bishop of our, I should say your, intention and have made an appointment to see him Wednesday week. Will that suit?'

George, still confused by the turn of events, shook his head, and then hastily nodded. 'Why, yes. Yes of course.'

'My carriage will be at the church – that's convenient? – at midday.'

The following Sunday George told Sarah he had been bewildered, rendered almost speechless, by a brisk gentleman from Llanmaes, whom he had been asked to meet at Ash Hall. Sarah had been informed that her friend the curate had met a Mr Portrey in the small sitting room, but no more. Richard had said nothing. While ever courteous, he had become distant and uncommunicative in recent weeks, for which she was both glad and, especially when, at night, the pungency from her extinguished bedside candle lingered still, heavy-hearted. She felt a shock of understanding when she learned the request for a licence was in train, and, it seemed, out of her hands. George had begun to say how pleased and grateful he was for the generous intervention of Lady Margaret that would hasten the day they would be brought together before God, when she began her confession.

She did not name the father of the child, but made no

attempt to disguise him or otherwise mislead the man who listened intently, silently. When she had finished, he remained silent, head lowered as though uncertain of the ground beneath his feet.

'You have nothing to say?' she said. 'Perhaps that is for the best. Do not speak now. You will think of what I have told you: how could you not? Next Sunday, if you will walk with me, I will understand you wish us to continue. Let me say now, that is my desire. And I swear again, I will be true to you. Hush – nothing now! Next week we will know.'

As soon as they parted George knew. He almost ran after her, so certain was he. He wanted this woman whose knowledge of the world far exceeded his, who held herself erect, looked and spoke without false modesty or condescension, whose care for the children of another was warm and firm, and who was so clearly loved by them. There was yet no sign of the child she said she carried, so that he half-doubted what she had told him was a test of his resolution. Yet for several days he did not sleep easily. It had all happened so suddenly and, much as he had wished it, so unexpectedly. He had been carried along, unresisting certainly, like a twig in a fast-flowing stream. He had not sought the company of the daughters of farmers and farm labourers, having had little time to spare for such pursuits, and then, as the son of the Vicar, there was, he felt, a distance between him and them. Sarah was the only woman he had ever felt moved by, had ever wanted. And he could take her to wife, provided he would also accept her unborn child. Another man had known her, as he had never yet dared to imagine. Though with all his strength he pressed this phantasm down, like soft clay it oozed up at the edges of his thoughts. He would probably never forget, but he knew for the sake of their relationship, and his own sanity, he must suppress the desire to be told more, and think instead of the inestimable gift of herself that Sarah brought, and embrace the child as his own, unconditionally. It was a vow he made to himself, and though, too often at the start, his imagination betrayed him and he almost lapsed, he kept it. When Sunday came round again, after the service, he approached her smiling, and took her hand, and they walked out into the sunlight, where the men in a small group of parishioners, observing them, doffed hats, and the women, turning to one another, nodded wisely.

The following Wednesday, 19th August, prompt upon midday, a carriage drew up before the lych-gate and Ambrose Portrey leaned from the window beckoning the curate to join him. George had barely seated himself before Portrey said, 'I don't like the sound of that news of the French. Some of them seem intent on turning the world upside-down. What do you think?' George could not hide his ignorance of affairs in that distant place and thereafter, apart from some observations on the continuing fair weather and the condition of fields as they passed, neither had anything to say and the journey along the turnpike and into Llandaff passed largely in silence.

They were met, not by the Bishop, but his surrogate, Dr Benjamin Hall, chancellor of the cathedral, who first completed the form of application for a marriage licence, wherein Ambrose Portrey bound himself to the Bishop in the sum of two hundred pounds that no lawful let or impediment existed to the solemnisation of marriage between George Williams, Clerk, bachelor, and Sarah Jones, spinster, of the parish of Ystradowen, and then, hurriedly, passing the tip of his tongue lizard-like along his lower lip, wrote the licence in his own sloping hand. The marriage could follow as soon as convenient. With expressions of gratitude and bows, the gentleman and the curate left the chancellor's office and were soon hastening back along the turnpike.

The following Sunday George told Sarah what had transpired at the cathedral. Now it was simply a matter of deciding upon a day. He said, 'Let it be tomorrow.'

'We must think of the children. They will need to understand I am leaving, but that they will always be in my thoughts, and of course their father will need to find a new governess. I shall ask him to suggest a day when it will be convenient to release me from responsibilities I have always been happy to bear. And now the day is so close, I have a most earnest request to make of you, that after the wedding we go to my uncle in London. I have written to him explaining all and he has replied saying he will be pleased to welcome us and will see we have suitable accommodation.'

Taken aback, George did not know what to say and for a time they walked in silence. Then, 'What of my duties to the Church? I cannot simply abandon the curacy. Given time, I can possibly find one who will stand in my stead while we are away, but I would not do so lightly. It will not go well with the wardens and congregation. Yet, if that is what you wish ...'

'Thank you.' She smiled and pressed his hand.

It was some time later, thinking of their conversation, George realised what Sarah intended – not that they should for ever leave the Vale, but that her child would be born far enough away for no slightest rumour to reach Ystradowen, and the infant would return to the village as *their* child.

The marriage was solemnised on Tuesday, 3rd September 1789, the vicar of Pendoylan, another Aubrey church, officiating.

A crowd of witnesses assembled to sign the register, among them Richard Williams, George's brother, Ambrose Portrey Esquire, representing Lady Margaret Aubrey, John Lewis, churchwarden, Mary Edwards, newly appointed governess at Ash Hall, and, at the head of the list, in a fair, well-taught hand, was the signature of Julia Frances Aubrey.

Immediately after the service George and Sarah left for London, where, a few days later, John Jones, Sarah's uncle, laughing, pointed out to them a page in the *Gentleman's Magazine*, which bore the heading 'Marriages of Considerable Persons', announcing the unions of noblemen, bankers, lawyers, merchants, soldiers, clerics, about fifty in all, including eighty-year-old Mrs Bromwich, widow of a papier-maché manufacturer of Ludgate Hill, worth £1,000 per annum, who, despite the best efforts of her children, had taken, as her fourth husband, her coachman, James Wheeler, 'a stout young man aged about 25'. In the midst of all these happy couples, and to their vast surprise, they found: 'At Ystradowen, co. Glamorgan, the Rev. Geo: Williams, of Maendy, to Miss Sally Jones, of Ash Hall.' It was the only notice from Wales.

Metropolitan readers of the magazine would have been surprised to learn Sally was not daughter, nor relative of any sort, of the owner of Ash Hall, and the Reverend George Williams was an impecunious curate.

PART TWO

I

ON THEIR WAY to London, George, unaccustomed to the headlong advance of the mail coach, had at first felt ill at ease, rocking in the close confines of the crowded interior. The weather being fine, he sought Sarah's permission to leave her and take for a while an outside seat, where, occupied with his thoughts, he viewed the changing scene as a meaningless blur while the straining horses plunged onwards. There was much to think about. At the next change of horses he returned to his wife's side, windblown but little refreshed and, holding her hand, whispered in her ear.

'My dearest Sarah, what shall we do? In London … what shall we do to live – the two of us, and soon, sooner than I dare think, a child too?'

His anxiety pricked her. 'Why, we must place our trust in the kindness of my uncle, and his great knowledge of the city. He will, I feel sure, secure accommodation for us and means whereby you may obtain employment.'

George was little reassured. 'I am a clerk without a living, allowed but twenty pounds a year by the Reverend Thomas, whom I have never yet seen but is mercifully prompt to advance the sum, and a share of the lesser tithes he has not himself the time to gather. In our absence he will find another to take my place. For the rest, I am, and I thank God for it, able-bodied and used to hard work in the fields, but you have taught me not to expect ploughing, sowing and reaping, and the care of beasts, other than those herded to market, in the midst of London streets.'

Although already well aware of his concerns, her husband's urgency precipitated a spasm of fear that seemed to Sarah like a stirring in her womb. She clasped his hand tightly. 'We must be trusting – and patient,' she said.

The first breaths of putrid, soot-laden London air were nauseating, the noise and bustle of thoroughfares wearying to all the senses, the expense of the carriage from Paddington to Piccadilly alarming. Although she had once been well used to city life, to Sarah the return was shocking. George was stunned. But when, near the time expected, they arrived at the army clothier's elegant premises, the dark, miasmic cloud lifted. John Jones, his eyes moist with suppressed tears, embraced Sarah as a father would a long-lost daughter and shook George warmly by the hand, congratulating him on his marriage.

'You are among the most fortunate of men,' he said.

And George, looking at his wife, now recovered from her initial perturbation and, with flushed cheeks and shining eyes, delighting in her reception, saw how lovely she was.

'I am, sir, I am indeed.'

They soon learned that arrangements had been made for their arrival. Only a hundred yards or so from where they stood, in Swallow-street, which branched off Piccadilly, an adequately furnished apartment and the services of a maid of all work had been obtained for them. It was neat and clean and would certainly serve their needs for as long as they chose to stay in London.

George was anxious to explain their circumstances. That was

not necessary John Jones assured him. He fully understood, having been informed by letters from his niece and from another, whom he did not care to name, but who had their best interests at heart. Sarah bit her lip and, colouring, smiled upon her husband.

'If my dear uncle tells us so, I am sure all will be well. You know already how, when hardly more than a child, I was entrusted to him, and how he taught and encouraged me, made me his housekeeper, put me at my ease in company. Everything I am I owe to him.' She took her uncle's hands and would have raised them to her lips had he not prevented.

'Ah, your father,' he said, suddenly reminded, 'a dear brother. Although I was his elder by several years, we were deeply attached. As one without children of my own, it was a joy to receive the privilege of protecting his daughter. His own correspondence fell off in the last year and I assumed he was busy with that new project he believed would bring wealth to the family. I had no news of his passing until your letter reached me.' For a while he could not speak, then, 'Come, come,' he said, tears unchecked coursing down his cheeks, 'let us take tea and afterwards we will go together to your new home.'

Their rooms on the second floor of a large dwelling house were as they had been told. They would not need to purchase new furnishings and bedding. Jane, the maid, a widowed countrywoman, originally from Cornwall, round-faced and red-cheeked, had lit the fire and was busy with broom and duster. She would come in daily to cook and clean according to their needs. Through the tall windows, smirched with soot on the outside, as through a mist, they glimpsed below the people, carts and carriages passing by on the road.

But it was not a busy thoroughfare and soon the sound of

vehicles and pedestrians became so much a part of their lives as to be barely noticed. It was far less easy to become accustomed to the powerful stench of London, which could be ameliorated by strolling among the crowds in Hyde Park and Green Park with its reservoir lake, but dissipated only by lengthy walks into the countryside. As the weeks passed Sarah became less inclined to contemplate the greater distances and more to busy herself at home, preparing for the baby. With Jane, she arranged and re-arranged furniture to her satisfaction, ensured both rooms were properly clean from floor to ceiling, and that any object or utensil capable of shining shone indeed. She, too, shone, with happiness.

Near her, George was more than content, but at the start, whenever they were apart, he was assailed by doubts. All their needs seemed to have been anticipated, and were met without call upon either his skills or bodily strength. It was not the way of things he had expected as husband, provider. Life had taught him there must be a day of reckoning, and he feared deeply that, when it arrived, he would not be ready to meet it. Moreover, having worked every day since boyhood, he had no use for leisure. One morning, in the first week of their residence, he found himself walking up and down outside the army clothier's shop peering in at the window where gaudy officers' uniforms and hats and campaign equipment were displayed. At length, when he saw the proprietor entering from the back of the shop and joining an aproned servant examining some new merchandise, he went in and, after a cordial exchange of greetings, summoned the courage to ask, 'Is there some employment for me here, or anywhere to your knowledge where I may earn the wherewithal to repay all the kindnesses Sarah and I have received at your hands?'

Smiling, John Jones drew him aside, pointing to a gleaming mahogany box, exquisitely made, with a pristine brass nameplate on the lid and, within, an array of silver-stoppered bottles and all the tools and instruments a gentleman might need in camp or bivouac. 'My dear man,' he said quietly, 'I beseech you, do not think of settling debts. There are no debts. In the best and brightest of worlds your wedding would have been preceded by a marriage settlement and Sally would have brought a handsome dowry to your union. There are those mindful of a deep obligation to Sally, and I count myself among them. You see, it is we who are indebted to you.'

George swayed, half overcome with conflicting sensations: relief, gratitude, love, incredulity.

'Take my hand,' said John Jones, 'let us have no more talk of debt. You are new here and London has much to offer – not least to a man of the Church. We have ancient churches and cathedrals full of wonders. St James's, our parish church, which you will have passed in walking here this morning, though plain enough without, has great beauties within. You might make yourself known to the clergy there. Give them my name – they will tell you I am a faithful member of their congregation.' And as they moved together, hands still clasped, to the shop door, 'My fond good wishes to your dear wife.'

George had indeed noticed the church on their arrival, for it was almost opposite the corner they turned into Swallow-street: a long wall in dark red brick with a fine gated entrance and, behind it, a building constructed of the same reddish brick, which had a square tower from the summit of which rose a short, sharp spire. Beneath the grey-slated roof of the nave was a row of simple arched windows. It was, as Mr Jones had said, plain, very plain, though a good deal larger than any parish church in George's experience. Ystradowen, he calculated, would fit easily into the nave and leave room for a sizeable congregation.

The following Sunday George and Sarah walked arm in arm to matins. They were disappointed not to find her uncle among the congregation, but the inside of St James's, which Sarah knew of old, was a wonder beyond her husband's expectation. The great half-cylinder of the ceiling, delicately poised on slim pillars with no cross beams, seemed almost to float high above his head, and all around wood panels of stalls and pews and gilded scrolls and escutcheons gleamed in pale morning sun and candlelight. Above the western end of the nave, beneath the tower, the organ reposed in a vast case of wood intricately carved with figures and garlands of leaves and fruit and flowers, and at the eastern end, beneath a wall almost wholly window, was a white marble altar. George, entranced by the spectacle and the sonorous chords of organ and echoing voices raised in prayer and psalm, felt for a moment the touch of grace.

After the service, the priest, divested of his voluminous surplice, stood at the door greeting those of the congregation with whom he was familiar. He was a tall, swarthy man approaching middle age, his dark hair greying, his face rounder than it had once been and waist thickening. He lived well, loved the sound of his mellifluous voice soaring to the great arched ceiling and resounding the length of the nave. George bowed to him and vouchsafed that, as a fellow man of the cloth, though of the humblest sort, he sensed the mind of God revealed in the calm beauty of the place. There were those who would disagree the priest replied, but it was gratifying to find some at least who viewed with sympathy the design of the architect.

'This is my first visit,' George said. 'My wife, Sarah, and I will be resident in the parish for a short time only, pending the birth of our child. But you will know, perhaps, my wife's uncle, John Jones, who is, I understand, a regular worshipper here.'

'Indeed, we are very happy to know him – a munificent gentleman of great discrimination. He finds much to admire in our church. I did not see him here today. I hope that doesn't mean he is unwell.'

'No, I think not,' said Sarah. 'Perhaps he is abroad, where his business often takes him.'

'While we are here, residing in Swallow-street, only a few yards away from this door, is there aught I could do with the time at my disposal within or on behalf of the church?' George had steeled himself to ask the question. 'This must be an unusual request, but I beg you will consider it. Full of wonders as London is, I would far prefer to do God's work in this place than wander the streets without aim or purpose.'

'Welsh, I think. Oxford? Which college? Jesus at a guess.'

George was humiliated by the question. 'No college.'

'Ah, I see. A noble sentiment, to share in God's work here.' The words ascended and hung a while in the vault. 'But I cannot think we have a role to engage you. However, I thank you warmly for the intention and you can be sure I will make enquiries and give further thought to your request, and of course let you know should anything occur. I trust we shall see you and your dear lady at evensong – or next week.' He bowed, and as the last worshippers trickled away, turned and, head high, strode down the long nave towards the altar.

George returned to St James's often, at first in the hope that he might after all be invited to help there in some way, but quite soon he realised there would be no further response to his request. He was a village curate, inducted at the instigation of a dying father, whose plea the bishop could hardly refuse. What had he to offer other than a humble heart? No learning, although the Bible and prayer book were familiar since childhood. On his daily walk, whenever his route brought him near the church, he would enter to think and pray. Almost alone, kneeling, or seated on a long bench watching sunlight through clear windows travelling over polished wood and gilded ornaments in the tall spaces of the great church, where every last sound awoke echoes, slowly he began to be aware of the presence of God as he never had before.

The sky had darkened and rain streaked the sooty windows. They sat either side of the fire sipping tea, the silence broken only by the occasional clatter of pans and crockery in the kitchen where Jane was beginning to prepare a meal with a pie purchased from a nearby purveyor of baked-meats. George was neither hurt nor disappointed at the response to his request, having expected no more from a great church, priested as it must be by learned men. He placed his cup and saucer on the side table and knelt before Sarah, clasping her hand.

'I am glad St James's has no need of me,' he said. 'Since we have been given the means to live here in comfort, I should spend the months that lie before us awaiting the birth of your child by your side. We are blessed by fortune in this: I cannot foresee another time in our marriage when we can be together, unburdened by responsibilities.'

Sarah looked at him, seeing a good man, an honest man, who would work hard and be faithful to her, just as she had thought at their earliest meetings. 'Yes, we have been fortunate.' She placed his hand to her cheek. 'We cannot know what lies ahead, so let us do what we can with this – holiday. Cares will crowd around soon enough. I doubt we shall visit London again. While I am still able, we should explore a little more. When I lived with him here, my uncle showed me wonderful places, like the tombs of the kings in Westminster Abbey and the wild animals in the Tower of London. Perhaps I can show them to you. And once he took me to a theatre to see *Romeo and Juliet*, a play by Shakespeare. It was wonderful. Would you like to do that? I can ask Uncle John where we might be best entertained.'

In the course of his meanderings, unaccompanied by Sarah as her time neared, at Covent Garden George discovered Noble's Circulating Library and for three shillings purchased three months' membership. He read then as he had never read before. The days shortened and fogs thickened, or else wind and rain made walking unpleasant, even in the parks near at hand, so that they increasingly stayed closer to their fire. With candles lit, George delighted in reading aloud to Sarah, who lay on a settee, a broad cushion supporting her back and a blanket over her legs. For all the strangeness of their coming together, they were happy.

The dark-haired child was born healthy in the middle of a mild January – a boy. They pondered what to name him. Thinking it would please Sarah, George suggested Thomas, after her late father, or possibly John, for her uncle. But Sarah was quite certain: the child should be George, as befitted a son, the firstborn in the family. Uncle John expressed his pleasure at finding mother and child well and presented them with a handsome gift of money that allowed them to remain in London 'until the boy would be strong enough to travel'. He was baptised on Easter Day, 4th April 1790, in the carved white marble font of St James's, Piccadilly. A week later, George, Sarah and the baby journeyed to Ystradowen and Maendy Uchaf, where the third bedroom had been made ready for them.

Esther, rejoicing in the status of grandmother, but with eyes somewhat dim, was surprised to find the child such a weight in her arms. Scenting the honey scalp and running her fingers through the plentiful dark hair, she said how well she remembered her own children at like age, and 'Ah,' she said, 'he follows my father, who had a head of black hair well into later life. And that mouth, too, I do believe resembles him – but the nose, that's his own father's nose.' Looking at George, and then turning again to the bundle in her arms, stroking the baby's short, flat nose, 'Yes, it is, yes, it is,' she said.

Richard, returned from a day's work in the fields, and hiding ineffectively a brotherly resentment that he had been left with the labours of two in George's absence, protested he was not clean enough to hold the child, but said he looked well, for a baby. Sarah he greeted warmly, for now there were two women, one young and strong, to share the work of the home, the stone-floored kitchen with its oven-grate, the back kitchen and its bread oven, the dairy, the henhouse, and the garden, where there were gooseberry and currant bushes, and apple and pear trees readying to blossom.

Sarah returned the warmth of her welcome, content that all was turning out as she had hoped and gratified to find Maendy Uchaf much like her own home, the farm in Llangan where she had been a happy child. She would be happy here, too, she resolved. Life in London and Ash Hall was over. She had come back to her roots in the Vale. It was a good place to begin married life.

I I

IN MATTERS AFFECTING his niece, John Jones, as a friend of the late Sir Thomas, had been pleased to serve as young Mr Aubrey's London agent. It was a delight to see her again, he wrote to Ash Hall, one he had not anticipated, and to meet her husband, a gentle, serious young man, who he was sure would stand by her. Then in January he had written again to announce the birth of a son – news that gave Richard Aubrey considerable satisfaction. Shortly afterwards, the army clothier had been gratified to receive, from a Welsh drover employed for the purpose, the purse of gold and silver coins that had enabled the couple to delay the baptism and extend their stay in London until April. Richard was pleased to hear the child was named George, as people would expect. He looked forward to watching him grow – at a little distance – and perhaps bringing a gentle influence to bear upon his education.

There was the difficulty that Sally's husband was a curate, receiving twenty pounds a year from his patron, who by his own labour also earned a share of the modest income from tenancy of a small farm. He had taken the trouble to enquire about Maendy Uchaf and had learned that, in addition to the farmhouse with garden and rickyard, it had four fields, a total of little more than fifteen acres. In normal circumstances it would provide enough to live on, but a bad year or two could be ruinous. To provide a secure home and an education for the child, the curate would need an incumbency. He was young and inexperienced in orders for preferment, and his qualifications for priesthood were undeniably weak, though that was not unusual in the Vale, but something would have to be done. Richard decided he would put the problem to Aunt Margaret, who had already been helpful on his behalf.

And then he thought again. Following his aunt's command, he had denied himself the comforts of visiting Sally at night, and been far cooler in his dealings with her during the day, while encouraging her marriage to a poor curate without prospects – all to hide his indiscretion. What he had done was contrary to urgent promptings of mind, heart and body, which nagged him still. He had paid for his aunt's sense of propriety, for his obedience to her word: a large portion of his happiness had left with the children's nurse and governess. They had missed her, too. Only the day before, Julia had asked when Sally was coming back. Brother John would not have heeded their aunt, would have kept the woman as wife or concubine. Like any number of his landed friends, Sir John was careless of proprieties. With wealth and position, one could afford to ignore the gossip and strictures of others. But he was not like them, nor could he afford to be. His aunt had suggested he look for another young woman, one of his standing, to marry and take to bed. He had looked, but there was no one like Sally. No, not yet – perhaps never. He recognised that he had been filled with bitter envy on the day he interviewed the poor curate, but that was no reason to condemn Sally, and his own child, to a life of penury. He would go to his aunt. This time the problem was far simpler and she had the means of solving it.

As it transpired, there was a difficulty. Along with land and property in the Vale, Sir John had inherited from his father the rights of patronage of several churches. When Aunt Margaret proposed that at the next convenient vacancy Richard should ask his brother to show favour to the curate of Ystradowen, he refused.

'I prefer not to involve John,' he said. 'He will want to know why, and even if I were to tell him, he will out of ancient spite make the gift elsewhere. I am sure he will readily find far better qualified clergy to take possession of his churches. There isn't really a great deal to commend the Reverend George Williams, except that he is an honest, modest sort of fellow, who is clearly fond of Sally and prepared to put up with, what shall we say, inconveniences, to support her as wife – with my child into the bargain. He has never sought reward for this, marriage to Sally being reward enough, he says. That, I firmly believe, is the truth. It is one of the reasons I feel inclined to help him. The other affects me nearly: I want to be sure my child is not reared in an impoverished house, and that his mother, to whom, as you know, I owe a great deal, has a measure of security and comfort in her life.'

'Very well. As I do not have rights of advowson donation to any church, when an opportunity arises I shall endeavour, on your behalf, to influence those of my friends who do possess them. We shall see if we can find a living for your honest curate somewhere in the Vale.'

Not long after the interview with his aunt, Richard, as his brother's grudging representative, was informed that the Reverend Nehemiah Hopkins, aged rector of Llantrithyd, the Aubrey family church neighbouring the Plas, had fallen gravely ill, and shortly afterwards that he had died. This did not appear the opportunity he was seeking: it was obviously a church in the gift of his brother, who, as he had told his aunt, would not be accommodatingly open to the notion of admitting an unlettered local curate to the living. But later the same day his hopes were raised by the unexpected arrival at Ash Hall of a breathless rider bearing a letter from Lady Margaret. It was to inform him that patronage of the rectory and parish church at Llantrithyd did not reside with Sir John, but with Thomas Edmondes of Llandough Castle, who held in trust a ninety-nine-year lease on a number of parts of the estate, including this right, as a result of a transaction between their respective grandfathers almost fifty years before. 'I believe it is in the interests of the family to place Rev. Geo: Williams in the rectory,' his aunt had written, 'and I shall therefore hasten to Llandough Castle and see what can be done to persuade Thomas Edmondes to that course of action.'

Richard smiled at the vision of his aunt's breakneck coach ride, sparks flying from the horses' hooves, as she thundered from Llanmaes to Llandough. 'God speed!' he whispered.

The following day another perspiring rider appeared, sealed missive in hand. His aunt had been successful. She did not need to persuade, far less browbeat, Thomas Edmondes. Within minutes he was able to lay before her a copy of the deed his grandfather and old Sir John had signed and, having read it, he pronounced himself content to accept her direction in the matter. The Edmondes family had gained ownership of Llandough Castle not many years before, having accumulated wealth as lawyers and businessmen and Thomas had learned as a young man that Lady Margaret should be received with the deference due to ancient lineage. He had not heard of the death of the Reverend Hopkins, but undertook to attend at once to the drafting of an appropriate document addressed to Richard, Bishop of Llandaff, which he would be pleased to carry to Llanmaes for joint signing.

'And who is to be the fortunate new incumbent at Llantrithyd?' he asked. 'Why, the Reverend George Williams, of course,' said Lady Margaret, brooking no further discussion of the topic.

Edmondes, who knew nothing of the named cleric and had not begun to think of a rival successor to the Llantrithyd living, smiled and shrugged disarmingly. 'So be it,' he said.

A letter, dated 23rd April 1790, in appropriately convoluted language and an elaborately elegant secretarial hand, prayed that 'the Right Reverend Father in God Richard by divine Permission Lord Bishop of Llandaff would be graciously pleased to admit and canonically to institute George Williams Clerk to the rectory and parish church of Llantrithyd and to invest him with all and singular the rights, members and appurtenances thereunto belonging'. It was signed and sealed by Margaret Aubrey and Thomas Edmondes in the presence of witnesses and despatched with all possible speed to Llandaff.

A week later, the time allowed for the two surviving children of Nehemiah Hopkins to mourn and bury their father and clear the premises (his wife having died many years before), George and Sarah moved into the rectory. Of goods and chattels they had very little: in addition to Sarah's treasured possession, the small pastoral painting by Morland, there was a pair of plain wooden chairs, the bed they had slept in at Maendy Uchaf and the table on which George's father had written his sermons. With his brother's help, George disposed these few sticks in the empty rooms of the echoing house.

The baby, plump and well fed, lay content in his familiar

cradle, almost asleep. The new rector and his wife stood in the doorway of their home, said 'Thank you' to their helper, and waved as he turned at the garden gate. It was a glorious early spring day. On the threshold of a new life, George embraced Sarah.

'God be praised,' he said.

Sarah smiled. 'Amen to that!' she said, and, wondering how much human agency was involved at the Good Lord's behest, 'We have much to do.'

Llantrithyd Place, a noble mansion, seat of the Aubreys from Tudor times, stood in a hollow, and close, a little above it to the east, church and rectory, side by side. Richard Aubrey was an early visitor. He was not familiar with the rectory, having had business with the church and the parson only infrequently. His brother had slight enough interest in the Plas, a rare beauty in Richard's eyes, which would have sat well among the colleges of Oxford, and none in the two buildings that were its near neighbours, which he well knew, for decades past had been in the gift of another.

The unexpected, firm knock at the door startled Sarah. Shading her eyes with her hand and peering into the morning sun, she recognised at once the outline of the figure silhouetted on the doorstep. 'Mr Aubrey,' she said, 'we are very glad to see you.'

He was uneasy. 'I don't want to disturb,' he said. 'I've brought a letter. It's from Julia Frances – and there's an interesting scribble from her brother that I'm not entirely sure about.'

'Do come in. My husband will be pleased to greet you. Will you take tea with us? We are not quite settled, but we have a chair and table and teacups. And there's young George – you know I have had a child since leaving Ash Hall? Perhaps you would like to see him?'

'Ah, yes. Yes, I suppose.'

The new rector had appeared behind Sarah, extending his hand, smiling. 'The warmest of welcomes to you, dear sir,' he said. 'I am barely acquainted yet with the church, but have viewed the handsome memorials in the nave with astonishment, and know already of its ancient connection with your family. I am deeply privileged … honoured … filled with gratitude …'

Voicing his feelings aloud, he was suddenly overcome, almost to tears, and fell silent.

'The letter,' said Richard, handing it to Sarah. 'You see you taught my daughter well: letters must be properly addressed, "To Mistress Sally, The Rectory, Lantrithyd", and sealed.'

'I am most happy to receive it and shall keep it safe until I can read it privately. And I shall reply. Be sure to tell Julia that – and Thomas. Now, you'll take tea?'

But Richard begged to be excused and seemed about to turn away when struck by an afterthought. 'The baby,' he said, 'I almost forgot. It would be churlish not to greet the newest of newcomers to the rectory.'

Following Sarah, he passed through the empty wood-panelled inner hall to the kitchen, where a low fire burned and a kettle was singing on a trivet close to the bars of the grate. George lay in his cradle, which had been drawn up to one side of the hearth. He was awake, stirring slightly, turning his dark head and flexing the fingers of both hands.

'A fine looking boy,' said Richard, ' – my congratulations to you both. Let me see. There must be a gift to mark this occasion.' He searched in a waistcoat pocket and produced a gold coin and put it into one small hand, which grasped and held it. 'Ah, you see how he holds on to money. A good sign, surely.' Then, sensing Sarah was about to protest, he added, 'No, no – it is my pleasure. Let it purchase something he needs – or keep it for him if you prefer. Now, I have business at the Plas on behalf of my brother, and must leave.' So saying, and with no more than a token gesture of farewell, he turned away, strode through the hall and out of the door, closing it behind him with an echoing bang in the emptiness that startled the baby and made him cry.

Some time later, Sarah still rocking the child in her arms, George said, 'Mr Aubrey was very generous, but had little to say to us in our new situation. I expected him to have words for me about my pastoral responsibilities, how they might embrace the great house and so on, but he didn't so much as look my way while he was here. Did you not think him somewhat disdainful?'

'I thought it was kind of him to call, and of course his gift to our son was indeed generous. No, I did not find him disdainful. Really, much as usual. I am sure he is a shy man. You have met, but are hardly on familiar terms. When he begins to know you better, you will see a change in him.'

There was much to be done in their new home, but George was filled with hope and expectation: the bird of good fortune had perched on their shoulders. With money remaining from their residence in London, under Sarah's direction, furniture and kitchen things were acquired sufficient to make the house comfortable and fitting to their needs. More slowly, George learned about his parish and the ancient church dedicated to St Illtyd now in his care, the preservation and maintenance of the chancel being his personal responsibility. His churchwardens told him the parish extended over fourteen hundred acres and included about forty dwellings large and small, and some two-hundred-and-fifty people. His father had been a curate for many years before his appointment as vicar of Penlline, and now, in such a short time, he was rector of Llantrithyd, a living of one-hundred-and-twenty pounds a year, the possessor, for as long as he lived, of a spacious, fine parsonage, a kitchen house, a brewhouse, a well-built stable, a large barn, a garden, an orchard and a fifty-two-acre glebe, more than three times the size of Maendy Uchaf's fields, to farm and stock as he pleased; and both great and small tithes for the parish were due to him, to collect and keep. He had never dared dream, far less think ambitiously of such a transformation. He could hardly understand, he told Sarah, how, without fresh effort or inspiration on his part, such a change of fortune had so swiftly come about. One day, it seemed, he had been a poor and lonely curate, with a brother and widowed mother scraping a bare living from the land, and the next united to a wife, his partner in life, with a child, and wealth far beyond that which his father had commanded. He would endeavour to deserve what bounteous God had ordained, by caring for the church, succouring the sick and needy of the parish, and uplifting the souls of all. Later the same day, he thought again of the gifts he had received. The first and greatest was Sarah. He was required only to reconcile himself to loving a stranger's child and all else followed. Alone in the church, he knelt to offer a prayer of thanks.

III

THE NEW RECTOR was disappointed to find his pastoral duties did not extend to Llantrithyd Place. He passed by the old mansion house daily, gazing down on its long tiled roofs and tall chimneys, lit by sun or shining with recent rain, and longed to see within. Sarah told him she had once been received there by Sir Thomas Aubrey, father of Richard, though the old man was then sick and soon to die, and how grand and stately it was. If its present owner, Richard's older brother, Sir John, were to visit, perhaps he would be called upon to pay his respects and give an account of himself and his labours in the parish. He had paused to view the Plas one day, with much these thoughts in mind, when he was accosted by a stranger, shorter than himself, George thought, but broader, and rather stouter, in knee breeches, coat and waistcoat of good blue stuff and a broad-brimmed soft hat, for it was June and the morning sun was high.

'A fine old place,' said the stranger. 'I was there to meet Sir John when he came down a little while ago. Took my dear wife along with me. Do you know he gave me – I can't say how many dozen of beer. Just like that, on a rich man's whim. Seemed amused by the whole business. Pardon my intrusion on your thoughts: I'm John Perkins of Pentra.'

'Ah, Pentra – an admirable, large farm. I have wondered who the gentleman owner might be and have had it in mind to call, as I intend to call on all my parishioners, especially those whom I have not yet met at the church door. I have recently become rector here.'

'What remarkably good fortune I have in meeting you,' said Perkins and went on to explain that he and his wife had a child awaiting baptism, but his wife, Bessy's, illness following the confinement had so far prevented them bringing the baby to church.

'There is no need,' said George. 'I will happily come to Pentra Farm and perform all due rites there.'

In the absence of a resident master at Llantrithyd Place, Perkins looked on the rector as his only social equal, and one who was, like him, a newcomer to the village. Thus began a lasting friendship. They walked together often, discussing the weather, assessing the quality of arable and pasture, and the condition of stock and crops. Perkins was interested in the news coming out of France, a topic to which the rector had given scant attention. He and Sarah had arrived in London less than three months after the fall of the Bastille, when the coffee houses were noisy with debate about events across the Channel, and Sarah's uncle, the army clothier, wise in the world of business, was already contemplating the possibility of fresh contracts, but they were hardly aware of the turmoil just then beginning. By January 1790 news of the flight from France of aristocrats and wealthy landowners, and the pillaging and destruction of their homes, had changed the minds of those who had at first greeted the revolution with some enthusiasm. Perkins, who had properties elsewhere in the Vale as well as his sixty-acre farm, and much to lose if similar madness gripped Britain, was on the side of the ousted nobility. He earnestly sought to persuade his friend of the rightness of this view, and called upon him to use the pulpit to instruct his congregation accordingly.

'I've read there is some sort of declaration in which all citizens are said to be equal. What nonsense! We all have our proper place under God and king. Who knows what ills may befall the nation if we undermine good order? And that isn't all. Did you know they've abolished tithes in France and are selling off church lands to the highest bidder? Some of the scoundrels over there are desecrating churches. They've forced King Louis out of his palace and have him at their tender mercies in Paris. What do you think of that?' he cried, the warmth of his passion seeming to inflate his natural ebullience until his cheeks were quite red.

George, mindful of his new, enhanced position as clerk in holy orders, and of the prayers he led in church for His Majesty and the royal family, felt John Perkins, who was perfectly hot in his assertions, must be right. In his mild way, he could not think how to respond, but shook his head to show how shocked and saddened he was. Obliged to confess he knew very little about France and its revolution, he said he hoped it would not bring violence and distress to British shores.

'Ay, that's the fearful thing,' said Perkins. 'What if the plague spreads? Who knows what storm of ills may blow across the channel? We should inform ourselves lest we are of a sudden bowled over, when with warning to prepare we might avoid a wreck. What say you we subscribe to a newspaper, which we can share – perhaps read together or pass to one another?'

George agreed. 'I should be obliged,' he said, 'if you could choose which newspaper might best suit our purpose and arrange the subscription, in which I will gladly join with you.'

'I have the very thing in mind,' said Perkins. 'The *London*

Gazette, a weekly newspaper, and a reliable one at that – "official", you know. It will be sent to us by post. We shall probably need to collect it from Cowbridge. Shake hands on it. I'll make the arrangements and let you know your share of the costs.'

George had been swept along by his new friend's enthusiasm, and committed to he knew not what expense. But with his stipend and his tithes (so long as there was no revolution!), he was among the wealthiest in the parish. And he was sure Sarah, too, would be interested.

So it proved. She had been accustomed to sitting quietly in London coffee houses while conversation, often heated discussion, whirled about her. She had listened, with gradually increasing understanding, to arguments for and against political reform, to the opposing views of Whig and Tory, to voices raised in support and denunciation of William Pitt, and much more, sometimes quite scurrilous talk and malicious gossip. When, while they were drinking tea, George told her of the plan to share a newspaper, she said it would be good for him to be well informed. A man in his position in the village should be. Who knew when he might be in the company of people of standing in the neighbourhood, and would be looked to for an opinion?

It was an unexpected response and he was struck to silence. Not for the first time he gazed at her with an expression close to wonderment. That he had wed a woman of such refinement and knowledge of the world, yet one so modest, warm and loving, was little short of a miracle.

'My dear Sarah,' he said at last, 'this place I have gained, though in all honesty I hardly think I have earned it, is yet new to me. I have not been ambitious, other than in desiring you.

I did not see my path in life extending farther than curacy at Ystradowen and labour with Richard in the fields of Maendy Uchaf, and in a blink, I have been translated to a different place, wonderful, rich with promise. I do not know whether I have the wit and wisdom, and faith, to perform what is expected of me, but with you by my side to counsel me, I shall not stint in my endeavours.' He knelt at her feet, an attitude of worship, his arms clasped her waist. Sarah smiled, bowed her head and kissed his cheek. 'We shall do well,' she said. 'We shall do well, together.'

At the beginning of October, Sarah told George she was sure she was to bear another child.

IV

LONDON HAD GIVEN George Williams experience of comfort and, in the home of John Jones, a display of wealth in furnishings, paintings and books exceeding anything he had previously imagined. It had also shown him, down narrow ways off stately thoroughfares, a glimpse of indescribable filth and degradation. Beyond his schooling he had grown up on a farm, little more than a country labourer, until his sick father had nominated him curate, to officiate in his stead. And suddenly, unexpectedly, he had found himself married to a woman whose knowledge of the world and ease in society were so much greater than his. He confessed himself simple and ignorant; there was so much to learn.

Sarah's new baby, the first born in the rectory for many years, attracted the attention of the village. It was a boy, a brother for George, who was, all agreed, a sturdy child. With a little assistance from Dr Bevan of Cowbridge and Sarah's maid, the newcomer entered the world on April 17th 1791, the Sunday before Easter. At the first of his lusty cries, George hastened upstairs to embrace his wife and soon after to take his son in his arms. He saw what hair the healthy newcomer possessed was fair, even a little golden, perhaps as his own had been when he was new born.

He and Sarah had spoken about names for the child. Surely, a girl would be Sarah, like her mother, George had said, but

Sarah herself preferred Julia Frances, after the pretty, dark-haired child that neither time nor distance could erase from her memory. If it were a boy? Neither expressed a preference and, when the time came, it was the august presence of Dr Bevan that inspired George to suggest an outlandish name, but one with roots in earlier generations of his family.

'Let's name him Bloom,' he said. 'I have a distant cousin named Bloom in Cardiff, a doctor who has made his way in the world. It may do the boy some good to be named after a respected citizen of the town. I would rather like to see him grow up to be an apothecary-surgeon. What think you, Dr Bevan?'

'Why, yes, I suppose, Humph!' said Bevan, taken off-guard by the question.

'Bloom, Bloom,' said Sarah, as though testing, balancing it on her tongue. 'A family name? Well, why not? Bloom he shall be, born at the time of spring flowering, the blossom of our mutual love.'

George could have wept at the words. She is truly beautiful, he thought, her soft glowing cheeks, her hair bountiful, loose over her shoulders, and amazingly fresh after her ordeal. The child still in his arms, he leaned over the bed, to embrace his wife once more, while Bevan shuffled his feet and the maidservant blushed and smiled.

George's friendship with John Perkins progressed apace. But the *London Gazette* was not a success. It arrived at the post office in Cowbridge twice weekly and, at eight pence each issue, more expensively than the joint subscribers anticipated. Events abroad were dealt with briefly and infrequently and the friends soon tired of court circulars, parliamentary election results, diplomatic movements, lists of army commissions and bankruptcies, and Acts of Parliament. They read avidly only the occasional publication of the prices of corn, barley, peas, oats and rye in various parts of England and Wales.

Reluctant to give up the project, Perkins said he would seek advice and a few days later, as he and George were taking tea together in the comfortable kitchen of Pentra farmhouse, he said, 'I met young Mr Aubrey the other day and he said he was pleased to learn we two and our wives had become friends. We were talking about burning lime for the fields and how it might be to our financial advantage if we got together to lay in stocks of coal for the burning. I said, with the glebe to farm, you too might be interested, and that we had already joined forces to purchase a newspaper, but had been disappointed by the *Gazette*. I was bold enough to ask what he would advise to keep up with events at home and abroad in these threatening days. Why the London *Times,* says he, and if you will, I'll make a third in sharing the subscription – We'd be delighted, said I.'

Again George felt he had been led into a situation he had not bargained for and at somewhat greater expense than previously, but when he spoke contritely to Sarah about the new arrangement, she said she was glad he would be on friendly terms with Mr Aubrey, for it would do them nothing but good.

A few days later, on a fine June morning, Richard Aubrey called at the rectory. He had been passing, he said, having business at the Plas, and had brought the children with him for an outing to see the gardens and ponds. They had become excited when he told them that Mistress Sally lived nearby, and wished for nothing so much as to see her and her new baby.

And suddenly, there they were: Thomas Digby, just seven,

already a young gentleman, and Julia Frances, past her tenth birthday, glowingly dark-haired and dark-eyed, in an embroidered gown of pale green silk. For a moment they were silent and uncertain, then as Sarah opened her arms Julia ran to her embrace and, more slowly, Thomas came forward solemnly to shake her outstretched hand.

'My, how you both have grown,' said Sarah, 'and how wonderful to see you.'

Behind them, their new governess stood silent. She was, Sarah saw at a glance, an older woman, grey haired, thin lipped, dressed in black – possibly a widow. The children, quickly at ease in an old warmth, chattered, saw the baby asleep in his cradle and thought he was a very Bloom indeed, and clapped his older brother, George, essaying strides far too long to remain upright without the support of the maid bending over him.

Richard Aubrey drew the rector to one side. 'John Perkins has persuaded you to share in his plan to follow the news from France? Goodness knows what ill he anticipates may fall upon these islands from that eruption of evil. But he is right: it is as well to be informed, and I am glad of the opportunity to join you in the venture. I wrote to my brother about it. Sir John, who, as you will know, is a Member of Parliament and much taken up with newspaper reports, does not usually have patience to assist others, but on this occasion he has been obliging. He has arranged for the *Times* to be sent down in weekly bundles – it's a daily, you see – at our expense, of course, though shared by the three of us that will not be exorbitant.'

'Mr Perkins and I are indeed fortunate to have your help and guidance in this, and the aid of Sir John. When you next write, please give him our thanks.'

'The arrangement will bring us closer together,' said Richard, 'and I am glad of it. You may know of the debt of gratitude I owe your good wife: no less than the upright, good sense of my children. You must come to Ash Hall, where we can talk at greater length.'

The visit had been unexpected but was welcomed for all that by Sarah, who was overjoyed to see her former charges, and rather to his surprise, by George, who had previously thought Mr Aubrey brusque and unapproachable. This occasion had not been marked, on one side, by dismissive condescension, and on the other by excessive humility. They could never meet as equals, but now, it appeared, there might grow between them a pleasant acquaintance, even in time friendship.

V

IN THE WEEKS and months that followed, the friendship between the rector and John Perkins grew firmer and spread in a strong tide among other members of the families. They took tea at one another's homes two or three times most weeks, so that Bessy, who presided, plump and voluble, over the tea table in the painted wooden-floored parlour at Pentra, soon became familiarly at ease with the Reverend George, while at the rectory, in much the same way, though with a more reserved demeanour, Sarah came to know Mr Perkins. And then the womenfolk began exchanging visits, when the conversation was mostly about their children and neighbourhood gossip that servants brought to their attention.

On one such occasion when Sarah came alone because both children, George and young Bloom, were miserable with colds and had been left in the care of the two housemaids, Bessy told her about the terrible anxiety she had suffered some two years earlier when, at her husband's urging, she had allowed Kitt, the oldest of their children, to be inoculated by Doctor Bevan.

'He was almost three years old at the time,' she said, 'and it was dreadful the fever he suffered. I wept and prayed for days and cursed myself for agreeing to it. And John said nothing, but, oh, his looks, his misery. He had read all about it, you see – he's a great reader, my John. Interfering with nature I swore it was, but with Bevan here all hours of the day and night and the two of us nursing him, at last he was well again. I don't know that I could go through it again, but John was right, you see, in the end; yes, he was right. And now we know Kitt will never catch the smallpox.'

At first, Sarah had been unsure where the story was tending, but when she understood, she found herself wondering whether it might be worth finding out more about this way of protecting children from a disease that killed many and disfigured those it spared.

For the men too, taking tea was a time for gossip and, usually it seemed, grumbling about weather and crops, though both gentleman farmer and rector rarely had reason to complain. Their arable land was as good as any in the parish, and as well tended, for they could afford to employ labourers and had time and knowledge enough to survey the fields and see all done to their satisfaction. Two or three times each week they would walk their properties, often together, strolling and talking, pointing with their sticks at this and that doing well, or not as well as might be expected. To George's surprise, for he had not yet shrugged off the lowliness of his former standing, it was a friendship of equals. He found he was allowed to have views about husbandry, and about parish highways and such, which were harkened to with the same attention he gave to the assertive pronouncements of John Perkins. Soon they were helping one another as the need arose, by lending a cart, or a pony to attend a mart, sharing in the purchase and transport of coals and the production of lime for the fields, and in the newspaper.

It was agreed the *Times* was a great success. The bundle

usually arrived at Pentra a week or more after it had first been delivered to Ash Hall, so that the events in Europe that most gripped John Perkins and, by a sort of contagion of interest, soon occupied the thoughts of the rector, had often occurred a month or more before they first read of them. It was mid-August when they saw the news of June that the French royal family had fled Paris, and then been identified at Varennes and forced to turn back, October when they read how, a month before, the beleaguered king had been forced to recognise the revolutionary constitution.

'A disgrace!' Perkins shouted from the depths of the paper, his hands shaking with rage. 'No good will come of this, you mark my words. What is our army doing about it, I should like to know.'

It had been mid-September in that year of wonders when George Williams was presented to the living of Llantrithyd before a chance meeting with a fellow cleric at the mart in Cowbridge made him fully conscious of his expectations henceforth as the recipient of both great and lesser tithes. A search among parish documents uncovered a copy of a terrier of 1764, which had been agreed locally and confirmed by the consistory court at Llandaff, declaring the share of produce due to him. Quantities of stock and crops of all kinds were listed, except that there was no tithe for hay; rather, each in-dweller of the parish should yield him one penny per acre of hay, each out-dweller five pence per acre. The tenth stook of wheat, barley, oats, peas and beans would be his, one tenth of all wool and every tenth lamb; one calf out of season, or else twelve shillings and sixpence in lieu; twelve pence for every milch cow kept; eight pence for every barren cow; sixpence for every heifer at first calving; a penny on the fall of every colt, horse or mare; one tithe pig of every seven at fourteen days old ... poultry, eggs, apples, pears, summer and autumn fruits, honey and wax, the list went on, ending with a tithe from the water mill where grain was ground, and from the orchards, gardens and premises of the Plas. It was too much to take in at first and he read it again and again. He had been grateful for the share of the lesser tithes the absentee rector of Ystradowen had permitted him while he was still a curate, but this represented wealth indeed.

John Perkins looked at him quizzically when he asked in all innocence where and how such loads of produce could be stored. 'You have that fine barn,' he said, 'for settlements in kind, but I think you'll find most people will prefer to agree with you a rate of payment in coin, if they have it, for each acre or bushel or whatever.'

The meetings with his parishioners on All Saints, the day tithes were paid, was another wonder. The rector returned to his home, incapable of uttering a word, sat at the table and beckoned to Sarah. Looking up at her, smiling, but with tears in his eyes, he produced stacks of coins from pockets and small leather pouches, and laid them out upon the broad oak surface.

'We must start keeping accounts,' she said.

The weight of money in the hand was another new experience, one that delighted and induced a hunger. Before the first year of his tenure of the glebe had ended, the rector had decided he would let the greater part of it, some forty-seven acres, retaining only five acres of meadow for his own use. William Smythe, a townsman of Cowbridge, who owned fields in Llancarfan, was looking to augment his holdings of arable land, and had the means to pay the rent, was pleased at the bargain.

With this unprecedented wealth George purchased a riding horse and accoutrements at the market in Cowbridge. He knew enough about horseflesh to judge it was a sound beast of some nine years, and its price reasonable. After a lifetime of careful economy he was not inclined to extravagant expenditure. He also began to hunt, following the encouragement and advice of Richard Aubrey, who from childhood had been accustomed to hunting on his father's extensive estates.

'I know you take pleasure in walking heath and copses on fine autumn days, as I do, and a little sport from time to time will kindle excitement, which is no bad thing. Besides,' he added, looking sombre, 'we do well to become familiar with firearms and their use in threatening times. If you'll permit, I'll obtain a musket for you.'

George admitted that shooting for the pot was not part of his experience; there had never been a weapon of any sort at Maendy Uchaf, nor even a fishing rod. He would need to be taught.

'It will be my pleasure,' said Aubrey, clapping him on the back.

A week later one of his men brought the rector an invitation to walk the land about Ash Hall. Perkins was already at the house when George arrived and on the table in the big kitchen lay three weapons, one considerably longer than the other two.

'This is yours,' said Aubrey, handing George one of the shorter muskets, 'and here is a pouch with a dozen cartridges. I got them at Cardiff when I was doing my public duty at magistrates' court. We can settle up later – there's no need for haste. That's the sort of weapon used by the army. Exactly like mine. It's reliable as long as you look after it – clean it properly. Perkins' is a bit older, has a longer barrel, but there's not much difference in weight.'

George examined the object in his hands: polished dark wood, three-and-a-half-feet of steel barrel, engraved brass plates, cock, flint, pan, trigger, rather less than five feet over all. It was, of its kind, handsome. He smiled as he weighed it at arm's length: about ten pounds.

'Let us try a shot or two in the field beyond the garden. The stock have been moved; there's nothing to take fright,' said Aubrey, 'or, Lord help us, to shoot accidentally.'

They stepped out into a day clouded but fair, with a steady breeze from the sea glinting in the distance and, farther off, the dark outline of the Somerset coast. Perkins, who had been unusually quiet while Aubrey was handing the weapon to George, roused himself, demanding a target to demonstrate his prowess. He, too, had hunted from boyhood. The field was called Tair Onnen and the three ash trees that gave it its name stood in a line together forty yards from where they stood, their fine green canopies already thinning at the very thought of winter.

'Aim at the trunk of the middle tree,' Aubrey suggested.

'Too easy. Never mind.' Perkins loaded the long barrelled gun with practised efficiency, took casual aim and fired. A loud report sent a fountain of rooks cawing into the air from a tree in a neighbouring field, and a cloud of thick smoke enveloped Perkins for a moment before the wind dragged it away.

'Your turn,' Aubrey turned to George. 'We'll train you like the soldiery.'

For an hour he followed the repeated instructions: pull

the cock back halfway, check the flint in its beak, tear off the clenched end of the paper cartridge with the teeth, empty its black powder and shot into the muzzle, followed by the wad of paper, ram it home with the rod slung beneath the barrel, replace the rod, pull the cock back to its full extent, dribble a dusting of fine powder in the pan and close the frizzen lid upon it, raise the weapon to the shoulder, aim, pull the trigger. Although he had been warned, he was still caught unawares by the noise of the explosion close to his ear and the musket butt's kick to his shoulder. He learned to mitigate the recoil, but the soreness lasted two whole days and the bruise longer.

'The army use 0.75 calibre ball,' said Aubrey, 'but that's little use for hunting. Even if you were to hit a small target, like a hare or a woodcock, which is very unlikely, you would smash the creature to pieces. That's why we are using shot. Let's see how well you two have peppered the tree.'

'I don't think I shall ever perform that drill as neatly, and quickly, as you manage,' George said.

'It's just practice. It will come.' Perkins preened, quite himself, busily cleaning inside the long barrel of his gun with the rod. 'You need to do this every time you shoot or residue from the repeated explosions will build up in there.'

George returned to the rectory elated. The musket had a ruthless beauty. Its wood and metal gleamed. It was perfectly formed to accomplish its murderous purpose. Like a good scythe you could hold it balanced ready for use in an outstretched hand. Sarah was less impressed but listened attentively as he recounted the events at Maes Tair Onnen, and smiled as, child like, he unbuttoned his shirt to reveal how his shoulder had suffered. She was pleased, too, because she saw how friendship was growing between her husband and Richard Aubrey.

They hunted together during the autumn months, George sometimes with Aubrey, sometimes Perkins, sometimes all three. Muskets at the ready, they walked together from stubble field to hill, from copse to covert. From time to time they returned with a hare or two, or perhaps a plump bird, but often they came back after a good airing with nothing in the game pouch, but much talk about near successes and occasional mishaps. There was the occasion when Perkins slipped while they were crossing a steep field. Unable to stop himself, he tumbled, and his plump form, weighted with greatcoat and scarves, rolled and bounced over and over to the foot of the slope, and lay there, arms and legs working like an overturned beetle, as he struggled to get up. His stout clothing had protected him and he had come to no harm. Only his pride was hurt – especially when his companions, who, fearing for his safety, had rushed down to him, found he was uninjured and laughed at the comic surprise of his descent.

From time to time, George donned a coarse smock to help his brother Richard, who still farmed Maendy Uchaf and was glad to know he was no longer required to share harvests with another. The issue of the farm lease remained in abeyance, since it appeared that neither Sir John Aubrey nor his steward, Mumford, could yet be bothered to demand its renewal at increased rental so long as the existing rent was promptly paid. For George, although he loved his brother, it was no longer a concern. He had been a diligent labourer in the soil and first sight of the glebe had filled him with joy and ambitious plans; now he turned his back on farming without regret. He would ensure that the ditches and field drains and hedges of his meadows were regularly attended to, that clover was sown and hay cut and safely stored. He would buy a riding horse or two, perhaps in time a simple carriage. And to please Sarah he would put in hand the recovery of the rectory garden, little more than an acre of good south-facing land, sloping gently towards the shallow valley bottom, bounded to the west by the neat dry-stone boundary wall of the Plas and on the other sides by a quickset hedge in need of trimming. These were tasks, given time, he might easily accomplish himself, but he decided he would find a stout labourer to undertake the work at his direction and, if she expressed any, to Sarah's wishes.

Not long after reaching this conclusion, while visiting dilapidated cottages at the end of a narrow, muddy lane, he came upon a young man he thought he recognised, who was alternately slashing with a hook at an overgrown hedge and digging at previously unbroken soil in its shadow to extend a small garden plot. He was tall and thin, had tow-coloured hair that sprang in cropped tufts from his long skull and, as he looked up, revealed a pronounced Adam's apple.

'Ah, Reverend Williams, you've come up in the world,' he said, his deep voice hoarse with the effort of his labour. 'You don't remember me, I suppose.'

'Yes … we have met I feel sure, but I cannot think where.'

'Perhaps you recall my grandmother – Elizabeth Morgan, long dead now, and that farm in Ystradowen that's gone like her and nothing to show for it.'

The smoke-filled empty room, strangely echoing voices, his and the old woman's, his sense of failure, came back in a rush. He looked more closely at the young man: there, under fair bushy brows, the squinting eye.

'Why, of course, I remember … from Llancarfan was it? You are …?'

'Lewis … Richard Lewis.'

'I am glad to number you among my parishioners, though I do not recollect seeing you at church. What has brought you here?'

'A woman, of course. What else? Didn't a woman fetch you to this place? That's what I hear.'

George, angry that this ragged, unprepossessing fellow should presume to speak coarsely to him about Sarah, and uncertain what exactly he meant, felt his colour rise. He was about to reprove him sharply when he thought again of the old woman, beyond fear of God or man, on the borders of death, and the gawky boy, her sole companion. 'Could you take on some gardening work at the rectory?' he said.

VI

I N THE DREARY early months of the new year, 1792, Aubrey at Ash Hall, Perkins at Pentra Farm and the Reverend George at the rectory, each in his turn, read of events in France with increasing concern. At first George had been sure the Vale could not be affected by the troubles of a far country. To him, it was like reading Gibbons' history of Rome, a book he had borrowed from the circulating library in Covent Garden, dramatic and absorbing, but of no consequence. Almost from the start his fellow *Times* readers had been grimly apprehensive or enraged and, as the weeks passed without any change or diminution in the turmoil, he had caught their unease.

The newspaper had reported food riots in Paris throughout the winter months: the entire population seemed on the point of eruption. At the end of March, they read of the recent official announcement that a new mechanical means of execution had been approved, the guillotine. It seemed the French did not relish seeing their criminals kicking at the end of a rope; they wanted justice to mete out a swifter, bloodier death. 'Chacun à son goût,' said Richard Aubrey, smiling wryly. In April the three met at Pentra, shaking their heads, murmuring to one another, 'I told you so': France had declared war on Austria. The violence was spreading.

Rather to her disappointment, Sarah was afforded no opportunity to read the newspaper, but as usual, when he returned, George conveyed to her the news, with his fears for the future. It was Bloom's birthday. His father saw he was a happy child, but restless in the maid's arms, watchful, head and shoulders twisting this way and that, wanting to be put down so that he could crawl to some destination he had in sight or mind, then demanding to be picked up by the maid to see what could be seen from the height of her arms. Rejecting the beribboned bone ring bought for the purpose, he chewed his fingers and dribbled copiously. His brother George, sturdy and usually firm on his feet, was persuaded to give him a birthday kiss, but the kiss ended in a pinch and a scold and both cried. Tea was served and sweetmeats for the little boys.

The rector looked upon his healthy children, the doting maids and his wife smiling at the head of the table, and silently thanked God for home and family. Again, he thought, it was she, Sarah, who had wrought all, *all*. How could he possibly reveal the depth of his regard for her. He had planned to make a pleasant garden where she and the children could walk on fine days, and it was beginning to take shape, for Richard Lewis, although he appeared ungainly, was capable of working well enough once he had been shown what needed to be done, and so long as he was being watched. He told himself, if there was aught he could do about it, Sarah should have a home of which she could feel proud. She still recalled from time to time the paintings that decked the walls in the home of her uncle. He resolved that she, too, must have paintings to add to the precious Morland landscape that glowed in a quiet corner of the rectory. There and then, he devised a plan: he would write secretly to John Jones asking his advice and help.

It was early June when Sarah mentioned her desire to protect the children from smallpox. George had heard from John Perkins how he and Bessy had gone through the torments of hell when they had asked Bevan to inoculate the first of their children. It was his own fault, he had said, because of his confounded reading, that he had been persuaded it was a good thing. And, indeed, he was forced to admit, all had turned out well. Their Kitt had recovered, was as good as new, better really, because he would never now fall victim to the dread disease. In recent days, Sarah had been speaking again to Bessy, who, with the pain of anxiety largely forgotten, had said how watchfully and tenderly they had needed to nurse Kitt, which was only to be expected, and that she and John were glad now they had summoned the courage to get it done.

Young George was a beautiful child, tall for his age and sturdy, his dark hair falling in loose curls to his shoulders. He was talkative, quick on his feet and agile enough to demand the alert attention of the nursemaid lest he get into scrapes about the house and especially in the garden, where walls were being rebuilt. He was surely strong enough, Sarah told George, to withstand inoculation, if they took great care of him, but her husband was not immediately persuaded. 'I'll ask Perkins about it again,' he said. 'He told me the idea came from something he read.'

A day or so later, as they were standing at the top of a field on a low hill overlooking Pentra, watching a pair of labourers whitewashing the walls of the farmhouse, he put the question.

'I was reading about a physician called Mead,' Perkins said, 'Richard Mead – in London. Became very famous – and rich! Was the old king's doctor, and Queen Anne's before him, and Isaac Newton's. Anyway, fifty or sixty years ago this was, he had the idea from his studies that if you *gave* healthy people the smallpox, the illness would be less dangerous than if they caught it the normal way and, once over that, they would be immune from the contagion.'

Down below, two figures in labourers' smocks were dipping broad, long-handled brushes into a large tub and sweeping up and down then across the farmhouse walls, white on white, making no observable difference so far as the watchers on the hill were concerned. One climbed a ladder and, bending, with a smaller brush painted under the thatch and around an upstairs window, moved the ladder and repeated the operation.

'He got permission to infect seven condemned criminals in Newgate,' Perkins continued. 'With one of them, a young woman, he got some matter out of a ripe smallpox pustule and pushed it up her nose and she had a dreadful fever and headaches and then got over it. With the others he made a small cut here or there on the body and put a thread of cotton dripping with pus into it.'

His friend's reaction of disgust prompted him to hurry on.

'It was all right. Just the same as before, they all had fevers, rather less severe than the girl's, and in a few days, a week, they were out of them and healthy again.'

'And then what happened?'

The figure of a woman appeared from the farmhouse door and stood, hands on hips, surveying the work, pointing from time to time at some omission or blemish.

'There's Bessy keeping an eye on things.' Perkins chuckled, 'She doesn't miss much around the house.'

'Yes, I can see. And then what happened – with Mead and his Newgate birds?'

'Why, they went to the gallows. They were free of the threat of smallpox. Like dogs, might have rolled in it without harm. But they couldn't 'scape the rope.'

George looked doubtful. 'That is not an edifying tale,' he said.

'I understand you, but just think: they had performed a useful service, probably for the first time in their lives, but they hadn't paid their debt to society. Now, Mead said that the best subjects for inoculation are young children, sound in wind and limb, and born of healthy parents. That's what persuaded me to ask Bevan to operate in that way on Kitt. I haven't regretted it – and our Edward's next in a few months' time.'

George reported the conversation to Sarah who, rather to his surprise, was no whit discouraged. 'What will it be?' she said. 'A little scratch and a fever – we will have Bevan's help to deal with that – and then it will be over and our boy will never catch smallpox. I think he will grow up to be grateful to us. Perhaps we could wait another few weeks, when he'll be three, and then have it done.'

On 13th July, Bevan, somewhat less bulky than the rector remembered, and bowed, with flowing white hair and beard, came out from Cowbridge to examine his patient.

'Firstly,' he said, 'we must be sure the young man is in good health. To inoculate a child who is already unwell would be tantamount to a death sentence.

'Has he shown any slightest sign of illness? His nose, his throat? No coughs or sniffs? How about his bowels?'

Young George was standing close to his mother's chair, and the doctor, kneeling on the floor with some difficulty, peered at him through his spectacles. The child stared at the doctor and before Sarah could intervene grasped the white beard and pulled hard.

'Don't fret,' said Bevan, removing the child's hand from the tangle of white hair as Sarah gasped, caught between laughter and concern, 'he's quicker than me, and strong. He appears well enough, that's sure. No negative indications?'

Sarah shook her head. 'None.'

Placing one broad palm on the heavy oak table, the doctor struggled to his feet. 'A lively lad, bright too, I'll wager. If you are ready to go ahead with inoculation, then it shall be done – tomorrow if that suits you.'

The rector looked at his wife for the least sign of doubt. Over the dark head of the child seated on her lap, who, one finger to his lips, still watched the doctor closely, she smiled and nodded.

'Very well, tomorrow let it be,' he said.

Before he left the rectory, Bevan described how he had inoculated the Perkins children and repeated the story the next morning. He would need to make a small incision in the arm or the thigh, no more than the sort of scrape a child gets in tumbling about, on which he would place a small patch of infected lint held in place by a bandage. The boy would soon forget about this dressing and the maid could remove and burn it by the end of the day.

'And what happens next?' Sarah asked.

'Why, nothing – for perhaps two weeks or rather more. Then the fever will begin. You must summon me at the first sign of a change in him so that we can take steps to ameliorate the condition.'

The weather being fine and warm, George wore a sleeveless

dress, which would allow the doctor more easily to operate on his upper arm. The child was content, secure on his mother's lap, his head, gently averted from the doctor's preparations, laid on her bosom. He gave a small cry as the blade nicked his arm and a bead of blood appeared, but he didn't struggle. Tears welled in Sarah's eyes and she held him close as Bevan applied the lint and bound it in place.

'There,' he said, 'all done.'

Sarah was incapable of speech, but her lips moved, 'Thank you.'

'It is a dreadful thing,' she told her husband when they were alone later, 'to expose your own child to pain and injury. I know we believe it is for the best, but I do not think I shall be able to go through such torment again.'

'But George is well: see how he plays, without a care.'

'Go to the church. Pray he remains well. Pray for us all.'

A week passed, a week of fair weather during which haymaking began in fields near the rectory, and doing the rounds of Perkins' fields, George saw how wheat and oats were well advanced towards harvest in another month or six weeks. Under Sarah's watchful gaze, young George and Bloom played and sometimes squabbled together just as before. The maids, who had been warned to be alert to any change in George's appearance or behaviour, returned from walks with the children to say no, they had noticed nothing untoward. He was as lively and curious as ever, into everything, they had to be like hawks with him. Sarah began to think it would turn out well after all. She need not have been so anxious.

On the twelfth day George was listless, and then unhappy, whimpering. The toys and little games he so enjoyed with his mother could not rouse or distract him. A message brought Bevan quickly to the rectory.

'Yes, it's beginning,' he said. 'Feel his brow. He's already a touch feverish. Poor lad, he doesn't know what's going on. He will be aching you see – arms, legs, back, especially his back.'

On the sofa, George lay in his mother's arms, whining. Then he struggled to get up, walked a few unsteady steps and fell, crying pitifully.

'To bed with him,' said Bevan. 'I'll let a little blood to steady his fever, before it gets a grip. Get a towel or some rags for me.'

'Dear God, let me take his pain,' Sarah whispered. 'Let me take his pain ... let me take his pain ...'

She stood in the children's bedroom, her back to the door, wretched, while the doctor found a vein in the smooth, plump thigh and in a moment produced a thin flow of blood some of which he caught in a shallow vessel while more stained bright red the cloths packed about the wound.

In a few minutes more, the bleeding stopped. 'Burn these,' he said, 'and I'll wash this away at the pump.'

He returned to announce that he had done all that could be done for the moment. 'Let him be watched closely. Applying a cold compress to the brow might ease the ache there, in his head. He will not want to get up: you see how his energy has drained away. I'll come tomorrow morning.'

Throughout Bevan's visit the rector had remained in his study, his head bowed over Bible and prayer book. What could he do for the child? Wait and pray. They had been warned this was how it would be, but that did not save them from the terror they felt. He joined Sarah in the bedroom and sought to comfort her, but she was stiff, unyielding, would not be comforted. Not knowing what to do or where to put himself, he felt useless. He left the rectory, walked into the churchyard. Early glimpses of sun had disappeared and cloud was building from the south. Long grasses, green and grey, with feathery heads, lapped against headstones, the ancient yew, a hollow ghost of a tree, spread tortured boughs where straggling tufts of dark foliage alone expressed its will to persist. At length he told himself the child was in God's hands. Whatever physician could do, Bevan would do; whatever tenderness, whatever nursing was needed, Sarah would supply. 'God's will be done,' he said aloud to the hunched stones.

Sarah remained at the cot's side throughout the night, alert to the slightest sound or movement from the child, comforting him through bouts of feverish restlessness and pain. Her outward calm cloaked an agony of emotion. At first light it seemed he fell into an exhausted sleep, or unconsciousness, and still she watched. Bevan came early, through grey drizzle, asked how the night had passed and saw at once the boy's fever remained high. 'I think I might let a little more blood,' he said. And after that, when his patient lay in the cot limp, like a dead thing, 'Has he drunk some water? It won't be easy, but if he can take a spoonful or two of gruel with honey a few times a day, it will help to keep up his strength, and that's important. And you,' he turned to Sarah, saw the dark rings under her eyes, ' – you must rest. Let your husband, or one of the maids, watch for a while, with strict instructions to call you if there is the slightest change in his condition.'

A small bowl was brought and the child stirred and helped to sit up in the cot to be fed, though such was the pain of swallowing, much of the sweet, milky gruel dribbled down his chin. But the doctor was satisfied. 'Keep it up,' he said, ' – a little and often is best. I'll return tomorrow morning and hope to see improvement.'

After Bevan had gone, Sarah abandoned her watch to lie fully clothed on her own bed. Barely ten minutes passed before she was sharply awakened by a cry from the maid who had taken her place. Little George had vomited and was in an agony of retching. Throughout the rest of the day Sarah and one or other of the maids struggled to feed the child, whose strength had so ebbed he could not hold his head up without help, and soon after watched, helpless, as he vomited. Flat red spots had begun to appear on his face and arms. On the third day, Bevan found it hard to hide his concern, but he assured Sarah and the rector that what he and they were doing was the best that could be done. They must be patient and persevere.

On the fourth day, soon after dawn, the sickroom still lit by candles, Sarah was startled by a different sound from the restless child, a choking gasp, and when she held up a candle to look more closely, she saw his eyes were rolling in his head and his limbs jerking spasmodically. As she bent to lift him in her arms, the movements subsided and his body lay inert. She hurried to bring George to the room and with tremulous voice tell him what she had seen.

The boy lay still as though asleep but his eyes were wide. Far from diminishing, his fever was higher than ever.

'Perhaps the crisis will come soon and then he will begin to mend,' George whispered. 'I pray his pain will end soon.'

Sarah looked at her husband with frightened eyes. 'We must help him now. What can we do to cool his little body? Help me strip these bedclothes away, take off his nightshirt. Stir the maids – tell them to bring water, a large bowl of cold water.'

Naked, the child appeared shrunken, his face smaller, the

dark hair matted. Sarah held him tenderly as the maid washed head and face and body with a cold wet cloth, over and over, until the furnace within him began to die down. Returned to the cot, he lay still.

'I think he's sleeping,' the maid said.

'Please God, let it be so!'

When the rector returned the room was calm. It was another day of heavy cloud, but already light enough for the candles to be extinguished and their wisps of smoke to hang visible in the foetid air. 'Quite soon Bevan will be here with us again,' he said. He took Sarah's hand. 'Let us pray together for our son.' And they knelt beside the cot and prayed silently in the stillness of the house.

As they rose to their feet, with a wail and then a strangled cry, under their helpless gaze the tiny, naked body began threshing about, the limbs flailing, the head jerking, for what seemed an eternity before it quietened to waves of shivering and finally lay still, the dark eyes rolling back.

'My God, my God, what have we done?' said Sarah, while her husband moaned and rocked on his feet.

Before Bevan appeared at half-past-eight of the clock, three more convulsions, each more prolonged and terrible than the last, had seized the child. By nine o'clock he was dead.

Sarah was beyond speech, beyond tears. Hour after hour she sat staring blankly at the empty cot, and when lifted and drawn away down the stairs, she remained silent as one turned to stone. George out of his own misery strove to offer solace, but she was deaf to his tender urgings to care for herself as to his prayers for God's help and guidance in their hour of need.

'Why, why?' he said, voicing her agony, and then, 'God's

will be done, Sarah. God's will be done.' But his appeal did not move her. It was only when he bade her think of Bloom, who had been kept away from the sickroom and access to her while young George lay, as they now knew, dying, that she at last stirred herself.

'Bring my baby to me,' she said, and when he was brought and placed in her lap, she held him close, laying her cheek on his fair, coppery head. Sensing the intensity of emotion in her breast, the child lay still in her embrace, while she clung to him as a frail support in the wreckage of her existence. It was only then, when she began once more to consider life beyond herself, that Richard Aubrey swam into her thoughts.

Should she inform him his son had died? No, there would be no need: the dreadful news would have reached him already. Everyone knew Richard was in some sense Sir John's deputy at the Plas and St Illtyd's, the Aubrey family church; little occurred in Llantrithyd without intelligence of it reaching Ash Hall. That Sally, wife of the rector, who had been governess to his children, had lost her eldest due to inoculation would very soon be known. She could not guess how he would react. He had taken pains to ensure the child was brought safely into the world and had no material needs. He would grieve of course, because he was a man of sensibility, and then console himself that he still had Julia Frances and Thomas Digby, legitimate heirs both. Perhaps in time she would write to her former master, to express her sorrow that what she had intended as a safeguard for young George's future had turned out so badly. 'God forgive me: in the pride of my certainty about things beyond my knowledge, I killed him,' she thought, and vowed to dedicate herself to the care of Bloom, the child in her arms, and other children that God in his mercy might give to her and her true husband. She was not then aware that she had conceived in those calm days between the fatal inoculation and the first signs of the fever that destroyed her firstborn.

George wandered aimlessly around house and church, not wanting to be far from Sarah and yet fearing the coldness and the distance from her he had experienced during the days of George's sickness. From the moment she had first given the child into his arms in their room in London, he had taken him as his own. What had been a bargain between them before marriage became an inseparable part of his love for his wife. He grieved in earnest for a child not of his loins, one he had seen grow quick to learn, and handsome, a boy of infinite promise. He thought of his parents and how they sorrowed for their lost children, his younger brothers and sisters, all save Richard, and how his father, whose faith was strong, yet thanked God for all his mercies. He would strive to do the same.

He was strong with John and Bessy Perkins, strong with neighbours and churchgoers, strong too in reaching out to Sarah, so that she knew he would be near when she felt she could turn to him again. But on 2nd August, the day of little George's funeral, he was struck down with he knew not what ailment of body or mind. He could not rise. He turned his head to the pillow and wept. When Sarah, moved by the depth of his sorrow, came to console him, he said, 'I have thought about this day and now it has dawned I know I cannot commit his body to the grave. God forgive me, I cannot.'

An urgent message was sent to Cowbridge, and on a bright, breezy afternoon with high, scudding clouds, the child was laid to rest by the curate of that place, the Reverend William Thomas. From an upstairs window, the rector observed the small crowd gathered in the churchyard, the curate in billowing surplice, Sarah at the head of the grave. In a while they dispersed, leaving two labourers to their work and Sarah to walk alone, slowly, through the tall, waving grasses back towards the rectory. She did not see, nor did the observer of the scene in the upstairs window, a tall, hatless, dark-haired man, standing with bowed head, close behind the broad, hollowed trunk of the ancient yew.

VII

THE HEALING OF hearts after young George's death was slow. Guilt kept the wound fresh, for it was their doing: Sarah, who had seen (and, oddly, admired) Bessy Perkins' pride in having saved her son for the future from the ravages of smallpox, and George, who so implicitly trusted his wife that his unease at exposing the boy to danger was quelled. They would never forget the child's suffering, never forget their complicity in it, but the layering of daily duties, frets and cares became, as it were, a bandage masking their pain, until at length it waned.

Caring for Bloom, who for a short while searched for his brother and then, as infants do, forgot, kept Sarah occupied in the present, and within another month she became certain she was again pregnant. She was glad; life would go on. She had not the slightest regret that she had married this kindly, thoughtful man, who had taken her, when others would have turned away, unconditionally. That he was devoted to her she knew; she would return his devotion.

Although he had divested himself of the cares and physical labour of cultivating the glebe (and was more than happy to collect the rent), the rector had ecclesiastical and parish responsibilities enough to occupy his days. His churchwardens, Morgan David and Evan Meredith, reappointed year after year, preferred to discuss issues in their first language, Welsh.

They were stout and reliable men of the Vale, but in the frail later years of his long life, the Reverend Hopkins, George's predecessor, had been less than punctilious in reminding them of their duties to the parish and, being only human, some they had overlooked. The audited accounts revealed men and boys had been paid bounty on the carcasses of vermin – polecats, pine martens, hedgehogs, magpies – while the collection of the church rates from householders and landowners, on which so much of the work of the church depended, had been less than assiduous and the sums had declined. The grazing of sheep in the churchyard had raised some pence for poor relief but not succeeded in trimming grass around the tombstones. The two bells tolled, faultless after centuries of use, but the ropes had frayed, and tiles had fallen from the slant belfry roof and the roof of the nave. The great family memorials of Mansells and Bassetts, which so attracted the attentions of especially young parishioners, had been worn bare of paint in parts. Communion wine and candles were needed. The church silver had tarnished and many prayer books were badly worn. More worrying than these physical signs of neglect were the empty pews at services. David and Meredith crushed their soft hats between gnarled hands, shuffled their feet on the ancient, worn stones and mumbled apologies. There had been backsliding, they conceded, and they had been remiss in not enquiring after absentees, who might, after all, have been ill and needy. They would do better, they said. They would attend to the collection of rates at once so that the poor could be relieved.

George had continued visiting parishioners with prayer, cheer and help, if it lay within his power, where it was needed. He was invariably well received. The parish needed a younger, active rector, all agreed. But his first attempt at alleviating poverty out of his own pocket had not been entirely successful. Richard Lewis had turned up in the rectory garden regularly enough, and was observed to be working steadily. But the job was taking far more time than anticipated and, when paid, he peered at the coins in his hand, seeming always surly and ungrateful. The rector could not understand this, was quite sure, were their positions reversed, he would labour hard and cheerfully to please his employer.

In the midst of the usual brief observations on the weather and the state of crops, John Perkins noted in his diary, 'Rev. Geo: Williams's boy out of inoculation died'. He also wrote to George and Sarah expressing heartfelt condolences. Although she wanted to embrace and console Sarah, Bessy could not bring herself to visit the rectory. She, too, was afflicted with guilt, because she felt responsible for putting the thought of inoculation into Sarah's head, and for having in Kitt the example of a healthy survivor – and henceforth constant reminder of her lost child. Nevertheless, on the third Sunday following the burial of young George, at his insistence, Bessy went to church with her husband. After the service, the couples met in the porch and while other members of the congregation moved past, averting their eyes, after a moment's hesitation, the couples embraced, and wept on one another's shoulders. Their relationship was renewed from that moment, though it was never quite as free and open as it had been between Sarah and Bessy. Soon it became usual for the maid or Sarah herself, the weather continuing fair, to walk with Bloom as far as Pentra Farm where there would be a welcome and some refreshment before the walk back. Bloom, now an only child and receiving more attention than he had while his brother yet lived, was suddenly sturdy on his feet and talkative. Bessy Perkins, unconsciously redemptive, fussed about and, if she were allowed, spoiled him.

The friendship of the men, which had not reached that level of intimacy characteristic of the female sex, soon slipped into its former social ease. Perkins brought a bundle of newspapers to the rectory so that George could acquaint himself with the way the world had turned during the weeks when their usual arrangements had been suspended. There had been terrible news. Revolutionaries had attacked the Tuileries Palace and arrested the French royal family, but retribution would surely follow, for Austria and Prussia had invaded France.

'We must hope for a swift end to this bloody rising,' said Perkins, thumping the table before him. 'They have had their own way far too long. They need to be taught a lesson, then we shall soon see sense and common decency restored.'

He was clearly moved, and a week or so later elated when the *Times* told them the great French fortress of Verdun had fallen to Prussian troops. The way west into Paris was open. The re-establishment of good order and punishment for malefactors could not be far off. But all they had read together before was as nothing to the reports carried by the latest editions of the newspaper that Richard Aubrey unfolded before them after they had taken tea together at Pentra. They told of atrocities that had occurred during the following week when, out of rage at the Prussian victory, or fear of an enemy within, prisoners held in Paris gaols, including members of the aristocracy and priests, were massacred and, with the most horrible display of triumph over those unable to defend themselves, their bodies mangled and heads paraded on pikes.

'"Bodies are piled up against houses in the streets",' Perkins read aloud, "'and near the prisons, the carcasses lie scattered in hundreds. Every person who had the appearance of a gentleman, whether stranger or not, was run through the body with a pike. A ring, a handsome pair of buckles, a new coat, or a good pair of boots, in a word, every thing which marked the appearance of a gentleman, and which the mob fancied, was sure to cost the owner his life.'"

He looked down at his own plump, well-dressed form, 'By God! We cannot let this lie. We have to fight these animals – worse than animals! – in their lair, or risk their madness infecting these shores. What say you, Mr Aubrey? Williams?'

A deep flush covering his face, he had risen from his chair and was striding to and fro, his fists clenching and unclenching, occasionally smiting the air, as though about to explode. Aubrey, who had read the report earlier, was stern and silent. George, hand to mouth, was shocked and sickened, but he, too, had nothing to say.

Later, before the altar of his church, he prayed for the alleviation of suffering on a foreign shore, to which, not long since, he had given no thought at all. Now, his view of the world enlarged, he felt pressing in upon him concerns far beyond the narrow bounds of his parish. He had barely recovered from the misery of bereavement, but what was his grief compared with that felt by thousands of decent people in France whose loved ones had been taken from them and had lost everything? He felt inadequate: what could he do for them but pray? What might be asked of him, if the madness John Perkins feared did spread, he could not tell. He trusted God would show him when the time came.

Before the end of September they read of the abolition of royalty in France and the proclamation of the First Republic.

Paris was controlled by the mob. In December, Louis XVI came to trial before a body that called itself the National Convention, accused of treason against his own country and people. He was found guilty, and on 21st January he climbed the scaffold, where the thunder of drums drowned his last words before he bowed his neck to the guillotine. The *Times* reported he had died with manly fortitude and resignation, and demanded action to preserve the Constitution.

'Amen to that,' cried John Perkins, florid and brandishing his fists. 'At last others are beginning to feel as I do – that we must fight to preserve our way of life.'

Richard Aubrey declared it a dreadful catastrophe, adding that every royal family in Europe was now under threat. But folk in the Vale knew only that it had been a miserable winter. Having more pressing concerns in the daily struggle to stay alive, few paid much attention to news that reached their ears slowly, as a distorted babble from a great distance. At St Illtyd's, the rector led his congregation, wrapped as well as they could be against the cold and wet, in prayers for the late king's soul, though his attention was not undivided.

He, too, had other things on his mind – duties to church and parish never previously required of him. The care of the poor and sick he had always discharged as well as he was able, but now he must ensure there were supervisors to see that the Poor Laws were properly applied, and collect Poor Rate Tax from those who could afford it. He must have an eye for the condition of parish roads and ensure two Surveyors of the Highways were appointed and any necessary work carried out – and there always was work to be done in and around the church. Steady drips on the paved floor reminded him of the urgent need for maintenance of the roof. The rain, which seemed incessant, had penetrated in three places, one in the chancel, where the repair would be at his expense. Above all, he must care for wife and child – a change he had not thought of, hardly dared contemplate when, not long since, he had been curate of Ystradowen. That was responsibility he rejoiced in, although, as he had learned, it could bring pain that pierced through and through as well as joy.

In France, on 1st February 1793, the National Convention declared war on Britain. There was no longer need for rallying calls from the *Times*. With the next bundle of newspapers, Richard Aubrey had received a rare letter from his brother, saying Pitt and his government could no longer wait and hope for a successful counter revolution in France. They must surrender to the enemy, or go to war, again, notwithstanding the recent American fiasco, regardless of cost. And the cost would be great, for both army and navy were hugely outnumbered and not fit for action. What if France moved to invade at once? What could be done?

'As before in times of war,' Richard said when they met at Ash Hall, 'the answer will be to embody the militias county by county. Sir John thinks I should have a role here in Glamorgan, and it may be that our sharing the *Times* will have to end – for which I shall be truly sorry, for I have enjoyed our meetings. In any event, for the time being it is the Lord Lieutenant's duty to submit an annual return of men aged eighteen to forty-five from among whom a regiment will be raised by ballot. Those chosen will serve for five years, and be uniformed, armed – and paid, of course – at the government's expense.'

'Splendid, splendid,' said Perkins, rubbing his hands vigorously. 'Everyone must do his share. Now we'll see what the French are made of. Not very much, I suspect.'

Mr Aubrey looked at him, seemed about to say something, then shook his head. He had private concerns: Aunt Margaret had been struck down in the midst of her usual gallop through life. Bustling upstairs to prepare to meet guests, she had suddenly fallen to her knees and, if it had not been for the maid accompanying her, might well have tumbled down into the hall, which would probably have killed her outright. As it was, she was little more than half alive, a dreadful paralysis having seized her down the left side and robbed her of speech. Richard hastened to visit and found her held half-sitting in bed by heaped pillows, but incapable of movement. She gave no sign of having recognised or even seen him, her one eye drooping, her mouth sagging to the left. He held her hand for a time as her maids sobbed quietly. A woman of spirit, she had led a bold, full life, untrammelled by husband and children, deferring to no one, though everyone in the Vale deferred to her. As major leaseholder of the Aubrey lands, she wielded power and pleased herself. Behind her back, some said she might as well have worn breeches, but her taste in clothes was feminine, from time to time extravagantly so. Usually merry and brisk, but never to be trifled with, she was accustomed to having her way. It was not strange that Thomas Edmondes, in his castle, had accepted her recommendation that the Llantrithyd living should pass to an inexperienced curate of whom he knew nothing.

Richard anticipated the Vale estate would revert to his brother, as it did on her death in the second week of February, but Sir John could not spare the time to attend her funeral. Many others, high and low, the grieving and the curious, were present, filling the little church and standing among the graveyard stones as the rector conducted the funeral service.

The Reverend Williams, conscious of Lady Margaret's long life over almost eight decades of a turbulent century, and more deeply affected by his knowledge that it was to her he owed his presence on this sad occasion, wept openly at the interment.

Having drawn closer to Richard Aubrey, sharing the *Times*, hunting with him from time to time (though often enough returning from a long walk without having raised their muskets), George had formed an entirely different impression of him. He was a gentleman, and of a wealthy family, but not self-important, of superior intellect, but thoughtful and kindly, and patient with the views of others. Always a good sign, his servants were prompt, careful, and cheerful. He inspired loyalty. Sarah had been very fond of Julia Frances and Thomas Digby, his children, and he could understand why.

It was feelings such as this that led George to ponder his exemption as a clergyman from the militia list.

'I don't see why you shouldn't join,' said Perkins. 'I'm sure there's a place for all the able-bodied, regardless of employment or calling.'

'But should I consider it my primary duty to be here with my flock or, in these days when danger threatens every parish, to serve alongside those who are listed to leave home and family, or have indeed volunteered, to defend us? Will you leave Bessy and the children – if you are among the chosen?'

In April the following year, Lieutenant-Colonel Richard Aubrey became commandant of the Glamorgan Regiment of Militia. John Perkins had been among the drawn men but found himself a substitute among casual labourers on his farm and bought himself out. After much heart-searching and extended discussions with Sarah and his churchwardens, the

Reverend George Williams offered his services as chaplain to the regiment.

He had long been conscious of his initial debt to his father, who had nominated him to serve as curate. At that time it promised little beyond the addition of work in church and parish to labour in the fields of Maendy Uchaf and the Penlline glebe. He had bowed to his father's wishes and, once installed, had done what he could. He had not sought or even hoped for preferment, but it had come, suddenly, soon after the most wonderful change that had linked his life with Sarah's. As rector of Llantrithyd, he was now in a position to extend to his brother Richard the same advantage that his father had given him. With God's will and guiding hand, he too would prosper.

Richard visited the rectory from time to time. He looked around at the spacious home with a mixture of surprise, pleasure, and a little envy. It was already well-appointed and paintings of rural scenes in gilded frames decked the walls. One, in an autumnal setting, had a hunter, musket at the ready, and his two dogs, with humble cottages in the background; another two depicted dilapidated cottages and ragged peasants labouring in fields or under burdens. It was as though the artist (he peered more closely – 'G. Morland') was inviting us to consider the reality of rural existence: the warmly clad man of leisure with his gun and pointers did not connect with the lowly dwellings and bent and weary figures of those who travailed.

Sarah considered the thick-set, darkly-bearded young man. He was oddly unlike George, who was lean, fair and clean-shaven. It was, she mused, rather like the contrast in appearance between young Bloom and their poor dead child. Bloom now had another brother, born in March 1793, who had again been baptised George, with fervent prayers that for his and his parents' sake he would be spared the fate of a life cut off in infancy. He thrived in the long, hot summer of his birth year, and became a lively, adventurous one, quickly on his feet and reaching out with his arms to follow Bloom in whatever he was doing, which occasionally led to quarrels. He wailed if left behind when Bloom was taken for a walk and Sarah soon concluded it was better if the maids waited until George was napping before setting forth, or else both children went together. Richard was fond of the boys and vowed to protect and help them while he had health and strength. Bloom ran to him when he visited because his uncle would often walk him around the garden, or take him on his knee and tell him a story, usually about some creature of the woods or fields. The tale of the magpie that would follow him about and pluck hair from his head to make a nest was a favourite.

Richard was surprised when his brother, lately returned from church, still clad in cassock and bands, beckoned him into his study, murmuring, 'Would you be a curate?'

Richard, not sure he had heard, looked at George.

'Would you be a curate? I can offer you forty pounds a year, which is more than our father was able to afford me from his meagre stipend. But money is not the prime consideration. You know well serving God and His people means sacrifice with no promise of reward. If you are prepared to accept the life, I shall be pleased to nominate you curate here, to take my place when I am absent. What think you of that?'

'How absent? You would not abandon Sarah and the children.'

'No, of course not. It seemed right and proper that I should offer myself as chaplain to the militia, now mustering under the command of Mr Richard Aubrey, who as you know has been a good friend to us. His family has lifted me up, caused me to be inducted into this living. I owe him much. There is another reason. I have learned a little about the bloody turmoil in France and fear an invasion of these islands will tip us all into the abyss. Clergy are exempt from the militia list (and this would apply to you if you are content to be nominated), so as a man of the cloth I cannot fight – but I can stand among the ranks and pray with and for those who will defend us. That the list for Llantrithyd will be displayed on the doors of my church only increases my sense of obligation. I do not know how often I shall be called upon and how much time I shall spend away, but I shall rest easier if, in my absence, you have the cure of my parish and are close at hand should ever need arise within this house and family.'

Richard looked keenly at his brother. 'If I were married, I do not think I would be capable of leaving wife and children, as you now propose, without being commanded to do so,' he said. 'But it will be no hardship for me to help here in this house when help is needed, and I shall strive to serve the parish as you would wish. I thank you warmly, dear brother, for the nomination. You will need to help me equip myself for the task ahead.'

'Gladly,' said George, rising and embracing him. He was relieved: the decision had been made and the first step taken in securing home and parish against the possibility, or likelihood, of his absence, whenever it occurred.

The rector had been gripped by a sense of urgency and did not realise how long it would take for the bishop to respond to nomination of his brother. When at last a reply came, it was not what he had hoped for. The chancellor at Llandaff (for it was he who wrote at the bishop's direction) declared that Richard would be appointed deacon in the first instance and, all being well, occupy a curacy at Llantrithyd in due course. George would need to be patient, a second letter said to his reiteration of the request accompanied by a full account of the reasons that had led to it. There was no more to be done. Besides, the mustering of the Glamorgan Militia was proving, in Mr Aubrey's words, 'a devilish slow business': he would carry on with the affairs of the parish, with Richard by his side assisting and preparing for the future.

The summer and autumn of 1794 was a blessed time for George and Sarah. They were prosperous and comfortably settled, and they and their children were in good health. In John Perkins and Bessy, they had friends who gave them pleasant companionship. They met almost daily when the weather was fair, walking the children, taking tea together at Pentra or in the rectory. Bessy seemed to Sarah an admirably simple soul, incapable of deceit, and she enjoyed the older woman's company, because she was a busy, bustling woman. Home and family life – husband, servants, children – swirled about her. And she was a teller of tales, a merry gossip, so that conversation with her often broke up in laughter. John bustled too and, from time to time, he and Bessy ran athwart one another, like two small, sturdy vessels under full sail steering for the same narrow channel. The collision, when it came, resulted in some noise but no rancour. In a minute or two they found their usual good spirits and embraced with fond smiles. Without ever mentioning them, George recognised his friend's faults. He was self-important, bumptious, rather fiery, though only in words, not deeds. But he had, too, a lively, curious mind, was generally affable, and, George could not help remarking, was proud of his wife and family. There was something child-like about him. He enjoyed playing games with his two little boys, and with Bloom, who was often in their company. It was Perkins who took Bloom, on his third birthday, out hunting hares – though they never saw one – while a special tea to mark the occasion was being prepared. Bessy, George and Sarah gathered in the garden at Pentra to wave them off, rotund John, with game pouch and long musket and little Bloom trotting by his side, carrying a smooth, peeled stick over his shoulder, like a marching soldier. They laughed together at the sight, and Sarah wiped a tear from her eye.

When the men went coursing, the rector, Perkins and Mr Aubrey, as morning mist was rising and the sun still lay low on the horizon southwards, they met with more success. Aubrey's brace of greyhounds unfolded their long legs and jumped down from the dog cart to flush and chase the hares. It was a brave sight: greyhounds at full speed, eyes fixed on the nimble prey, twisting now this way, now that as the hare dodged and veered, and the spray rising from their racing paws silver in the sun. Occasionally, as Aubrey waited still to receive his orders, there were whole days of companionship, and they often dined together, taking turns as host at Ash Hall, Pentra or the rectory, until the last week of October suddenly turned cold. A bitter wind from the east killed at once the few remaining ornamental blossoms betrayed by a fine, warm autumn, and scourged the last leaves from the trees.

So began the worst winter in decades. Fierce westerly gales drove inland from the stormy coasts. Ships were wrecked at sea and trees, uprooted, smashed the roofs of cottages and blocked roads. Almost without pause, the wind shifted, howling now from the north. Only the desperately needy ventured outdoors.

In a lull, dreadful frosts descended, so deep and lasting that apples hoarded under cover in lofts were spoiled frozen. Heavy snowfalls prevented movement in December, again in February, and again in March. Food was scarce because much of a good harvest had been bought to feed the military. The families of farm labourers starved.

VIII

RICHARD AUBREY, COMMANDANT of the Glamorgan Militia, mounted on a fine bay gelding, cantered into the parade ground of Maindy Barracks on the outskirts of Cardiff, past half-a-dozen carriages in a line close to the heavy entrance gates. Straight-backed, elegant, in the uniform and insignia of Lieutenant-Colonel and tricorn hat, he pulled the horse up smartly, kicked his feet from the stirrups, leapt lightly from the saddle and handed the reins to a stableman who came running up, saluting. A ripple of applause arose from the small crowd gathered near the carriages, well-dressed men with their wives and daughters, several holding parasols, for it was a sunny, warm day in mid-May. It was as though after a terrible winter and uncertain spring, the curtain of desolation had been fully drawn aside to reveal trees and hedges green and floral ready for the next act. The spectators had come to watch the purple-uniformed militia at drill and musket practice. It was a splendid sight, flags flying, drummer-boys drumming and the fife band playing, columns of men marching and counter-marching, wheeling and stamping together at the turn, the steady beat of their feet, commands ringing out and, at regular intervals, from butts in the distance, a cloud of dark smoke rising, quickly followed by the echoing bang of a platoon's muskets firing together.

Aubrey swept off his hat to acknowledge the clapping and

hastened to the task of inspecting his men. He was admired by the citizenry and as popular among the newly-mustered ranks of the militia as any commander is likely to be. Uniformed, he cut a fine figure, and he set an example in his energy and attention to detail, whether with his men in drills and on manoeuvres, or at his desk attending to their proper equipping and provisioning. He was respected as a firm and fair leader and very few were foolhardy enough to risk his wrath, which could be terrible, by laziness or insubordination. He selected officers and non-commissioned officers with great care and relied upon them to maintain the standards he had set. At first he had been exasperated by delays through the long, harsh winter in bringing together men from all parts of Glamorgan and ensuring they understood what was expected of them. More than half the six hundred eventually assembled had little knowledge of the English language, and few of those who did were familiar with the instructions and commands in military usage. To overcome these difficulties he did not spare his officers, and the sergeants and corporals beneath them did not spare the men. The drilling was intensive and fatiguing, every action repeated a dozen, a score, a hundred times, until they could have been performed in pitch darkness, or the dense smoke of a battlefield, faultlessly. Yes, there had been delays but, Aubrey told himself, more time given to preparation now would benefit the cohesion and effectiveness of the corps later. And so it proved.

Although, because of the delays, the Reverend George Williams had time enough to reconsider his intentions regarding the chaplaincy of the militia, he remained true to his word. Once winter relaxed its grip and the ways were clear, he had arranged with Colonel Aubrey that he would ride over to

Cardiff every third Sunday and conduct a simple service in the drill hall.

On the first of these occasions the great open space, lit by a range of tall windows down one long side, was fitted with a dais upon which a simple lectern was installed. Watching the hall filling with uniformed men led in platoon after platoon by their officers, aware of all those faces assembling before him rank by rank, George, accustomed to the echoing intimacy of small village churches, felt overwhelmed. Do priests of St James's in Piccadilly feel like this, he wondered? Is this what an actor feels – at that great theatre in London, where he had seen – What was it? – such a spectacle. What does an actor do, gazing out over his audience? Why, he acts. He is no longer himself, he enters another and it is the other that speaks. As the thought came, he raised his voice and spread his arms in greeting and invocation, a gesture he had never made before and, as one, all the bare heads before him bowed. Prayers for God's strength to hold them firm against a cruel foe, prayers for their safety and the safety of country, family and friends, prayers for king and royal family: after each the Amen rumbled through the building. A bubble of excitement rose in his breast. When it was over, he felt both elated and fatigued. For that short time he had been transported out of himself – with God's help, he had no doubt. He had assumed the role of chaplain.

Early in 1796, because large numbers of men, fit and well-trained after several months in the militia, were leaving to enrol in regiments of the line, a supplementary militia list was pinned to the church door at Llantrithyd. Such was his fate that John Perkins was drawn again. After a search in the neighbourhood, he found another substitute and paid ten pounds to the Lord Lieutenant of the County of Glamorgan to obtain his release. He was, he said, a man of property and exceedingly busy providing valuable crops to feed the military and the population at large. Much as he would like to serve in the militia, he could not, in all conscience, be spared.

The Reverend Williams's contact with the militia remained intermittent while the regiment was based in Cardiff and was then broken at their first deployment to the outskirts of Bristol, where they were engaged in manoeuvres with elements of the West Country militias. He found himself torn between loyalty to a peripatetic military parish at a time when Britain was threatened with invasion, and holding fast to the one sure thing in his life, his wife and growing family. Sarah's fifth child, another boy, baptised Philip, had been born in December. She had been free of troubles while carrying him and the birth was uncomplicated. To ease her burdens as mother and housekeeper, a third maidservant, and, because Julia Frances, their much-loved daughter was but fifteen months old, for a time, a wet nurse, were employed. Although George told no one of his agony of uncertainty, Colonel Aubrey, who seemed to sense his torment, assured him that militia commanders were expected to call on local parsons wherever they were encamped to perform the duties of chaplain, if one had not been appointed to the regiment, or if the appointed chaplain were not immediately available.

'And that,' he said, 'is what we will do until we have a settled posting and headquarters, when we shall inform you.'

They were out partridge shooting on Ash Hall land, he and George, with Perkins, somewhat out of breath, trailing behind. They had emerged from a copse and were climbing a steep meadow along the diagonal of an old sheep track, Aubrey's two white and tan pointers bounding along beside them or snuffling the grass. It was mid-September, the sky grey with thin, high cloud. The field faced south towards the glinting, gunmetal sea and the farther Somerset shore, where Aubrey's regiment resided under canvas. It was, for him, the last of five days' leave of absence to attend to family business, which had doubled since Aunt Margaret's death. The day was warm enough for the rector to be well aware of the encumbrance of musket and ammunition pouch, but his tall companion, after months of physical activity in all weathers, strode forward effortlessly. He had been talking about the changes that had occurred in France, of the emergence within the previous year of a new military leader, Napoleon Bonaparte, who was either blessed with good luck or remarkably gifted. He had led the French army into Italy and defeated the Austrians in the north of that country. There was no immediate threat to Britain from overseas, but feeding the large number of men now under arms was causing strife, particularly in the cities of England.

'If you have corn to sell,' he said, turning to the figure behind, 'you will sell it at the best price. Is that not so, Perkins?'

'Why, yes, indeed.'

'So you sell to the army?'

'Ah – yes, yes.'

'Well, I can tell you rations for the militia are by no means plentiful, and it means the price of flour in places like Bristol – many of the big cities in England – is so high that bakers have stopped working and, even if you have the money, you cannot buy bread. There have been riots in Manchester and Sheffield, and we have seen the militias deployed not against the French, but against our own people.'

Perkins shook his head. 'Troubled times, troubled times,' he said. 'Even in the Vale we have been plagued by vagrants. You see them out along the turnpike, in the lanes and the woods, ragged men and women, sometimes whole families trailing along. It's a surprise we haven't come across any today.'

'They are hardly to be blamed for being destitute,' said George. 'They come looking for succour, but we have our own parish poor to relieve and have not the means to give to others.'

'I have told Joseph, my gamekeeper, to put some coins into the hands of our poorest by offering threepence for every partridge nest they can spot in field or hedgerow, which explains why we are heading in this direction. Thank God, it appears we shall have a good harvest; perhaps the worst is over. Look there, Jess is pointing, and that rascally son of hers seems to be getting the idea. At least he's quiet.'

The bitch was stock-still, head raised, tail extended, eyes fixed on a low bush fifteen yards off, and the dog beside her also still, but twitching with impatience.

'Ready? George, your shot.'

The low voice was enough. A pair of plump birds burst from the bush, ascending steeply, wings a grey blur. Without thought, almost without aim, the rector brought his musket to his shoulder and squeezed the trigger. He did not see what happened next as the kick of the explosion spun him off-balance on the sloping ground. Ears ringing, he recovered his position in time to see the dogs snatching up two bundles of feathers.

'Bravo! Good shot!' said Aubrey.

'Well done, George,' said Perkins, clapping him on the shoulder. 'Can we sup with you tonight? There's nothing like a few hours' rough shooting to give a fellow an appetite.'

They dined at Ash Hall. The master's study had been prepared, fire and candles lit, because the evening was cool and the light was fading even as they arrived. The partridges were declared fine eating and George was toasted as a marksman – an accolade he protested he did not merit: 'Fortune, pure and simple.' The wine was savoured.

Perkins rose to pledge friendship. His face had acquired a roseate hue from good food and drink and the warmth of the room. 'Our companionship has placed us among the most fortunate of men in these harsh times,' he said, 'and if, as seems likely, we must henceforth meet less frequently to share a newspaper or tramp the fields together with dog and musket, let us not forget this day.' And tears welled in his eyes.

'Come, come,' said Aubrey, 'we will not forget. I'll wager George will not forget two birds with one shot. Eh, George? Another glass of wine? Then I'll see the carriage is brought round to take you safely home.'

As they were about to part, he drew the rector to one side. 'A quick word, George. I must express the gratitude of the regiment for your volunteering to become our chaplain, but I have been thinking further on the subject. I appreciate the sacrifice involved.'

'No more than your own.'

'Ah, that's the point George. Yours is far larger. I do not have a wife at home. I have the children, very precious to me, but with the help of the family I have made acceptable dispositions for them. I shall miss them, and rather hope they will miss me a little. But it's different, you see. You have parish responsibilities here and, above all, you have wife and children, still young children. In all honesty, I would not leave Sally, your precious Sarah, if I were in your shoes. You see our friend, for all his belligerence, will not quit his farm to defend the realm. Please do not protest. What I have said is not merely to caution you, but to tell you I will not have you permanently attached to the regiment. I will not add you to the strength – I will not pay you the customary six shillings a day or whatever it is. The title you can have, if you will take it on those conditions, and there may be times and places when you can join us, and I will let you know, but that must suffice. The parish and its church have long been dear to my family. You were appointed to serve them, and serve them you shall.'

Perkins had struggled into his greatcoat and the carriage was at the door. With firm handshakes and mutual wishes for good fortune and the bounty of God's blessing, they parted.

IX

EARLY IN MAY, the Glamorgan Militia marched east from Wells in Somerset to Kent, all their baggage and equipment trailing behind. They tramped across Salisbury Plain and on through Basingstoke and Aldershot, Reigate and Sevenoaks, to Canterbury, over two hundred miles, in mercifully cool weather. It took them twenty-four days.

'Do you know the French army marches at twice our speed?' Colonel Aubrey was addressing a gathering of his company commanders. 'Of course, we could travel more quickly if we were not obliged to linger while our baggage trundles up. I am reliably informed the French infantry live off the land. I doubt the good people of Canterbury and the other towns and villages we have passed through, would be as welcoming if they knew we would be demanding the contents of their larders and the comfort of their beds. But then, the French are moving, and moving damned quickly to the attack, while we are preparing to defend. We are to remain here or hereabouts for two months, perhaps more. I will have all done orderly while we are under canvas: tent lines to be straight, routes about the camp clearly marked, all stores well protected, latrines properly dug and maintained. You know all this. I demand the highest standards. Fate has placed us in fields that belong to two inns. Their doors will be open for the men and the temptation will be great. Let me be clear: I will not tolerate drunkenness and rowdy behaviour. Any man disgracing the uniform can expect, as a minimum, fifty lashes. Make sure they know and understand this. Stealing from farmyards and village shops, at least a hundred lashes. Fighting with villagers or members of other militia regiments camped nearby, similarly. You have been through this before in the West Country and, thanks to your vigilance, we came away with an untarnished reputation. See to it there is no backsliding. Ah, yes – I almost forgot – and the married women in camp are not to be pestered. They have their work to do, cooking or laundering, and must be left in peace to get on with it. It's all in fun, the miscreants may say, but we have seen how much trouble it can cause. At the merest hint, you must be sure to put a stop to it at once.'

His first task had been to respond to an urgent request from the Marquis of Bute, the Lord Lieutenant, to send a small party of experienced men and drummers back at once to Glamorgan to beat up enthusiasm for joining a line regiment, the 44th Foot, and, that done, to supervise the training of a fresh batch of militia at Maindy Barracks. Having newly arrived at the defensive stronghold in the south-east of England, where, if invasion came, the French would almost certainly land, no one present volunteered to make the journey back. In the end Aubrey made the selection himself: two captains, four subalterns, two sergeants and six corporals, men he could ill afford to lose, and with them, as required, four drummer-boys, to thunder the call to war at town squares and market places all over the county, wherever a crowd might gather. They were to engage men and urge them to join the fight, offering a bounty of seven guineas for service 'to the end of the war plus six months'. The more that joined the quicker it would be over, was their message. In six weeks, their duty done, they returned with a ninety-eight new militiamen, the beneficiaries of twenty days' intensive activity on parade ground and shooting range, followed by a long, quick march to Canterbury. With them came the regimental chaplain.

The Reverend George Williams arrived on a sturdy cob that carried him and his baggage at an easy amble. He had spent his days on the road moving up and down the column, sometimes on foot leading his mount, exchanging a breathless word or two with the marching men. At rests he had circulated among groups, talking to them about homes and families left behind and the noble cause that had demanded this sacrifice, to defend the land from the cruelty of a rapacious foe. And, with the utmost sincerity, he gave them the assurance of God's protection. Often, at these times, he found himself in the company of men for whom he was obliged to employ his limited command of the Welsh tongue, relying upon them to help him when he stumbled.

At camp headquarters he was greeted formally by the Colonel Commander, and, soon afterwards, privately embraced as a friend by Richard Aubrey, who said, 'You will not remain with us long. That is not a question, it is an order.'

'I wish to fulfil my obligations to the regiment and, I do not hesitate to add, in these turbulent times, to God. I have left Llantrithyd, church and parish, in the capable hands of my brother, Richard, who has recently been inducted as curate.'

'Since we have been here, companies have taken turns to be marched in good order to attended services at the great cathedral. You might accompany the next parade. It is an ancient church of great beauty. I was struck deeply by its history and atmosphere, and I am sure you will be equally impressed. You have joined us just in time, for we are about to be deprived of that experience. In the next week we are to strike camp here and march to the fortress at Dover, where we shall be part of the first line of defence against any attack from across the Channel. I have been told no further moves are in the offing, and that we shall be worked hard there, though in what capacity was not made clear. In any event, there is a drill hall at which you can lead the regiment in prayer, while we find our bearings and establish connection with some local church and pastor.'

'But surely now is the time when I could truly begin to be of service to the regiment.'

Aubrey was thoughtful for a moment. 'I think not,' he said. 'I fully understand you have been careful to appoint your brother, who, I have no doubt, is a worthy man, as curate to fill your place at Llantrithyd. Nevertheless, you will not join us indefinitely. Now tell me your news. How does your family fare? What intelligence from the Vale?'

The movement of the regiment and its equipment from Canterbury to Dover, no more than twenty miles along a road used for centuries by marching men, was accomplished in two days without untoward incident. They reached their destination in a long summer evening, the light beginning to fade. Before them lay enormous castle walls, with many tall towers and, deep within, the upper floors of a great keep where a few early lights revealed the presence of windows. Beyond, the darkening sea stretched to the horizon and France, while below, a town lay gathered around a harbour and, beneath a headland to the west, pale cliffs glimmered. Few of those halted and at ease gazing at the fortress could not call to mind mostly ruinous ancient castles close to their homes, but the scale of this structure and the many evidences of activity within its walls filled them with wonder.

'You have come twenty miles,' called an officer of the garrison, 'and,' pointing towards the farther horizon, 'if that was a land road out there instead of a sea road, in another two days you could all be in France. But you be thankful for this stretch of water. If it wasn't wet and deep, Napoleon's army would be here tomorrow morning. Look sharp, you have huts to sleep in tonight, if you can stir yourselves to unload the baggage before nightfall.'

'Confounded impudence.' The militia's company commanders had been awaiting the Colonel's orders and resented this interference, but the men, obedient and eager to be settled, were already moving to familiar tasks and making their way towards the darkened huts.

Richard Aubrey had ridden forward some time before to meet the commanding officer of the castle. Colonel William Twiss, clad in the liberally gold-braided red coat with black facings that identified him as an engineer, greeted him with the mumbled utterance and fleeting smile of a man with much on his mind. He was seated at a long table bearing plans and charts illuminated by lamps and candles and, in the silence that followed, Richard noted his bushy eyebrows, eyes that sloped downwards away from the sharp keel of a prominent nose, and a similarly downturned, short mouth. 'You are Mr Aubrey,' he said, extending a hand across the table, without rising and with no more than a glance at his visitor. 'Please excuse me, there is much to be done before the invasion, which seems inevitable. I am told Napoleon has assembled well over a hundred thousand men just across the Channel. What he's waiting for I cannot say, but I am glad of it. Every day's grace allows us to be a little better prepared. And that's where you and your men come in.'

For the first time he looked up. 'I'll wager a fair percentage of your regiment have experience of mining.'

'I don't know. We don't enquire about such things. I suppose it's likely.'

'I'll come to the point. I need miners who know how to blast rock safely and strategically, and who are familiar with the use of pick and shovel below ground, to dig tunnels in the chalk beneath the castle, because that is the only way we shall be able to accommodate, within the safety of the walls, the numbers of men we need to repel an invasion force of the size we expect.'

'My regiment has been trained to bear arms and fight. They have not marched across England to dig tunnels.'

'Nevertheless, that is what they will be required to do – first and foremost. They will have fighting enough when Napoleon makes up his mind. If we are lucky he will give us a chance to build barracks in the chalk to house another two thousand men.' And gesturing towards a map spread before him, 'The plans are ready. With those extra men, and artillery mounted here, here and here, covering what will almost certainly be his invasion route, we'll give him a battle.'

'I see,' said Aubrey.

'Yes. You would do well to speak to your company commanders. I need the experienced miners, who know what they are about, to lead teams of diggers. You can draw up the teams. Everyone is to do his share. Tell them, they will in all probability be digging for their lives and for the preservation of the kingdom. And this must start tomorrow morning.'

Aubrey returned crestfallen to his quarters. This was not what he expected, but he had imbibed a sense of urgency from Colonel Twiss, and respected his judgement. He drafted orders accordingly and had them delivered at once. In the morning, the regiment was informed what lay before them, and the selected men assembled. By ten o'clock the first teams were equipped and stood with picks, mandrels and shovels at the site where the tunnel would be driven, initially a long incline fifty feet into the chalk, fifty feet down below the level of the cliff top on which the great castle had been built in the time of Henry II.

As Aubrey anticipated, it went badly with the men, who had been entertained by the party returned from Wales with stories of how, back in February, local Pembrokeshire volunteers and militia had rallied swiftly and put on such a strong show of readiness to resist that a well-armed French invasion force of some twelve hundred men landed near Fishguard had surrendered with hardly a shot fired. It was a good story, especially the part where the French mistook women in tall black hats and red shawls for soldiers, and one woman captured a dozen French troops. It was said the militia would be honoured.

'We might have been there,' they grumbled, 'instead of digging holes in this place.'

'No honours for moles.'

The regimental chaplain volunteered to speak to the men, even to take up a pick and work beside them, but was told it was neither necessary nor desirable. Militia must be ready for any task.

Aubrey asked, 'Have you seen the church within the castle walls? You might look around it. See if it's possible to gather the men there on Sunday.'

He had been abroad early with Colonel Twiss, who took him to the roof of the castellated keep to view the position his men would defend when the attack came. As they mounted the final flight of stairs, Twiss had said, 'I shall have arches built below here to reinforce the ceiling, and that will allow me to place heavy cannon on the roof.' At that hour, on a dull day, though the sound of breaking waves, hush … hush, carried inland, the sea was hidden in grey mist; but the defences stretching out to the cliff top, circuit after circuit, culminating in the great curtain wall, were clearly visible. In his survey of the scene, Twiss had pointed out nearby St Mary's de Castro, the church by the castle, and close to its east wall the taller tower of a Roman lighthouse, where in ancient times beacons were lit to guide ships to the harbour. Napoleon would not need such guidance: with a good glass, in reasonable weather, he could see castle and harbour from the coast of France.

'Our navy will ensure the French are denied an easy passage,' Twiss had said. 'And with our numbers enlarged, thanks in part to the efforts of your men, we shall have a force to match any that come ashore.'

Impressed by the commandant's confidence, Aubrey returned to his captains in higher spirits than he had left, for the colonel of engineers had laid his plans well, and even if his Glamorgan men were disgruntled by their part in them, they would certainly make an important contribution.

On that first day, the former coal miners appeared at the end of a shift with clothes, hands and faces mired grey. 'Well, there's a change anyway,' they said, grinning. The labour was not as hard, nor as dangerous, as mining for coal, but each day still left them dry and drained. Through the weeks that followed, company after company, shift after shift, the tunnel expanded. And that was only the first. Seven tunnels were planned, each twice as high as the tallest soldier, shako and all, and broad enough to provide floor space for rows of beds and storage and, in the expected emergency, ease of passage for a column of men fully armed and accoutred.

The chaplain returned downcast from his inspection of the church. 'It's beyond use,' he said, 'an empty shell. And even if the roof were sound, it's too small to hold more than a couple of dozen men. And because of the crowding of all accommodation here within the castle, there is no room anywhere to hold a service. I shall have to think of another way of reminding them they serve king and country under God's will and protection.'

Aubrey, feeling the burden of a hundred and one concerns and not inclined to be sympathetic, told George not to worry himself about it, by which he meant not to worry him.

The next day, the chaplain appeared at a meeting of company commanders with a plea. It was high summer and the large tent was filled to capacity. A feeble breeze through the open door did little to ameliorate the sticky heat within. The officers were glad their conference was ending and were beginning to gather hats and papers when the chaplain raised his voice.

'The men are all day long engaged in burrowing like badgers and return to the surface exhausted,' he began. 'It is precious work they do as we face the prospect of invasion, but they are not able to come to me – so I have been thinking how I might take the Christian message to them. We know now the French have turned from God and defiled churches – it is hideous to contemplate – and having completed the long journey here, I cannot stand idly by and see His word neglected among our soldiery. Will you allow me a few minutes of prayer with them at their work? Surely they must rest some time during their labours, if only to take a little food and water and regather their strength. I swear I shall not delay them one moment longer from their task.'

The colonel looked wearily around at his officers. Some shook their heads, others shrugged. They had nothing to say. 'I suppose we can allow the attempt,' he said. 'My own feeling is that the men would prefer to be left in peace for the few minutes they have to take breath and refresh themselves a little. You could find,' he addressed George directly, 'you *could* find you have a revolt on your hands. If that does happen, I will not be able to blame or punish them. You will simply have to give it up. I don't doubt most of them, probably all, pray privately and decently.'

'"Where two or three are gathered together …"'

'Yes, yes, have it your way, but only if, or for as long as the men are prepared to accept your subterranean ministry. Make your arrangements with the officers in charge.'

The chaplain broached the first tunnel through a partially built casement, which would be the entrance and guardroom, where mortar was being prepared for another course of bricks, and descended the shallow incline. He was accompanied by one of the older militiamen, who, despite a splinted broken forearm, was carrying and tugging an empty, brass-bound, wooden ammunition box as best he could. The way was badly lit by lamps alternately left and right at twenty-feet intervals, the tunnel walls between them barely visible, the high roof not at all, but two hundred yards ahead there was the glow of many lamps and candles and the sounds of iron striking rock, shovels scraping, occasional shouts and the voices of many men, a constant hubbub, faintly echoing, rising and falling. As he drew closer to this activity, a louder cry, taken up and passed along, bade the men to stop working. It was time for their snaps. Then he saw the scaffolding, men clambering down, the polished fresh hewn walls gleaming, thin dribbles of water here and there, two score men, four platoons he guessed, half a company, jostling as they unwrapped their packs of bread and cheese and opened flasks and drank thirstily. He began to understand Richard Aubrey's reluctance to allow him into this brief pause in their seven hours of strenuous activity forty-five feet below ground, in another world.

So occupied were these ghostly figures in the flickering lights that his presence had gone almost entirely unnoticed. But he was there among them and would try what he could do.

'Jack, place the box just here, if you please,' he said to his breathless assistant, and mounting it a moment later, called, 'Let us pray for God's blessing.'

The voices gradually subsided to a silence in which the dripping of water alone could be heard.

'Our Father … ' he began.

'Yn Gymraeg.' A deep voice from a gloomy corner startled him. Was it a request? An order? An expectation among these men?

He began again: 'Ein Tad, yr hwn wyt yn y nefoedd …'

To his amazed vision the forty-odd men sank to their knees

and took up the slow chant. Tears filled his eyes. 'Amen,' he said. 'Amen' came the answering chorus.

There was little more to be said, no time, no words to express the emotion he felt there, while the pulsing light of lamps and candles held the long darkness at bay. He held aloft his hand in the familiar, ancient gesture of blessing: 'Boed i Dduw fendithio eich gwaith. Bendith Duw hollalluog a fo gyda chwi, y Tad a'r Mab a'r Ysbryd Glân.'

'Amen.'

The kneeling men rose and, amid a shuffling of feet and the clatter and rattling of regathered tools, the Reverend Williams stepped down from the wooden dais.

'Where in Glamorgan do you come from?' he asked the small group standing nearest him.

'Cwm Tawe,' said one, ''Dowlais, Merthyr,' another, 'Cwm Rhymni', a third.

'Which parishes? Who are your vicars? I would like to tell them of our prayers here today.'

'No vicars,' said the Dowlais man, 'chapel us.' And, as work began, the deep voice from the gloom rose again in a hymn tune, in a moment taken up it seemed by the whole body of men, and the tune, the strong Welsh words, followed the chaplain and Jack, hauling the ammunition box, along the sparsely lit tunnel back towards the surface.

George repeated his journey into the underworld five times, visiting five different half-companies of men hacking at the chalk, who were, in the main, quiet and respectful, joining his prayer sometimes in Welsh, sometimes English, but never with the same galvanising effect as on that first occasion. He had not long emerged from the fifth visit, when an urgent message from home reached him. There was regular communication between Lord Bute, Lord Lieutenant of Glamorgan, and militia headquarters in Cardiff, and Lieutenant-Colonel Aubrey, and occasionally personal messages to and from senior officers were included in the bundle. So it was George learned that his daughter, Julia Frances, was ill.

Sarah would not have written had the matter not been serious. Even so, out of a sense of duty and personal obligation, George was reluctant to ask for leave of absence. On receiving the news, Richard Aubrey, thinking of his own dear Julia Frances, the child Sarah had nurtured before marriage took her away from Ash Hall, was moved to impatience with the chaplain's protests about unfinished work among his militia parishioners. He ordered him to leave at once and return only when it was certain all was well.

The cob had been well nourished and regularly exercised at Dover Castle. The riders who carried the mails warned him not to neglect feeding and watering the horse. It was a fine, strong beast, they said, and if he kept a steady trot, he might travel forty miles a day – but he would be very stiff and sore, because he was not used to life in the saddle. He nodded understanding of their advice and warnings, but was resolved: he would press on as hard as he could, and hope to reach Llantrithyd within a week.

Early on the morning of the sixth day after leaving Dover, George entered a sombre house. Julia Frances had died on 25th May, the day he received Sarah's letter, and was buried on the 27th by the curate of the parish, his brother Richard. Cast down as he was, he did not press his wife to tell him what had happened. On the day he had left the rectory, Julia Frances, a happy child of some eighteen months, who already bore a marked resemblance to her mother, had been in good health.

When he and Sarah were alone, speaking softly to one another, 'She was of infinite promise,' he said. 'I felt she would grow as bright and resourceful as you have always been. I prayed every step of the way that I would find her recovered when I reached home. God has willed otherwise; she will be an ornament in heaven.'

'It was the whooping cough,' said Sarah. 'It seemed at the start no more than a cold, the sort all children get. The boys asked constantly about her – they played together so well – but we kept them apart. When her cough's better you'll play again, I used to tell them. It will go, I thought, but a week or so later, the cough was worse and then it became terrible – and she couldn't find breath. That was when I wrote to you. It was as though she was drowning. I never thought to care again as I did when George died. Oh, but I have cared, and wept. Your brother was very kind. He came daily while she was so ill. We prayed together.'

In the long silence that followed, George was thoughtful. 'I shall not hasten back to Dover,' he said. 'Colonel Aubrey was most anxious I should be by your side when I told him about our little girl. He will understand.'

George did not return then to the regiment. At the beginning of October, when the pain of their loss had withdrawn into itself under the weight of daily concerns for the parish and their three surviving children, and he might have set out, a personal letter from Aubrey expressing condolences over the loss of their child conveyed the intelligence that the Glamorgan Militia, their task at the castle complete, were about to leave

Dover for another, as yet unnamed, south coast town. There was no purpose in him returning to the regiment when nothing was certain. Notwithstanding his sense of duty unfulfilled, the rector became contentedly reconciled to the role of parish priest, husband and father.

The militia's departure from Dover was delayed. Such were the vagaries of military life in times of war. When they did move, in the spring of 1798, it was only as far as Ashford. They marched in good order, drums beating, flags waving, out of the castle, which looked much the same as when they had first observed it, but had been transformed underground with a network of bricked tunnels, where soldiers were already garrisoned. Their route led them past Dover harbour, over the now fortified headland beyond, and along a narrow coast road, the sea visible to the left for much of the way, through Folkestone and Hythe, before they turned inland along a fine turnpike. From a little distance, Ashford lay about a low hill, a tall church tower rising from the cluster of dwellings with the North Downs behind. It was a march of thirty-five miles, which, with all their equipment and baggage, they accomplished in two days.

Within the town, accompanied by the rolling clatter of drums, they tramped smartly through a market square under the stares of citizens, crossed a bridge over a clear river and made for the top of the hill, which was crowned with a man-made tump, a barrow, where they made camp. The men looked about them and smiled at one another: it was a pleasant enough place on a calm late-April day, until the view of the sea glimmering but twelve miles away reminded them of the serious business in hand. Once again, they had been given the role of pioneers. They were to begin the building of barracks to hold four thousand men. Their drill and musketry practice had not been neglected at Dover Castle, but they had toiled, platoon after platoon, for long weeks and months and were hardened to it. And their company commanders were well used to the organisation and supervision of men, who had come, unwillingly in the main, to defend the kingdom, but found themselves digging, hewing, trenching, building walls, like so many masons' labourers.

And again there would be parades and drill. In this the Colonel was punctilious: 'Fifteen rounds of ball and flint to be issued to each private,' and 'Every man will parade with his firelock well flinted,' ran daily orders.

'I will not have sloppiness,' Aubrey reminded his company commanders, concerned there should be no lapse in standards following their move. 'See that every man has his hair well tied. This must apply equally to you. Your own hair should be dressed without powder and with queues. How else can you insist the men grow their hair long enough to tie back neatly? And I want no flamboyance among you in the tying of silk handkerchiefs about the neck. You are not on stage in a theatre, or in a box for that matter, trying to impress some lady. You *are* setting an example in the way you dress and behave.'

On that day at Ashford, as, the first task done, they had looked along straight lines of newly erected tents, 'At least we'll be in the open air,' some privates said. 'Yes, in the wind and rain,' said others.

When will this all be over and we can go home? was the thought that ran through all.

X

NEWS OF WHAT was happening on the battlefields of Europe was slow reaching London, slower still to travel beyond the capital. Among the rural poor, preoccupied with the harsh reality of living from day to day, it was unimaginably tardy and vague, so that Napoleon became a grotesque bogey to threaten misbehaving children. But readers of the *Times* learned that in France, following his army's victories in Italy, he was proclaimed a national hero, and that, under his leadership, Switzerland had been overrun and its independent cantons merged into a republic on the French model. It was said the Corsican had begun to see himself as the leader of an empire as great as that of Rome and that it had turned his head and given him strange ambitions to outdo the Caesars. In May 1789, with an army of thirty-eight thousand, he had set out to conquer Egypt. It seemed nothing could stand in his way, until the British navy under Admiral Nelson destroyed the French fleet at the battle of the Nile.

This setback at sea led to postponement of Napoleon's plans to invade the south coast of England, but soon after, Lieutenant-Colonel Aubrey learned from urgent despatches that a French force of rather more than a thousand men had landed at Killala Bay in the north-west of Ireland. Its aim was to reinforce the armed rebellion that had broken out in several Irish counties around Dublin and, by raising a popular revolution, sweep the English out of Ireland, which would then become a route to invasion from the west. But on 8th September 1798, the combined French and Irish army was brought to bay at Ballinamuck, where they faced seventeen thousand British troops, led by General Lake and Lord Cornwallis, who (as Aubrey's brother, Thomas, told him) had surrendered to Washington at Yorktown in the American War. On this occasion he was the victor. The French general, realising their cause was hopeless, ordered his own men to lay down their arms. They were taken prisoner to Dublin, while the Irish were hunted down and killed on the battlefield, or else imprisoned and executed later. But Ireland was recognised as an Achilles heel and once the rebellion had been ruthlessly put down and a semblance of peace restored, the government in London decided it could not rely on compromised Irish militias in the event of another insurrection.

In May 1799, after six months spent constructing the permanent camp at Barrow Hill, Ashford and, at Appledore on the edge of Romney Marsh, another six helping to dig a canal to improve transport of weapons and ammunition, the Glamorgan Militia set out for Portsmouth. At news of this posting, Richard Aubrey, as he had promised, wrote to the Reverend George Williams. There would be a return to normal duties, which should have afforded him the pleasure of welcoming their chaplain to the regiment once more. But, alas, this could not be, because they were about to embark for Ireland. He had probably heard of the troubles there, now ended thanks to prompt and firm action – well, in order to ensure the present peace was kept, the Glamorgan men would replace a regiment of Irish militia based at Fermoy in County Cork, who would take their place on the south coast, where there was no danger of them turning their coats to join a local uprising. For the chaplain to accompany them across the Irish Sea was, he feared, out of the question.

When, six months later, the regiment left Fermoy, its officers were lavishly praised by a section of the populace for 'checking every irregularity of the lower classes', and the other ranks for their 'honesty and sobriety'. It was an honour of sorts, and Richard Aubrey was satisfied that the clarity and firmness of his command had produced the desired results. To the cheers of a small crowd, the militia marched out of town and onward, through a cold and miserable winter, via Clogheen, Clonmel and Kilkenny – and then Carlow. There, they were told, the previous May, the army garrison had been attacked from all sides, but in the end hundreds of rebels had been killed and another hundred or more, taken prisoner, executed afterwards.

'We'll show them,' said the Glamorgan company commanders. Heads up, muskets at port, the column marched smartly through the centre of the town behind their mounted commandant. Their boots crunched on the paved road to drums beating loud and fifes shrilling in an echoing space. It was as though the town had emptied. Sidelong glances of the marching men picked out dark figures in doorways and down alleyways, but there were no cheers in Carlow. Those who might have cheered were afraid to show their support for British troops, and the rest would sooner have thrown stones than flowers.

'It was the same at Naas,' Colonel Aubrey wrote again to his friend the rector, '– near-empty streets and a heavy, sullen atmosphere. But we are in the last months of our duty on this benighted island. I shall not be sorry to leave. I have been told that after Dublin we shall embark for Liverpool and from there march south. I can hold out no promise, but the time may be approaching when you can rejoin the regiment. I shall look forward to the pleasure of your company and your news of events in the Vale.'

There was still work to be done. The regiment took its turn at supplying the guard at Dublin's parliament buildings. In the aftermath of the rebellion, bloodily put down, these were politically sensitive times. The men selected for duty were made aware they served as no mere ornament to the gates and doorways of grand buildings: lives were at stake, not least their own.

It was with relief that Richard Aubrey sailed for Liverpool in May 1800. He had lost no men in battle or civil dispute, for the Irish had been cowed, their leaders executed, or hoodwinked into compliance with British law. Yet, by the time it reached Hereford on the march south to Cardiff, the corps had been almost halved in size, so many on their return having volunteered to join line regiments. It was as though, for all the dismal weather under canvas, the constant wariness and occasional moments of high tension, they had come to terms with service overseas and were ready for more. It would surely be a good deal warmer on the continent of Europe, for Napoleon had returned from his expedition to Egypt and was now undisputed leader of France.

The four hundred or so who remained sank into the familiarity of barracks and routine at Maindy: drill and musketry practice, day after day, in all weathers. On Sundays, the Reverend George Williams, come in a trap from Llantrithyd, led them in prayers in the hall as before. He had become rather plumper, more prosperous in appearance, the commandant noted, and more sure of himself. The news of his parish and those adjoining in the Vale, was far from good. The winter of 1798–99 had been dreadful, snow lying in the shadowed parts of fields until May, and frosts in June. In July some rivers burst their banks. The hay harvest was very poor and wheat yields were low. It seemed the elements conspired with the worst mankind can inflict upon itself in wars and rebellions to reduce the poor to greater depths of destitution. They had suffered terribly and even now many were dependent on charity to survive.

They were speaking in the Colonel's comfortable quarters. Aubrey had been poring over maps of a route to Pembrokeshire in preparation for the regiment's next move. 'Things are as bad, probably worse, in the rural parts of Ireland,' he murmured, pushing charts and papers aside.

'I am ever busy among the poorest of the parish,' George said, 'and do what I can to direct relief where it is most needed. But when I visit cottages that would not provide decent shelter for animals, far less the starving, ragged families that dwell in them, I feel helpless because I do not know how to raise them up. The men – and the women – work, when there's work to be had, but the price of a single loaf has risen so high … '

'It's the war,' said Aubrey. 'Blame it on Napoleon and his ambition. But blaming doesn't help, does it?'

The chaplain shook his head. 'I am among the most fortunate of men,' he said, 'to have been called to serve God, as I truly believe, for how else could I have found myself speaking here with you, and secure in the affections of a dear wife and family.'

'Tell me how Sally fares.'

'Ah, my Sarah: happily she is well, very well, and sends you warm greetings on your return to Wales. If all could but speak, the words our younger children too would join the chorus of greeting, and say how grateful they are for the gifts you sent to mark their births. Thomas, let me see, born in December '98, is eighteen months, and our youngest, Owen Glendour (I hope you approve his princely Welsh name) six months. Your insistence that the regiment can do well enough without a permanent chaplain on the strength has caused the rectory to be filled with children's voices, like a bush full of nestlings. I have to shut myself in my study to escape their constant chirping and chatter. Bloom and George and Philip are all breeched and thoroughly boyish – too boisterous on occasion, but good friends, you know. I often wonder what will become of them all. Will any follow me into the Church, as I followed my father? Sarah is a wonderful mother to the whole brood. She has taken it upon herself to teach the older boys to read and write.'

'Yes, I thought that might happen. Please tell her I have received good reports of Thomas Digby and Julia Frances and expect to see them soon.'

On another of his visits, after morning service in the drill hall, George fell in with two captains of the regiment, who, having dismissed their companies, were making their way back to the messhouse. They were ready to talk about the tour of duty in Ireland recently ended. It had been little to their liking because, although there was no outbreak of violence, towns and villages seemed constantly simmering with hate between the Protestant community, who had secured all positions of authority and what little wealth there was, and the Catholic, who found their subservient position and poverty worse now than before the rebellion.

'That's what they bought with all the blood that was shed – a life more impoverished and circumscribed than before,' said one.

'The atmosphere was bad – poisonous,' added the other. 'We had to be constantly on our guard. No man was allowed out of camp alone. Always at least two, and with weapons ready. And a couple of times each week we sent out a detachment on parade, a lieutenant with perhaps a hundred men, each with thirty rounds of ball to remind them we were there and ready for anything.'

'The rising in the north-west was doomed. How could they have expected that even with a thousand or so Frenchmen and a couple of light cannon that rabble would win the day against the British army. Most of the Irish had nothing better than billhooks and pikes made out of scythes and the like,' his companion added.

'The rebels got what they deserved, but most of the French got away scot-free. Once they saw it was all up, they showed the white flag and were happy to be marched prisoner to Dublin. And then shipped back to France. At the first chance they'll be blazing away at our ranks again.'

They agreed it was a sorry business, and keeping the peace in Fermoy had been a ticklish affair, but the Colonel had kept his balance, dealing even-handedly with both communities.

'More important,' one said, 'he kept the whole regiment up to the mark, made sure every man jack did exactly the same. Firm, oh yes, very firm, and fair. You couldn't ask more than that.'

'Yes, I know,' said George, 'honest, fair and clear in his intentions. He will make up his own mind and not shirk from telling you what's best. But with all that, kind and thoughtful for others.'

They nodded agreement. At the end, they told him, when it was time to go people thanked him, said the regiment had done a fine job – even a few of the Catholics. But they were glad to get away. Glad to be home.

The militia's stay at Maindy was short. In October 1800 the regiment marched to Swansea, and thence, a few weeks later, to new headquarters at Haverfordwest, where, as Colonel Aubrey had determined, they were well placed to respond should an emergency occur, like the landing at Fishguard Bay in 1797. There were roads, though mostly of an indifferent sort, poor in bad weather, south to the great harbour inlet at Milford, west to St Bride's Bay and north to Fishguard, and over the months ahead they rehearsed, and rehearsed again, forced marches to all three. That was Colonel Aubrey's way. 'We will not leave things to chance,' he told his company commanders. 'If the need arises we will be ready to march and know the best route to meet any trouble.'

But there were no more alarms. In March 1802 the Treaty of Amiens brought the war to an end. The Glamorgan Militia returned to Maindy Barracks and was disembodied. The men returned to their homes. There were celebrations up and down the land. Everyone hoped to see taxes and the cost of food reduced and, indeed, the harvest that year was good and prices dropped. In the Vale a great burden was lifted from the shoulders of ordinary folk, though for most it would take more than one good harvest and many months to regain the losses of the war years; some would never recover.

In the church at Llantrithyd, the Reverend George Williams

led prayers for lasting peace. The text for his sermon was from Isaiah chapter 2, verse 4: 'And He shall judge among the nations, and shall rebuke many people: and they shall beat their swords into plowshares, and their spears into pruning hooks: nation shall not lift up sword against nation, neither shall they learn war any more.' As he spoke of grief for the nation's losses, hope for the future and trust in God, he looked out over a congregation swollen by the return of men he had last seen among the ranks of the militia, and to the back of the church where a pew was occupied by his entire family, Sarah, their children, and their two maids. This was peace hard won and desperately precious. His fervent prayer and the chorused, loud 'Amen' echoed among ancient rafters.

Little more than a year later the conflict began again.

PART THREE

I

T HE THREAT OF a resumption of hostilities had precipitated another listing of names, another ballot and, in April 1803, the Glamorgan Militia was again embodied under the command of Lieutenant-Colonel Richard Aubrey. In May, Britain declared war on France.

The rector visited his friend at Ash Hall, where preparations were in hand for his imminent departure for Maindy Barracks, and found him in a sombre, reflective mood. His children had not joined him at the family home they now remembered but hazily. From time to time during the long years of his militia service, he had visited them at certain grand houses in Buckinghamshire where, for almost a decade, they had been given into the temporary guardianship of his older brother. Sir John, caught up in affairs of state, was himself little enough at home and they had fared as best they could under the care of housekeepers and tutors. This was an outcome Aubrey had not imagined when, as he told himself, he abandoned them. He knew not whence it came, but he preserved within himself an ideal vision of a family that gathered together frequently and were at ease in one another's company. He might have re-married, he sometimes thought, bitterly, if he had been strong-willed enough to face down his older brothers, neither of whom was a pillar of moral rectitude, and defy Aunt Margaret.

'My children were twelve and fourteen when I left and

have gone on growing up without me,' Aubrey said. 'It is the greatest regret of my life. And I tell you again, had I a wife like your Sarah, I could not have been dragged into this endless war, far less have volunteered, in any capacity. Thomas Digby will achieve his majority later this year. He is a fine young man, about to graduate from St John's, Cambridge – the malign influence of a tutor, I suspect. I thought Julia Frances would be married by now. Had she been here with me, I would have ensured she met the right people. They are both thoroughly Englished, of course – as I was myself before I brought my wife to this place. I knew about Llantrithyd, but these last years with the militia, hearing Welsh spoken daily in the ranks, have made me conscious of my roots. I regret now my inability to speak the language. At times, the little I have proved particularly useful: when you need to pull a man up short, or praise him, it comes better in his own tongue, the one his father would have used.'

'You have inspired them – and curbed their grosser tendencies. They know you will hold to your word, without fear or favour.'

'Do you think so? It is true I seem to have come to terms with the business of soldiering far more easily than I dreamed at first. My brother Thomas was the soldier. I was … I don't know what I was, or what our father expected of me. One for the Church, perhaps. Now, at any event, it is back to war.'

'I hope you will allow me to serve the regiment as before – on the same conditions, I hasten to add.'

Aubrey shook his head in wonderment. 'Why do you persist? It isn't that I do not appreciate your loyalty, and value our friendship, but there really is no need. Nevertheless, I shall not prevent you from joining us, briefly, on my terms. If it happens we are based at no great distance from here, and circumstances are otherwise propitious, I shall write and let you know you may come – if you still wish to. But there must be no sudden, unannounced arrival of the chaplain when we are in the midst of military business. Let us agree on that and say farewell, for I must hasten. Give my greetings to Sally. Let us hope this war will soon end and we can be reunited here in the Vale.'

But the hopes were frustrated and the earnest prayers of a suffering population remained unanswered. In the weeks that followed the fourth embodiment, the militia was drilled, driven and moulded into a corps ready to defend the realm, and then posted. In June, having marched via Winchester, sore-footed and with aching shoulders, the regiment skirted the town of Gosport, which the many who had been farm labourers for much of their lives saw at once was surrounded by fine, productive land, passed two broad branches of a tidal inlet edged with silt gleaming ruby in late afternoon sun and, through the long summer evening, with practised skill, made camp in what they were told was Stokes Bay Lines. Broad and inviting, Stokes Bay was considered a vulnerable position, a possible landing site within an hour's march of Portsmouth, where fifteen thousand enemy troops might be rapidly disembarked and assembled in fighting order within a few hours.

The next morning, with more time to look about, they found themselves on a swathe of flattish coastal land, behind which lay a band of shingle decked with scattered islands of coarse grasses and low bushes, and before, an undulating beach of pebbles and more shingle stretching south to Gilkicker Point and out into grey sea. Portsmouth harbour lay a few miles to the east, over their headland, the other side of Gosport town. That was what they, with thousands more, had come to defend, for Portsmouth, with its deep-water entrance and sheltered harbour and dockyard was essential to the navy's control of the English Channel. Those who, released from duty, first crossed the bridge over the longer of the two inlets and threaded their way through the narrow streets of Gosport to the quayside, returned with eyes and minds still full of the wondrous sight of scores of vessels, large and small, at anchor, more still moving stately under sail in and out of the harbour mouth, and everywhere teeming activity among masts and spars, weaponry, barrels, bales and boxes. Soon everyone had been to gape at the fine dwellings, the ropehouse, and the great brick storehouses on the Portsmouth side, and ask his companion what was it that made the rhythmic thumping sound that carried across the water. 'Ah,' a passer-by would say, 'that's a steam engine you can hear, where they're a-making pulley blocks for the ships.'

Re-orientated and satisfied, the regiment settled to its duties, its parades and gunnery practice on the Browndown army firing range. This posting did not have the constant threat, a presence humming like a fine blade vibrating in air, that Aubrey and his company commanders had been aware of in Ireland, but there was scant ease for any. General John Whitelock, commander of the Portsmouth and Stokes Bay garrison, was a small, spare man with a high colour and scarred and twisted face that bespoke a belligerence out of proportion to his size. A stern and arrogant disciplinarian, he published an edict to his command reminding all ranks that, in time of war, even trivial offences could be tried by court martial. Aubrey, seeing at once this was no idle threat, took pains to ensure the grim information was thoroughly understood by the entire regiment, Welsh and English speakers, and, somewhat against the grain, cautioned his officers to come down hard on the slightest hint of backsliding.

Each in its turn, the companies were marched on Sunday through the grid-like pattern of Portsmouth streets to the cathedral overlooking the town, to pray for the health of the king, for God's protection and peace at the last. No call went out to the regimental chaplain. In November, with the threat of attack somewhat diminished by the onset of winter and life under canvas increasingly harsh, the regiment was withdrawn into winter quarters at Haslar, the enormous brick-built naval hospital around Gilkicker Point on the western side of the harbour entrance.

Officers and men quickly became well accustomed to the routine and the ground they had been sent to defend. In January 1804, Colonel Aubrey reported to the general that he had full confidence in the regiment's ability to play its part whatever threat should arise.

'I should hope so,' said Whitelock.

'I assume we shall return to the Lines, under canvas, with the end of winter – April perhaps.'

'You should assume nothing of the sort. We cannot allow militiamen to stagnate in the familiar. They grow slow and idle.'

'I must protest …'

'You can protest as much as you like.'

In March, the regiment, all its baggage and equipment, two dozen wives and almost as many children, moved east along the coast, some eighty miles to Pevensey. When Aubrey was told of this next destination, he thought at once of his remote ancestor, Saunder de St Awbery, brother to the Earl Marshal of France, who had stepped ashore at Pevensey with William the Conqueror in 1066. He did not divulge this piece of family history to Whitelock. Having given the orders, the general sat looking at him with raised eyebrows, as though expecting appeal or expostulation, and then observing the flicker of a smile on his subordinate's lips, which he misjudged to be sardonic, dismissed him with a scowl and an airy wave of his arm.

The militia's initial camp at Pevensey was within the perimeter of an ancient castle reduced to ruin. There was little else: a village of fewer than two hundred folk in a single, short row of houses, the High-street, running away from the old castle gate down a slight hill to a bridge crossing a stream. Later they occupied barracks near a silted harbour, close to a long sweeping bay. This was the tempting shoreline that had brought the Normans to the place and, centuries earlier, the Romans, who had built the first castle walls, still just discernible here and there like a palimpsest of fortification beneath the Norman builders' masonry.

The sea had retreated leaving areas of flat, quaking marsh, reeds and brackish lakes and pools, and beyond, a mile or two inland, where the ground began to rise, clearly visible on a fine June morning, was a dark mass of woodland. In times of peace, the shore would have been a place of contemplative delight, shingle spreading, and glistening in the sun, away into the distance. But this was war and the threat of invasion imminent. Through 1805, the regiment was constantly on the alert, detachments standing guard along shingle shore and cliff top as far as Hastings, while the main body of men in shifts were engaged in digging deep foundations and then constructing seven squat 'Martello' towers evenly spaced about the vulnerable bay. It took a million bricks to build each tower, forty feet high, with walls fourteen feet thick. It was all hammering and shouted orders, rumbling carts and creaking harness, tumbling logs, clatter of iron tools, voices, noise and movement, and behind, unceasing, rising in the interstices of racket and hubbub, the grating roar of waves on pebbles. At last, a cannon on a rotating platform at the top of each tower stood ready to meet the enemy at any angle, if he dared approach.

In November news arrived that Admiral Lord Nelson had died while leading the British fleet to a great victory against the combined French and Spanish fleets off Cape Trafalgar on the south-west coast of Spain. At a meeting of senior officers, Aubrey learned that the destruction of French naval power would certainly make Napoleon think again about invading Britain. In a matter of weeks, intelligence arrived that the great 'Army of England' gathered on the French coast at Boulogne had been given fresh orders to march east: the invasion was again postponed, indefinitely. Over the next six months, militia regiments on the south coast were withdrawn for duty elsewhere. Thus, in April 1806, the Glamorgan regiment settled once more in Bristol. There, in rotation, companies manned the heavy cannon at the harbour forts of Avonmouth and Shirehampton, and, far less cheerfully, guarded hundreds of French prisoners-of-war crammed into Stapleton Gaol.

Eventually, Colonel Aubrey wrote to the Reverend George Williams to say that they were now, and for the foreseeable future, within reasonable distance of Llantrithyd, and that, if he were 'still inclined to sacrifice the manifold delights of home and family to perform the duties of chaplain to the regiment – for a month, no more', then he would be welcome to share for that while the discomforts of their Bristol barracks. George replied that he would be honoured to do so, recruited his brother Richard, now curate at Ystradowen, to fill his place, and made his peace with his churchwardens over what he promised would be a brief absence.

He joined the regiment on 1st September, going at once to see the commandant. Once alone, in private, they shook hands again, warmly. Although at first, because of the strength of his feelings for Sarah, Richard would happily have seen the scrawny, unprepossessing clergyman dead, having accepted there was no other way, he had made himself reconciled to her marriage, and had seen George Williams for what he was, or could be, an honest, loyal friend, and faithful servant of his God and Church. His brothers and Aunt Margaret, on the other hand, he never wholly forgave. Three years had passed since their last meeting and the rector was shocked by the change he observed in Aubrey. Although more than forty years old when they first met, he had then the appearance and vigour of a much younger man. Before the war had properly begun, spectators on the parade ground at Maindy Barracks remarked on his youthfulness of gait and figure. Now his friend saw that, while the smile came readily, charming as ever, he was grey-haired, hollow-cheeked and, when he stood, round-shouldered as though bent under a heavy burden.

'I did not think your duties here would be so arduous after your exertions on the south coast, with the enemy across the Channel, only a few hours distant.'

Richard looked gloomy. 'There are other considerations,' he said. 'Here, we have to be ever ready to maintain order among our own people. The folk of Bristol, a turbulent lot, are daily on the verge of riot. You may say this is only to be expected with a four-pound loaf of bread costing eighteen pence. How can the poor live? Well, how, indeed? But it means garrison duties are severe on officers and men. And we have to be constantly alert to prevent men smuggling spirits and tobacco to prisoners, some of whom have money to spare for bribes. I will not have that kind of indiscipline, which will certainly lead to trouble. And then we keep losing good men because of the bounty now offered to tempt them into line regiments.'

George was rendered speechless by this unwonted outpouring of troubles.

'Let's put all that to one side,' said Richard, seeing his discomfiture. 'You have come in good time, for the latest addition to our strength needs to be baptised. No, not a heathen recruit, but the son of one of our longest serving sergeants.'

So great had been the changes among officers and other ranks in the years since George had previously lodged with the regiment that, apart from the commandant, he saw scarcely a face he felt he knew. Within a few days, by visiting companies in their quarters and speaking to men off duty, he began to be recognised among them. On the following Saturday, at the regimental messhouse, before a large assemblage of officers and men, and a few wives and older children prattling in Welsh among themselves, he baptised the son of William and Mary Vaughan. The baby was a few weeks old, largely bereft of hair but well-formed and sturdy in appearance. Having fed recently, he submitted placidly to being placed in the chaplain's arms, and cried out only when, on his being named 'James Horatio', a hearty 'Hurrah' and applause broke out. Thereafter, at the Colonel's gift, all drank to his health and long life.

The happy occasion served to establish the return of the chaplain and the institution of Sunday services for those of the regiment who were not on detachment duty. On other days he prayed with and gave what help he could to those who were sick or injured, and rode out to the forts at Shirehampton and Avonmouth.

He spent more time at Stapleton Gaol. He flinched from admitting to himself that he was drawn by curiosity, saying that it was his Christian duty to give succour to those who suffered adversity, friend or foe. Some prisoners were still nursing wounds, some grievously ill, because disease spread rapidly in the close confines of prison, and to these he would have offered the Word of God, if he had found any who were receptive. All but a desperate few turned away. It was not that they could not understand him; rather, they would not accept his English God, or, often enough, any God. Communication was rarely difficult, because a good many spoke some English and those already proficient were teaching the language to others.

He asked two guards if he could meet some French officers to explain his godly mission.

'No, Reverend, I'm afraid we don't have any officers here,' came the answer. 'They are billeted at inns and houses round about. Won't be mixed in with your common soldier. Have to give their parole they won't go wandering off, that they'll stay within a mile of town.'

'And keep an evening curfew,' added the other.

'Of course, given the chance, some will keep walking, heading for the south coast, hoping to find a fisherman or some such, who will accept a coin or trinket to ferry them back to France.'

'That's treason.'

'Yes, I suppose it is, Reverend, but money in the pocket can be a powerful persuader. Still, we haven't had any go missing so far.'

Fresh groups of prisoners were marched in every few days, usually in threes and fours, once or twice in a straggling column of perhaps a score. George saw the prison become more crowded through the month of his stay.

'Still it's much better here than for those poor devils, hundreds and hundreds of them, cooped up in the hulks down in Portsmouth. We saw them there didn't we, Dai?'

'Smelt them, more like. I swear, if the wind was right, you could catch the stink of those hulks from the quayside.'

Prisoner exchanges offered hope to the newcomers, but all soon realised an early end to their incarceration was not to be expected. It would be months or even years. The sensible would become reconciled to the gates and bars of Stapleton and follow the example of others in making the best of an unavoidable bad situation. Some set up as teachers, instructing those who could not how to read and write. Some made pretty boxes out of unwanted oddments of wood, some gloves from scraps of fabric and, with their small profits from selling the work to Bristolians who came to gawp at the imprisoned enemy, bought more materials to make better articles. Some became highly skilled at carving the beef and mutton bones that piled up outside the cookhouse into intricately fitted miniature ships and houses and eventually almost anything the whim of a customer suggested.

George learned their basic needs should have been supplied with money paid by the French government, but the transfer of funds was at best uncertain and could not keep pace with the growth in the numbers imprisoned. That they must shift to supply their own food and drink was borne upon them and so they worked to pass the slow grinding of time and ameliorate their incarceration. Their ingenuity in so doing was a source of fascination to George, who wondered how he would fare in a similar situation. Not half so well, he thought.

On the eve of his departure, George found Richard Aubrey in his quarters poring over charts and papers by lamplight and told him what he had seen at Stapleton, and how he had been moved. 'Yes, moved,' he insisted, 'by the demonstration of man's genius for invention, although deprived of liberty, in the direst circumstances.'

'I would be better pleased had they employed their inventiveness at home,' said Richard. 'You will find me disinclined to love my enemy. He has cost me the best part of my life, and I grow increasingly resentful of that. Do you not see that, as their gaoler, I, too, am imprisoned? I am weary of this war and, God knows, my straitened circumstances are as nothing compared to the sufferings of untold thousands of our countrymen and their families in towns and villages, who may have the freedom to wander in search of work and bread, but would give thanks on their knees for the shelter and rations our prisoners enjoy.'

George was shocked to silence. For some time the only sounds were the rustling of paper and scratching of a pen. 'We all pray … ' he began.

'Yes, George, I know you pray … You leave tomorrow: I wish you joy of your wife and family. Tell Sally that I still think of her and my own children, together, as once they were.'

The rector returned to Llantrithyd chastened by the experience. The following summer, no letter came from Bristol, inviting his presence at the militia barracks. In January

1808 the Glamorgan regiment's tour of duty there came to an end and they marched through a bitter winter to Taunton, where they camped under canvas.

For the Glamorgan Militia at Taunton, the month of March 1808 began in traditional manner with celebration of St David's Day. As the mess room at the camp was too small for the elegant entertainment planned, the hall at the Castle Inn was hired and appropriately decorated for the occasion. Among invited guests were General Watson and General Wilkie, and a half-dozen colonels and majors from other militia and line regiments deployed in camps and barracks within easy reach of north Somerset, as well as officers from recruiting parties touring towns and villages nearby. Colonel Aubrey, contriving to be both merry and dignified, presided over the dinner and a programme of Welsh songs, sung, he said, 'by true and loyal Welshmen – Cymru am Byth'. The first describing miraculous powers and acts of St David 'and written by a famous son of Wales, Sir Llewelyn (whom the English know as "Leoline") Jenkins, who was born in Cowbridge, Glamorgan, only a few miles from my own dear, ancestral home, Llantrithyd' was saluted with generous and prolonged applause. It was an evening free of care and replete with good humour. The health of guests and the regiment was drunk, rousing choruses were sung, tales were told and there was cheerful banter.

It was the story he heard when the festive evening ended that Aubrey found most interesting. Watson and Wilkie, who joined him in his quarters for a nightcap, had earned their promotions on an ill-fated expedition to the south Atlantic a few months earlier. They had been attached to battalions of two line regiments that had sailed the best part of five thousand miles to augment a British force already established on the banks of the River Plate. The plan was to attack Buenos Aires, overthrow the Spanish occupying power and claim the region for Britain. The combined British force was commanded by General Whitelock.

'You may have heard of Whitelock,' said Watson.

'Yes, I have indeed. More than that, I have served under him – at Portsmouth. It was not a happy experience. I do not wish to give offence in speaking of a man for whom you may have high regard, but I have drunk well in excellent company, and I will tell you the truth of my observation. I found him a martinet, as coarse-grained as he was self-opinionated. Really rather unpleasant.'

The generals smiled. 'You give no offence to us I assure you,' said Wilkie, while Watson looked at the floor between his outstretched legs. 'I will say it,' said Wilkie to his companion, and turning to Aubrey, 'your honesty does you credit – as does your judgement of the man.'

They went on to tell a story of failed strategy, incompetent leadership and, in the end, a humiliating defeat and surrender which deprived the British force even of land they had previously held. 'We were fortunate to get away with our lives,' Wilkie concluded. 'Of the eleven thousand good British soldiers who took the field, a quarter lie dead in South America.'

'It is not yet common knowledge,' said Watson, stirring himself and clearing his throat, 'but Whitelock is facing a court martial. Proceedings began at the end of January and continue to this day. We should know the outcome before the end of the month. I may say the evidence appears to be going against him, but I beg you will be discreet with this intelligence.'

'Of course, I understand,' said Aubrey. 'It is not wise to speak of failures of command and dreadful losses while there are battles still to be fought – abroad and, it may yet be, here at home.'

'Abroad, certainly,' said Wilkie. 'The 38th and Watson's 69th are preparing now for battles ahead, probably in Spain. There we should join the command of Sir Arthur Wellesley, a general as unlike Whitelock as you could hope to find.'

Soon after, the carriages were called and with expressions of gratitude for hospitality and good comradeship, the generals left. Richard Aubrey turned over in his mind the information he had received. It could not affect him or his regiment, though his intuitive dislike of General Whitelock seemed to have been justified by subsequent events. But this was not a cause for self-satisfaction, so great had been the calamity and the number of lives lost. With that sobering thought he put the whole sorry tale aside.

A fortnight later, in the middle of the month, when he awoke on Friday morning, his throat was raw, the familiar beginning of a cold. There was no surgeon on the strength to prescribe treatment, and, he thought, even if there were, he had never known medicine or blood letting to ameliorate the condition or abbreviate its course one jot. He was urged by the group of senior officers he met daily to take sick leave and rest until the worst was over. He said he was well enough and carried on, until a week later, his cough unremitting, he began to feel feverish and such weariness that, in spite of himself, he took to his bed.

A surgeon from the town was called, who prescribed laudanum to ease the cough and procure him some rest. In another week he was seized with shaking chills and incapable of taking food or of drinking more than a spoonful. The surgeon came twice and then three times daily, but could do nothing to arrest the progress of the illness, which he now feared was pneumonia. 'What can be done?' he was asked. 'Pray,' he said. The patient's breathing was rapid and, from his groans, painful. Laudanum no longer brought relief. For four days more, barely conscious, with no breath to speak, he lingered, while his officers came one after the other to his bedside, praying for him. Quietly, on 31st March, he died.

News of the death of Colonel Aubrey reached Maindy Barracks the next day. It was greeted at first with disbelief and then with an outpouring of grief from all connected with the militia. A few hours later, messages reached Richard Mumford, steward of the Aubrey estate in the Vale and Sir John's representative, and it was he who told the Colonel's agent at Ash Hall and servants at the Plas in Llantrithyd. The housekeeper at the Plas tearfully conveyed the information to the rectory.

To Sarah it came as a physical blow, so that she could neither speak nor weep. George wept openly and the younger children gathered around him, perplexed. They did not know Mr Aubrey and could only wonder why their father, whose daily duty was to visit the dying and comfort the bereaved, was so profoundly moved. It was the shock, he explained, and the sense of loss of a noble character and greatly esteemed friend. And he wept again.

Sarah afterwards said she had sensed something amiss, a weight, as it were, hanging over her. In private, she recalled her journey to Ash Hall and first meeting with Richard at the door of the house – what a striking man, so full of life, though with a burden of sorrow of his own – and all that had passed between them in the years that followed. She knelt and prayed for his soul, then threw herself on her bed and she, too, wept.

On its journey from Taunton, the coffin, draped with the regimental flag, was accompanied by Captain Adjutant Irving and Captains Lucas, Jones and Sheldon, men who had served several years under Aubrey's command, black sashes angled across their red uniform coats. They stopped first at Maindy, where fellow magistrates of Cardiff came to pay their respects, and where the party was joined by four drummers bearing black draped drums. On a blustery day, with clouds hurrying from the south towards the line of hills in the distance, a fresh team of black horses pulled the carriage carrying the coffin along the turnpike and, accompanied by a solemn drumbeat, slowly through the narrow lanes to Llantrithyd. In the silent village street, men doffed their hats and bowed their heads as the cortège passed them, drawn on to the church by a single bell tolling slow.

As the flag-draped coffin was raised from the carriage, the low hubbub of voices rising from estate tenants, household servants and parish officials gathered in the churchyard, died away. On the shoulders of the captains, it was borne down the path curving through the clustered gravestones, past the ancient yew and to the church door, where the rector stood, with a tender smile of welcome on his tear-stained face.

'Ah, you have come home,' he whispered, reaching up to touch the oak boards, and then, raising his voice and turning under the arched doorway, 'I am the resurrection, and the life, saith the Lord: he that believeth in me, though he were dead, yet shall he live: And whosoever liveth and believeth in me shall never die.'

The mourners in the churchyard filed after the coffin, and his voice rose above the shuffling feet, 'I know that my Redeemer liveth, and that he shall stand at the latter day upon the earth. And though after my skin worms destroy this body, yet in my flesh shall I see God.'

In the nave, flagstones had been raised, and standing at the head of the steps leading down to the Aubrey vault were Mumford, Sir John's agent, and two young straight figures, both tall and dressed in black. The church was silent as priest and burial party moved towards them.

'We brought nothing into this world, and it is certain we can carry nothing out. The Lord gave, and the Lord hath taken away; blessed be the name of the Lord.'

Handling the coffin with exquisite care as though it was itself the husk that lay within, the captains bore it down to a lamplit shelf in the vault and returned to stand at the head of the steps while the rector and the two young people descended.

'Forasmuch as it hath pleased Almighty God, in his wise providence, to take out of this world the soul of our deceased father and friend, we therefore commit his body to the ground; earth to earth, ashes to ashes, dust to dust; looking for the general Resurrection in the last day, and the life of the world to come, through our Lord Jesus Christ.'

The scattering of dry earth and small stones from a box made ready within the vault barely reached the ears of those who listened above.

Thomas Digby and Julia Frances seemed numbed by the occasion. Duty had taken their father away from them when they were yet children and deprived them of the guidance of his wisdom while they were becoming acquainted with the world. That they did not really know the father they had now lost for ever made them uncertain of their own feelings, and when the rector asked if they would like to address the congregation in tribute to him, they shook their heads. Mumford had earlier offered the explanation that, such was the press of parliamentary business on their uncles, Sir John and Captain Thomas Aubrey, neither could be spared to attend the funeral, hence the presence of both the Colonel's children, all the way from Buckinghamshire. He too declined the offer of a moment to speak about Richard.

'You will not mind,' said George, 'for my heart is full, if I do so myself?'

Again no response was forthcoming, apart from a shake of the head. He stepped up into the pulpit and, looking out over the expectant, upturned faces, offered a silent prayer and took a deep breath.

'Richard Aubrey was known to you all, known as a friend to many. I have been told he bore his final illness with the utmost resignation. He was Colonel Commandant of the Royal Glamorgan Militia, and one of his Majesty's Justices of the Peace for this county. He died far from his home here, to the unspeakable grief of his surviving relatives, and the no less anguish of his regiment, which he had commanded for fourteen years with the greatest satisfaction to that very respectable and well-disciplined corps, and infinite credit to himself. He was courteous and affable to all who served under him. He was kind and compassionate. He had the wisdom of knowing how to keep soldier-like order without having recourse (except in very few instances) to the physical punishments, which I have seen far too frequently employed by commanders of other regiments.

The brave captains that you have witnessed performing a final act of loyalty and friendship here today told me that, as soon as it became known their loved and esteemed Colonel had lost his final battle against destructive sickness, there were groans and lamentations throughout the entire corps.

'I have on occasion shared with him the honour and responsibility of sitting on the magistrates' bench and have witnessed his persuasive powers of argument, his firmness and wise judgement. In private life his social virtues shone with such lustre as to procure him the esteem and admiration of all who were honoured with his friendship. As a gentleman he was polished in his manners, as a scholar, lively and instructive, as a friend, sincere and unshaken. His hospitality was scarcely to be equalled: in his neighbourhood he was charitable without ostentation. He was never happier than when he was able to relieve the distress of the poor, wherever he went, by feeding the hungry and clothing the naked. He died as he lived, a true Christian.'

Another deep breath could not hold back his tears. The silence hung in the church until he was saved by the constancy of liturgy.

'I heard a voice from heaven saying unto me, Write, From henceforth blessed are the dead who die in the Lord: even so saith the Spirit; for they rest from their labours.' He paused: 'And the blessing of God Almighty ...'

Mumford and the two young people were at the church door, about to leave, when the rector caught and detained them. Julia Frances was as tall as he, Thomas several inches taller. Dark-haired, dark-eyed, both looked upon him with mild uninterest.

'You are leaving at once – for Buckinghamshire?'

Neither answered. It was Mumford who said, 'They are returning to Chilton, by way of Bath, tomorrow morning.'

'You have time to take tea at the rectory with Sarah and me? Sarah – Sally – has such clear, fond memories of you as children. I do beg of you spare a little of your time to greet her. She has often wondered aloud how you might look now, and whether you remember her. It is but a little distance… just beyond the church wall.'

Again it was Mumford who spoke. 'We have business, of course, at the Place, but I believe there is time,' he said, 'for a short visit.'

The pair said 'Thank you' to the four officers of militia, standing stiffly to attention, while Mumford pressed a few small coins into the hands of the youthful drummers, then they passed through those of the congregation who had remained in the churchyard, with slight inclinations of the head acknowledging bows and murmured condolences on either side. George led the way along the path to the creaking side gate and into the terraced rectory garden, still winter bare.

'This way, this way,' he said, ushering them up the steps towards the house and, as he opened the stout oak door, called, 'Sarah, we have guests.'

Although she had prepared herself for the eventuality, Sarah was for the moment bewildered by the two strangers who met her anxious, affectionate gaze with bland looks. Both were so tall, and dark, dark-haired and dark-eyed. Julia Frances had the aquiline features and generous mouth of her father, but Thomas, she felt, must be more like his mother, round-faced, but swarthy, rather undistinguished. Indoors, on a day becoming increasingly gloomy, their mourning intensified their colouring.

'We must light the lamps,' she said, signalling to her maidservants. 'Please come to the table. Tea is being prepared. You will take tea?'

To her surprise, they looked to Mumford, who said, 'Yes, a little reviving tea would be most welcome.'

'I was going to say how long it is since I last saw you, and how you have changed,' said Sarah, 'but you know that. I wonder, do you remember me at all?'

Julia Frances answered. 'I remember quite a great deal of Ash Hall, especially the winters there on top of the hill, the ice and snow, and how our father once was caught in the snow and came home more dead than alive. And how we kept warm by the great fire in the kitchen, and practised reading and writing.'

'H'm,' said Thomas, after a pause, 'yes, the winters.'

He drank his tea and looked around the room. 'You like paintings.'

'We have three George Morlands,' said George, 'and some other rural scenes, rather fine, as you can see. We are fond of paintings, aren't we Sarah?'

Thomas smiled. 'Quite a collection,' he said, smiling again.

Sarah seemed discomfited. 'Will you be returning here to the Vale?'

Neither answered her question. 'I think not,' said Mumford. 'That is part of the business to be discussed. And, since time is short, perhaps we had better make a start. Thank you for the tea.'

Brother and sister added their thanks and, passing the curtseying maids without a glance, made their way to the door.

'Goodbye,' they said together, and in a moment they were gone.

George and Sarah sat silent at the table while the fine blue-and-white patterned tea bowls and saucers were carefully removed.

'Were you glad to see our guests?'

'I am afraid they have been ruined,' said Sarah. 'The fourteen years spent in the unloving care of their uncle have extinguished the generous instincts they possessed as children and replaced them with a supercilious attitude to people and things. Had he been here today, I truly believe their father would have been grievously disappointed at the manner of their comportment.'

'Thomas seemed interested in your paintings.'

'Far from it, I fear. He could barely restrain himself from laughing at our presumption. No, Richard is in his grave: I shall treasure his memory, but Ash Hall, those children who were once his delight, and all else, are best forgotten.'

In July, as though swiftly to purge away Richard's memory, Ash Hall, its land and contents were sold at auction.

III

THE OLDER SONS of the rector and his wife were not at home at the time of the funeral. George and Philip attended the grammar school at Cowbridge, as their father had done. They had often heard him praise its ancient foundation, full two hundred years before, and its reputation as a place of learning where famous men had received their early education. Sir Leoline Jenkins, he told his boys, had been a pupil, and Evan Seys, a great lawyer in the time of Oliver Cromwell, and Sir John Nichol, of whom their mother spoke from time to time, another man of the law, even now owner of the splendid mansion and estate at Merthyr Mawr. They were unimpressed but, as each became old enough to start, arrangements were made for him to spend the weeks of term with their grandmother. After the surrender of the lease at Maendy Uchaf, Esther had moved to a small, sparsely furnished cottage in Cowbridge High-street, a short distance from the school. This was doubly convenient, the rector said, enabling the boys to attend lessons regularly and be on hand to help their grandmother when help was needed. After the rectory, it was a comfortless lodging, but they put up with it.

The eldest boy, Bloom, had finished his schooling. He had been an apt enough pupil, but was not bookishly inclined. At seventeen he had no ambition to enter the church. Nevertheless, this was what his father intended for him.

When the young man achieved canonical age, he would be nominated curate, as the rector himself had been by his father. The rector's earlier nomination of his brother had been a notable success, for Richard had been advanced to the living of St John's, Newton-Nottage, some little distance off, near the coast, and he had no doubt the Bishop would accede to further proposals.

Bloom had developed a sturdy form and was thriving in the work of fields, barn and stables. He had transformed the grazing land of meadow and hill, which was all his father had wished to retain of the glebe for his own use, into productive plough, growing barley and oats, turnips and potatoes, crops that had become increasingly valuable year by year as the war continued. In this task he had been aided principally by Richard Lewis, who, by an unusual stroke of fortune, had avoided successive militia lists. When Bloom told him his father had volunteered to serve as regimental chaplain, he had laughed aloud. As for enlisting, he did not give a fig, he said, for king and country.

'The French have got rid of the so-called aristocracy – wasters of the wealth of the land – and all that goes with it: titles, liveried servants, shiny carriages that ordinary mortals must scurry away from or be trampled down. We should do the same. Ours condemn the petty misdeeds of the workers who keep them in their fine houses, while they live scandalous lives. Hypocritical moralisers all of them. They think the gift of a few paltry pence to a beggar a great act of charity. And we are expected to go to church and pray they will live long to rule over us. What rubbish! We don't want charity; like the French, we want equality, a fair division of land and wealth. But we have no voice. No one heeds the poor. It wasn't like that in ancient Greece.' He paused for breath, red-faced. Spittle had gathered at the corners of his mouth.

Bloom was taken aback by the vehemence of his speech. 'That sounds like sedition,' he said, his voice guardedly low. 'My father is magistrate as well as rector. You had best not say that sort of thing in his hearing.'

'I care not for the Church. What has God done for us here, and the thousands – millions – all over Europe suffering pain and starvation in this endless war?'

'You must blame your friends the French for that.'

It was not that Lewis had proved himself a ready and proficient labourer on the land since George had first employed him as gardener at the rectory. That had been an act of Christian charity, though (whence he knew not) he had a nagging sense of obligation to the man. More than once he had examined himself closely on the matter, and there was nothing, really nothing, he owed Lewis, who, for his part, did not disguise a lack of deference. The customary touching of the forelock, with him, was over-elaborate and invariably accompanied by a malevolent grimace. It was just that he could not expunge the memory, from early in his curacy at Ystradowen, of the bitter hopelessness of a woman, aged before her time, and a surly, gangling youth in a bare, smoke-filled room. The aura of resentment that hung about Lewis had not dissipated with the passage of time, nor had the rector's kindness in employing him been repaid by honest effort. He did what he was bidden to do by his master's son with ill-grace and at his own pace. When, at harvest, more labourers were employed, he was equally sour and uncivil with them, so that, if they could, they avoided working alongside him.

Lewis lived in a ruinous cottage a mile or so from the village, where a spinster, Ann John, kept house for him, and bore his children. When reproved for this immorality, Lewis curled his lip and, with his turned eye, directed such a look of scorn at the rector that he was reduced to silence. Lewis's attitude and expression invariably made him uncomfortable. It was as though this ill-clad field labourer esteemed himself superior to his employer. Whence came this sense of self-importance? Although never, of course, discussed between them, George surmised it was founded on Lewis's belief that he was the rector's intellectual superior. Nevertheless, he continued to pay the man – not much, it was true – but then, he reasoned, could it be said of Lewis 'the labourer is worthy of his hire'?

To advice he should marry Ann John, the man remained obdurate, but he did eventually yield to the rector's urging that the latest of his children, though born out of wedlock, should be baptised for the sake of his immortal soul.

'I do it to please her,' said Lewis, nodding in the direction of the woman, who stood, head bowed, by his side. 'But not in church. I do not come to church; nor does my woman. We do not need any sanctimonious tying of the knot. And I will not bring a child to church. Let him find his own way there in his own time, if he will – I won't stand in his way. For the good of *your* soul, you would baptise a child of mine. Very well, but you will do it on my terms and under my roof.'

Perplexed, the rector agreed and soon after came alone to the dilapidated, weather-beaten building in a clearing at the end of a narrow lane. He had seen more soundly roofed hovels for oxen. Thatch, patched with bracken, sagged over stone walls where whitewash had weathered and faded. The door hung at an angle and two small windows were curtained with sacking. But the garden appeared well-tended and productive, a cock and four or five hens scratched about a bare earth yard before the door and occasional grunts and snuffles from somewhere behind the house told of a pig quartered there. There was a threshold of sorts, a length of wood against which the door would rest when closed, and earth, uneven, though tamped and trodden to firmness, extended inside to floor the single room. A great box containing bed and bedding for the entire family occupied much of the space. At the further end was a chimney breast at the foot of which a wood fire flickered in an iron basket. Near the fireplace was a table, a chair and a stool, and a few shelves held some pots.

An earthenware bowl containing water had been placed on the table, and stiffly beside this concession to the rite stood Lewis and his woman. He was dressed for work, while Ann John, haggard and bedraggled, had covered her head with a square of dark woollen material. The child lay still in her arms.

'Ann and Richard, the older ones, are out,' she said, ' – looking for blackberries and nuts. They do their best to help.'

'Let us get this over and be done with it,' said Lewis. 'We know what we're here for, let's not waste time.'

George swallowed, 'Nevertheless,' he said, 'there is a form that we must observe ... I call upon God to bless this home and ...'

'On, on!'

'Forasmuch as all men are conceived and born in sin ...'

Lewis groaned.

' ... and that our Saviour Christ saith, None can enter into the kingdom of God except he be born anew of Water and the Holy Ghost: I call upon God the Father, that of his bounteous mercy this Child may be baptised with Water and the Holy Ghost, and received into Christ's holy Church.'

He hurried on: 'Let us pray. Our Father which art in Heaven ...' His voice alone rose in the space sweetly redolent of wood smoke. 'Amen,' he said. 'The collect for this occasion ... '

'No,' said Lewis. 'No collects.'

'Will you name this child?' He took the bundle from the mother and looked down into wide-open blue eyes in a pale, puffy face, the hair hidden by a cotton cap.

Lewis's voice was fierce. 'Aesop Charidemus.'

In the pause that followed a stick crackled and a little flare of flame lit the fireplace and the dark chimney surround. 'Very well,' the rector said. He gently pushed back the cap from wisps of fair hair and, scooping water from the bowl, let drops fall on forehead and scalp. The blue eyes blinked but the child uttered no sound. 'I baptise thee Aesop Charidemus, in the name of the Father, and of the Son, and of the Holy Ghost. Amen.'

'That's enough,' said Lewis.

George ignored the intervention. 'We yield thee hearty thanks, most merciful Father, that it hath pleased thee to receive this infant for thine own Child by adoption, and to incorporate him into thy holy Church.'

Without another word he handed the babe to its mother and walked out into light and air, drawing in deep breaths and striding briskly down the path and away.

Later that day, after they had supped in the comfort of the rectory, George told Sarah how, against his better judgement, almost against his will, he had agreed to baptise Lewis's new baby privately, at his cottage, and what had transpired.

'Aesop Charidemus. What on earth possessed Lewis to give his child that name?'

Although he was satisfied that the child had been received into the Church, it had all been deeply troubling. 'I swear the man will be my nemesis,' he said. 'But why? What have I done that he should look upon me with such bitter malice. I have never harmed him: *I employ him* – when most others would not, because, as Bloom constantly reminds me, he is not a good worker, seeming to hate every task.'

'He is an unhappy man,' said Sarah, 'and an envious one. Perhaps he was brought up with expectations of a better life. You are everything he could wish to be, and your charity increases his bitterness towards you. Seeing you fills him with resentment, against you, against the world, against God.'

'Then I am sorry for him, and sorry for the woman he will not make his wife. And sorry for the children. No matter how deep his animosity, I will not cut him off. I will continue to offer him work, however grudging his effort.'

Five weeks later, Lewis came to the rectory door bearing a small wooden box of his own making. Burned into the lid with a red hot poker were the words 'Aesop Charidemus'.

'You claimed him for the Church,' he said, ' – here he is for burial.'

IV

RICHARD AUBREY HAD been clear from the start that George's chaplaincy was not formally recognised. He was welcome to think, and call, himself chaplain to the Glamorgan Militia, but his name would appear on no list and he would not be paid for his service. With Richard's death, the rector no longer felt the sense of obligation that had been strong in him, and allowed his unofficial and intermittent connection with the regiment to come to an end. So many changes occurred among officers and men that soon there were few who had any recollection of him, and in a couple of years none. No one enquired after him.

His interest in the progress of the war did not diminish. He and John Perkins subscribed together to another newspaper – the *Cambrian*, a weekly, which had begun publishing in Swansea in 1804. It could not match the *Times* for the range of events reported, nor for the speed of their transmission to a public eager for news. Its tardy, less detailed reports of the military conflict were, nevertheless, better than nothing, and, by way of compensation, it contained information about people and places in south Wales (ignored by the *Times*), which for the most part had previously arrived, slowly and often distorted in the telling, by word of mouth. So the two men shared the *Cambrian* and, from time to time, in the old way, discussed issues of the day. The closeness of their friendship had waned somewhat because Perkins had acquired a larger farm, Tŷ Draw, farther off, so that he didn't as often pass church and rectory and was much busier than formerly in the management of his many acres.

Whenever he and George met, the allies' battles with the armies of Napoleon were uppermost in their minds and filled their conversation. Not long before the death of Aubrey, they had read how Napoleon had removed the Spanish king, Charles IV, and raised in his place the more pliable Ferdinand VII: ' … with unspeakable indifference to the desires and needs of the people of Spain.' Perkins was beside himself with fury. 'A day of reckoning will surely come,' he said. 'Please God, let it be soon.'

'Amen to that.'

Soon after, Perkins was again stabbing his finger fiercely at the newspaper. 'See here,' he said, ' – that French ogre would never be satisfied with a Spaniard on the throne, even one who had bent the knee to him. He has snapped his fingers and dismissed his puppet, Ferdinand, and who do you think he has put in his place?'

George shook his head.

'Why, his brother, of course! What's his name?' He peered at the paper: 'Joseph. Yes, there it is – Joseph.'

The *Cambrian* was scathing in its denunciation of this abhorrent act, and voiced its enthusiastic support for bands of young heroes who, in Spain and Portugal, took makeshift arms to sting the French in surprise attacks. But it needed a British army, under the command of Sir Arthur Wellesley, to force the enemy out of Portugal in August 1808 and set an example to the Spanish, who, in Napoleon's absence in another zone of the everlasting war, expelled the oppressor from Madrid.

When this news reached the *Cambrian* and its readers in mid-September, it was greeted with euphoria. That, alas, was short-lived. Napoleon returned with fresh men and retook the capital. The British attempted to intervene, but early in 1809, while his troops were being rescued by the navy, Sir John Moore was mortally wounded at Corunna and it seemed that the entire peninsula was once more at the mercy of the French.

War was hydra-headed, its horrors erupting now in Bavaria, Prussia, Austria, Portugal and Spain. Long columns of men marched across Europe taking at will the resources of the land, and assembled in battle formation to fight, with dreadful slaughter on both sides and the terrible destruction of town and country. There was heroism and cowardice, fine leadership and crippling incompetence – as bad as Whitelock's in South America, or worse. In July 1809 a military expedition set out to strike docks, shipbuilding yards and arsenals at Flushing and Antwerp, directly opposite the Thames estuary, where Napoleon was planning to equip his fleet for a new phase of the war on the sea. After initial success, lethargy and indecision left most of the force encamped in a mosquito-ridden marsh on the island of Walcheren. Few were lost in battle, but by September, first the *Times* and then the *Cambrian* and other provincial newspapers declared the whole affair a national disaster, for in scores and then hundreds men fell victim to malaria, typhus and dysentery. By October, of more than forty thousand who had set out, fewer than five thousand were fit for duty. In late December the ague-stricken remnant returned to Britain.

The rector, whose turn it had been to read the newspaper first, was deeply distressed, while Perkins was appalled. 'Who was the leader of this debacle?' he asked.

'It says here General Lord Chatham, Prime Minister Pitt's elder brother. As well as destroying the French fleet and its suppliers, the expedition was intended to turn Napoleon from his planned invasion of Austria, but it was to no purpose because he had already defeated the Austrians at Wagram.'

'Chatham you say – a man of military experience?'

'He has long been involved in army and naval affairs, but has had no military duties in fifteen years.'

'It is intolerable. What's to be done?'

'I cannot say. No one seems to know. But think of the poor men.'

Later the same day, as he and Sarah sat close to the fire on an evening of autumnal chill, George recalled his visits to sick and injured militiamen in the scattering of short weeks he had spent as chaplain. As he recalled the scenes and the stench of sickness, the comfort he had in wife and home was as a reproach to him.

'I saw some of them suffer horribly, heard their groans and cries, and how they called aloud for their mothers, and longed to see wives and children once more. I could pray for them, mop a fevered brow, but beyond that, nothing. It filled me with grief and frustration. And to think of those hundreds and hundreds of men in that ghastly marsh trembling with fever, sick and dying – and the dead – all heaped together, while I am here ...' He covered his face with his hands and his body shook with weeping.

He and Sarah were settled, their family complete. At ten, Owen Glendour resembled his mother in his calm competence. As each of the children in turn, he had become his mother's favourite, the one read to, the one who had carried a horn-book on a ribbon, the one whose head was gently touched as he bent over chalkboard or paper and pencil. But in Owen's case it was different, no one supplanted him. He alone had retained the fair hair of his infant years that curled when wet. He had been quick to talk and, having acquired the trick, talked through each day to whoever came close – parents, siblings, servants, strangers – or, if none could be found to listen, to himself, in games he played indoors and out. He had early learned to read and Sarah happily plied him with books – 'to keep him quiet for a few minutes' she would say, smiling. She was sure he was ready for school and just as sure she would miss him, more than any of the other boys, when, in another year or so, that time came. During the week, Thomas, who was eleven, had joined Philip, already fourteen, in the spartan lodgings of their grandmother's cottage, occupying the bed vacated by George and Bloom and taking their quota of Latin and Greek at the grammar school with fortitude, as they were bidden, but little enthusiasm.

While they waited for the embrace of the Church to give final direction to their lives, the two older brothers had work enough to occupy them in the rectory's barn, stable, brewhouse, garden, orchard and glebe. Their father was the precedent and pattern for their youth and prospects. From early childhood he had been familiar with the liturgy and a casual observer of the manifold responsibilities of a parish, but he had been a farm labourer until precipitated into curacy by his father's mortal illness. These postponed expectations suited Bloom, who had grown brawny with work and took pleasure in surveying a well ploughed field, flourishing crops, a sound, sweet-smelling barn, and healthy stock, but George was less content. He was impatient with life, sought progress speedier than the slow churn of the seasons. When once their father had absorbed and meditated upon its contents, both read the *Cambrian*. Bloom turned at once to news of farm sales and auctions, agricultural markets and prices, and only glanced at the rest.

It was the unfolding stories of the war in Europe and across the wider oceans that held George's attention, and in the spring of 1811, when he was just eighteen, he announced to his father that he would enlist – in the army, navy or marines, he was not yet sure, but he was certain he wanted to be part of the adventure overseas. Sarah was distraught.

'You are precious to us,' she said. 'I beg you will not throw your life away. You no longer have to fear the militia ballot, and it would be foolish to be tempted by a mere twenty pounds bounty to volunteer for it. Your father needs you here, and I need to know you are safe. You cannot have considered the monotony, the boredom of life in barracks or on ship, or the exhaustion and terror of long marching and fighting.'

'I assure you, from my own observation, and from what I have been told, the life of a soldier is hard and comfortless,' his father added. 'You are treated like a brute, called upon to obey, at once, no matter what the order. You no longer have a mind of your own. A minor breach of discipline may be punished by fifty – even a hundred – lashes. I would like you – I urge you – to consider more deeply what you will undoubtedly lose as well as what you think you may gain by enlisting. You are young, please do not make any precipitate, rash commitment. If you are still so minded in another year, we will discuss it again.'

Mother and father saw how their response had hurt and angered their son, who felt himself a grown man able to make his own decisions. They agreed that, if he held to his purpose, much as they deplored it, rather than risk estrangement, they would not stand in his way, but seek to advance his opportunities of a career in the army. Young George carried on as before working the fields and the yard alongside his brother, but he was quieter, less cheerful, as though he begrudged his labour. When a task brought him and Richard Lewis together, a whole morning could pass without a word exchanged.

The war in Spain, the outcome of which had been in doubt for so long, victory falling now to one side now the other, began to turn decisively in favour of the British under the leadership of the recently ennobled Arthur Wellesley, Lord Wellington. The *Cambrian* was eloquent in his praise. In July his army won the battle of Salamanca and in August they entered Madrid virtually unopposed. Napoleon seemed to have abandoned Spain; he was at the head of a great army advancing on Moscow. Before the end of the year, the harvest complete, young George's nineteenth birthday approaching, his father drew him to one side to ask whether he had changed his mind about his ambition to go for a soldier. He had not, he said. Indeed, he was now more firmly resolved than ever that he would leave home, leave Llantrithyd, and see as much of the world as he could.

'Then, although it grieves your mother and me, we will help you so far as we are able. I wish Colonel Aubrey were alive still, for he would surely have offered counsel and even, perhaps, recommendation. But I shall address myself to the task of purchasing a commission for you. It will, I fear, require a great deal of money, more than I have at present. If you will be patient a while longer (for we have also to consider your brothers' and sisters' needs and the calls of church and parish),

I will gather the necessary funds and seek advice elsewhere concerning a suitable regiment.'

The young man's reply was to clasp his father in his arms, declaring whatever befell him, nothing could change his love for home and family.

In March 1813, George Williams became an ensign in the Third Battalion 60th Regiment of Foot. The commission cost his father four hundred and fifty pounds and, for a time, left the family in somewhat straitened circumstances. Hearing the news, John Perkins invited himself and Bessy to take tea at the rectory. They brought with them their two youngest, a boy and a girl, who looked like twins, dressed alike, both plump, round-faced and round-eyed with long, straight, brown hair, although the boy was older by fourteen months.

Perkins shook his friend the rector warmly by the hand while Bessy embraced Sarah, saying, 'Oh, you will miss him. Such a lovely boy. I met him, passing by, the other day – such a sturdy well-set-up lad.' She took a deep breath, straightened herself and puffed out her ample bosom. 'Oh, he'll look grand in uniform. Will we see him today?'

Sarah, suddenly choked with emotion, could say only 'No, he's left …'

'I told you we should be late, Bessy,' said Perkins, 'and I did want to see him in his uniform.'

'He left us well covered in his greatcoat, against this interminable winter, and is presently visiting his grandmother in Cowbridge to say farewell,' George explained. 'He will stay there overnight and take coach from the Bear early tomorrow. We shall indeed miss him – miss him terribly.'

'I am sure you will,' said Perkins, ' – a valiant young man. How I love to see our brightest and best fighting the French tyrant. Barbarous Napoleon may be but, with God's help, and noble hearts, we will overcome him.' He was quite flushed with excitement.

'We pray only that he will return whole to us,' said Sarah, her voice hoarse, little more than a whisper.

'A mother's fears – we understand,' said Bessy, reaching out to touch the other's pale hand.

Sarah turned and bade the maid bring tea, and they sat and drank in near silence, for neither George nor Sarah could think of the usual mundane things that make conversation between friends. Perkins would have spoken at length about the latest news of Napoleon's armies and the ruin of Europe, but the quiet of the room and the sad, introspective looks of the rector and his wife unnerved him. He and Bessy soon gathered up their children, who were being entertained in the kitchen, and prepared to leave.

'Let us know how young George takes to soldiering,' said Perkins cheerily, 'where he's posted and so on. The 60th you said? It's mightily interesting.' And with more handshakes and embraces, they left.

As they walked away past the shallow terraces of the rectory garden, where, despite the long, cold winter, low yellow and white spring flowers studded the grass, Perkins said, 'I thought they would be proud to see their son go off to fight. It was more like a funeral.'

Wracked with anxiety, Sarah could not raise her spirits. In occasional letters George told of his new life. He was in the Third Battalion, which had many former militiamen in its ranks, though none from the Glamorgan regiment. At nineteen, he was not the youngest: many of the officers and, he thought, most of the men were no more than twenty. Even the youngest among them, a boy of fourteen, was obliged to carry the same knapsack and accoutrements as men nearly twice his age. Battalion officers usually dined together. He had been assigned to No. 7 Company under Captain Wilson and Lieutenant Baldwin, both of whom had experienced battle during the regiment's duty in Spain, and were 'good men', he wrote, 'firm and fair'. They got on well together. They had regimental drill four days a week, from first light (rising at four-thirty in the morning) until nine. Inspection of arms was very important. Two days were spent in brigade movements, musket and cannon practice. It was a full life: he went to his bed exhausted and 'slept like a babe'. With many new recruits, like himself, there was much to be taught, much to learn, before the regiment could be deemed ready for action. The regiment's commanding officer, Lieutenant-Colonel Henry Gilbert, a tall, steely man with an imperious gaze, had told battalion and company commanders that, although no information had come down regarding their next posting, there was not a moment to lose, for when it came *every man must be ready*. George missed the warmth and comforts of home (life under canvas seemed somehow temporary and precarious), missed his brothers, missed his father and his mother. But he was happy doing what he wished to do and, he hoped, earning the respect of fellow officers and the men of the company.

These cheerful letters did little to lift the gloom that had fallen upon the house with George's departure. And when, in May 1813, the *Cambrian* quoted a *Times* report that, in the previous autumn and winter, Napoleon had left a quarter of a million dead on Russian soil, it gave Sarah no satisfaction. It seemed that, in his latest adventure, Napoleon had gained at best a hollow success and then suffered a prolonged disaster. After defeating the Russian army at Borodino, he had advanced to Moscow, only to find it had been abandoned and left in flames. In September 1812, the winter already closing in, he had begun the long march home. As the army dragged itself mile after weary mile through ice and snow, thousands more died from cold and in sporadic attacks from an enemy accustomed to the bitter weather. War brought only destruction and appalling loss on all sides. Always the loss of loved ones, for were French soldiers any less loved by wives and families than British? The rector equally found himself in no mood for celebration when Perkins, waving the newspaper like a flag as he walked towards him, shouted, 'Now we have him.'

There was news, too, of a new coalition of forces being formed against Napoleon: perhaps, indeed, the turning point had been reached. But, returned once more to France, the Emperor hastened to recruit and train another army, and in mid-October 1813 led it against the combined forces of Austria, Prussia and Russia at Leipzig, in the largest battle Europe had ever seen. Half a million soldiers took the field, and one hundred thousand were killed. It took a fortnight to cart away the dead. For miles around, the country was devastated and many weeks later the desperate citizens of Leipzig were still dying of starvation and sickness.

In the same month as the battle of Leipzig, at long last, George learned he was to serve overseas, but not in Europe. He was in the half-battalion of the 60th that would sail to the Caribbean to replace the garrison on the island of Tobago. This deployment was not greeted with pleasure by most of the officers and men. All their training had been aimed at joining the fight against Napoleon, and now he was weakened and the allies were closing in on him, they had looked forward to being engaged in the final push that would destroy him. But instead of a short voyage east across the channel, they would be sailing far, far away west and south to the tropics. There, too, the French were a dangerous foe, and, since 1812, so were the Americans. British plantations on Caribbean islands, British trade interests, had to be protected.

All this, and his disappointment, young George expressed in letters home. Such was Sarah's terror of Napoleon that, at first, she greeted the news with joy. Then she thought of the dangers of the long sea voyage and the tropical heat and strangeness of her son's destination. She knew nothing about Tobago – had not even heard of that island, although Jamaica was a familiar name. She made regular purchases of sugar from the West Indies and, from time to time, cotton goods and even a little rum to make punch for special occasions. She knew, too, of the reliance on black slaves to work on plantations, and she deplored it. The transporting of slaves chained in holds from their African homes halfway around the world to be sold at auction to plantation owners had ended a decade before, but she had read that many already there were still treated worse than beasts, and denied the consolation of the Christian faith. It was abominable, she thought, and now, if God in His mercy delivered her son safely to this island, he would find himself in the midst of such inhumanity.

Sarah had done all she could to persuade her son against becoming a soldier, but there seemed no way of preventing it. She still feared, she said, they would not see him again. Her husband found that tender concern for her well-being was met with faint smiles, but did little to ameliorate her suffering. At his request they prayed together daily for God's blessing on their son, and clung to hope, a straw in the turbulent current of war.

V

BLOOM SEEMED PLACED on Earth to work with the soil. He found contentment in labour in the fields for its inherent promise of the rewards of harvest. He loved God's creatures for their individual beauty and companionship, and for their bounty in flesh and eggs, fleece and feather. He had not the slightest hesitation in taking the produce they gave, nor yet in despatching those beyond usefulness, or killing vermin, or game for the pot. Passers-by would stop and watch Bloom ploughing, cutting corn or scything hay, such was his mastery of the tasks. They admired, too, his easy command of horses and cattle, sheep and dogs, even the poultry in the yard. He treated all the same, with kindly affection, feeding and sheltering them as well as he was able and, without threats and whipping, insisting upon their bending to his will. His father and mother acknowledged with smiles that, even as a young boy, he had been every inch a farmer.

And he had added to the talent God gave him, seeking the advice of neighbours and observing how some farms failed where others succeeded and flourished. He enlarged his fields, made every foot productive by digging up hedgerows and ploughing where once they stood. He saw how John Perkins limed his land and, having from childhood been a talkative favourite of his, was allowed to share in the purchase of limestone and coals for lime making. On the first occasion, it excited him to watch as Perkins' men stacked the kiln with layers of coal and stone and waited with some impatience while it burned continuously for a week or more, and then longer while it cooled, before he could take his quota and strew it on the fields. His father, who had never done this, praised him for the increased yields it gave and encouraged him to read and weigh in his own judgement farming advice in books and newspapers. From the writings of a man called Jethro Tull he learned the virtue of hoeing and practised it assiduously. In his hands the hoe was a live thing. It was one source of his discontent, anger even, with Richard Lewis, that the man would not hoe with the vigour necessary to cut weeds and break up soil to a fine tilth. Lewis would stand there, leaning on his hoe, a tall and angular scarecrow, without interest in the work or energy to perform it, while Bloom's hoe flashed in and out and around the precious crop. They quarrelled over this and other daily tasks, Bloom castigating the labourer's sluggish idleness, while Lewis peered superciliously into the middle distance and muttered under his breath. The rector was often advised by his son that employing him was money wasted and, from time to time, faced with a demand for his instant dismissal. To these challenges the father had always the same answer, 'Be forbearing. He is an unfortunate man, deserving of our pity. He has little; we have much. We can afford to be generous and forgiving.'

When the threat of being turned away from garden or glebe was removed, Lewis offered no word of gratitude, no expression of relief. Rather, his slant smile grew more sardonic, the scorn more visible in his roaming eye.

The rector was pleased to see how ably his eldest boy farmed what remained in his hands of the glebe. He often praised and thanked the young man for his labour, but was disappointed not to see in him an eagerness for Holy Orders. Often Bloom came in from the fields fatigued and, after eating, would be persuaded to take up Bible or prayer book. Seated comfortably in an armchair or the settle in the chimney corner, he would soon be stunned by sleep, his head slumped forward, his breathing regular and deep.

Observing this, 'He is a fine boy,' George would say to Sarah, smiling indulgently, 'but I wish he could be persuaded to save a little of his strength for study. It's his future, after all, I plan for.'

When Sarah mentioned this to Bloom (for she did not trust her husband to do so), she added that to be merely a farm labourer would be to deny his ability to serve God more purposefully, and limit what he might achieve in life. In reply, he asked when the lease was due to expire on that greater part of the glebe rented by others, for he was certain he could make a prosperous farm of the whole of it. On one such occasion, she pressed him to look ahead.

'What of marriage?' she said. 'Do you not want a home of your own? If you spend your days labouring on the land, what woman might you take for wife, do you think, to give you children? The daughter of a farmer or farm labourer will be the height of your reach. I do not mean to deny their worth, for that would be to deny myself, and some are most certainly very good, pleasant young women, capable in the home but, if my experience is a guide, without ambition for the babes they bear. What do you expect, what do you hope your children will become when they are grown?'

Bloom did not know. He shook his head: 'Surely there is time for both,' he said. 'Time now to make our land as productive as it can be, and time yet, when I am a little older, to be made curate. And, perhaps then, time for marriage and children – when we must see at last how they will turn out.'

The winter of 1813–14 was the most dreadful even the old of Llantrithyd could remember. Snow had lain on the ground for weeks, drifted in glossy waves over hedges and fences, filling lanes and rendering the turnpike impassable to carts and coaches. At last news arrived from other parts. In London, during the worst of it, the frozen Thames had supported a Frost Fair with booths selling sweetmeats, toys, books, all things, along a wide road crossing the river. Bonfires had been lit on the ice, and an ox roasted on one rumbustious night, and there had been ballad-singers and acrobats and jugglers – and pick-pockets. The rector read of it with amazement. That anyone could have found pleasure in such cold was beyond his understanding. A large number of his older parishioners, having died of cold and sickness, had lain unburied for weeks, because the earth of the graveyard had become rock, and he was moved by the helpless suffering of their families. He was grateful that Esther, his mother, had died at a great age, peacefully in her sleep, early in December before frost had sealed the soil, and had been interred alongside his father in the church at Llansannor.

The locked-in season had seemed endless. Then, at the end of February, an unexpected thaw released floods that threatened to inundate all and, suddenly, it was unseasonably warm. In the same month, on the continent of Europe, Napoleon's beleaguered army had fought and won a series of battles against far greater forces without deflecting them from their goal, and in the last days of March, Paris fell to the allies.

On 6th April, the Emperor abdicated. Louis XVIII became king of France and Napoleon was exiled to Elba.

This time the news came quickly. On 9th April, the day before Easter, the Foreign Office in London announced the abdication and a day later reports of the event had reached the Vale. The rector was about to order a triumphant peal of bells, when he heard them: his churchwardens had anticipated him. A large, cheering crowd soon gathered where the road widened, fringed with cottages, just above the church. Young and old, women and men were embracing one another, weeping and laughing, throwing hats in the air. 'Hurrah!' they shouted and 'Heddwch! Heddwch!' Yes, peace, at last, peace. Children gazed open-mouthed at transported parents, or ran about wildly, crying out with their sharp voices. New arrivals, grasping the meaning of the joyful noise, fell on their knees in the dust and prayed aloud, giving their thanks to God. And some were bewildered. The war had been part of their lives for so long they could not remember a time when Napoleon and his great armies were not an imminent threat, the cause of painful taxation, food shortages, poverty, unrest, the absence of their menfolk, some to be lost for ever. And those poor fellows who had returned maimed would not forget the terrible fighting, but surely now better times were coming, peace and prosperity.

Perkins and Bessy had driven at speed from Tŷ Draw in a pony-trap, the former in an ecstasy. 'At last, at last, George,' he shouted, leaping down and grasping his friend warmly by the hand. 'I shall never forget this day. We have beaten the ogre, brought him down, down to the dust.'

So great was his enthusiasm he had forgotten Bessy, whose request for help to dismount the trap he could not hear above the noise of the crowd, until the rector directed his attention to her predicament. Both husband and wife were formidably rotund and when she clutched at his hand to take the long step to the road, he staggered backwards so that they performed together an inelegant dance and were saved from falling in a heap by the crowd they swayed into. Then all laughed together. And above all the hubbub in the little square the church bells pealed out.

George's own delight was sobered by Perkins' exuberance, but he remained smilingly courteous. 'Come, take tea with us,' he said. 'We haven't seen you and Bessy together for a long time. Sarah will be glad to welcome you.'

He hoped tea and the quiet of the rectory would be calming, and for a short time it was. But while Sarah and Bessy were content to talk about their children and exchange village gossip, Perkins could not restrain himself. He caught George by the elbow and pulled him away. 'Let's talk in your room,' he said.

Once there, he could speak of nothing but the war. 'I knew we had him,' he said, 'once Wellington had fought his way out of Spain and into France.'

It was always the British heroes, or the French villain, he spoke of, not the fighting men, the poor foot soldiers, the wounded, maimed and dead. George, mindful of his soldier son, could find hardly a word to respond.

'Where is this Elba?' said Perkins, 'this place where Napoleon will kick his heels in exile? Do you have an atlas? Allow me to point a finger at it and gloat a while.'

George did not possess an atlas, but Perkins could not rest until one had been found. 'Send to the Plas,' he said, 'they will surely have one there that you may borrow for an hour.'

Luckily, business in the vicinity had taken Sir John's agent to the great Aubrey house and when the request came he found the stout volume in the library and delivered it into the servant's hands, with earnest demands for the greatest of care with a precious book. It did not take long for Perkins to find a map of the Mediterranean, but Elba proved more elusive. It was only when the rector put on the eyeglasses he had needed for some time when reading and peered at the page that it was found – a small island between Corsica and Italy.

'Ah, it's good to think of him there. Not much of an empire, eh?' said Perkins. 'Though I must admit I'd be happier if it was farther off from the coast of France. Be that as it may, we have him.' He was euphoric, and mistaken.

Notwithstanding the vagaries of weather, during the war years farmers in the Vale as elsewhere had benefited from the high prices fetched by crops and stock, but prices of wheat, barley and oats almost halved once hostilities ceased, the army began to shrink, and imports of food increased along the open seaways. Families that had survived well enough on smallholdings found they were self-sufficient no longer and the men went out begging for work at larger farms.

In late summer 1814, when every man was needed to bring in the harvest, suddenly Richard Lewis was missing. After Bloom had returned to the rectory grumbling that he had been absent for three days, George, fearing the man was ill, hastened to his cottage to provide succour. But Lewis was not there. His woman explained that he had received a message saying a relative had died. She could not tell what or how close was his kinship to the deceased, but he had set off at once for Llancarfan, his family home, in hope of a legacy.

Beyond the cottage clearing, a thin mist still clinging among the trees was quickly dispersing, and the sky above was blue with high, slow-moving white clouds intensely bright in the sun. The rector hoped Lewis would return with a bequest that would bring ease to his family, remove the heavy burden of resentment he bore against life in general – and give himself release from the sense of obligation he felt towards the man. What if he received a legacy and decided to stay in Llancarfan? The thought stopped him in his tracks, but then, he told himself, though unmarried, Lewis had been faithful to his woman for years and would surely remain so. Only a beast would desert her and the children now.

He put the ugly thought aside and looked about him. It was a fine day for harvesting. He had not worked in the fields for many years, but why not this very day? Why not take Lewis's place? He knew he was somewhat stouter than when he and his brother, Richard, worked the land together, and admitted to himself that, unused for many years to labour, his back might creak and his hands blister. But he would never forget how to ply scythe and hook, how to fork a sheaf on to a wagon, how to build a stook. He was ready to put off his priestly outer garb, roll up his sleeves and help Bloom and the harvesters already gathered.

He found them in a field his son had enlarged, so that it now seemed rather narrow and long, extending up a slope to one of the higher parts of the former pasture. It had a fine crop of barley, about a third of which was already cut, for the work had started not long after first light, when the hairy heads of grain were damp with dew and decked with jewelled spider webs. He walked briskly up the slope between stooks roughly capped with straw against a change in the weather, and emerged into bright sunshine and the sounds of harvest: the harsh whispering of scythes through dry stalks and the chatter of men as they swayed to their task. He was greeted with doffed straw hats and touched forelocks, and 'Bore da. Bore da, Mistar Rheithor.'

He was quite breathless and obliged to wait before gasping, 'And good morning to you, a good morning, indeed.' Turning to Bloom, he said, 'I've come to help you, if I can. What would you have me do?'

'There is no need … but, if you will, why not help bundling up and tying sheaves.'

Usually the task of those incapable of more exacting toil, it was less than George had prepared himself to face, but necessary, and he soon settled to the pattern of activity, following the advancing line of men wielding scythes, bending to pluck up by armfuls the cut barley and bind it in sheaves with stems of roughly plaited straw. Soon his tender hands were sore and bloodied from grasping the stiff, coarse stems, but when the men in the line paused to drink and take a little bread and cheese, he begged to be allowed to try if aught remained of his old skill with the scythe.

The borrowed tool was fitted with a cradle. There had been no such thing when he was young and working the land, but he had often watched with interest how harvesters using this strange device cut swaths of grain or grass and laid them neatly in rows extending behind as they advanced. Even with the additional bows of the cradle that altered the feel of the thing, and despite the passage of years, within a few strokes he felt an old skill begin creakingly to return. Balanced on spread feet, arms straight and body turning from the waist, he aimed to make a straight cut low to the ground. It should be second nature, he thought.

'Da iawn, Mistar Rheithor.' The small chorus of voices gave him the chance to pause. He knew they were laughing at him, and would have called back, 'No, not very good: you should have seen me handle a scythe when I was younger,' but lacked the breath for it. In his pride he worked harder and faster, striving for the easy rhythm in the task he had known more than twenty years before, until his face was blotched pink and bathed in sweat and his heart thumped fast. An ache spread across his shoulders. Soon after, sensing the blisters on each palm at the apex of thumb and finger, he stopped and, still wordlessly, smiling his gratitude, handed the instrument back to its owner.

He showed his wounded hands to Bloom. 'I can still do the work,' he said, 'but at some cost. My hands are not hardened as once they were.'

'You must not tell Mama I did anything to encourage this.'

'No – it was my own doing. And, if at the cost of no more than bloodied fingers and some loss of breath, I shall not regret it. You have done well here: it will be a good harvest. What do you think? Will it yield ten, or twelve, bushels an acre?'

Bloom glanced over the enlarged field: 'Nine – perhaps ten. Ten would be a good return on seed. We shall see.'

The rector smiled, observing the thoughtful judgement. His son was a man and, dressed for the fields, with the brawny look of a man, and an easy air of authority about him. He would make a fine clergyman. The talk of the men, and the frequent sound of sharpening-stone on blade faded as he walked down the field to the far gate and out into the lane.

Sarah was startled by his appearance when he arrived at the rectory. 'Whatever have you been doing?' she said, 'You are covered in dust.'

He had folded his coat and placed it with others at the side of the field before offering to help the harvesters and put it on again as he left them. He had been too breathless then to notice his breeches were no longer black.

'I'm afraid the blame lies with Richard Lewis,' he said, and he told her about his fruitless visit to the cottage. 'Since he wasn't there, and it was such a fine day, I thought I might stand in his place for a while. And look what my desire to be of service has brought me – dust stained clothing, and sore hands.' He presented palms and fingers for her inspection.

Sarah looked keenly at him. He was no longer young. Unaccustomed as he was to work in the fields, he had been foolish to attempt it. She saw her man, red-faced, damp with perspiration, his thin, grey hair plastered to his scalp. He was round and fleshy where he had once been spare and lean.

He shrugged his shoulders, winced and rubbed them, first the left then the right. 'My shoulders ache,' he said, 'but I shall be all right. I'll rest a while … perhaps think of next Sunday's sermon. It will soon be time to thank God for harvest.'

V I

THERE WERE TIMES when the rector thought of his youth at Maendy Uchaf. He had been no more than a farm labourer, without ambition, much as Bloom was now. He loved his parents and obediently studied Bible and prayer book to realise the ambition his father cherished on his behalf. Even so, being precipitated into the role of curate because of his father's illness was shocking, and his father dying so soon thereafter deprived him of the guidance he knew he needed as he began his task in the Church. For a long time he felt no confidence standing before the altar or in the pulpit. He cared for his parishioners and visited the unfortunate to bring them what comfort he could, but was well aware he lacked ease in their company. He was quite sure he would have remained a curate forever, had it not been for the merest chance that brought Sarah to the church at Ystradowen. What followed had all flowed from their meeting. Each day he thanked God for bringing her into his life. Everything he owed to her: the great privilege of the rectory, friendship with Richard Aubrey, one of the finest of men, chaplaincy with the Royal Glamorgan Militia, a seat on the bench of magistrates at Cardiff … his dear children.

The war ended, it was possible to think of the future once more. The rector wanted no more than what he had. He was perfectly consoled and content in body and spirit to be with Sarah, sitting near the fire early on a chill autumn evening, candles already lit, reflections flickering on polished surfaces and gilt picture frames. But Sarah was restless. It was time, she thought, to talk about what the children might do in the days opening out before them, in a world released from the horror and travails and trammels of war. And, as so often, led by her, they talked. Sooner now rather than later, Bloom would surely become reconciled to a curacy, and follow his father into the Church, but what of the others? Owen, the youngest, had been praised at school. 'He might go far,' his teachers had said. He had talked early, his mother remembered, and had a way of noticing things, pointing out things, asking questions endlessly, telling others, even strangers, if his mother or father were not nearby, about a story he had read or heard, or invented, or some creature or plant he had observed on a walk.

'What shall we do with him?' Sarah said. 'He's fifteen; soon, or perhaps already, of age to be apprenticed, but in what calling and where?'

George peered at the fire, as though the answer lay there, and shook his head. 'University,' he said, 'and then ... ?' The Church again loomed in his thoughts.

'Why not ask advice of your Williams kin when you are next in Cardiff?'

'Apothecary? Surgeon? I don't know. Can't he aim higher than that? Though it's true my cousin has prospered in the town. Come Thursday, I shall be seated beside him on the Bench. Perhaps I could ask him then what sort of apprenticeship we might seek for Owen, and where best to find it.'

'Philip and Thomas,' said Sarah, 'are not cut out for further years of study. It would go hard with them I fear. But, much as I love them, I would not have them linger here in the Vale, to slide into farming for lack of other opportunities. I shall ask

Uncle John in London whether there are openings in drapery and tailoring. Now the war is behind us, I doubt the trade of army clothier, which made him, will be quite as prosperous, but as you ask your cousin, I shall ask my uncle how best to help our sons forward.'

Within two months, arrangements had been made for all three. Through the good offices of John Jones, living in semi-retirement and considerable luxury in a grand house on Piccadilly, the two older boys, Philip and Thomas, were apprenticed to his cousin, Henry Jones, who had successful drapery shops in Bridgend and Neath. Neither boy was enthused at the prospect and they left home reluctantly, Philip saying, since go he must, he would travel farther in pursuit of his fortune as soon as he was able. Owen Glendour, at the recommendation of Bloom Williams, surgeon and alderman of Cardiff, was apprenticed for five years to Benjamin Gustavus Burroughs, an apothecary with an extensive practice in Clifton, Bristol.

The rector and his wife did not speak about Ensign George of the 60th Foot, although he was constantly in their thoughts. His first letter conveyed both the dreariness of long, empty days at sea and the excitement of arriving at a tropic island. All the family read it in turn, some several times, before it was placed safely in a small mahogany coffer, in anticipation of others that would follow it. And some did, though none had the same fascinating detail about the sickening turbulence of the ocean and the wonder of arrival on a strange shore. The captain's chart, which officers had been privileged to see during the voyage, revealed how, after calling at Road Town (a village rather) at the end of a sheltered inlet on Tortola, largest of the

Virgin Islands, for fresh water and supplies, their vessel skirted the long chain of isles curving round towards the coast of South America. Their destination lay almost at the very end, only the larger island of Trinidad standing between it and the mainland. Tobago was small, they learned, only twenty-five miles long and little more than six wide, but even so, strategically important. That was why the regiment had been posted there: it was only in 1803 that the island had been recaptured from the French. His first sight of its northern parts, rugged hills clad with dense forest rearing out of blue sea under an intensely blue sky, filled him with excitement, but they had sailed on to the south-west, where the terrain was far less hilly, and into Rockly Bay and the harbour of Scarborough, the main town of the island. As soon as stores and equipment were landed, they had set out, the ground seeming to undulate beneath their feet after so many weeks at sea, for Fort King George, only about a mile along a good road around the bay. This was to be headquarters for the duration of their stay.

The island had many wonders, from the clarity of the sea water, in which fish like jewels could be seen slipping through their salty element, and the white sands fringing the shore, to the many sugar plantations with their windmills for grinding the cane. He wrote, too, of strange birds – the largest gulls that any had ever seen, with enormously wide wings, and tiny, long-beaked creatures that hummed as they hovered, wings a rainbow-hued blur, sipping nectar from gaudy flowers. And beyond the fort, close to the edge of plantations, at the side of every road, were dense, pathless forests, seething with ugly insect life. But the most profound shock to his senses was the presence everywhere of black slaves. For every white face, he wrote, and underlined, you see fifteen or twenty black. There was even, to his immense surprise, a militia regiment of blacks in scarlet uniform coats and long white trousers.

Young George had posted his letter on 21st November 1813. It arrived at the rectory on 5th March 1814, at the end of the appalling winter. His younger brothers read it avidly, striving to imagine the wonders he described, and silently speculating on future voyages of their own, now the war was over, but it had shaken Sarah to the core. Soon after reading it, she wrapped herself in scarves and woollen mantle and walked out alone along the muddy lane below the church. Her lovely son, that straight, handsome boy, was far away from any possibility of influence she could bring to bear, any sacrifice she might make, to ensure his preservation. And she feared for him, feared dreadfully. She counted herself among the most fortunate of women. Throughout her childhood and young life she had been blessed, by God's grace, or by fate or fortune. It had come about strangely, but she had married a good man and their union, too, had been blessed in so many ways. They had mourned two of their children, and those losses grieved her still, but many families in the village had fared far worse. The suffering and death of poor little George, her first-born, had left the deeper scar, because she was responsible for it by persuading her husband to interfere with God's will. Was that *hubris?* (Richard Aubrey had used the word, speaking of his brothers.) She did not know, but certainly she had paid for it in tears. And must we also pay for gifts received at God's hand? Many such had come to her and she feared the day when the bill would be presented and settlement demanded. Sarah did not share these thoughts with her husband and family, but they were a constant presence in her mind, lurking there in the shadows to bubble up when least expected. Then she would fall suddenly silent and, if she could, steal away to be alone. She would bully her simple mind, thrusting down the rampant fears, denying they had their origin in her Christian faith. It was superstition, like the childish lore that magpies brought bad luck.

Young George continued to write from time to time to assure them he was well and give some flavour of his experience. Wearing uniform in such heat was punishing for officers and men alike. He was obliged to enforce the rule in this as in other matters, and could not do so without obeying it strictly himself. He now realised they had arrived in Tobago towards the end of the wet season, when heavy rain combined with heat so that it sometimes seemed they were living in green soup. And other creatures moved about in this sodden atmosphere far more easily than any soldier could, creeping insects and flying insects that stung and bit and dropped into food and drink. But at the end of December the rains ceased, it became cooler and garrison life resumed its usual routines and rhythm, with drills and parades and gunnery practice. Officers had been invited to the mansions of plantation owners and afforded every hospitality. He had seen for himself the ease in which the owners lived, their every whim, indoors and out, attended by black servants, scores of them on some estates. The houses were richly furnished with goods brought all the way from shops and manufactories in England. He thought his Mama would be impressed by their luxury, as he had been. Perhaps not for the soldiery, but life could be sweet on a tropic island.

The length of time between letters increased, but each was read many times before being neatly refolded and placed in the mahogany box. On 1st December 1814, the young ensign wrote describing the evils of a second long, enervating rainy season, and how the entire garrison looked forward to the drier, somewhat cooler weather soon to arrive. He wondered when the regiment would be returning home. Now that Napoleon had abdicated and, as they had been reliably informed, the war against America was soon to end, there was less reason to keep a large garrison on the island, especially since the black militia had been trained and equipped to put down insurrection if the slave population were to rise against its white masters. He wished everyone at the rectory the happiest of Christmases and said how he would be thinking of them all in snowy Llantrithyd.

As was usual, this letter took almost three months to reach his family. They read it and prayed together that God would soon bring him home to times of peace. The next from Tobago arrived in May. It came from Ensign Williams's commanding officer. It told them briefly there had been much sickness in the garrison during an unusually prolonged rainy season and he had died of fever on 27th February. He had been a good soldier, steady and reliable in all circumstances and likely, had he lived, to have merited early promotion.

George, his face suddenly drawn and white, handed the folded page silently to Sarah. Even as her fingers touched it, she knew, and feeling as though she had been struck a violent blow in the pit of her stomach, bent, clutching at herself, and would have fallen if her husband had not caught her.

The few words of praise at the end of the letter did nothing to alleviate the family's suffering at the loss of a much loved son and brother. Sarah felt her heart broken a third time.

She turned to her husband in hope of solace. 'That he should have lain among other tortured souls, like him sick and dying, with no tender hand to cool his brow, no loving arm to comfort him, no one to pray for him – I cannot bear it. And now he lies there in the earth of that dreadful island, thousands of miles from home – oh, the thought of it,' she held her hand to her heart and looked beseechingly at him, 'gives me such pain here.'

But the rector was dumb. Inspiration (heaven-sent, he supposed) sometimes saved him when he feared the words he needed would never reach his tongue, but on this occasion, though he would have sacrificed his soul to save her from suffering, it did not come prompt on his wish. He was conscious of a dull ache in his chest, and a terrible tiredness, and believed the loss had left him, too, broken-hearted. Neither as husband nor priest could he give her ease. His whole being gestured towards her: he would have gathered her in his arms and rocked her as a father soothes a hurt child, but watched helplessly as she covered her face with her hands and wept.

Then, at last, he was moved to say, 'The bell will toll for him. He is not there, on that island. He will hear the bell in heaven and know how we love and miss him.' And they fell into one another's arms.

Perkins and Bessy, at Tŷ Draw, heard the slow tolling borne to them on the breeze and wondered who had died. Gossip among the servants soon alerted them to the tragedy that had befallen their friends and they came to the rectory to offer their condolences. They had known young George from infancy and loved him as well as any outside the family could. Perkins approached Sarah and took her hands in his, and could not speak for weeping. And for a while, quietly, the couples communed, sharing their memories and their grief.

Had the ensign lived to return across the Atlantic, he might well have found himself on a battlefield in Europe, for on 10th March 1815, London newspapers carried the alarming information that Napoleon had left Elba and landed in the south of France with a force estimated at ten or twelve thousand men. He had, in fact, slipped away from the island on the day before George died in Tobago, and came ashore on 1st March at Golfe-Juan, a Mediterranean bay between Cannes and Antibes.

Perkins was beside himself, raging at the rector as though responsibility for the disaster lay with him. 'How could Bonaparte be allowed simply to walk away from exile and all the promises he made?'

'Well, he didn't walk from Elba,' said George, taken aback by his friend's ferocity and nervously rubbing the sudden heaviness in his chest, 'but you saw yourself how near that island is to France. And it seems he has many friends and supporters.'

'Yes, yes – but what will the allies do now? We have to lay this – this demon, once and for all.'

He looked hard at George, who was silent. Then, 'Can't stop,' he said, ' – have to watch over men I have digging up hedges. The more land we have under cultivation, the better we shall feed the army.' With an airy wave of the arm he strode away down the garden path, hat in hand, his round head perched like a pumpkin on an absurdly tall white collar.

The rector, at his open door, watched the plump retreating figure and thought how, by enclosing commons and extending plough, the landowner, too, was well fed. Bloom, working in the glebe, had done as much for him. He bowed his head as a sense of guilt stole over him.

Rumours spread about Napoleon's progress through France, some saying he had been met by superior forces and sent back into exile, others that he was closing in on his goal, the imperial throne in Paris. Definitive news reached London on Good Friday, 24th March, and Llantrithyd a few days later. It told how he and his men had set out from the coast along rough mountain roads, climbing in great loops up to alpine passes, and then north, again over difficult terrain, covering thirty-five to forty miles a day. Near Grenoble he had encountered a regiment sent by the king, Louis XVIII, to stop his progress. Instead they greeted him with cries of 'Vive L'Empereur' and changed sides to swell his ranks. It was a pattern that repeated itself, and so, without a shot fired, his advance continued. He had entered Paris, the *Cambrian* said, on 20th March, and the king had already fled.

Not long since, towns and villages up and down the land had been celebrating victory over Napoleon, but now the congregation at the little parish church in the Vale prayed again for peace. They feared once more the cost of the war in increased taxes, deaths and ruined lives. Maimed veterans of the conflict were often to be seen in the streets of towns and villages, drunk on their sixpence-a-day pension. Former soldiers still able to bear arms were being recalled to the ranks, fife and drum bands were rousing men to enlist, the Glamorgan Militia was re-embodied.

Sarah, still in mourning for her son buried in the tropics, where they could never pray at his graveside, found some small satisfaction in knowing that her other boys were in apprenticeships. But while war persisted they, too, were in danger. George, though he found it difficult to express his love and concern for her in her misery, watched her tenderly.

Through the last days of the long winter and the still dark, chill evenings of early spring, they sat either side of the fire, for the most part silent, while George searched his wife's face for a sign that she was ready to reach out to him so that he could embrace and console her. He saw how, quite suddenly, her hair had become grey and, as she was without appetite and ate little, how candlelight caught cheekbones and the concavities of her face. He studied her minutely, thought her more beautiful in her sorrow than when they had married.

Summer ventured in changeable and cool, and the rhythms of the year on the land repeated themselves. Cattle had been turned out in the meadows rather later than usual, barley and oats sown and, into May, potatoes planted, fallow fields ploughed, rye grass and clover broadcast on the turned brown soil. Then, as the young green crops sprouted, came the labour of hoeing and weeding, again and again. At the beginning of June it was time once more for burning limestone and spreading the fields with the chalky product of the kilns. Then haymaking began in fair weather.

Meanwhile, in Europe, armies massed. It seemed Perkins' earnest desire for a final battle would be satisfied – but what would be the outcome? The *Cambrian* boasted the allies' superior forces, Russians, Prussians, Austrians, British, but singly and in combination they had outnumbered the French in the field before, and lost. Besides, the Russian and Austrian armies were far to the east, and the clash of forces, when it came, would be in the west, close to Napoleon's seat of power.

All was resolved in the third week of June. News quickly spread that Napoleon had been defeated. Copies of the *Times* rushed on the mail from London reached the hands of sitting magistrates in Cardiff, including the Reverend George Williams. He read how, in a battle near the village of Waterloo, south of Brussels, that had begun in the sodden aftermath of a violent thunderstorm and lasted three days, 16th to 18th June, and was for some time in doubt, the combined forces of Prussia and Britain had finally overcome the French. It was reported fourteen thousand lay dead on the field and there were innumerable wounded. Wellington and Blücher, the Prussian general, were celebrated as heroic leaders. There was loud rejoicing: again the bells pealed out, again bonfires leapt in the darkness. Again, rivers of tears were shed for those who would never return and those who came back broken in body and mind. By the end of the month, all who cared to know had learned that Napoleon had abdicated a second time. It was mid-August before Perkins was satisfied that the former emperor of France had gone for good, banished to St Helena, a small island thousands of miles away in the south Atlantic. 'Let him swim back from there,' he crowed, with immense satisfaction.

The Reverend George Williams descended the path of the rectory garden, as he had done for almost a quarter of a century. The garden was unkempt. Richard Lewis, returned more bitterly churlish than ever (and presumably empty-handed) from Llancarfan, had been allowed to take what he wanted of the produce and had neglected to replant or to hoe the rest. At the bottom step of the shallow slope he turned right through the gate into the graveyard of his church, where he saw the grass had grown apace between the headstones. That, too, needed attention. Perhaps, for a few pence, Lewis could be persuaded to cut it. Or should he find someone more reliable? He passed the shaggy, twisted yew, like sculptured sinew, and at the church door turned the handle and heard the familiar grind of old metal on metal and the resonating clap in the space beyond as the heavy door swung open and the latch fell back into its iron loop. He left the door ajar; his churchwardens would soon join him. It was August, pleasantly warm outside, but chill within the ancient walls. He walked down the aisle, glancing at the grand memorials to Bassets and Mansells, the plaques in brass and marble commemorating scions of the Aubrey family and, a little breathless, steadying himself with one hand upon the altar rail, knelt, and prayed for guidance. There, still kneeling, head bowed, he drifted off into a reverie, in which he was young, walking down a summer lane with his brother Richard, pursued by the raucous chatter of a magpie.

He was stirred to full consciousness by the creak of the church door and the sound of concerned voices speaking low, and footsteps approaching up the nave. Pushing on the altar rail, he raised himself and turned to greet Thomas Morgan and David Jones, the recently appointed churchwardens.

Morgan addressed him in English. 'Terrible thing happened at Will Meredith's place,' he said. 'Their little boy William, out in the yard when the beasts were being moved, was trampled by a bullock, killed. Oh, they've had a bad year and this is the worst yet.'

'The boy did nothing to upset the creature,' Jones added. 'It just went for him they told me. You know how you've got to watch out for cattle, even cows can turn nasty. Might have been maddened by flies – lot of them about just now – or anything.'

George remembered – Richard, the magpie, the good, old plough horse, the flies: a coincidence. 'I shall go over to the

Merediths as soon as we have finished here.' He shook his head sadly, thinking how dreadful, what agony they must be in. 'I must see how I can help.'

The business was soon concluded: collection of the Poor Rate and charity to the needy, and the state of the highway, summer being the best time for inspection and repair. The rector realised he was very tired. Perhaps, he thought, the great sorrow in the Meredith family was affecting him, his sympathy for them drawing strength from him, although they were not regular churchgoers. As the clatter of the door closing behind Jones and Morgan echoed among the roof beams, he pondered on the many early deaths that came to his ears, and he thought of his own dead, his and Sarah's. He was heavy-hearted. Climbing the steps up the garden to his door was a labour and he was glad to sit in a chair near the half-open window, feeling the breeze on his cheek. Sarah and the maid brought tea. They already knew about little William Meredith – only four, the servants said, and a lovely child: 'Bad news travels quickly.'

'I shall go and see them – this afternoon,' said George, '– after I've rested. I think I'll ask John Perkins to take on the job of surveyor of the highways.'

He had walked the roads himself, noting the many deficiencies in the aftermath of a hard winter, and organised labour for the repairs needed from Llantrithyd's share of the tolls collected at the turnpike gates on the road between Cardiff and Bridgend. Suddenly he could not contemplate doing all that again. The appointment was in his gift, and Perkins, who was both officious and efficient, might be glad to receive it from him. He had already given up beating the bounds of the parish, having begged Mumford, the agent, to take on the task of leading the churchwardens and the usual crowd of boys and a few old men strongly attached to the tradition. He had in past years enjoyed the jollity of the occasion, but it was good to relinquish responsibility, to let things go, as he seemed increasingly inclined to do. He would never take up a scythe again, of that he was sure: the last attempt had taught him a lesson. Even harnessing and saddling his favourite riding pony, gently talking the while, in a kind of warm intimacy with the animal, could find him catching his breath. In the end, reluctantly, he had given that task to a manservant.

He had not been alone in thinking, once the war was over, a time of prosperity and content would surely follow. But there was no recompense for all the hardship and suffering it had brought and, after the celebrations and thanksgiving with the specially composed prayers circulated to all clergy for the great occasion, no general raising of the spirits. The war dead would not return, and those who had lost limbs and eyes were as maimed as before. In Cardiff, fulfilling his duty as magistrate at the Quarter Sessions, he saw them begging in the streets.

Perkins was gloomy and subdued. Like farmers the length and breadth of the land, during the war he had prospered on the high prices his produce brought at markets denied imported foods. Napoleon had hardly set sail for St Helena when the price of wheat began to fall.

'Without the need to raise, equip and feed an army, I thought at least taxes would be reduced,' he said. 'Everyone I spoke to thought much the same. And we were all wrong.'

He and George had read together about the government's borrowing from bankers and rich individuals to keep British soldiers in the field, but without fully realising what that meant, the enormous sums involved and the interest to be paid.

'People in towns and villages and farms – all of us – will have to trim our sails to settle the government's debts, and we'll go on paying year after year after year.'

Perkins' expression was sober. His natural ebullience had deserted him and he was less open than usual with his friend, partly because he could see his pounds and shillings dribbling away what with changes in the market and increasing taxes, and, partly because, while he was considering the latest depressing land tax assessments for Llantrithyd, he had calculated that, taking into account glebe lets and tithes, the rector's income was greater than his. He had revealed this to Bessy who was at first surprised and then a little soured by the discovery. Forgetting the rents he collected from his properties in other parishes, he decided that he, too, as owner of the largest farm in Llantrithyd, and constantly busy, felt somehow discontented. Though not enough to sweep entirely away long years of amicable association in which he and George had shared interests and activities as well as newspapers. Nevertheless, a coolness fell upon their relationship. He received the appointment of highways surveyor, an important role befitting his standing, as the rector assured him, with thin gratitude.

The coming of peace proved an affliction to many families in the parish. It was not the best of harvests. Wherever it was possible, the land had been given to wheat, and as the price of the crop went on falling, until its value had halved, the returns were unexpectedly poor. The larger farmers who commonly employed labourers for threshing during late autumn and winter had fewer jobs to offer. Both labourers and those tenant farmers, whose properties were small, were already finding it difficult to feed their families and preserve their stock. By the third week of October, there was no little discontent abroad.

Wherever men gathered, at an inn, on street corners, there were sure to be some voices raised against those who had led them into twenty-two years of war and could not now, or would not for reasons of their own, give them the assurance of a job and a wage. At this time of year, the rector would have raised his arms inviting the congregation to give thanks to the Lord for his bounty; instead he reminded them of their duty of submission to the law of the land and the will of God, and called upon them to pray for His mercy in the months ahead.

The urgency of his prayer seemed almost to stifle him, as though there was no room in his lungs for breath. He abbreviated his sermon on the Loaves and the Fishes, so that he was uncertain what he had said, nor did he realise how low his voice was.

Ears strained to catch his words, but they were received in rapt silence. It was then, in descending the two steps from the pulpit, dizzily, he stumbled and would have fallen had his flailing hand not found support on a pillar of the chancel. He stood there for a minute, two minutes, under the silent watchful gaze of his parishioners, until he had gathered composure and breath enough to dismiss them with a blessing.

'Dear George, are you unwell?' Sarah asked, hurrying forward once the congregation had left.

Colour was returning to his cheeks. 'Well enough, I'm sure,' he said, 'and I shall be quite myself when I am seated with you by our fire.'

With arms linked, leaning on one another, they walked slowly through the dusk graveyard and the little gate into their garden. As they approached the door of the rectory George stopped to draw breath. 'No matter what,' he said, 'you are my love, my consolation.'

First frosts arrived before October was out. The dry, clear weather encouraged those with dogs and guns to go a-hunting. In previous years, the rector and Perkins had often hunted, with indifferent success, and though the invitation came as usual to join his friend in walking the fields and copses, George did not have the energy for it. He was determined to serve Church and parish, albeit slowly and carefully, and saved his strength for that, resisting Sarah pleas that he should employ a curate. Bloom should have filled that role, but continued to find excuses to delay his nomination: 'Let us wait until the new year,' he said.

Light snow had fallen soon after dawn on the third Sunday of Advent. With little in the way of breeze, it settled evenly on roofs and paths, on already frost-stricken grass and bare branches. It was the season of the church that, in other years, the rector had taken most pleasure in, a time of looking ahead with fresh hope to the coming of Christ. But this year, it seemed, hope and expectation had been sucked out of it. His congregation was disappointingly small. People were gathered around their hearths, his churchwardens said, hugging their greatcoats more closely about them. 'God grant them good fires, and no shortage of fuel,' he said, and, rubbing his hands, agreed with them it was probably colder inside the church than outside. Once the candles had been snuffed, he was glad to leave for the comfort of his own hearth.

A little more snow fell Wednesday evening and through the night, and all was newly white the following morning and very still, with a strange expectancy in the chill clarity of snowlight. George had abandoned his study and, after breakfast, remained at the table, close to the fire, while the maids cleared away. He was still there, head in hands, drowsily reading his Bible, when a loud knock at the door stirred him. He heard voices: Sarah, who had been busy directing affairs in the kitchen, was greeting Mr Morgan, and a moment later she ushered him into the room.

'Why, Thomas,' said the rector, seeing his churchwarden's disquiet, 'what brings you here? Is all well at the church? Has there been some damage?'

'No, it's not the church. There's trouble up in the village. I think you ought to know about it. A crowd outside Jane Rosser's alehouse is making a lot of noise and shouting about the king and parliament … and the clergy. Very offensive shouting. I told them to hold their tongues, but there was no listening with them.'

'Don't you go,' said Sarah. 'They are no doubt drunk – at this hour, too! – and will find their own ways home soon enough, probably to bully their wives, when it's they who have been wasting what little money the family has for food and warmth at Christmas. Leave them. They won't stay long out of doors in this weather.'

'I'm afraid it's my duty,' said George, 'as rector and magistrate. Similar stirs have brought men before the bench in Cardiff. They come humbly enough, saying they meant nothing by the outrageous behaviour witnesses have testified to. But they have been found guilty – and punished. The Chairman tells them such excesses cannot be tolerated, and drunkenness is no excuse. I must go with Thomas and, if what he has seen and heard is still going on, I must warn them of the risk they run.'

Nearing midday, the sun was a faint incandescence in the pale grey above, like a candle, George thought, glimpsed through a mist-hung window. The world was created anew, cold and cheerless. In the graveyard, black stones had been thrust up by their protesting dead through unsullied white. Surrounding trees spread wide skeletal arms and fingers, black against the pearl sky. A pair of magpies circled and perched on a low branch to watch the two men pick their way carefully around the dark mass of the church.

'Damned birds,' said Morgan, almost to himself, ' – don't like them.'

Although warmly clad, within a few yards the rector had felt his nose and throat sting with each breath, and soon the chill penetrated to his core. He was glad to take the churchwarden's arm for mutual support as their uncertain footsteps wound up the slope to the church gate.

A hubbub of voices carried on the still air from the alehouse fifty yards off, where a dozen or so men were gathered, jostling together, stamping their feet and blowing on fingers and then calling out, 'Yes! Yes! You're right, man. Down with the lot of them.' As George approached he could see several of the noisiest were laughing, while some nearer the speaker were nodding their heads in agreement. A few ragged children were throwing snowballs at the group and then crying out and running off when one or other of the men turned on them with threatening shouts. One voice rose above the others in a long harangue.

'What! Do we sweat in the fields for a pittance? Is the work of our backs worth no more than a few pence? If you're content with that, you're less than men. Not much better than the beasts.'

A chorus of noes echoed in the frosty air.

'If I take a hare or a partridge, I'm a criminal. It's unjust! It's intolerable! If I were to take one of my lord's deer from his fine, walled deer-park – God forbid! What then? Why I'd be hanged. For feeding my children, I'd be hanged! What sort of life is this if you're hauled before the magistrates and whipped for taking something from a rich man's plot, something he wouldn't even miss, out of desperation to fill your children's bellies and stop their tears?'

In a moment's pause the speaker recognised the rector approaching, and George saw that it was Richard Lewis, dishevelled, and wilder-eyed than ever, foam flecking his lips.

'I've only to help myself to a cabbage from the parson's garden – a cabbage that I planted and tended – to get whipped for my pains.'

'But this is lies,' said George to Morgan, 'simply lies.' And his heart beat fast with the hurt and injustice of it.

'And he claims tithes. Do you want to give him a share of your labour, your hard earned bread? Why do we give tithes? For the privilege of going to church to thank God for the royals and parliament? What have they ever done for you and me? The French don't pay tithes. They aren't dragooned into church to say thanks for nothing. They don't have a king any more. They got rid of him and all his squandering crew. And a good thing too, I say.'

'This has gone far enough,' said Morgan.

'What have our kings and princes and lords and ladies ever done for you and me? And we have to touch our caps and bow as they deign to pass by – without so much as a glance at us, far less a coin for our trouble.'

George could not speak, but Morgan raised his voice, 'This is sedition,' he said, 'and we have a crowd of witnesses who can swear on the Bible that they heard it from your lips. I don't wish you ill Richard Lewis, but I warn you. You'd best go home.'

'He's very loud, especially in his drink, but harmless enough,' said one of the smiling bystanders.

'Take no notice, Mr Rector,' said another. 'We don't pay much attention to him.'

While George struggled for breath, Morgan said, 'It's cold out here. You'd all be better off by your own firesides.'

As the men began straggling away, Lewis stepped down from the alehouse doorstep and lurched towards the spot where rector and churchwarden stood together. As he passed them, with a grimace of defiance and malice, he put a knuckle to his forehead and, not content with that, added a low bow that sent him staggering backwards, his arms flailing, but he recovered himself and stumbled off laughing through the snow.

The rector was very pale. 'Thank you, Thomas,' he said. 'It is as well I witnessed all this, because we cannot be sure what will come of it. I shall keep my counsel. Although, if a report is made of Lewis's behaviour, I shall be obliged to say what I know. I have always treated him well, employed him when others would not. Now I am sure the man is an incorrigible scoundrel. I have had enough for one morning, as I'm sure you have. See, it is beginning to snow again. Go you home to your family and I shall go to mine.'

Flakes were floating aimlessly down from a darkening leaden sky as they shook hands and parted. Morgan watched doubtfully as the rector turned and moved slowly away in the direction of the church, a black figure, bulky in greatcoat and scarves, gradually receding in a fresh swirl of snow, then opening the church gate, closing it carefully behind and disappearing down the slope.

The gravelled path where firmer footing might have been found was hidden and George stepped tentatively, slithering much of the way to the lee of the church. He leaned against its ancient wall, gasping, feeling his heart race. His hands and feet were numb with cold but a cold sweat bathed his face and beneath the weight of clothing his body was clammy. He moved forward, out among the black headstones, each new-crowned with a layer of snow. The flakes were falling more thickly: he could barely see the gate to his garden, but it was not far off, and then he would be home. Only a few more steps, one foot carefully in front of the other. His heart was thumping with the exertion of keeping himself upright, he could hear it in his ears, feel it thud against the walls of his chest. The flakes were blowing into his face. It was so very cold. He could think only of Sarah, what it would be like to be held by her, close in her arms, warmed by her love. A great pang rose in his chest. He did not think love could bring such pain. 'Ah, my Lord, thy cross,' he would have said, but no sound came. In a searing explosion of love he flung out his arms for Sarah, fell headlong, and lay still. The heedless flakes spiralled down and clung to the black figure, and a lone magpie, which had observed this event, soundlessly spread its wings and flew off to its mate.

By the time servants from the rectory, sent out to look for their master, came upon the body, it was almost entirely hidden in the new fall. They carried him tenderly home.

Sarah, grief-stricken, had nevertheless to arrange the burial of her husband. She sent an urgent appeal to his brother Richard to officiate. The roads were bad: he would come as soon as he was able. It was as well there would be a delay, for the ground was frozen and digging the grave a prolonged and onerous endeavour. Eventually, 'the Reverend George Williams, Rector, was interred in the graveyard of his church on Christmas Eve, 1815, the service in the church and at the graveside conducted by the Reverend Richard Williams, younger brother of the deceased. Present at the graveside were deceased's sons, Bloom, Philip, Owen Glendour, and Thomas. After the burial, mourners presented their condolences and took tea with the Rector's widow, Sarah. Messages expressing great sorrow at the loss to family, church and parish were received from near and far afield.' Thus reported the *Cambrian* the following Friday. The next day Sarah began planning her departure from the rectory.

George's death had been a profound shock, raising again in her mind doubts about a loving God. She had known her husband was ailing. He had not complained, but had become slower in thought and action, as though preoccupied with some unspecified, nearer, concern. At the same time he had been more tenderly solicitous of her, as though she were the one in decline, sickening to death. She had never had reason to regret their marriage, had given herself to him wholly and forever. Now he was gone, she missed him, grieved for him, for her own sake and for his. But the resilience and inner strength that had been hers from childhood sustained her again.

The rector's widow had no claim on rectory or living; a new incumbent would soon be appointed to take on the cure of church and parish. She must begin a new life: very well, she would. Sudden death had robbed George of the opportunity to prepare his last will and testament. It was for her to ensure that along with the furniture, household effects, the pictures they had collected and proudly displayed, contents of barns and stable, everything, was listed and valued, sold or stored until a new family home was established. She could rely upon Bloom to help her; the other boys – her fine young men – were secure in their apprenticeships and would in due course make their own way in the world. Bloom would help her, but what future could he hope for now? His unwillingness to be nominated for ordination until he felt ready, despite his father's pleas, and hers, had rebounded on him. He had farmed his father's glebe with industry and skill and, since he was too old to begin learning a trade, farming must henceforth be his life and livelihood.

The winter had started badly and so it continued. While not the extraordinary cold of the previous winter, it still dragged on and brought frosts and snow enough to disrupt all manner of events and affairs in town and country. Sarah was grateful it delayed the arrival of the new rector; he would be inducted on Easter Sunday, 14th April. She wrote to her uncle in London, now an old man, seeking his advice about accommodation in the city, where (she thought) greater opportunities existed for her sons, once their apprenticeships were concluded. They would then need a house, as it was her ambition to keep the family together. Uncle John replied suggesting that, while finding a family home, she should initially reside with him. Moved by his kindness after so many years, she was glad to accept his generous offer and settled on a date for departure. It soon became known throughout the parish that the rector's widow would leave Llantrithyd on 20th March to join a rich relative in London.

On the Sunday before their planned departure, a day of cold and blustery showers, Sarah was preparing to leave the rectory and walk the familiar path to church for what would probably be the last time, when there was loud knocking on the door and the sound of excited voices outside. It was Thomas Morgan and his wife Margaret.

'You must come at once,' said Morgan, very flustered. 'There's a notice on the door – the church door – and I'm not sure what it means, whether it should be there at all. You need to come at once.'

Sarah took her hat and followed the couple as they hurried through the churchyard. It was yet early for the service, but a few were gathered around the door peering at a notice fixed with nails at the four corners, one tracing letters with his fingers and trying to spell out the words, while others stood open-mouthed. Several more were hurrying down the sloping path, alerted by the news that something strange – perhaps shocking, it was difficult to be sure – was to be seen on the church door. All gave way as Sarah appeared and stood silent as she read, and read again, such was the complexity of the legal text, a citation uttered by 'Benjamin Hall DD. Vicar General and official principal of the Right Reverend father in God Richard by divine permission Lord Bishop of Llandaff.' As she at last grasped its import, she almost swooned and gripped Morgan's arm to stop herself falling. A few days before, at Llandaff, Richard Lewis had sworn an affidavit to the effect that the Reverend George Williams, late rector of Llantrithyd, owed him ninety-six pounds in wages for his work as a farm servant. He therefore named himself the principal creditor of the estate and demanded first choice of the deceased's household goods and chattels.

Very few of those gathered at the church door could read, far less understand, what hung before them, pulling at its nails and bellying out in the stiff breeze. But eventually the gist at least would be known and whispered from one to another. Sarah knew envy of the prosperity she and her husband had enjoyed would give rise to a great deal of tutting and sly laughter among village gossips, but it was not the scald of public humiliation she felt. For the first time in her life she was enraged. That the ungrateful beast to whom George had shown every kindness should attempt to take advantage of her, to rob her, at a time of raw grief, was intolerable. Perhaps he imagined her naive and helpless: well, she would show him.

Bloom, who had arrived at the church tardily, as was his custom, was ushered forward to join his mother. As he read the notice, he flushed scarlet.

'Where is he?' he said. 'When I lay my hands on that villain, that cockroach, I will not spare him.' And he would have gone at once to find Lewis, but Morgan held him and his mother spoke low and urgently to him. This was a legal matter and would have to be handled not with fists and staves but at the consistory court in Llandaff. 'We must show that wages – and more – were paid. Did he think we would meekly yield to his lying allegation? He will get nothing. We must delay our departure, obtain the help of a proctor and put our case, before Reverend Hall if the Bishop himself is not present. You will ride to Llandaff on my behalf tomorrow and say what we intend to do.'

News of events at the church and the resolve of the late rector's family sped through the village. Shortly it became known that Lewis and his concubine and their children had fled, no one knew where. He did not appear at the consistory court and his claim was dismissed.

'Perhaps,' said Sarah, at home once more, 'he could see there would be no more work for him, since only your father would employ him. Yet I cannot understand why he claimed all that money was owed. What is it? Four – five years' wages? And how did he persuade the Vicar General there was truth in the allegation? I doubt we shall ever know. If he had come to our door and asked for five pounds, I would have given it to him, for your father's sake. Now he will have nothing.'

'He buried his small talent,' said Bloom. 'I got to know him well enough and never liked or trusted him. He was the sort of man who thinks fate or God has been down on him from the start and for all time. Nothing and no one could please him, and goodness knows Dada tried, and against my better judgement, so did I. He was filled with spite. The village is well rid of him.'

Two days later Sarah left by coach for London. James's, the carrier from Cowbridge, had been charged with the task of transporting all the furniture and fine things, the paintings, the silver, to London. Packed in covered wagons and sent on before, it would arrive several days after them. The apprenticed sons would follow in due course, once they had served their time. Given his share of the patrimony, only Bloom was left in the Vale, determined to make his way doing what he knew best and where he felt at ease.

VII

BLOOM HEARD OF his mother's death, aged 94 (she believed), at Hammersmith, late in April 1853. Hammersmith, he was told, lay on the western outskirts of London, along the Great West Road. It was as though she had sought a dwelling convenient for travel back to Wales, although she had never, until now, made the journey. The letter from his brother Thomas told how her body had been brought from London to Cardiff on the railway, and thence, in a black draped hearse, to Llantrithyd, where she was buried alongside her husband. A suitable gravestone had been ordered and railings to surround the plot. Thomas was at pains to explain that he wished Bloom had been present at the interment, but did not then know where to find him. It was only in the past few weeks that, by diligent enquiry, his address had been discovered.

Bloom was seated, still in his working clothes, redolent of farmyard, at the kitchen fireside in his cottage, tired after a long day's labour on Penylan Farm in Coychurch. But the farm was not his; it belonged to old Fred Evans, its last connection with the Griffiths family, his mother's relatives, having disappeared decades ago. Evans was a good enough employer, but not the sort to keep on a man who couldn't pull his weight. Each day, therefore, he rose early to tramp a couple of miles up a steep, winding path, when, at this time of year, with overcast skies and skeins of mist dragging over the hill, it was still gloomy, to join three or four others in repairing the depredations of a long winter: lopping trees, clearing ground for planting, spreading manure, dibbling potatoes. Soon it would be time to sow – barley, clover, beans, cabbages. Month by month, season by season, the work went on, and he was glad of it, even though he had to struggle to keep up with men twenty years and more younger.

He placed the refolded letter, a single sheet, on the deal table. At the other side of the fire his wife was darning and patching trousers and coats for him and their unmarried sons, George and Walter, who still lived with them, laboured on the land like their father and shared the upkeep of the cottage. They were good boys, both walking out with local girls and looking to settle down in places of their own.

Bloom had been just the same at their age. He had waved goodbye to his mother as she left in the trap for Cowbridge and the coach that would start her on the road to London. The rectory door clapped firmly behind him on the hollow echo of an empty house, and he felt, not robbed by fate, but free. Despite the unseasonably poor weather that spring after the fall of Napoleon, life was full of promise. He had taken the tenancy of a small farm in Llysworney at forty pounds per annum and believed he could make it pay – with good fortune, even handsomely. Llysworney, a village of much the same size and character as Llantrithyd, and about as far from Cowbridge, three miles at most, though in the other direction, welcomed him. He began at once attending the parish church, another dedicated to St Illtyd, and meeting his new neighbours. A farmer needs physical strength, energy, knowledge of husbandry and readiness to learn new methods: all these attributes he was confident he already possessed. He was also well aware that his livelihood depended on the vagaries of weather, soil, the health of stock, and the market for farm produce. He was, nevertheless, optimistic.

Soon after settling in his new home, coming out of church one Sunday, he met Mary, daughter of a good, thrifty family. He was almost twenty-six, she twenty-three, both of age to marry, and the timing seemed propitious. Within a few weeks he had won the affection of Mary and the confidence of Robert Rees, her father. More speedily than he had dared hope, a marriage was agreed and arranged. The wedding took place at St Illtyd's in the first week of May 1816, witnessed by Mary's father and her brother, George, who had been released for the day from labour at Court Lamphey, 'a very grand farm' he said, in the neighbouring parish of Ewenny. Despite squally rain, it was a happy day, and Bloom was immensely proud taking his bride to her new home. They had youth and strength, and a will to work: the future seemed bright. How could they know the summer before them would be the worst anyone could ever remember.

The letter from Thomas brought back old memories, as fresh as yesterday. He had not seen his brother, or any of his near kin, in over thirty years. Had he been the sort to write with news of marriage and children and the vicissitudes of farming in the Vale, no doubt his mother, or someone, would have replied. But he had been too busy living his life to write about it. Besides, although he could read and write well enough, he had always found books and quill-driving irksome. When one year became two, and then five, it seemed too late to start. After all, they might have begun the correspondence; why (if that's what it was) did they wait for him? He did not know how his brother had discovered where he now lived.

There must have been some lingering connection between Hammersmith and Llantrithyd through which enquiries were made. And so the letter, to his great surprise, had reached the cottage and Mary had placed it for him to see alongside his supper. He had eaten first before attempting to open it.

Thomas arrived in a hired pony-trap from Bridgend, where he had taken a room at an inn. He found Mary alone in the cottage at the side of Pentwyn-road. Bloom was expecting him, but did not know at what time. In any case, there was no question of taking a day off work to greet him. His appearance late in the afternoon threw Mary into a state of nervous confusion. She was not accustomed to receiving strangers, still less gentlemen strangers. The man she stared at had bushy side-whiskers and a flourishing moustache, and was attired in high-collared shirt and large bow-tie, dark frock coat, paler waistcoat decked with a gold watch-chain, and plaid-patterned trousers. He carried a soft crowned hat, as befitted a journey in rural parts, and seemed at once perfectly at home. His appearance and the confidence of his bearing were almost too much for her. Her first instinct was to hide until he went away. It was only when she had placed a cup of tea before him, and had time to peer more closely, that she saw the resemblance. If you looked past the whiskers, she said to herself, he was a somewhat stouter, and far more prosperous, version of Bloom.

Thomas, for his part, thought his brother's home a mean little house and the wife a mouse. But as he sipped his tea and looked about him he saw the brasses over the fireplace gleamed and the sparse and simple furniture glowed with the lustre of care. He attempted to engage Mary in conversation, but his strangely accented English confused her still more, and he had no Welsh. After a lengthy silence, having finished his tea, he announced that he would take a turn about the village and return when his brother would be at home. 'At what time would that be?' he asked. Mary smiled and shrugged helplessly. 'Ah well – anon,' he said, and with a little bow, touching his hat brim, he left. She heard him stir up the pony and watched from the front room window as the trap rolled off down the road.

A full two hours passed before Thomas returned, by which time Bloom and his sons had come in from work and, at the urgent prompting of wife and mother, eaten, washed and changed into Sunday best. The tall fresh-faced young men, both in their twenties and rather like their mother, were introduced, sheepishly mumbled a few words to their uncle, and hurriedly excused themselves, saying they were meeting someone. Mary, too, disappeared and in a little while creaking floorboards above told she had gone upstairs.

Notwithstanding the many years that had passed since they had last been together and the changes life had wrought, Bloom still possessed the ease of the older brother and, he noticed, a sturdier frame. At first greeting his broad work-hardened paw had seemed to swallow-up Thomas's soft, pale hand.

'Fine pair of lads you have,' said Thomas, 'you must be proud of them.'

'Yes, I suppose.' Bloom had not thought it a matter of pride. He knew pleasure at having seen them survive infancy, grow into strong, honest workers, and soon, if he had read the signs correctly, he expected them to leave home. 'Come into the front room,' he said. 'Mary's put a jug of ale and pipes and tobacco there, if you'd care for a smoke.'

She had lit another fire, too, Thomas noted, and he followed Bloom's example in drawing a spindle-backed chair away from the table closer to the hearth. They had, he thought, so little in common, and nothing to talk about, it was a mistake to come: the gap of years, of decades, was too great. But Bloom stretched out his feet towards the fire and busied himself with a clay pipe, motioning his brother to do the same.

'You'll take a mug?'

'Well, I … Yes, yes I will. Why not? Thank you.'

'You can see I'm still labouring on the land. There's no disguising that, is there? But Mary and me, we're pretty snug here. You'll hear no grumbles from us and the boys, as long as there's work to be had and health and strength to do it.'

The timbre of the voice had changed but the lilt, the Vale way of saying things, was unmistakeable. 'And what do you do, Thomas? Not dressed for ploughing!'

'No, don't have time even to look after our patch of garden.' He was going to add that he employed a man for that, but wisely (he thought), held his tongue. 'I had a sort of apprenticeship in the drapery business in London, and I was lucky after that.' He paused. 'Perhaps you remember our great-uncle, John Jones – or at least hearing about him. He was in the army clothier business, supplying uniforms and kit – not weapons, of course – for the soldiery. Anyway, he took me under his wing and started me off and I carried on with it. It's made me pretty comfortable.'

Having said it, he winced inwardly at his self-satisfaction and unwarranted pride, for he recognised he had been blessed by fortune built on the misfortune of others. He hurried on:

'Did a lot of travelling, showing what we had, what we could provide. There's always wars, always soldiers, more at some times than others, and they always want uniforms and the like. Business even brought me down to Wales, though not often.'

They both stared at the fire and sucked their pipes and took a draught.

'Yes, there's always wars, always soldiers to be dressed in their red. I didn't have Uncle John's luck of a war that went on and on – no new Napoleon to stir up business, but I did well enough out of it. And I walked out with a delightful young woman, my dear Jane, and married her. Had a little girl we named Julia Sarah – the old names. But Jane, I think, never recovered from the birth and she died – about eighteen months later. So I took my baby and we moved in with our mother who then had a house in Camberwell, another part of London, and I carried on working, while Mama cared for the child until she was a young woman, and then it was her turn to look after her grandmother. She's being courted by a man from Bridgend, a Richard Jones, distant relative of ours, who has a good business – drapery, as you might have guessed – and if, or when, they marry they may settle near here. Anyway, after years living with Mama, I met Ann and we got on very well together, so we married, with much affection and for companionship, and found a fine little house in Barnes, out in the country, close to the Thames. And being so comfortable there, I grew tired of constant travel in pursuit of business, so I sold up and put the proceeds into property. People always want to rent houses in London, so they might as well rent them from me. And that's it. Now tell me: when we left, you had a farm.'

'That didn't last long,' said Bloom. He took a long draught of ale and wiped his lips before he continued. 'I couldn't have picked a worse year to start farming on my own account. That year we barely saw the sun – a bad winter, nothing you could call a spring or summer, just constant cloud and rain and fog and then early, early frost, winter again, and the year was over. No matter how hard I worked, and it was just the same all around the Vale, there was hardly anything to harvest. With nothing to sell, I had no income. And without the means to renew the annual lease – yes, annual leases by then – I had no opportunity to recoup my losses. I had married my Mary in May, trusting we were set up for life, and the following March we were out of house and home, and I was looking for labouring work in the surviving farms round about. And that's how it's been ever since. Work here for a while, then you find you're no longer wanted and you have to move on. With Mary and the children to provide for, work always came first. It's easier now because the children are grown up and most of them are away, fending for themselves. So, I'm afraid you won't meet our daughter Mary, because she's in service at a big house in Llanharan, or her other brothers, William, who's away working on the railway, and Thomas and Owen Glendour, who labour on a farm Ewenny way.'

'Ah, the old family names again, including my own,' said Thomas. 'You have prospered in children. More than I managed. I'm sorry to have missed them. Perhaps there will be another opportunity.'

A sense of brotherly familiarity had begun to swell in Thomas's chest so that he felt a lump in his throat at the thought of that distant past when he and Bloom were just – boys.

'Going back to Llantrithyd for Mama's funeral, the first time since we left, was – I don't know – a bit of a shock, I suppose. It's so small. I didn't think it would be so small. But it brought back a lot of memories. The church is much as it was when Dada had it, but that grand old house, the Aubreys place …'

'Ah, the Plas.'

'It's falling into ruin, or fallen. It was beautiful. What waste. How did it come to that?'

'Do you remember Dada's friend, Richard Aubrey, son of the Plas? Probably not. I can't picture him these days, but I remember a few things. He led the Militia when Dada was chaplain. Well his son, Thomas Digby, the one Mama told us she used to nurse, inherited house, land, everything. That was strange, I thought, when I was told about it, for that same Richard Aubrey had two older brothers. You would have thought the heir would be a son, or daughter, of one of them. What do you make of that? Anyway, this Thomas Digby who inherited the Plas and everything decided to stay up in England where he had more land. Never came back. Didn't care what happened to the property in Llantrithyd. People have been helping themselves to stone and slate, and timber – and lead – for years. Not much you can do about it now.'

Bloom picked up a poker from the hearth, thrust it between the frets of the iron fire basket and stirred the crust of small coal covering the glow beneath until flames spurted up and a thin pillar of smoke spiralled up the chimney.

'"Shiggle the fire," Mama used to say.' Thomas smiled at the memory as his brother refilled their pots. They puffed at their pipes in silence for a while.

'When our mother left the rectory – and you went off to Llysworney – Philip and I were nearing the end of our apprenticeships. It hadn't been the happiest of experiences for either of us, but whereas I could see the possibility of a future living in the drapery business, if I could take advantage of family connections, Philip thought it promised nothing but endless effort for poor returns. The war had just ended and the seaways were open, so he decided to seek his fortune abroad.

Our mother thought he was throwing away opportunities he had earned by five long years' work for a pittance. But if that made her angry, she was distraught when she learned where he thought to go – to the Indies, the West Indies.'

Bloom sucked in his breath. 'Oh, dear – all that business about brother George again.'

'Yes, it went on for weeks, until he sailed, and there was no longer anything to be said or done about it. But he got on well in Demerara, became a sort of clerk, so far as I could make out, at a big plantation, and then he had the immense good fortune to marry the owner's daughter and heir. He was well set for life. He wrote from time to time, not often, to tell us the good things. Didn't mention slave revolts or anything like that we've heard of since. Then in (what was it, 1840 or '41?) a letter came from his wife, Sophia, telling us he had succumbed to a dreadful fever (just like George again) and died. They had no children. That was that.'

'Poor Mama.'

'Poor Philip – so close to returning to London and a life of ease, if not luxury.'

'What happened to Owen?'

'Ah, Owen – mother's favourite. As the youngest of us boys, I suppose that was inevitable. And he was the clever one – did handsomely in his apprenticeship at Bristol. Five years well spent, he told us, and fully licensed by the Worshipful Society of Apothecaries of London. Very grand. Set up first with a partner, somewhere near Cannon-street I seem to remember, and a couple of years later married a young woman called Sarah, like our mother, from a Welsh family originally – quite well off. Anyway, she came with a dowry and in no time Owen had split with his partner and set up on his own in

Doughty-street. You wouldn't know it, but a splendid street, fine gates at the entrance – as though you had gates at the end of the road here – and liveried porters to see you tidily in and out. He seemed set fair. And then Sarah died having their first – the child, too – and things went downhill. It's odd really. I'm sure he could have pulled himself together, made a fresh start – married again, as I did. Why not? But do you know what he did?'

Bloom shook his head.

'He gave up everything here. Sold the practice at a paltry price, such was his haste to get away – and went to Jamaica!'

Bloom started to his feet, coughing. 'God help us – how could he do that, after his brothers …?'

'No, no, this was several years before Philip died in Demerara. So far as Owen was aware, Philip was succeeding in the tropics, so why shouldn't he? He told me about the wealthy English in Jamaica, and Scotch and Welsh, too, who would give anything to have a good surgeon they could call upon. He expected to return a wealthy man.'

'What did Mama say?'

'Well, she wept, and begged him to reconsider, and warned him about the dangers. Had he forgotten what happened to George? And she was angry with him for planning to go to a place where money was made from the barbaric use of slaves. Not for much longer, he used to say, and anyway I've heard they are called apprentices now and have wages. Ha! wages, she said; then why do they revolt. "Mama, mama," says Owen, "we have riots in the streets here." And so it went on until the day he sailed. She was speechless when he came to say goodbye, and said hardly a word to anyone for days afterwards. It hurt her very badly. He was such a fine looking fellow, taller than you, but headstrong, you know. She told us she had a dreadful premonition.'

Thomas paused and relit his pipe. 'She was right. He wrote to tell us about Kingston, where he lived, and how he had premises and a number of wealthy clients. All the signs were good. We waited for the next letter from Jamaica, six months – more, and when it came just before Christmas 1836 – I remember it so well – it was from the governor of the island. Owen had fallen victim to yellow fever, a terrible scourge still prevalent there. It was a case of "physician heal thyself" – and he couldn't.' A tear rolled down his cheek. 'He couldn't.'

With heads bowed, they communed silently for a while.

'What happened to that evil scoundrel Lewis?' said Thomas.

'I don't know. I left the village just about the same time as you and no news of him came to Llysworney. I have never attempted to find out. I wanted revenge for what he did, or tried to do, and might have pursued him, but I had many other things … and in the end it didn't seem worth the trouble. I heard about our father's friend, John Perkins; he died only a couple of years later – 1818 perhaps, and his wife not long after that. But he left a lot of property in various parts of the Vale, which is why the news of his death was well known. I liked him a lot. Almost my earliest memory is being taken hunting in the copses by him, though we never caught anything. He was a bit of a blusterer, but full of good spirits, seemed to enjoy it all, even that shouting we used to hear – about if he had his way, the things he would do to set the world to rights.'

They sucked their pipes in another thoughtful silence.

Bloom sighed. 'I like to think of the old days in the rectory,' he said. 'Do you remember how we used to climb the gate to sneak into the Plas? Weren't we lucky to have a place like that to play in – the gardens, the woods, and the little river where we tried to catch trout. And the deer park? Do you remember the deer park?'

'I remember being chased out of it by some farm servants, one on a horse. And hiding in those great gorse bushes while the horseman slashed at them with his whip and running and running and nearly being caught. Though what would have happened if we had been caught? We would have been dragged before our father, I suppose, who would have thanked the men and put on his most serious face to deal with us. But he could never scold us, far less beat us. Left that sort of thing to Mama. He was such a gentle man. And kind. Though I remember he was very stern that time when you were caught pretending to be a ghost.'

'Mostly because his surplice was torn as I was struggling to escape. He was a big hairy man, the one who caught me. I did say sorry about that – but it was worth it, just to hear the screams when the two old ladies saw me being ghostly under the trees, and those other fellows I crept up on who simply took to their heels. I just tried it once too often. A lot of superstition in Llantrithyd then – people believing in fairies, hobgoblins, all sorts of things. Did you ever bathe your eyes in that spring that was supposed to give you wonderful sight? And what about that other spring, the one they built a sort of brick dome over. That was a wonder – beautiful cold water in the hottest weather, when every stream had dried to a dirty trickle.'

'The water of life,' said Thomas. 'My memory of those days is not as sharp as yours, but the closeness of our life then, as a family, I mean, lingers still. I think of our father and mother with such love and gratitude – Mama especially because chance kept me near her over the years. I watched her grow old – and very old. She didn't change. Oh, she became frail eventually, but she was so bright, so ready to be interested in what was happening in the world, what was going on with Ann and me and Julia Sarah. She was just the same as when we two were boys, right to the end, the most wonderful woman, and quite determined she must be buried with our father in Llantrithyd. Do you still have the Bible, Dada's Bible? I was quite envious when Mama gave it to you, just because you were the eldest.'

'Why, yes – yes, of course. It's been safe through all our wanderings around the Vale.'

With slow deliberation, Bloom knocked out his pipe and stood, the firelight casting his shadow on the wall of the darkening room. He opened the cupboard door in a small oak dresser, produced the thick, leather-bound book and laid it on the table before his brother. 'Here you are, just as you remember it, I'm sure.'

Thomas turned the leaves carefully. 'Ah, that's the first, I think.'

On the open page before him was a copperplate of an Old Testament scene, but that was not what he looked for. On the other side, a blank, the Reverend George Williams, Rector, had neatly inscribed the births of three of his and Sarah's children as they occurred, the day, the place, the time. There you are brother, and there am I, he said to himself. And so, on the next copperplate's blank side, more births. And then, in the way of things, deaths too, entered in the same rather elegant, flowing script, but less detail.

For minutes during which the only sound was the muttering of the fire and quiet sobbing, Bloom stood by his brother bent over the old Bible. 'I've put in the births of our children,' he said, 'and two who died almost as soon as born.'

Thomas saw that these later births and deaths had been recorded in exactly the same manner and style as the older ones. He looked at his brother's hands, broad and gnarled with decades of labour, yet they had not lost delicacy and skill in handling a pen. 'I'm afraid you have fresh entries to make,' he said, 'our mother's first. Will you do it – if I write to you with all the dates and places?'

Bloom nodded. 'Yes, you can be sure of that.'

The surviving sons of the Reverend George Williams, Rector of Llantrithyd, and Sarah his wife, looked at one another and, smiling warmly, shook hands in the twilit room.

About the Author

Sam Adams has been involved in Welsh writing in English since the late 1960s. He is a former editor of *Poetry Wales* and former chairman of the English-language section of Yr Academi Gymreig. His scholarly writing includes editions of the *Collected Poems* and *Collected Short Stories* of Roland Mathias, and three monographs in the Writers of Wales series, the latest on *Thomas Jeffery Llewelyn Prichard*, who is also the subject of several articles published in the *Journal of Welsh Writing in English*. He has contributed poems and well over a hundred 'Letters from Wales' to the Carcanet Press magazine *PN Review*. His work from Y Lolfa includes, in addition to *Prichard's Nose*, a collection of poetry and *Where the Stream Ran Red*, a delightful and moving history of his family and of Gilfach Goch, the mining valley where he was born and brought up.

By the same author:

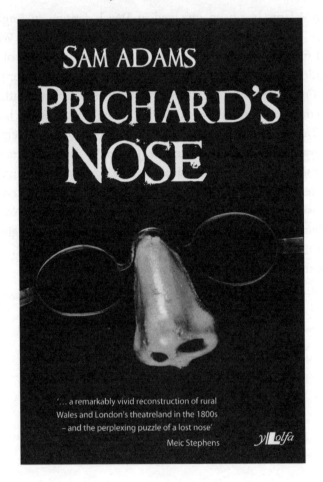

SAM ADAMS

PRICHARD'S
NOSE

'... a remarkably vivid reconstruction of rural
Wales and London's theatreland in the 1800s
– and the perplexing puzzle of a lost nose'
Meic Stephens

y Lolfa

£9.95

Praise for *Prichard's Nose*

'This is a masterly tale about a real, nineteenth-century teller of tall tales. Sam Adams's nose for the Welsh past is combined with his poet's eye to bring the story alive to all our senses.'

M. Wynn Thomas

'A beautifully written novel of mystery and literary detective work that takes us from rural Wales to the teeming London of the 1820s.'

Robert Minhinnick

'*Prichard's Nose* is engaging, smoothly written, and powerfully evokes a life lived at the tail of the eighteenth century and through the early decades of the nineteenth century in rural Wales and Regency London … The evocation of place and time is tremendously convincing … This is partly down to a sense of accuracy in detail and partly to the precision with which the feel of the language is so often caught … the feel of the cadence of the language of the time … [F]or its vivid re-imagining of places, times and a strange, elusive life, it remains a very good read.'

Christopher Meredith for *PN Review*

'A lyrical delight … Adams is as incapable of writing badly as a great tenor is of singing out of tune … [he] inhabits his characters beautifully and summons up great atmospherics in a novel that moves between a fine evocation of Welsh country life, the drovers' roads and the London stage in the early nineteenth century.'

Steve Dube for *Wales Online*

'I found *Prichard's Nose* to be a revelation … Sam Adams's story brings to the table … an overwhelming depth of subject, a fascinating portrait of one of Wales's less well-known cultural gems … a myriad of adventures … inspiration, fascinating prose and rich historical context at every step.'

Jack Clothier for *Gwales*

SAM ADAMS

WHERE THE
STREAM RAN RED

Memories and Histories
of a Welsh Mining Valley

£9.99

SAM ADAMS

Missed Chances

y Lolfa

£5.95